# *Illusions*

Nelda Jo,
Continue the
magic!

Marge Dickel

Sissy Marilyn
3/06

# Illusions

### SISSY MARLYN

Copyediting by Robert Ritchie

**WASTELAND PRESS**
Louisville, KY

# Wasteland Press

Louisville, KY
www.wastelandpress.com

*Illusions*
By Sissy Marlyn
Copyediting by Robert Ritchie

Front Cover design by Wasteland Press
First Printing – April, 2005
ISBN: 1-933265-39-6

Printed in the U.S.A.

## Chapter 1

# *Birth*

At 3:00 p.m., on a bright, sunny, pristine May fifteenth, a lovely baby girl was welcomed into this world by the Greathouse family. Her given name was Katherine Rose, but with much affection, this name was shortened at once to Katie Rose. Katie Rose was the name that would stick with her throughout her life.

Katie Rose was a petite six pounds, six ounces, and she was only eighteen inches in length. She had full, rosy red cheeks and tiny, pouting, pink lips. She had mounds of soft, dark hair covering her perfect, little, round head. Katie Rose seemed content from the moment she had taken her first breath.

Katie Rose was a much wanted and planned for child, unlike her older brother, Mason. Mason had been an awful surprise to his then unwed mother, Jackie Lynn. When she had first learned she was pregnant, Jackie Lynn wanted neither to be a wife nor a mother.

*Thank God Mason has a headstrong, convincing father!* Jackie Lynn acknowledged.

Mason's half Indian father, Abraham 'Long Wolf' Greathouse, had won Jackie Lynn over with his all-encompassing love. Long Wolf had made Jackie Lynn see how wonderful sharing her life with him, and their child, could be. He had also convinced her to become his wife.

Mason was now three years old. It had been Jackie Lynn's idea to add another child to their family. Long Wolf had been more than a little ambivalent about this suggestion. His reluctance was based solely on the fact that Jackie Lynn was forty-three years old. Long Wolf had feared for her health.

Jackie Lynn had little trouble whatsoever during her pregnancy with Mason. But Long Wolf had been aware that women past the age of forty were subject to more complications during pregnancy. Jackie Lynn had been unwavering, however, that Mason not grow up an only child, as she had.

*He's not going to suffer that terrible loneliness.* Long Wolf had been unable to persuade his wife otherwise. Jackie Lynn had even had her gynecologist personally call to reassure Long Wolf.

"Jackie Lynn has an excellent chance of having another uncomplicated pregnancy. Your wife is in perfect health, and more and more women are having babies after age forty", the doctor had relayed. This reassurance, plus the fact that Long Wolf was almost powerless to deny Jackie Lynn anything she truly wanted, left him agreeing to bring another child into the world.

*And what a beautiful child she is!* he silently determined, moments after Katie Rose had been born.

Long Wolf was now coddling his newborn daughter in his arms. Katie Rose was bundled in a pretty pink receiving blanket. Long Wolf kissed his cherished baby girl's small forehead.

*I wish your grandmother were alive to see you. She would be so happy to have a granddaughter. She always wanted a little girl. She will always be watching over you.*

Long Wolf's Indian mother had died the year before. Her death had somewhat ended his Indian heritage. She had lived on a Reservation, until her death, and Long Wolf had gone to visit her there often. Since his mom was gone, he no longer desired to return to the Reservation. Long Wolf's life now was with Jackie Lynn, his son and his new daughter.

His only other allegiance was to the family business, Greathouse Construction. When his father had died, many years prior, he had passed the reign of leadership to Long Wolf. Likewise, some day, Long Wolf planned to pass the company onto Mason.

Long Wolf was pleased that this second child was a girl. *Since we did not have another son, there will be no competition between my children for who will someday take over the company.*

2

*Still, don't you worry, my precious Katie Rose, daddy will take good care of you. You'll always be daddy's girl.*

\* \* \* \*

Only a day later, about 5:00 p.m., on a gray, overcast, rainy and stormy May sixteenth, Callista Elizabeth Roberts entered the world. The turbulent weather seemed to match Callista's tempestuous temperament. She greeted her parents with loud, immediate, piercing screams from her tiny, but powerful lungs.

Her face turned a bright red, reminiscent of a tomato. Callista appeared to be angry with her parents. Her birth had disturbed her peaceful stay within her mother's womb.

Callista's size made her birth difficult. She weighed nine pounds, three ounces, even though she was only twenty one inches in length. A few strands of blonde curls graced her otherwise bald head. Already, Callista had cried so hard, and so long, her lips were now a deep purple. Her cheeks were a dark crimson.

Her mother, Mary Julia Roberts, was a close friend of Jackie Lynn Greathouse. Mary Julia and Jackie Lynn had been friends for years before she met, and fell deeply in love with, Jonathan Roberts.

Jonathan had been one of the most gorgeous men Mary Julia had ever laid eyes upon. This man was slightly over six-foot tall. He had a slim but well-built body. He had short, jet black, curly hair and the most exquisite baby blue eyes she had ever had the painful pleasure to gaze into.

Jonathan and Mary Julia had dated for a year before he proposed and she accepted. They had married in an intimate ceremony, with only family and close friends attending the wedding.

Two years later, shortly after Mary Julia's thirty-eighth birthday, Jonathan had broached the subject of them having a child. He knew it would be hard a hard sell. Mary Julia had suffered through a sad and distorted childhood.

Both her father and stepfather had sexually abused her. Nevertheless, Mary Julia seemed to be over the pain she had endured. She also overcame her subsequent sexual addiction.

Jonathan's wife got over the distorted notion that she had to sleep with every man to feel loved. Mary Julia had learned to love herself, and she had faith in Jonathan. Mary Julia truly loved him as a partner, and not merely for the sexual favors they shared.

Thus, it only seemed natural that Jonathan and Mary Julia should have a child. "Your biological clock is ticking away," he reminded his wife. "We have built a loving and trusting relationship. It would be great to add a child to our lives. It would bond us together even more, if that is possible."

Jonathan had pulled Mary Julia into his arms then and whispered in her ear, "Think of the fun we will have trying to conceive this little bundle of joy." All the while, he nibbled little kisses over her neck.

*Jonathan is right about my biological clock*, Mary Julia had accepted. She was very thankful, at long last, to have the love and companionship of a good man. So, Mary Julia had agreed that that they should conceive a child.

*Hopefully, I can give Jonathan a fine son, like my best friend Jackie Lynn did for her husband Long Wolf. Except...what if I should have a girl?*

This reflection sent waves of terror through Mary Julia. *No! I'm not going to worry about that! I'm going to have a boy, and then I'll have nothing to be concerned about! Jonathan will do the* normal *things a father and son do together. Men simply do not know how to behave around girls.*

\* \* \* \*

Mary Julia tightly held her defenseless newborn daughter. She was checking and counting each of her fingers and toes. They were perfect. Mary Julia felt profound, heart clutching love for her robust little girl.

She carefully wrapped the infant back up in a soft, pink blanket. Mary Julia securely tucked the corners all around Callista's body. She cradled her daughter in a safe embrace, vowing to always protect her.

"Isn't she beautiful! She looks like her mother," Jonathan's words rudely interrupted Mary Julia's silent, loving vigil.

Mary Julia looked up to find Jonathan's face hovering over the top of their daughter. He had a wide, adoring smile on his face. *Did he say this baby looks like me? And he finds her attractive?!*

4

There was an odd, irrational panic arising within Mary Julia. She wanted to spring from the bed and dash away with *her* daughter.
*But it's* his *daughter also. Get a grip! Jonathan is merely admiring his daughter. The same as you were.*

"Mary Julia, I love you both so much!" Jonathan gushed. He bent to kiss his wife on the lips. Jonathan then planted a tender kiss on one of his new baby girl's faultless, rosy, little cheeks.

"I love you too, Jonathan!" Mary Julia replied with a bittersweet smile.

*Regardless of how much I love you, I'll do whatever is necessary to protect my innocent little beauty! I'll be a good mother to you, Callista. I'll protect you from all harm. No man will ever hurt you. This I promise you!*

## Chapter 2

# First Birthday

For the girls' first birthday, Flora Best and her husband Kenny graciously offered their house to host a combined celebration of the big events. Flora had briefly been married to Jonathan's father. So, technically, Flora was Callista's – or Callie as she was now being called – grandmother.

Callie was now a robust, twenty-eight pound toddler. She had a chubby face and plump arms and legs. Her head was now covered with soft, blond curls. Her eyes were a vibrant shade of blue.

Flora cared greatly for Callie's parents – Mary Julia, a dear friend of many years, and Jonathan, who had literally saved her life. Jonathan helped free her from his abusive father. So Flora accepted the title of 'Grandma' for their darling daughter with pride.

Flora and Jackie Lynn had been the best of friends even longer. Flora had watched Jackie Lynn spend years in and out of dead-end relationships. Then Long Wolf came into her friend's life.

Long Wolf had been as patient and loving as he was handsome. He was a big man, standing over six-foot tall. He also had very muscular arms and legs. He had the darker coloring of an Indian and short, thick, shiny black hair. His alluring, golden brown eyes instantly caught and held your attention, and his charming smile was heartwarming.

Long Wolf had managed to capture Jackie Lynn's heart, if not her soul. Both Flora and Mary Julia had been overjoyed when Jackie Lynn married and gave birth to Mason. Flora was no less thrilled to welcome their daughter, Katie Rose, into her extended family.

Katie Rose was still a petite baby girl. She weighed only eighteen pounds. The biggest part of her was her chunky upper legs. Katie Rose was still mostly bald, with only a sparse covering of dark black hair. Her eyes were a pretty bluish green.

Flora was affectionately known as 'Aunt' Flora for Mason and Katie Rose. This first birthday party, that she and Kenny were throwing, was intended to be only the beginning of watching these wonderful children grow to adulthood. Flora loved them all very much.

Flora considered both Jackie Lynn and Mary Julia to be like sisters. No one would have ever mistaken them as such, however. The differences in their appearances were too distinctive.

Flora considered herself short and thickset. She was only five-foot three and weighed 125 pounds. In Flora's opinion, this made her hips and upper thighs heavier than she preferred. Flora's breasts were on the small side but *thankfully* firm. Shoulder length, permed, short, loose curls softly framed Flora's face. Flora's most attractive feature was her extremely captivating, large, deep chocolate brown eyes. They immediately conveyed warmth to those who beheld them.

Jackie Lynn was the tallest, being almost five-foot eight, with a flattering breast line, an attractive waistline – especially after bearing two children – and long slender legs. Her luminous, straight, jet-black hair hung well past the center of her back. Her deep-set eyes were a seductive, emerald green.

Mary Julia was nearly as tall as Jackie Lynn. Her waist, while not tiny as it once had been, was still small. She had long sleek legs, and voluptuous breasts. Her body still had an hourglass shape. Mary Julia had long, golden blond, naturally curly hair. She had big, dreamy, sapphire blue eyes.

Flora and Kenny had been married only a short while – less than a year. After her horrendous marriage to Jacob, Jonathan's father, and Jacob's violent death, Flora never imagined she would marry again. Kenny Best had broken down that resolve with love and tenderness.

Kenny had been the exact opposite of Jacob in every way. Kenny was short and stocky. Jacob had been tall and lean. Kenny's eyes were a captivating, unique shade of bluish green.

7

Jacob's eyes had been an enticing sky blue. Kenny's hair was a sandy blond, peppered with gray and thinning a bit on top. Jacob had sported a full head of dark black, wavy hair. The most important way that the two men were different, however, was in their temperaments. Jacob had been mean-spirited, and Kenny was as kindhearted as any man could be.

Even so, Kenny's relentless quest for Flora's heart had still taken him two years. Fortunately, the wedded bliss he currently enjoyed had him believing that Flora had been more than worth the *every minute, of every hour, of every day* it had taken him to win her trust and love.

Flora had been forty three and Kenny forty nine when they had married. So, the two had decided that they would not try to have children. But Kenny was more than happy for them to share their lives with the children of Flora's dearest friends. Kenny realized that she considered them to be family.

So celebrating the girls' first birthdays at their house was a pleasure for both Flora and Kenny. They sat the girls in two highchairs, side by side, in the kitchen. Each was given a small, round, yellow cake piled high with white icing. There was a pink rose in the center that held a single lighted candle.

The adults and Mason sang an exuberant 'Happy Birthday' to the girls. Then the candles were extinguished and removed. At once, Callie reached out with both hands. She began demolishing her cake.

Callie cackled loudly. She appeared to be immensely enjoying herself. Katie Rose, on the other hand, seemed unsure what to do with her cake. She seemed mesmerized by how pretty it was. Katie Rose glanced at the adults and her brother in confusion.

She noticed Callie's laughter, so Katie Rose looked over to see what the other small girl was doing. Callie seemed to be having fun, so Katie Rose stuck one of her own tiny fingers into the frosting on her cake. Katie Rose placed that same finger into her mouth. A darling smile formed on her face, and Katie Rose began to tear into her own cake too, with shared enthusiasm and laughter.

The babies then began extending cake-filled hands toward one another, appearing to be attempting to feed each other. Kenny was videotaping the whole celebration, but camera flashes were still going off in all directions. All the adults were anxious to forever capture this one time, precious memory.

Four-year-old Mason, not wishing to be left out of the action, scurried toward the girls. Mason was a cute little boy. He was of average height and weight for a boy his age – three-foot tall and thirty-five pounds. He had jet black hair and handsome, golden brown eyes. He looked like a miniature version of his father.

Callie noticed Mason's approach first and began to play. She flung cake in Mason's direction. Katie Rose was quick to follow suit.

Mason was soon covered in cake also and squealing in response. He opened his mouth, daring first Callie and then Katie Rose to try and throw some cake inside. The girls did a much better job of getting cake into his hair, face and down the front of him.

The children were having the time of their lives. Mason willingly received the girls' abuse without attempting to retaliate. Long Wolf and Jackie Lynn had instilled in Mason a gentle sense of love and protectiveness toward his baby sister. It was only natural that the boy assumed the same must be true for small Callie as well.

A few minutes later, what remained of the cake was removed from the girls' destructive grasps. Mary Julia scooped up Callie and began to hurry off to a separate room with her. Callie began to cry.

At first, Mary Julia mistakenly thought she was angry about having to stop her play with the cake. But as she saw Callie's small hands reaching out toward Katie Rose, Mary Julia concluded that her daughter was crying because she did not like being separated from the other children. Mary Julia was alarmed that Jackie Lynn was allowing Long Wolf to take Katie Rose to change her clothes and *most likely diaper her*.

Jackie Lynn helped Flora wipe down the highchairs and tuck them away out of sight. Flora swept up the remaining crumbs from the floor, and Jackie Lynn turned her attention to Mason. She took him to the bathroom to clean him up as well.

Jonathan laid his camera down and had a seat at the kitchen table to await the return of his wife and daughter. Kenny had a seat with him. "So how is it that you get so lucky as to not have to do any clean up duty?" he joked.

"Mary Julia is funny about that," Jonathan admitted. "I suppose I should consider myself lucky. She doesn't believe it's a father's role to either change the baby, bathe her or dress her. Sometimes it's a little rough though, because I want to help her out. But she won't hear of it."

"I don't think I would complain if I was you," Kenny commented with a chuckle. "A lot of fathers nowadays would consider that to be a blessing."

"Yeah," Jonathan somewhat absentmindedly replied.

*It might be nice to be excluded from such duties if it were not for the fact that my wife does not want me to do* anything *alone with our daughter.* Jonathan found this more than a bit unsettling.

He rather painfully recalled Mary Julia's strange reaction when she came home one day to find him caring for their baby alone. Their daughter's nanny, Martha, had called him late one day at his pediatric practice to inform him that Callie was very fussy and appeared to be feverish. Jonathan canceled his late appointments and came home to check on the baby at once.

Since he was home, Jonathan dismissed the nanny. He had not called Mary Julia. She had been trying a big case in court that day. His wife was a lawyer at a prestigious law firm in town, and it would not have looked good if she had been called away because of her child.

Callie had not had anything seriously wrong with her anyway. Jonathan should have been an excellent judge of his daughter's health condition. He had been a pediatrician for many years. *More than likely, Callie is coming down with her first cold,* he diagnosed.

Jonathan gladly set to the task of trying to pacify his sick little girl. When Mary Julia got home from work that day, he had been rocking the baby in the rocking chair in their bedroom.

"Jonathan, what are you doing home?!" Mary Julia asked in a quite snappish voice. "Where's Callie's nanny?"

"Martha called to say Callie wasn't feeling well, so I took the day off and came home to check on her. Since I was here, I told Martha that she could go home," Jonathan explained.

"Callie's sick?!" Mary Julia inquired with apprehension.

She had charged toward Jonathan and practically snatched the baby from his arms. "Why didn't you call me?! Martha was told to *never* leave this baby! She should have stayed no matter what you said! I'll have to fire that woman!" she ranted.

"Mary Julia, calm down!" Jonathan commanded. He leaped to his feet and placed a consoling arm around his wife's shoulders.

"Callie isn't that sick. She is coming down with her first cold. That's why I didn't call you. And there was no sense in the nanny sticking around. I'm more than capable of caring for our sick child by myself. In fact, I was happy to do it. So don't be mad at Martha. She's a very caring woman and excellent with this baby."

"If Martha was so excellent with this baby, she would *never* have left her alone. She is supposed to keep an eye out and make sure nothing happens to this child," Mary Julia kept rambling, almost more to herself than to Jonathan.

Next, she strangely questioned, "Did you undress Callie?"

Jonathan gave Mary Julia a strange look but did not answer, so Mary Julia asked him again in a more harsh tone, "Did you change her?"

"Of course I did. As a matter of fact, I changed her twice. One was rather messy, but I muddled my way through pretty nicely," Jonathan replied with a smile, trying to lighten things up.

"I've got to go check her. You know how I feel about you doing that, Jonathan. Callie's nanny knows I specifically told her she was *never* to leave my angel unsupervised with *any* man."

Ending the relatively one-sided conversation, Mary Julia had disengaged herself from her husband's arm. She rushed away toward the nursery with Callie and left Jonathan standing all alone in a bewildered daze.

*What on earth! What's the big deal about me taking care of my daughter? What does Mary Julia mean by telling Martha that the baby shouldn't be left unsupervised with **any** man? I can understand that with a strange man, but I'm the child's father after all.*

Later, Mary Julia had calmed down. She apologized to Jonathan and told him she had overreacted because Callie was sick. But she stressed once more that a woman should be the one caring for their child. She also made Jonathan promise that he would call her at once if Martha ever had to leave again.

Jonathan had agreed to his wife's request, even though he had not fully understood it. *Mary Julia greatly loves our child, so maybe it is not so unusual for a first time mother to be a little overprotective.* It was certainly natural that she would have been upset that the baby was sick, and he had not wished to worry Mary Julia any greater.

*Things will probably get better when Callie is older,* he had found himself wishing.

Jonathan was still actively thinking about this strange past incident, when Mary Julia reemerged from the bathroom carrying their baby girl. Callie was still sniffling while her mommy wiped at her tears. She was now dressed in a pretty, pink, sun suit and tiny, little jelly sandals.

Right behind her, Long Wolf came out holding Katie Rose's small hand as she toddled along beside him. She was still giggling from her daddy tickling her while he had cleaned her up. Long Wolf had dressed Katie Rose in a lovely lavender sundress with matching ruffled panties and sandals. Jackie Lynn was a step or two behind Long Wolf. She was holding Mason back from charging into the room with excitement.

*Time to focus on your daughter's birthday again*, Jonathan told himself. He was pleased to be allowed to freely share in this celebration for the child he so adored.

It was time to give the girls their birthday presents. Long Wolf handed Katie Rose off to Jackie Lynn, and then took charge of Mason. He placed him on his lap, so the baby girls could be given their gifts without his son attempting to hog their attention.

## Chapter 3

# School Time

The next two years were gone in the blink of an eye. The girls were now three years old, and it was time for them to begin preschool. It was also time for Mason to start first grade.

Callie had thinned out a little, since she was an extremely active little girl, running everywhere to and fro. Katie Rose, on the other hand, while also being very energetic, had still managed to put on some weight. The girls were now closer in size, although Callie was still more full-bodied then Katie Rose.

Callie had thick, curly blond hair now and the prettiest, sapphire blue eyes, so like her mother's. Katie Rose also had a full head of hair now. Hers was a deep, dark black and straight as a board. Her eyes also favored her mother's, but they were a much more brilliant green than Jackie Lynn's.

Mason had tall, skinny legs, and his body was now a little on the slim side. Of course, he too was always on the move. He was becoming a handsome young boy, with an engaging smile and big, expressive, brown eyes.

Mason had attended preschool and kindergarten at St. Bernard Catholic School. Both Long Wolf and Jackie Lynn had been satisfied with this educational institution, so they had decided to permit Mason to go to grade school there as well. They also were planning on sending Katie Rose to preschool there.

St. Bernard's was Flora and Kenny's parish. Flora had been the one who had convinced Jackie Lynn to send the children to St. Bernard School. It did not hurt that St. Bernard School had a reputation for being one of the best in the area.

Mary Julia was troubled by the decision of where to send Callie to preschool. She debated whether she should send her young daughter to school at all. Despite St. Bernard School's great reputation, Mary Julia did not hold the Catholic Church as a whole in high esteem. She had heard far too many horror stories about pedophile priests.

*What if one of these monsters is lurking in the shadows at Flora's parish? Can I trust that Callie will be safe there?*

Nevertheless, Mary Julia could not keep Callie in a protected shell in her home forever. *Even if I hold Callie back from preschool, she will eventually have to start school somewhere. Private schools will likely shelter a child more than the public ones.*

Mary Julia had conceded that Callie could also attend St. Bernard's preschool. *It would be best for the girls to be together in preschool. This way, the girls can watch out for one another, even though they are so young.*

After all, preschool was only from 8:30 a.m. until 12:30 p.m. each day. *Callie will not even be lying down to take her nap until she comes home.* This fact made Mary Julia rest a little easier.

Both Jackie Lynn and Flora were happy that Mary Julia had decided to permit Callie to attend St. Bernard School. Jonathan had little say in the matter. Mary Julia had the final word on all decisions concerning their daughter. Jonathan had long since learned to silently surrender to this unspoken rule in order to keep the peace between the two of them.

On the children's first day of school, the seats of Long Wolf and Jackie Lynn's minivan were filled to capacity. Long Wolf was the driver. Jackie Lynn was in the front passenger's seat. Mary Julia and Flora sat in the two bucket seats directly behind them. All three children had been seated on the long rearmost seat.

Mason was willingly sandwiched between the girls' two booster seats. He was chattering on with excitement to the girls. He was telling them how much they were going to like *his* school. Mason seemed as thrilled for the girls as he was about himself starting first grade.

Jonathan had not come along. Mary Julia had assured him that there was no reason *whatsoever* for him to be there. 'After all, you have early appointments,' she had reminded him. 'There are

14

sick children and worried parents depending on you to be there. It should be a mother's role to see that a child gets to school and settles in alright.' As usual, Jonathan had bowed to his wife's decision. He had headed off to work to see other people's children, but his heart had ached a bit for what he had been missing with his own little girl. Jonathan would have loved to have been there to see his precious daughter start school for the first time. In actuality, he had hated missing any of the *firsts* in Callie's life. *I have to trust that Mary Julia knows best though.*

* * * *

Long Wolf released Katie Rose and Callie from their booster seats, and the children climbed out of the minivan and into St. Bernard's parking lot. Mason, acting the part of big brother, grabbed one of Katie Rose's small hands and one of Callie's. "I'll take them both in," he announced to the adults.

Mason began almost pulling the girls toward the preschool building. The girls freely went with him. He was Katie Rose's big brother, but Callie appeared to look up to Mason as if he was hers as well.

The adults fell into pace behind them. Long Wolf and Jackie Lynn exchanged a proud smile at the way their son was protectively taking charge of the girls. The children walked inside the classroom, and the teacher recognized Mason at once. She had taught him two years ago.

"Hi, Mason. How are you? Who have you got here with you?" she asked in a gentle, friendly tone.

"Hello, Mrs. Hamilton," he addressed with a broad smile. "This is my little sister Katie Rose and this is her bestest friend Callie Roberts. Callie is sort of like my other little sister; my mommy has known her mommy forever and ever."

"Well, it's nice of you to walk them in here," Mrs. Hamilton bragged. "Do you start first grade this year?"

"Yes, ma'am," he declared with a wide proud grin.

"Yes. And we need to be getting you to your room," Jackie Lynn spoke up. "It's time to say goodbye to the girls."

"Okay," Mason conceded. "Bye, Katie Rose. You be good for Mrs. Hamilton," he instructed. "She's really nice."

Mason gave his little sister a brief, sweet kiss on her cheek. Then Mason turned and discovered that Callie also seemed to be expecting a kiss. Mason sheepishly glanced at his father and saw him nod, so he gave Callie a small kiss also. The little girl squirmed and giggled with happiness in response.

Long Wolf and Jackie Lynn approached the girls then, hugging and kissing their daughter and reassuring her that all would be fine. Callie waited her turn at receiving their affection too. Jackie Lynn hugged and kissed the other girl as well.

Mary Julia rushed toward her small daughter before Long Wolf's arms had a chance to engulf her. Long Wolf was baffled when Mary Julia snatched her daughter away, but he concluded it was merely due to her excitement. He did not take her actions personally, but he should have. Mary Julia had not wanted Long Wolf to touch her daughter in that affectionate way; *the way a man does a woman.*

Flora gave the girls a goodbye hug and kiss and wished them well too. Before they left the girls for good, Mary Julia pulled Callie aside once more and whispered in her ear, "Remember what mommy told you, Callie. If any strangers approach you, even if it's a priest, you don't talk to them. You stay away from them, and you tell mommy when you get home."

Callie nodded in agreement, although she did not understand. Her mommy's words scared her, with their serious tone. Mary Julia's final hug was a little too hard, and she held on to Callie a bit too long.

Katie Rose smiled and waved goodbye as her parents, Flora, Mary Julia and Mason left, but Callie began to cry. Her mommy had frightened her, and Callie was not sure she wanted to go to preschool any longer. She only wanted to go back home.

"It's okay, Callie," Mrs. Hamilton assured her. "You'll have fun here. We have lots of pictures to draw and books to read. Then you will see your mommy later, and you can tell her all about what you did today."

Katie Rose stepped over to Callie and took her hand. She was trying to lead her to a rug that had toys spread across it. Callie gave her mommy one last, unsure glance. Then she gave in to Katie Rose with reluctance.

Callie followed after Katie Rose with tears still streaming down her cheeks. However, after Mary Julia left, the girls sat

16

down and began to play with the other children. Callie started forgetting the scary words her mommy had said to her.

# Chapter 4

# *The Name*

Nine-year-old Mason was not at home. He was out playing with some boys who lived in the neighborhood, much to Katie Rose's dismay. He had not wanted her to tag along.

Katie Rose felt she should be able to go wherever Mason went. Thus Katie Rose had complained, or actually she had whined, to her parents about this. Nonetheless, both had taken her brother's side and made her stay home.

Six-year-old Katie Rose was taking Mason's rejection hard. It had hurt her feelings that her brother did not always want to spend time with her anymore. Long Wolf tried to convince his little angel that Mason's abandonment was not due to him not loving her.

"It's just, as your brother gets older, he wants to play more with boys instead of girls. You ought to be playing with other girls instead of Mason and his friends. Little girls should be playing with baby dolls, and boys should play with cars and bats and such."

This did not set well with Katie Rose at all, and she candidly shared these feelings with her daddy, "I don't even like baby dolls!" Katie Rose professed.

"Katie Rose, that surely surprises me, since you have all of those pretty dolls on your bed, your book shelves and in the rocking chair in your room." Long Wolf tried to point out without success.

Katie Rose continued to bellyache, "But Mason has always taken me to play T-ball with him. He never left me at home. It's not fair!"

This was one of the reasons Callie was over today. Jackie Lynn had arranged for the two girls to play together more often. She and Mary Julia agreed to take turns having the girls at their homes on the weekends, to help Katie Rose make the adjustment to Mason's newfound independence.

When Katie Rose was invited to Mary Julia's, Jackie Lynn would often drop her off. On the other hand, when it was Callie's turn to come over to Jackie Lynn's, Mary Julia would stay the entire time that her daughter was there. She would use the excuse of wanting to visit with Jackie Lynn.

The only times that Mary Julia had ever left Callie at Jackie Lynn's house was when Long Wolf had been out of town on business. Mary Julia had even allowed Callie to spend the night on this rare and odd occasion.

Callie was visiting today, and the girls had decided, out of curiosity, to investigate Jackie Lynn's antique cedar chest. This was a place that Katie Rose considered to be a treasure chest, rather than merely another piece of furniture.

In this chest, her mommy kept all kinds of magnificent, interesting keepsakes, including many pretty cards and love notes from her daddy. Katie Rose and her brother's baby books were also among the magical treasures.

Callie removed Mason's baby book from the chest with eagerness. The girl was mesmerized by this older boy and was anxious to see anything that had to do with him. Katie Rose pulled out her own book as well, inquisitively wanting to compare hers to her brother's.

The girls took the books and snuck off to Katie Rose's room, as if they had items of great wealth. They sprawled across the bed, lying side by side on their bellies and placed their books down in front of them. Their knees were bent, with their feet pointing toward the ceiling; they were swinging their legs back and forth in perfect rhythm.

Katie Rose giggled, and she suggested they compare the two books page-by-page. Callie agreed with excitement that this was a great idea. "I'll count to three. You open your book, and I'll open Mason's. We will do it at the same time," Callie proposed. She was making it all into a fun game.

The girls had only turned about four pages in each book when Callie came upon a picture of an old Indian man holding

19

Mason high into the air. "What's this a picture of?" Callie asked Katie Rose. "Look, Katie Rose, who's the Indian man holding Mason? What is he doing with him?"

"I don't know," Katie Rose confessed with a little bewilderment.

She fanned through a few more pages in her own book to see if her mommy had put any pictures of her with an Indian in it. Katie Rose did not find any, so she looked again thinking she might have missed something. There was something written under the picture of the Indian man holding Mason. But the girls had both just started first grade, so neither could read very well – especially something handwritten in cursive and not printed.

"Let's go ask my mommy; she will tell us. Or we can ask my daddy; he will tell us," Katie Rose suggested.

She was interested in discovering what this picture might represent. It was put in Mason's baby book, so it must be something important. Her mommy put everything that was important into their baby books.

Callie slid Mason's baby book over in front of Katie Rose. They were not supposed to get into things at Katie Rose's house without asking permission first. Neither had asked to look in the old treasure chest.

Regardless, Katie Rose clutched Mason's book. She rolled over onto her side, sat up, and when her feet hit the floor, started a *determined* charge to find either her mommy or her daddy. Callie followed in hot pursuit.

The girls scampered down the hall. Both Katie Rose and Callie could hear their mommies' voices in the living room. As usual, Mary Julia was visiting with Jackie Lynn and Long Wolf while their daughters played together.

"Hey, girls, what's up?" Long Wolf inquired as he looked up to find the two girls entering the living room in a heated rush.

He was sitting in the chair that faced the hallway and the entrance to the living room. Jackie Lynn and Mary Julia were sitting on the couch against the opposite wall. It was rare for the adults to receive a visit from the two girls. They normally stayed to themselves, either in Katie Rose's bedroom, the playroom, or out in the fenced in backyard.

"Is everything okay?" Long Wolf further questioned. He had noticed the solemn expression on his daughter's face.

"Uh-huh," Katie Rose said with a nod. "I wanted to ask you or mommy something."

"Ask away, princess," Long Wolf initiated. He patted his knee to offer Katie Rose a place to sit if she so desired.

She approached her daddy with a wide smile and took a cozy seat on his knee. Callie stopped a short distance away. She turned her head to look at her mommy with bafflement. *Why is it okay for Katie Rose to sit on her daddy's lap but not for me to sit on my daddy's lap?*

On her first day of grade school, Callie ran with excitement to her own daddy. She had hopped into his lap, rambling on in delight about what had transpired that day at school. Mary Julia came into the room and spied her daughter snuggled against her father.

She was shocked that Jonathan would allow such inappropriate behavior. Mary Julia raced over to them. She took a tight hold of Callie's hand and ordered her to get up. Callie wanted to protest. But her mother's harsh tone of voice, as well as the painful grip she had on her small hand, convinced Callie to do as her mommy ordered.

'You started grade school today, Callie. You are much too old to be sitting on your daddy's lap,' Mary Julia explained to her. She had led Callie out of the room.

Yet now, here Callie stood watching her best friend, who was a whole day older than she was, sitting on her daddy's lap. Mary Julia understood the confusion she viewed in her daughter's eyes. *Callie must be remembering what I said to her about sitting in Jonathan's lap.*

"Come here, Callie. Have a seat with us girls," Mary Julia invited.

Mary Julia demonstratively patted the sofa cushion between her and Jackie Lynn. Callie had taken a seat on the couch, as her mommy had indicated. Mary Julia still believed she was, without question, right about prohibiting this kind of affection between Jonathan and Callie – *Or between Callie and any grown man.*

"Daddy, who is this Indian man holding Mason? Why is he holding him so high? Weren't you and mommy afraid he would drop him?"

ILLUSIONS

Callie attentively listened. Katie Rose was pointing to the picture in Mason's baby book and asking Long Wolf important questions.

"Where'd you get hold of this book?" Long Wolf inquired, giving his daughter a slight tickle to the ribs. "Were you and Callie snooping around in mommy's cedar chest?"

"Yes," she freely admitted with a giggle. Katie Rose struggled, and she vigilantly attempted to push her daddy's hands away from her ticklish spot.

"Stop, daddy! I mean it!" she was squealing in protest in her high-pitched little girl's voice. "I want to know who this man is and what he is doing with my brother. Please, can you tell me?"

Long Wolf was further amused by his daughter's intense seriousness concerning Mason's picture. He looked across the room at Callie and saw that she appeared to be interested in the story behind the photograph as well.

Long Wolf glanced at Jackie Lynn with a questioning look. She nodded her approval for him to explain the picture to their daughter. Long Wolf easily conceded, "Okay, I'll tell you girls the story behind this picture."

Before he continued he asked Callie, "Callie, do you want to come over and sit on my other knee?"

"No. She's fine where she is," Mary Julia surprised both Jackie Lynn and Long Wolf by abruptly answering for the girl.

They were even more amazed to hear Callie add, "Yeah. I'm a big girl now. I'm too old to be sitting on your lap." Even Katie Rose was puzzled by this bizarre comment.

"Alright," Long Wolf surrendered. "The story behind the picture is this. My mom, and Katie Rose's and Mason's grandmother, was an American Indian. So that means I'm half Indian and that means that you, Katie Rose, and Mason are part Indian as well. My Indian name, the name my mom gave me, is Long Wolf. My dad, who was not an Indian, named me Abraham Greathouse. When Mason was born, my mom was still alive so your mommy and I took him to the Reservation. The Reservation is the place where your grandmother and the other Indians live. When we took Mason to the Reservation, he received his Indian name. That's what this picture in Mason's baby book is all about. The chief of our tribe is the Indian man who is holding your brother, and he has just given Mason his Indian name, Running Wolf."

Totally transfixed by this story, Katie Rose asked with excitement, "So what is my Indian name daddy?" Long Wolf did not answer right away, so she was quick to add, "Why isn't there a picture of me with the chief Indian man in my baby book?"

"Well..." Long Wolf hesitated, this time looking to Jackie Lynn for help. She had a lost look on her face and merely gave him a shrug of her shoulders.

Long Wolf spoke now with a softer tone to his voice, "You see, Katie Rose, your grandmother died before you were born. I haven't gone back to the Reservation since she was buried there. So.... you don't have an Indian name."

Seeing the dismay in his daughter's eyes, Long Wolf attempted to helpfully add, "But we could always make one up for you if you want."

Katie Rose's beautiful emerald eyes, so like her mother's, darkened with disappointment. "No, daddy! I don't want some old made up name! I want a real Indian name like Mason has. I want the chief Indian to give me one, like he gave my brother. It's not fair that Mason got a real Indian name but I didn't. I can't help it that my grandmother died before I got here. I want to be an Indian like Mason and like you, daddy!!"

Katie Rose's angry outburst was unusual. She was a meek and agreeable child, but presently, she was very upset. Tears wrought from frustration and betrayal began to flow plentifully down Katie Rose's flushed cheeks.

Long Wolf could not stand this. Female tears always tore at his heart, whether it was his wife's or his daughter's. He had to do something to alleviate his daughter's pain. Katie Rose was the apple of Long Wolf's eye.

Long Wolf was, all of the sudden, ashamed that he had not taken his daughter to the Reservation. He should have had her properly inducted into the tribe when she was an infant, as he had his son. Long Wolf could almost feel his mother's spirit strongly disapproving of his inaction, and so it should be.

"Hey, sweetie, don't cry," he soothed.

Long Wolf enfolded Katie Rose in his arms and held her against his chest. He also kissed one of her wet cheeks. "Daddy will make it all better. I promise. How about if your mommy and I take you to the Reservation and have the chief give you a real Indian name like Mason's?"

Jackie Lynn was astonished by her husband's words. Long Wolf's heartbreak over losing his mother had made him inflexible about not returning to the Reservation. Regardless of her husband's sorrow, it was not right for him to turn his back on his Indian heritage.

It was even worse for Long Wolf to deny his children from knowing their heritage. However, Jackie Lynn had not pushed this issue. She had wanted to give Long Wolf significant time to grieve first.

"Really, daddy?! Do you mean it?" Katie Rose exclaimed. Her head sprang off his shoulder and her eyes studied his invasively. She was trying to determine if he was telling her the truth or not.

"Yes, honey. Daddy wouldn't lie to you. If your mother agrees, then we shall go," Long Wolf assured Katie Rose. He rubbed her back, and with gentle strokes, he wiped the remaining tears from her face.

"Mommy, can we go? Can we please??" Katie Rose half begged.

"Of course," Jackie Lynn replied with eagerness. She gave her daughter an agreeable nod. Then Jackie Lynn looked directly into Long Wolf's eyes, and she smiled with love.

"When can we go? Can Callie come too?!" Katie Rose began impatiently firing additional questions.

"We'll go in the summer, since you and your brother are both in school right now. Both Daddy and Mommy will take a few days off from work, and we will plan a special trip. As to Callie, I have no objections to her coming along. That is, if her mommy and daddy give their permission," Long Wolf told them all.

"We'll see," Mary Julia was swift to tell Callie. She had seen her daughter's expectant eyes gazing up at her.

Mary Julia was thinking that she and Jonathan had not taken a trip anywhere since before Callie was born. She also contemplated the wedge that she had driven between her husband and herself. Jonathan had not appreciated Mary Julia removing Callie from his lap and telling her she was too old to be sitting there. Mary Julia hugged Callie to her side with affection.

*I had to put you first, my sweet daughter. Regardless of how your daddy might have felt. But would a family trip this summer help to mend the rift that stands between Jonathan and me now? I don't see where it would hurt.*

"I'll ask your father, and if it's okay with him, then we'll *all* make plans to go along to the Reservation with Jackie Lynn, Long Wolf, Mason, and Katie Rose," she relayed to Callie and everyone else.

"Yea!!" Katie Rose cheered in a loud and animated voice. Callie joined in immediately.

"Thank you, daddy!" Katie Rose screeched in a high pitched voice. She proceeded to give him approving kisses on his forehead, on his nose and lastly on his lips. This was the way she was used to kissing her daddy each night as he tucked her into bed before she went to sleep.

Mary Julia squirmed with uneasiness in her seat as she watched what she deemed unsuitable physical affection between Long Wolf and Katie Rose. *I need to find a way to convey my concerns about this to Jackie Lynn. She wasn't abused as a child, so she does not comprehend the evil that can lurk in a man's heart. She doesn't understand how important it is that she watches over Katie Rose very carefully, even when she's with her own father. I need to find a way to make her understand this, before something terrible happens to Katie Rose.*

Mary Julia was relieved when Katie Rose hopped down from Long Wolf's lap. Callie leaped off the couch and the two girls formed an elated embrace. They held on tight to one another, bouncing up and down in splendid delight in front of the adults. They were celebrating, with youthful excitement, the thrilling trip to come.

# Chapter 5

# *New Identity*

That summer, Long Wolf was determined to keep his promise to Katie Rose about visiting the Indian Reservation and having her properly inducted into his tribe. Mason was excited about the trip as well. He had been so young the last time he had been taken to the Reservation, right before his grandmother's death, that he did not remember his visit there at all. Presently, Mason's nine-year-old, male mind actively imagined all kinds of fun and adventure in visiting a real live Indian Reservation.

Mary Julia, Jonathan and Callie, as well as Flora and Kenny, were supposed to be making the trip to the Reservation along with the Greathouse family. As Jackie Lynn's extended family, they were all looking forward to witnessing Katie Rose's ceremonial tribal renaming. Jackie Lynn was happy they were going to be there with them.

Flora and Mary Julia had also come along when she and Long Wolf had been remarried on the Reservation and when Mason had been welcomed into Long Wolf's tribe. Neither Mary Julia nor Flora had been married then, so they had rode in the car with Jackie Lynn, Long Wolf and Mason to the Reservation. Her two friends had even stayed in a teepee together, beside Jackie Lynn, Long Wolf, and Mason's teepee, on the Reservation grounds.

This time, however, each individual family would be traveling separately, and only the Greathouse family planned to stay overnight on the Reservation. Mary Julia and Jonathan were going to take Callie and stay at a nearby hotel. Flora and Kenny had decided to do the same, and they requested a room near the

Roberts' room. The hotel was a couple of miles from the Indian Reservation. It was nothing fancy, but it was nice and quaint.

Long Wolf and his family left on a Friday, as soon as he had gotten home from the office. The Reservation was eight hours away. Long Wolf drove a little over halfway and stopped for the night at a Holiday Inn.

Long Wolf planned on getting up early the next morning to drive the rest of the way, in order to arrive early midmorning. Mary Julia, Jonathan, and Callie were supposed to start off early the next morning with Flora and Kenny following them in their own car. They would arrive late that afternoon. Katie Rose had wanted Callie to ride along with her and Mason, in her parent's car. Then Callie could have stayed the night in the hotel with them, but Mary Julia had not allowed it.

'You girls will have plenty of time to spend together once we get to the Reservation,' she had reasoned with Callie.

Mary Julia pitied Callie. Her daughter would probably get bored riding eight hours with no other children in the car to interact with. Regardless, Mary Julia would not chance sending Callie with Jackie Lynn and Long Wolf.

*After all, Long Wolf will be spending the night in the same room as the children. I've seen firsthand how he is with his own daughter. I won't have him kissing, hugging and fondling my daughter. I hope that some day Jackie Lynn doesn't discover that this man has harmed Katie Rose. I pray to God that it's all innocent, but I won't take that chance with my precious little girl. No....Better that Callie is a little bored than risk something terrible happening to her. I'll find some way to entertain her.*

\* \* \* \*

Long Wolf and his family arrived at the Reservation about eleven the next morning. The incredible view at the Reservation was always breathtaking. There were miles of trails among wooded acres. They seemed never-ending.

The Indians used these trails mostly for hunting, hiking and horseback riding. Nearby, to the west, was an unspoiled stream. As you turned to the east, all you could see, or so it seemed, were miles of beautiful mountains.

# ILLUSIONS

The Indians still mostly lived in securely constructed teepees, but further up on the hillside was a settlement of small log cabins. The outdoor lifestyle of these people was overwhelming to believe. It always took Jackie Lynn by surprise each time they visited.

It was hard to conceive of such picturesque land and people living together so peacefully. There was no traffic, no loud noise from trains or buses, and no rushing pedestrians trying to reach their next destination. There was only tranquility.

Long Wolf's people welcomed them with warm hearts, but Long Wolf's heart was once again seized by intense sorrow. The Reservation had always been his mother's home. There was this certain emptiness without her to greet him.

Long Wolf also felt guilty that he had not visited his mother more often. He wished that she could have lived long enough to have seen her beautiful granddaughter. He could still picture his mother's heartwarming broad smile with vividness. Long Wolf could also imagine the feel of her big warm arms, engulfing him in a bear hug. He was shaken by how much coming back to the Reservation made him miss his mother.

"Long Wolf, are you okay?" Jackie Lynn asked, always in tune with his emotions.

"I miss her," he shared.

Long Wolf was never afraid or ashamed to share anything with his wife – especially his feelings. Jackie Lynn felt free to share everything with him as well. It had taken Long Wolf a great deal of time and effort to get Jackie Lynn to this point. They now shared a close, nurturing relationship. Long Wolf could not even begin to imagine loving another woman as much as he loved Jackie Lynn.

"Your mom was a wonderful woman," Jackie Lynn proclaimed with a forced smile. She closed the space between her and Long Wolf, and she reached to console him, stroking his back. "I'm glad we have come back to the Reservation. This is hard for you, but your mother is looking down at us right now and is happy to see us here. She is thrilled that you are having Katie Rose inducted into your tribe. Your mother would have loved her so much, and I'm sure Katie Rose would have adored your mother. I wish she was still here too."

28

"I know," Long Wolf replied. He gave his wife a grateful embrace, holding on to her a few moments for comfort. As Long Wolf released Jackie Lynn, he placed a tender kiss upon her forehead. "Thank you," he murmured.

"For what?" Jackie Lynn inquired.

"For being here by my side. For sharing my pain. For being a part of my life. I love you and will continue to love you forever, Jackie Lynn," Long Wolf professed with tenderness. He was fighting to remain strong and contain his emotions.

"I wouldn't want to be anywhere else but by your side. I love you too, Long Wolf," Jackie Lynn responded. She enfolded him in another secure hug.

The children had scampered several paces ahead of their parents. They had found themselves surrounded by a group of curious Indian children. Katie Rose was a little frightened by this and concealed herself with shyness behind Mason's back. Mason was not at all scared. On the contrary, he was as *curious* as his Indian counterparts if not more so.

"Hi," he said, raising his hand in an effort to wave at them.

Most of the Indian children continued to stare at him. One boy, who looked to be about Mason's age, or maybe only slightly older, stepped forward and replied, "Hi. Most of them don't speak English, but I do."

"Oh," Mason acknowledged. He was surprised to learn that the other children could not understand him.

"I am Soars Like an Eagle. Are you Indian, or are you visiting someone here?" the other boy questioned.

"I am Indian, and so is my dad," Mason explained.

"So what is your Indian name?" the boy continued to interrogate. He acted as if he did not believe that Mason was Indian.

Mason was embarrassed, because he could not remember his Indian name. He looked helplessly over his shoulder, trying to ascertain if his mother and father were nearby. He was relieved to see that they were approaching.

"Dad," Mason called. He motioned for Long Wolf to catch up with him and Katie Rose.

"Yes, Running Wolf," Long Wolf replied to his son, as he and Jackie Lynn caught up with their children. Long Wolf had called Mason by his Indian name on purpose. It seemed appropriate considering where they were.

Mason was relieved to hear his dad refer to him in this manor. He turned back to face the Indian boys, beaming with happiness. With pride, Mason announced, "This is Long Wolf, my dad, and I am Running Wolf. Dad, Mom, this is Soars Like an Eagle. He is the only other kid that speaks English here."

"I'm glad to meet you, Soars Like an Eagle. Who is your father? Does he live here on the Reservation, or does he have relatives who have brought you here to visit?" Long Wolf inquired. *This other boy speaks English, so he must not have been raised on the Reservation.*

"My father is Fighting Bear," the boy acknowledged. "He lives here on the Reservation. I come to visit him for a month and a half each summer. When I am grown, I want to live here all the time. For now, my father says I must live with my mother. Unfortunately, she lives far away from here," he revealed with discontent.

Long Wolf knew Fighting Bear. He had not been aware that this younger man had come back to live at the Reservation. Fighting Bear had left years ago when he had fallen in love with a woman on the outside.

Things between Soars Like an Eagle's father and mother evidently had not worked out. So Fighting Bear had returned to make the Reservation his home once more. Long Wolf was glad this man was bringing his son here each summer and sharing his Indian heritage with him. Once again, Long Wolf was glad he had brought his children here.

*I'll have to make sure I return with them more often after this visit. It is important that they know their Indian heritage.*

"Soars Like an Eagle, would you mind showing my children around the Reservation while I go and talk to the chief for awhile? And if either of them should need me or their mother, will you bring them to the chief's teepee?"

"Yes, sir," he consented without hesitation.

Soars Like an Eagle was happy to encounter other children who both spoke English and did not live here. Lots of times, he felt intimated by the other Indian boys. They were so much wiser in the Indian way of life than he was. This was Soars Like an Eagle's chance to show off for this other boy. It was even okay with him if the little girl tagged along too, although he was not much for playing with girls.

"Mason, you look out for your little sister," Long Wolf reminded him. "If she wants us for anything, then you bring her to us. Okay?"

"Sure," Mason assured his parents.

He was eager to be on his way. He had no fear of this new place. Mason was overcome with tremendous inquisitiveness. He could not wait to start exploring this place with the other Indian boys. Mason was certain that he could do this and still make sure Katie Rose was okay. He would never allow anything bad to happen to his little sister.

"Come on, Katie Rose. Let's go. You'll be fine. I promise," he told her, tugging with anxiousness at her hand.

"Okay," she conceded.

Katie Rose trusted her big brother. Mason would never promise her she would be okay if she would not be. He would look out for her, and her daddy gave the impression that she would be safe as well.

Katie Rose was curious about this place also. Katie Rose smiled and waved goodbye to her parents. Then she and Mason and the other children started off in the opposite direction of her mommy and daddy.

* * * *

Mason and Katie Rose played for hours with the Indian children. Soars Like an Eagle showed Mason how to shoot a bow and arrow. The boys would pretend to be hunting. The girls would pretend to fix meals for everyone, from what the 'brave warriors' brought back to them.

Katie Rose wanted to try hunting too, but Soars Like an Eagle gruffly informed her, "Girls do not hunt. You prepare the food."

Katie Rose did not like this boy much. He was much too bossy. She also deemed him to be rather unfriendly. She was a guest, and he would not even share his toys.

If she and Mason had been home, Katie Rose would have voiced her opinion to Soars Like an Eagle. However, they were only visiting this place, so she held her tongue. So, as usual, Katie

Rose played more with the girls than she did with the boys. Unfortunately, none of the girls spoke English, so Soars Like an Eagle had to interpret for her. Katie Rose hated this, because she wanted nothing from this selfish Indian boy.

\* \* \* \*

For her induction ceremony, Katie Rose was given a buffalo skin dress and moccasins to wear. The dress was ornately decorated with red, green, blue and yellow beads around the neck and running down the center.

*The dress is beautiful.* Katie Rose thought with glee, as she gazed at it.

Once she was dressed, a large group of Indian girls of various ages was sent into the teepee with Katie Rose and Jackie Lynn. The girls were all dressed in buffalo skin dresses as well. However, their dresses were plain. There were no special, pretty beads outlining the neck and front. Katie Rose felt exceedingly privileged.

The girls directed Katie Rose to have a seat on the cot. Then they gathered around her and began to work their magic. Some began to paint her cheeks, forehead and chin with many lines of vibrant blue, red and yellow colors. Others brushed her long, straight, shiny, coal black hair. Another girl carefully pulled her hair back in a ponytail. Still others began weaving dried yellow and blue flowers throughout Katie Rose's hair.

Katie Rose could not remember ever feeling so special. At home, she shared a lot of her special events, such as her birthday, with Callie. Katie Rose did not mind sharing these times with the other girl, but she was pleased this big event was for only her. *Me alone!*

When they were satisfied she was ready, the girls motioned for Katie Rose to follow them out of the teepee. Mason and her daddy were waiting on the other side.

"Wow! Look at you!" Mason exclaimed.

He circled Katie Rose. Mason teased his sister by giving her ponytail a slight tug. "You look like a real Indian!"

"A lovely squaw," Long Wolf added, raising a camera. "Mason, put your arm around your sister. Let me get a picture of the two of you."

Mason did as asked, but he was surprised to find he was slightly jealous of his sister. He wished he had not been inducted into the tribe as a baby, so he could also be dressed as an Indian and get to participate in the ceremony. It seemed unfair to Mason that he had had to participate when he was too young to enjoy and remember it.

"Is Callie here yet?" Katie Rose asked. She was anxious for the other girl to see her in her Indian garb and makeup.

"Callie, Mary Julia, Jonathan, Flora and Kenny are all waiting for you by the bonfire," Jackie Lynn answered.

"They are watching the tribal dancing. The dance is to welcome you. After you join in the tribal dance, the chief will take you aside and assign your Indian name to you. Then you will officially be a member of this tribe," Long Wolf added. "So shall we go and join them?"

"Yes! Let's go, daddy!" Katie Rose squealed in a high pitched voice. She was overcome with excitement. She skipped toward her parents.

The four of them set out with Katie Rose energetically leading the way. She was practically jogging. Katie Rose was so overcome with exhilaration that she hardly appeared to care if her parents or Mason were even following. Katie Rose was impatient to participate in what was to come next.

She set off into the dark of night, entering a well-worn trail that was dimly lit by flaming torches. These torches were only placed every few yards. The trail wound into the woods. Even though there were large, intimidating shadows cast before her, Katie Rose had no fear.

She was making a mad dash along this path. Soars Like an Eagle had showed her and Mason earlier where the ceremony would take place. It would be at a spot called Big Rock in a nearby clearing in the woods. The rhythmic sound of the pounding drums was also a dead giveaway as to where to head.

Katie Rose drew to a rapid stop at the opening of a large circle of people. She was giving her brother, mommy and daddy a chance to catch up. Katie Rose was also taking a second to take in an awesome sight.

All of the Indians in the tribe stood in a giant circle. In the middle of the circle was a roaring bonfire. Groups of Indians took turns dancing all around it.

33

ILLUSIONS

Since it was dark, the flames from the fire seemed to illuminate the brightly colored feathers in the Indians' headdresses and the paint on their faces. They looked like a human kaleidoscope. Katie Rose's astonished eyes found this all so beautiful.

"Wow!" she gasped.

Long Wolf gave Jackie Lynn a wide smile. He was delighted to see the awe on his daughter's face. "Well, go on, Katie Rose. They're waiting for you," he coaxed. Long Wolf gave Katie Rose a gentle shove into the opening that stood before her.

Katie Rose roamed through the channel with eagerness. This space had been left open on purpose so she and her family had easy access to the center. A giant man wearing a massive, multicolored, feathered headdress approached Katie Rose. She looked apprehensively toward her father and mother.

"He's the chief, sweetheart," Long Wolf reassured her. "You'll need to go with him. It's okay. We'll be right behind you."

Katie Rose looked at the strange man's large outstretched hand. A smile appeared on her face. She took this man's hand and allowed him to lead her forward through the opening in the crowd. They reached a raised rock platform, at the midpoint of the circle, and ascended upon it. The chief made a hand signal, and the drums were brought to an instantaneous halt.

Katie Rose only understood English, so the chief spoke to her in her native tongue and not his own. "Welcome, daughter of Long Wolf." One of the braves, who also understood English, translated the chief's words to the tribe in their native tongue.

"Your father has expressed your request that we make you an honorary member of our tribe. According to our custom, the chief is to name the children of the tribe. I, Chief Ironhorse, along with the help of the gods, will do so tonight. It is a picturesque, clear night and the gods of the night sky, moon and stars appear to be looking with pleasure down upon us. I will ask for their assistance in knowing what name would best suit this young squaw."

He raised his head, stared wide-eyed into the bright sky and chanted for a few moments. Then he lowered his head, closed his eyes and was silent for several more. Katie Rose never took her sparkling green eyes off this man. She was mesmerized. She was so engrossed that it startled her when he spoke again.

"Daughter of Long Wolf," he addressed once more. "The gods have spoken. Your tribal name from this day forward will be Emerald Sea. Emerald because of your captivating emerald eyes, given to you by the white woman who is your mother. Sea because you will grow in your heart and in knowledge to be strong as the waves of the mighty sea."

As suddenly as they had stopped, the drums began again with a fierce and joyous beat. The tribe began to chant and dance around this precious little girl. Long Wolf and Jackie Lynn were pulled into the dance by other members of the tribe. The celebration had begun.

Mary Julia, Jonathan, Flora and Kenny were all laughing and rocking to the beat of the music as well. By this time, other tribal members began playing actual musical instruments. A young boy and a man played guitars; an old man played a harmonica; an old woman played an antique looking violin.

Katie Rose was spellbound by the celebration of becoming a real Indian girl. She momentarily forgot that Callie had come along for the occasion. Callie stood apart from the others watching her friend dancing in circles with joy. She was furious.

*I can't believe that Katie Rose has forgotten all about me. They all have.*

Callie felt lonely and hurt. She and Katie Rose had always celebrated everything together. She did not know how to handle being left out of this special event. She hid in the shadows and sulked, harboring mean thoughts toward her friend.

# Chapter 6

# First Fight

Katie Rose finally noticed Callie standing by herself near a tree. She took off running to her friend, her arms outstretched to embrace Callie. But Callie was infuriated with jealousy by this point.

Callie stepped aside, just before Katie Rose reached her. She stuck her foot out to trip her friend on purpose. Katie Rose went tumbling to the hard, course ground.

She began crying before she even hit the ground. After Katie Rose rolled over and saw her skinned up knees, her wailing became even louder. Callie had fallen to the ground too, as if Katie Rose had hit her instead. Tears were streaming down her cheeks.

Callie called out to her mother, "Katie Rose pushed me; help me mommy, please!"

Mary Julia scurried past Jackie Lynn. Reaching the girls first, she dropped to her knees and knelt beside Callie. Mary Julia cradled her daughter with tenderness in her arms. She was giving Katie Rose the most evil look and shaking her finger at her.

Mary Julia scolded, "Katie Rose, you deserved to fall down and get hurt for pushing Callie."

Katie Rose looked up at Jackie Lynn as she was reaching down for her. Her big green eyes were sad and confused. There were dirty little streaks on each of her cheeks where the tears were still flowing. She started to relay to her mother how Callie had tripped her, but Jackie Lynn did not give her a chance.

She also began to reprimand Katie Rose, telling her it was not nice to play so rough with Callie. Jackie Lynn pointed out how it had only led to the two of them getting hurt. Katie Rose dropped her head in defeat, but her father came to her rescue.

Long Wolf placed his hands on Jackie Lynn's shoulders and gave them a soft, yet firm squeeze. He was swift to stoop down between his wife and daughter and announced, "Katie Rose has something she needs to say about what has transpired here."

In hearing this, Katie Rose raised her head and divulged to both her father and her mother that she had not pushed Callie. Without delay, she also added that she had seen Callie standing all alone and had hurried over to give her a hug and share the dancing with her. "But I tripped over something and fell. I never meant to push or run into Callie. I couldn't help bumping into her as I fell."

Finished telling the small lie, Katie Rose looked over to Callie for approval. She could not fathom that her best friend could have intended to trip her and make her fall. Nonetheless, Callie would not even look at Katie Rose.

Instead, Callie started crying to Mary Julia anew. She whined about how she was so hurt by the way Katie Rose had pushed her down and how she had ruined her new dress. Of course, there was not a scratch on Callie, and her dress would be fine after she stood up and brushed it off.

Jonathan had reached the scene by then, and Mary Julia instructed him to pick up their daughter and carry her straightaway to the car. "But don't hold her too closely," she added. She scrambled to her feet and scampered off toward the parking lot on his heels.

Long Wolf could see the disappointment in his little girl's eyes as they took Callie away. The place that he had been standing had provided the perfect vantage point to view the entire scene that had unraveled. Katie Rose had lied to all of them about bumping into Callie. Long Wolf had seen Callie stick out her foot and trip his daughter.

Mason and Soars Like an Eagle came walking up. Flora and Kenny were headed their way too. When Mason got close enough, he spied Katie Rose upon the ground. He also noticed her scrapped knees and tear-streaked face. Mason demanded, "What happened? Katie Rose, are you okay?"

"Why don't you tell your brother what happened, Katie Rose?" Long Wolf spoke, adding, "Just make sure you tell him the truth."

Long Wolf arose from his squatting position, and Jackie Lynn rose beside him. She was giving him a confused look. Jackie Lynn could not decipher what Long Wolf was trying to get at. First, he had come to Katie Rose's defense when Jackie Lynn had been admonishing her for playing too rough. But now, Long Wolf seemed to be trying to get their daughter to confess to this very thing.

Long Wolf placed his arm around his wife's shoulders and pulled her close to his side. Placing his mouth close to her ear, he explained in a whisper, "I saw what happened."

Katie Rose stared up into all of the eyes that were watching her. All of these people were waiting for her explanation. *I can't keep lying. I only lied to protect Callie, and she didn't even appreciate it.*

"Callie tripped me," Katie Rose blurted out. Frustrated tears sprang to her eyes once more. "I was only coming to give her a hug and get her to dance with us all, but she stuck out her foot and tripped me. I don't know why."

Long Wolf crouched back down and put his arm around his daughter. He hugged Katie Rose to his side, "Shh...no more tears, Emerald Sea," he instructed in a quiet voice. "I'm glad you told the truth. Lies never solve anything. You need to remember this. Not only was Callie wrong for tripping you, but she shouldn't have lied to us about what she did. I understand why Callie behaved so meanly to you. Callie felt left out, since the two of you usually share everything. She was jealous of you since you were getting all the attention. You asked her to come here, but then in all the excitement, you forgot she was here. Didn't you?"

This was true. All at once, Katie Rose felt guilty about having ignored her friend and leaving her out of her celebration. She always enjoyed sharing everything with Callie. Sometimes it felt as if Callie were her twin sister instead of merely a close friend.

"I didn't mean to, daddy," Katie Rose attempted to assure him with sad eyes. "I love Callie. I didn't want her to feel left out or jealous."

"I know, sweetie," he said, giving her another reassuring squeeze. "Callie shouldn't have acted the way she did. She needs to learn to control her temper and not let jealousy get the best of her. The two of you can't always share everything. You'll discover that more and more as you grow older. We need to go tell Callie's mommy and daddy exactly what transpired, so they can talk to her about her behavior. The two of you also need to apologize to one another. Okay?"

"Okay," Katie Rose obeyed.

Long Wolf stood and helped his daughter to her feet. All of the sudden, an idea came to Katie Rose. *There is something I can do to make things better between Callie and me.*

"Daddy, can I go ask the chief something before we go?" Katie Rose made a strange request.

"The chief? What might you want to ask him? What's he got to do with this disagreement between you and Callie?" Long Wolf interrogated.

"You'll see," Katie Rose told him with renewed optimism. "Can I go see him, please?"

"Make it quick," he concurred.

Katie Rose was off running almost before Long Wolf's words of permission were out of his mouth. "What is she up to?" Jackie Lynn asked.

"I don't know. But I'm sure we are going to find out in a few minutes," Long Wolf replied. "Kenny...Flora, can you lead us to your car? That's where Mary Julia had Jonathan take Callie. She is more than likely planning on all of you leaving now. I hope the children can settle things between themselves and all of you will stay."

"I certainly hope so," Flora agreed. "It would be a shame to have to leave over some small spat between the children. It would be best if Mary Julia had Callie stay until the children could reconcile anyway. Children fight. But they also make up. That is, if the adults stay out of things. Sometimes Mary Julia is much too overprotective of Callie."

"In more ways than one," Long Wolf commented.

He was contemplating Mary Julia's warning to Jonathan not to hold Callie too closely. *Mary Julia was hurt by her own father, but it is terrible the way she drives a wedge between Callie and Jonathan. I don't know how Jonathan manages to stand it.*

Katie Rose was scuttling toward them again. She had the chief's hand, and she was pulling him toward them all. "Now we can *all* go see Callie," Katie Rose announced. There was a wide, accomplished grin on her face.

Long Wolf did not have a clue what his daughter might be up to, but he was happy to see Katie Rose smiling once more. "Flora...Kenny, lead the way," Long Wolf instructed. They all fell in line behind them, heading for the parking lot.

They came face to face with Jonathan first. He was headed back inside the Reservation. "Mary Julia sent me to get Flora and Kenny. She wants to leave," he explained with regret.

"No! You can't leave!" Katie Rose protested. "The chief is going to make things all better for Callie."

Jonathan looked toward Long Wolf for an explanation, but Long Wolf merely shrugged his shoulders. "We all need to talk about what happened," he told Jonathan. "And the children need to apologize to one another. After that, if Mary Julia still feels you should leave, then so be it."

"Okay," Jonathan concurred with ease. He was not anxious to leave anyway.

Jonathan agreed with Long Wolf. *The children should mend their fences, and we should all put this small incident behind them. So what if the girls had a fight. Fights between the children are bound to occur from time to time.*

Jonathan turned and walked with them toward the car. Mary Julia was sitting in the backseat, still cuddling Callie and consoling her. Jonathan softly knocked on the window to gain her attention.

Mary Julia was startled, because she had not expected him back so soon. She looked out and saw all the others, and she was even more surprised. Mary Julia released Callie with reluctance and opened the door.

"What's going on?" she asked in bewilderment. "I only sent you to get Flora and Kenny. Jackie Lynn, Long Wolf, I'm sorry, but we should be leaving."

"No," Katie Rose objected again. "The chief needs to talk to Callie. Please let Callie come out and see him. Can she please?"

Mary Julia looked perplexed. Callie, on the other hand, was intrigued. She wanted to be able to talk to the chief. She wanted him to talk to her, like he had to Katie Rose.

"Mommy, can I talk to him. I want to. Please?" Callie began to plead.

40

"I don't know, Callie. You've been through a lot tonight," Mary Julia began to disagree.

"It will make me feel better, mommy. Really it will! Pleeease!!!!"

"Okay. But only for a second," Mary Julia conceded with hesitation.

She wanted to make her daughter happy once more. However, Mary Julia intended to keep a close eye on this Indian man. He would not be allowed to take her daughter anywhere apart from them all.

Callie slid across her mom's lap, and she scrambled with excitement out the open car door. She ran past Katie Rose, without a glance, and she approached the big Indian man. Callie showed no sign of fear.

"Hi, I'm Callista Roberts," she told him. Callie offered her hand in greeting.

"Hello, Callista Roberts," the man greeted in a deep, authoritative voice. The chief gave Callie a brief handshake. "I have been asked to come see you by Emerald Sea. You have a troubled heart because she now belongs to our tribe, but you do not. Emerald Sea considers you to be a sister to her. She asks that I make things right by also including you in our tribe. She asks that I do this by giving you an Indian name as well. Is Emerald Sea correct? Do you desire to be included as one of us too?"

Callie turned and looked at Katie Rose in astonishment. *How did she know? I've been so mean to her.*

She wished she could take all of her mean actions back. Tears stung Callie's eyes. Katie Rose rushed over to her friend and pulled her into a tight embrace.

"I'm sorry, Callie," she told her. "I didn't mean to leave you out."

"I'm sorry too," Callie said. "I didn't mean to hurt you." The two girls hugged and cried together for several moments.

"Chief Ironhorse," Katie Rose addressed him, as she turned toward him. She kept one arm staunchly around her friend though. "What is Callie's Indian name?"

"Callista Roberts, sister of the heart to Emerald Sea, your honorary tribal name will from this day forward be Golden Fire. Golden as the lovely, long curls which frame your face. Fire because you are a force to be reckoned with. You will always be welcomed by the tribe." He was silent for a few moments and then he invited, "Now, why don't you all come back in and enjoy the celebration? It will not only be for Emerald Sea but also for Golden Fire. Come, let us celebrate."

Long Wolf had wanted Callie to be punished for her behavior. But it had been more important to Katie Rose to let Callie know that she loved her and valued her friendship about all else. He was proud of his daughter. If Katie Rose could let the incident drop, he could as well.

Mary Julia was still standing by the car. She was trying to decipher what had transpired. She was also ascertaining if she should let everything else go by the wayside.

"Can we go back in, mommy?" Mary Julia heard Callie asking her. Katie Rose had pulled some of the feathers from her hair. She was trying to make them stick in Callie's.

"Yes. We'll go back in," Mary Julia granted. "But no more roughhousing. Okay?"

"Okay!" Callie agreed. "Let's go, Katie Rose!" Callie grabbed Katie Rose's hand and starting to pull her along.

Mason and Soars Like an Eagle followed behind them. The adults brought up the rear. They were all glad to see that the girls had mended their rift, and they were all glad to be able to relax once more.

They were all looking forward to having more fun. Mary Julia would not totally relax, however. She was mindful of the fact that she would have to keep a close eye on Callie. There were way too many strange men around.

*If I had been keeping a closer eye out over Callie in the first place, none of this would have happened. It won't happen again. I'll keep Callie safe. She can have fun, but I'll still keep her from harm. Always!*

## Chapter 7

# *First Kiss*

The girls' eleventh birthday was fast approaching. Callie proposed that she and Katie Rose should ask their parents if they could have a sleepover party. Then they could invite all their friends from school.

This sounded like a wonderful idea to Katie Rose. She and Callie had heard some of the girls at school talking about having sleepovers at one another's houses. These get-togethers sounded like great fun.

The girls approached Jackie Lynn to ask about the party, and as expected, Katie Rose's mommy seemed to be fine with the idea. Thus the girls brought up the idea to Callie's mommy. Mary Julia was far less than thrilled with this plan.

"You are much too young to start this sleepover business," she informed her daughter.

Mary Julia began pacing back and forth in front of them. She contended, "There was nothing wrong with the pool party we had last year for you girls. It went over well. All your little friends liked it. Why don't we do that again? You can still invite all of your friends from school. I'm sure Kenny and Flora wouldn't mind you girls coming to their house again. She loves being included in your birthday celebrations, and they have such a nice pool."

"I don't want another *damned* pool party, mommy!" Callie snapped.

Katie Rose stepped back from Callie in disbelief, but more in fear of what Mary Julia was going to do next.

"Callista Elizabeth Roberts! What came out of your mouth?!" Mary Julia demanded to know. She dropped to her knees and grabbed Callie by her upper arms to give her a hard shake. "You had better watch it, young lady! Or you'll have no party at all."

Mary Julia stood up and stared at her precious little girl with scrutinizing eyes. *Where in the world is she learning such language? She isn't hearing it from Jonathan or me. Could it be coming from Mason? After all, he is a teenager now.*

Mary Julia was not comfortable anymore when he was around the girls. He had grown so much in the past year. Mason was well over five feet tall now. His voice was beginning to change, and he was even growing a little hair above his lip.

*He's becoming a man. I need to make sure I keep a close eye on that boy around Callie. She trusts Mason, and like all men, he may take advantage of her innocence some day.*

"I'm sorry, mommy," Callie apologized with haste. She realized she had been pushing things much too far.

*I'm not settling for another damn pool party*, she was determined. *That's for little kids. Katie Rose and I are getting too big for that. I will somehow have to convince my mom.*

Callie lowered her head, pretending shame. When she looked back up at Mary Julia, there were big tears streaming down her pink cheeks. Callie had long since perfected the art of crying on command.

Many times, turning on the waterworks was the only way to get her mommy to agree to something she genuinely wanted. Having a sleepover at Katie Rose's house for her birthday was definitely something Callie wanted. "Katie Rose already told all our friends at school that we are having a sleepover at her house for our birthdays. All our friends have already told Katie Rose they will come."

Katie Rose stood there shaking her head back and forth in shock. Regardless, Callie continued with the lies. "They all have sleepovers all the time now. I'm the only one who isn't allowed to. I just won't have a party this year. I'll stay home all by myself." With that, Callie plopped down in a chair, put her head in her hands and began to sob, her shoulders vigorously shaking.

"Katie Rose should not have been asking girls at school to come to a sleepover for the two of you before you girls got the approval from your parents. I'll have to talk to Jackie Lynn about this. Maybe Katie Rose will be the one who is staying home alone on her birthday, while you go to a pool party with all of your friends at Flora's," Mary Julia stated with wrath. She was looking at Katie Rose's unhappy and bewildered little face with condemnation.

Callie's protest was immediate. "No, mommy!" She raised her head from her lap, wiping her eyes with the back of her petite hands. Callie studied her mother with intense, pretty, watery, sapphire eyes, so like Mary Julia's.

"Katie Rose and I always celebrate our birthdays together. It isn't her fault that she told everyone about the party. It's mine. Her mommy said it would be okay. I figured if Jackie Lynn was letting us have it at her house than it would be okay with you. Besides, you're always telling me I'm a big girl now – too big to sit on daddy's lap, too big to be hugging him, too big to kiss him goodnight. So I figured if I'm too big for all those things, then I must be old enough for my first sleepover party. Some of the girls at school that are coming to the party still hug and kiss their daddies. I've seen them do it when their daddies pick them up at school. If they are still baby enough to do that, then how come they are old enough for a sleepover but I'm not?"

Callie undeniably had a point. *How can I tell her she is too old to be affectionate with her father and not allow her to do what all the other girls her age are doing? I can't.*

"Alright," Mary Julia approved with misgivings. "I'll allow you to have a sleepover for your birthday at Katie Rose's. But you need to understand that this doesn't mean you will be allowed to start attending them at all your friends' houses. You can invite them here if you want to for special occasions like this one."

"Oh, mommy! Thank you!" Callie proclaimed. She sprang from the chair and threw her arms around Mary Julia's waist. "This will be my best birthday ever!"

*I truly hope so*, Mary Julia wished. *Callie will be fine. She'll be surrounded by a whole group of girls. She won't be alone with Long Wolf or Mason. Mason – I need to talk to Jackie Lynn about him. I'll get her to agree to keep him away from the girls. He is much too old to be hanging out with these little girls. Jackie Lynn still sees him as a little boy, but he's capable of*

45

*harming some young girl now. I need to make Jackie Lynn recognize this.*

Mary Julia tightly squeezed Callie to her. Looking down, she was happy to see the wide, satisfied smile that had appeared on her daughter's beautiful face. She did not notice the sly wink Callie gave Katie Rose.

\* \* \* \*

Jackie Lynn was hanging up the phone when Long Wolf walked into the room. Her face was locked in a hard frown. Jackie Lynn was shaking her head, and she was hissing. It was clear to Long Wolf that Jackie Lynn was livid.

"What's wrong, hon?" he asked. Long Wolf took a seat beside her on the couch.

"That was Mary Julia. She called to tell me that she had given Callie permission for the sleepover here at the house for the girls' birthdays," she began to explain. "Then she asked me if Mason would be here. I told her I was sure he would be. He never misses the girls' birthday celebrations. So she asked me if that was such a wise idea. Then she went on to point out how Mason is becoming a young man now and probably should not be hanging out with a bunch of young, innocent little girls. Especially if they are going to be in their pajamas spending the night here. She even had the nerve to ask me if Mason had been cussing in front of the girls. She said Callie used a cuss word out of the blue today. She couldn't imagine where else she might have heard it, except for maybe from a teenager. Naturally, Mason is the only teenager she is ever around. Can you believe this? She's making Mason out to be some sort of foul-mouthed pervert! Who does she think she is?! I'm so angry right now I could scream!!"

"Jackie Lynn, honey, you are screaming," Long Wolf pointed out, with a slight smile, half-teasing.

He needed to help diffuse his wife's anger. She and Mary Julia had been friends for many years, and Jackie Lynn knew how this woman was when it came to her daughter. Mary Julia had merely pushed the wrong buttons this time.

Mary Julia had launched an unwarranted attack on their son. Jackie Lynn was willing to listen to a lot of things from her dear friend. Mary Julia was like a sister to her. But Mary Julia unjustly attacking one of her children crossed the line.

"Do you think it's humorous that Mary Julia is attacking our son?" Jackie Lynn questioned, her eyes dark with fury.

"Of course not, sweetheart," Long Wolf assured her. He reached out to caress her hand. "You are getting much too upset over this though. You know how Mary Julia is. You also know why she is like this about men. She is scared to death of any man being around her daughter, even Jonathan, who is the girl's father, for Christ sakes. She sees Mason is growing up. So isn't it only natural for her to set her paranoid sights on him now. It's nothing personal against him specifically I am sure. It has to do with all men. Deep down you know this. You are rattled because you feel you must protect Mason's honor. But, my dear wife, you must consider the source. Am I wrong?"

"Eew!" Jackie Lynn howled in exasperation. She wrung both hands into fists in her lap.

Jackie Lynn hated it when Long Wolf was so logical, especially when he was right. "Okay. Let's say for the sake of argument, or not arguing in this case, that you are right. What are we supposed to do? Send Mason away for the birthday party? Keep him away from Callie from now on? How do we explain this to Mason? He looks at Callie as if she was his little sister too. I can't imagine that Mary Julia actually thinks anything else when it comes to him."

"Did you tell Mary Julia how you feel about all this?" he inquired.

"No. She threw me for such a loop that I ended up telling her I would talk to Mason about it all. I led her to believe she was right. That's part of the reason I'm so angry. I should have confronted her and told her how wrong she was. Why didn't I?"

"You know the answer to that as well as I do. You didn't confront Mary Julia or tell her off because what she is saying is crazy. Mary Julia is saying these things because she is disturbed. We've all ignored her strange behavior since Callie was born. Even Jonathan has for much too long. But we do this because Mary Julia does what she does, and says what she says, out of fear. She can't stand the thought of something terrible happening to Callie the way it happened to her when she was a child. You getting angry and screaming at her isn't the answer. You know

47

that," he pointed out with calmness. Long Wolf also placed a reassuring arm around Jackie Lynn's shoulder.

"Then what do you think the answer is?" she dared to ask. Jackie Lynn was significantly calmer now. Long Wolf always seemed to know what she needed to hear to keep her on track.

"I honestly don't know," he admitted. "But the solution to our immediate problem would be to send Mason away for the girls' sleepover."

"But, Long Wolf..." Jackie Lynn started to object. Long Wolf placed a gentle finger on top of her lips to silence her.

"Please let me finish," he requested. "We'll let Mason celebrate the girls' birthdays with the group. He'll get to sing happy birthday with all of us here together and have some cake with ice cream. He can even watch the girls open their gifts. But he should spend the night with Flora and Kenny. They'll be here for the celebration too. They can take Mason home with them when they go. They'd love to have him over. He will get to swim late into the night and be spoiled rotten by them. Mason would far rather be doing that than hanging out in the house with a group of eleven-year-old girls anyway. Mary Julia is right in some respect about that. He is getting too old to be hanging out with a group of little girls. Flora always jumps at the chance of having either of the children stay the night at her house. She loves to spend time with them."

"Okay. That solves the problem of the party. You're right. Flora would love to have Mason as her houseguest for the night, and I'm sure Mason would love to go spend some time with her and Kenny. But what about after the party? We can't send him away from his home every time Callie is around."

"You're right. I don't see this as being much of a problem. Mason doesn't spend that much time around the girls anyway. Mary Julia's biggest concern is about Callie spending the night with Mason around. Since he'll be gone for the sleepover, she won't have to be worried about this. Going forward, I have a feeling Callie won't be allowed to spend the night over here anymore. That's the way it's always been. Callie has never been permitted to spend the night when I've been home. This isn't a coincidence. So see, my dear, there actually is no reason for you to be all upset. The problem is solved," Long Wolf egotistically professed.

SISSY MARLYN

*Not even close*, Jackie Lynn was privately meditating. *Long Wolf is right. We all have consistently looked the other way at Mary Julia's strange behavior. Now, things are coming to a head. I let her distrust my husband. Jonathan has allowed her to dictate his relationship with his daughter. Now, she even fears Mason. Where will it all end? What is this all doing to Callie?* The biggest question, which still remained, was what was she going to do about all of this?

"Jackie Lynn, it's best to let it go," Long Wolf interrupted her thoughts. He gave her a tender squeeze. "Considering all the things you told me that Mary Julia suffered at the hands of men when she was a child, it's remarkable that she handles things as well as she does. She is always going to have deep-seated fears towards men. It's extraordinary that she learned to trust Jonathan enough to settle down with him. You can't expect her to stop fearing for Callie's safety. You're going to have to accept this. You can't let her comments get to you. Take them with a grain of salt, as you always have in the past."

Deep down, Jackie Lynn had to admit that Long Wolf was right. *What can I do? Jonathan is Mary Julia's husband, and the father of their child, and he accepts things as they are. How can I expect any more than that? I can't. Mary Julia has a right to raise her child the way she sees fit. If I make an issue of this, I could not only jeopardize our friendship, but what about the girls? What good would that do any of us? I'll put it aside, as Long Wolf suggests.*

She gave her husband a brief, warm kiss on the cheek.

"What's that for?" he asked with a crooked grin.

"For always knowing what I need to hear. Have I told you lately how much I love you?"

"You just did," he said with a chuckle, his smile widening. In all the years they had been married, Long Wolf never got tired of hearing those words come from his wife's lips.

"I love you too," he said and planted a lingering kiss on her lips.

\* \* \* \*

Mary Julia and Jonathan brought Callie over to Jackie Lynn's an hour before the birthday party was to begin. Callie ran

49

off with Katie Rose while her mother and father helped Jackie Lynn and Long Wolf do some last minute preparation for the girls' celebration. The girls hurried down the hall toward Katie Rose's bedroom, but Callie stopped at Mason's bedroom door instead.

The door was closed. Callie had stopped because she could hear the sound of a acoustic guitar being softly strummed. She could also hear Mason's voice singing some tune. Regardless of the fact that it was rude, Callie opened his door without knocking.

Mason was sitting on the other side of his bed. He was facing the window, so his back was to the door. He was engrossed in his music, so Mason never noticed that the door had been opened.

Katie Rose turned and stood beside Callie in the open doorway, with a questioning look on her face. Callie put a finger to her mouth to silence her friend. She could tell that Katie Rose was about to ask her what she was doing.

Callie did not want Mason to know they were there. She was enjoying eavesdropping on him. It was a thrill to be able to share in his secret world of music.

All at once, his voice went from baritone to soprano. "Darn it!" he cursed. The boy's voice was changing, so it was not unusual for it to alternate between low and high without warning.

Katie Rose forgot Callie's call for silence and giggled at her brother. Mason spun his head around in dismay. "Can't a guy have any privacy around here?!" he growled.

Mason sprang to his feet. He pulled his guitar strap loose and carefully laid the instrument on the bed. "I don't remember hearing either one of you knock or telling you to come in. Why are you standing there so quiet, spying on me? I'm glad I'm going to Flora's tonight and don't have to put up with a whole bunch of you little brats."

"I'm glad you are going to Flora's too," Katie Rose snapped back. "You're mean and hateful, Mason. Callie and I don't want you here with our friends."

Mason always seemed to be saying nasty things to Katie Rose lately. He also made it plain that he did not want her around him. This greatly hurt Katie Rose's feelings, so she was glad to have this opportunity to express these hurts.

*Why is Mason going to Flora's and not staying around?* Callie had hoped that he would be here with them for the whole night.

As Callie watched Mason play the guitar and sing, she lost herself in her fantasies. She pictured herself sitting there beside him, with Mason singing solely to her. Over the past year, Mason had begun his transformation from a boy into a young man. Callie had developed an unrelenting crush on him.

Mason was the most handsome boy she knew. He had grown tall over the past few months – from barely five foot to five foot seven. He had the most gorgeous, shiny, wavy, neatly cut black hair. He was even growing a small mustache.

He made Callie's heart speed up and her stomach flutter when she looked into his striking, golden brown eyes. She hated that he only thought of her as a pesky little girl. She was growing up too.

Callie was almost five foot tall now. The girls had been the same height, but now Callie was taller. Katie Rose was still only four and a half feet. Callie had also slimmed down quite a bit with her jump in height. She still had a little baby fat, but it all seemed to be resting in the right places. Her chest had even begun to swell a little.

*You'd think Mason would notice these things with as much time as he spends around us girls. Mommy said I'm developing breasts. I could be your girlfriend, Mason. I'm not just a little girl.*

"Come on, Callie. Let's leave Mr. Rude and Nasty alone," Katie Rose said, tugging at her sleeve. Callie did not want to leave, but Mason did not give her any choice.

"Out! Both of you!" he shouted.

Charging toward them, Mason grabbed the door and started closing it. The girls lurched back as he slammed and locked the door in their faces.

"I hate him lately!" Katie Rose ranted to Callie.

Angry tears sprang to Katie Rose's eyes. She spun around and stomped down the hall, heading for her room once more. Callie halfheartedly followed.

\* \* \* \*

About half an hour later, Jackie Lynn came to Katie Rose's room. She surprised the girls by telling them that Mason wanted to see them in the living room. He wanted to give them his gift before their other guests arrived.

The girls vacated the bedroom with curiosity. They found Mason sitting in the living room on the sofa. He was holding his guitar.

"I was working on my present for the two of you, which is a song, when you little snoops tried to sneak into my room," he explained to them. All at once, Katie Rose was engulfed with guilt. She regretted the irate words she had spoken to her brother.

"I'm sorry for what I said earlier," she told him in a quiet voice. Her face turned a little red with embarrassment. She and Callie sat down in two recliners across from Mason.

"That's okay. Just knock next time," he said, giving her a forgiving and reconciling smile. Callie's insides melted as she gazed at it.

*Mason is so cute. He should be an actor. He's as cute as, if not cuter than, some of the stars I have pin-ups of on my wall.*

Mason had begun taking guitar lessons three years ago. Now, not only did he play the guitar quite well, but he had also started experimenting with writing songs. Katie Rose normally hated this, because it meant that he would spend hours alone in his room and not want to be disturbed by anyone.

Mason would come out of his room, but he would often take his guitar and go to Ralph's house. Ralph was his friend who played the drums in the school band. Away from school, he and Mason formed their own small band.

The two boys loved playing and singing Mason's songs together and dreaming of hitting it big as musicians. Long Wolf tried to assure Katie Rose that this was merely a phase Mason was going through. However, she was not as easily convinced of this as she might have been when she was younger.

Mason seemed to be growing farther and farther apart from her. Katie Rose did not like this at all. She was touched to find that Mason had written a song for her and Callie for their birthdays.

"The name of this song is *Brats in the House*," he announced with a playful chuckle.

"Mason," his father addressed in a stern voice, a disapproving frown on his face. Mason could easily hurt Katie

Rose's feelings these days. Long Wolf was not going to stand by and let him ruin her birthday.

"I'm only kidding," Mason was prompt to add with a snicker. "The real name is *The Birthday Song*. Much more appropriate."

"Much," Long Wolf was swift to agree. Jackie Lynn shook her head in agreement.

"Sing it to us, Mason," Callie chirped.

She squirmed a little in her seat with noted excitement. Callie could hardly wait. Her dream was about to come true. Mason was going to sing to *her*.

*It's a song for me, even if I do have to share it with Katie Rose.* "We'll both sit beside you while you sing to us," Callie brainstormed, wanting so badly to be close to this boy.

"Sounds good by me," he consented. "Come on over here you two."

Mason did want this day to be special for the girls. He still loved the two of them – *even if they were little pests most of the time.*

Callie sat down on one side of him and Katie Rose sat on the other. Callie was so overjoyed that she could feel her heart beating in her head. Mary Julia and Jonathan were standing together inside the door from the dining room. Flora and Kenny were standing to the side of them along one of the walls of the living room. Jackie Lynn walked over to stand next to Long Wolf, who was leaning against the mantel of the fireplace.

"Okay, everyone settled? Here goes. I hope you two like it…and that my voice holds up," Mason said.

He began to strum his guitar and sing:

"Happy birthday, Katie Rose. Happy birthday, Callie. This song was written just for the two of you. Two special young ladies who turn eleven this year. Who turn eleven this very year."

"Katie Rose and Callie, born a day apart…born a day apart. These two girls are now sisters of the heart… sisters of the heart." He followed with the refrain again. Then Mason eased into the second verse.

"Katie Rose and Callie, they've become the best of friends…the best of friends. Even though they argue, their friendship never ends….never ends." He followed with the refrain once more, followed by the third and final verse.

"Katie Rose and Callie, I will look out for them all their days...all their days. It's for them that this special song plays...this special song plays."

"Happy birthday, Katie Rose. Happy birthday, Callie. This song was written just for the two of you. Two special young ladies who turn eleven this year. Who turn eleven this very year...this very year."

Mason brought the song to a close then. Callie did not hesitate to throw her arms around Mason and kiss him. It was not a long kiss, but it was a kiss directly on the lips.

Mason looked stunned as Callie pulled away. Mary Julia became choked on her own saliva, which distracted everyone in the room. Mason hardly had a chance to react before Katie Rose hugged him and kissed him on his cheek. Mason thought this was much more appropriate.

"Thank you, Mason!" Katie Rose squealed, tears in her eyes.

"It was fantastic!" Callie chimed in. She kissed Mason again, but on the check this time.

Mary Julia could remain silent no longer. She frantically called out to her daughter, "Callie, that is enough!"

Mason was merely trying to justify the whole experience. *It must have been the excitement of the moment that made Callie accidentally kiss me on the mouth. I'm sure she didn't mean anything by it. I'm glad they are both so happy.*

"I'm glad you both liked it," Mason said with a wide smile. He gave them both a final, conclusive hug. Then he was on his feet and heading to his room to put his guitar away.

"Good job, son," Long Wolf praised, patting him on the back as he passed.

"I'm so proud of you," Jackie Lynn chimed in. She gave her son a brief hug and kiss before Mason could make his escape.

Flora grabbed him and hugged him also. Kenny gave one of Mason's arms an affectionate squeeze as he passed. Jonathan gave him thumbs-up and a pat on the back also.

Mary Julia stood apart from the others sizing up this young man. *Thank God, Mason is going away this evening. Callie is much too innocent to be around a boy this age. I bet he liked it when she kissed him on the lips. I bet Mason would love the opportunity to teach her how to really kiss. He'll never get that opportunity. I'll see to that.*

She turned, without a word to the others, and returned to the kitchen to finish some last minute preparations for the girls' party.

# Chapter 8

# *The Sleepover*

The official birthday celebration came to an end, so Mason departed with Flora and Kenny. Jonathan took Mary Julia by the hand and gave her a little pull to suggest they head home. Mary Julia went along with him reluctantly. At last, the sleepover could begin.

The girls headed to the basement and spread sleeping bags all across the carpeted floor. None of them planned to sleep though. The idea was to stay awake all night, or most of it anyway.

Katie Rose slipped a popular movie, called *Dance City*, into the DVD player. Mesmerized, the girls all watched the popular, young, male star impressively swivel and shake his body, as he danced his way through the movie. They all cackled and discussed their undying love for this gorgeous movie idol.

After the movie ended, they listened to a variety of CDs, some hip hop, some pop and even some country. They also played a few games, Trivial Pursuit, Uno, and Scrabble.

The hour grew late and they began to get tired. So they changed into their pajamas and sleep shirts. They were all intent on settling into their sleeping bags and talking and giggling the rest of the night away.

As one of the girls, Glenda, slid into her sleeping bag, she remarked to the others, "Ouch!! I can't lay on my stomach. It hurts my chest too much. I'm growing boobs, and they are sore as hell!"

Katie Rose glanced at the stairs to make sure her mommy or daddy was not anywhere in sight. Then she warned the girl, "Glenda, you shouldn't use that kind of language."

"What? Boobs? Or hell?" the girl challenged. She laughed at Katie Rose in ridicule.

Katie Rose looked at Callie with helplessness. Callie was the one that had invited Glenda to their party. Katie Rose did not particularly like this girl.

Glenda was a heavy girl, who appeared to take delight in picking on others and pushing them around. She also cursed quite often. Katie Rose was intimated by her. She basically tried to stay out of Glenda's way. Callie, on the other hand, for some unbeknownst reason, had befriended the girl.

Instead of helping to end the conversation or steer it in a different direction, Callie announced, "I know what you mean, Glenda. I'm getting them too." Callie stretched her nightshirt tighter against her body to try and show the others that she was no longer a flat-chested baby.

Glenda began to howl with laughter. "Hey, Katie Rose, go get a magnifying lens, so we can see what Callie is trying to show us. Why don't you try again, girlfriend, when you truly have something to show."

Then Glenda crawled back out of her sleeping bag. She sat on top of it and dared to unbutton her pajama top. "Now, here are some real boobies," she proclaimed with pride. She placed a hand under each small, rounded mound and showcased her breasts to them all.

Katie Rose could feel her face growing red hot. She was both shocked and embarrassed. "Glenda, put your clothes back on!" she hissed in a quiet voice.

Katie Rose glanced up the stairwell again in fear. She fully expected to see her mom, *or God forbid, her dad,* coming down the steps at any moment.

The other four girls snickered and giggled in embarrassment. Callie was strangely quiet. Her glistening sapphire eyes, however, told Katie Rose that her friend was furious. Callie did not like to be showed up by anyone.

"You heard Katie Rose, Glenda, button up your shirt," Callie demanded with ire.

Glenda pulled her shirt back around herself and buttoned it again. All the girls seemed to be relieved that she had done this.

"Don't worry, Callie. My boobs are bigger because I'm a year older than you are. I'm twelve already, and I've even started my period."

At that comment, Katie Rose turned her head and looked around at the other girls in the room. They were all sort of dumbfounded. Glenda continued, "I'm sure you'll grow some real boobs when that happens to you. Anyone else want to share?" she challenged.

The other girls all nervously glanced at one another, and no one said a word. None of them, included Katie Rose, had started to develop yet. Katie Rose had been astounded to hear that Callie was developing breasts already.

*Surely, she hasn't started her period. Callie would have told me if that had happened. We always share everything.*

"Why don't we change the subject?" Callie suggested.

"Good Idea!" Katie Rose was prompt to second.

"Okay, little girls," Glenda conceded. She slid back into her sleeping bag, but Glenda lay on her side this time.

One of the other girls started talking about a popular teenage boy band that they all loved. Katie Rose revealed that she had a video of them. She sprang from her sleeping bag and slid it in the VCR for them all to watch.

Katie Rose was relieved that the last discussion had drawn to a close. She settled back into her sleeping bag to watch the video with all her friends.

\* \* \* \*

One by one the girls began to resistantly nod off. Callie observed them, fighting sleep with all her might. When she heard nothing but heavy breathing all around her, Callie was convinced everyone was asleep. She cautiously crawled from her sleeping bag.

Walking on tiptoe, Callie silently crept across the room to a large walk-in closet. She opened the door with care, listening for any sign of squeaky hinges. Callie entered the closet. She switched on the light and headed towards a shelf which held all of Katie Rose's art supplies.

There were boxes of crayons, colored pencils, water paints, coloring books, scissors, and most importantly, glue. Callie picked up the bottle of glue and studied it with a wide, devious smile on her face. *So Glenda thinks she is really something with her big boobs, huh? Well, I'll show her! Wonder how she will like having a whole head full of glue? She's lucky I don't glue her big mouth shut too!*

With pleasure, Callie turned with the glue held in both hands. She switched off the light and hurried from the closet. Callie softly closed the door behind her.

She turned the orange cap on the glue, opening it. Quiet as a cat scoping out its prey, Callie approached Glenda. The girl was now in a deep slumber.

Callie bent to her knees, directly over Glenda's head. She turned the glue bottle upside down and began to squeeze the sides. Callie had to stifle a delighted squeal as she watched the glue begin to trickle from the bottle.

She ran the bottle back and forth over all of Glenda's exposed hair. Since Glenda was sleeping on her side, Callie was able to cover almost all of it. She did not stop until she had emptied almost the entire bottle of glue.

Glenda soundly slept through the whole dousing. She hardly even stirred in her sleep. Finished with her revengeful tirade, Callie settled back into her sleeping bag. She rather quickly fell into a peaceful, contented, unremorseful sleep.

* * * *

Shrill screams awoke Callie with a jolt, late the next morning. Girls were scrambling from their sleeping bags all around her. Suddenly, Callie remembered what she had done the night before and knew exactly what was wrong.

Jackie Lynn and Long Wolf came running down the steps in a panic over the horrible screams. They were positive that something terrible must have happened to one of the girls. They soon discovered that they were somewhat right.

Glenda was crying and screaming and thrashing about. She was attempting to pry her glued hair loose from the side of her pillow. "My hair! What's in my hair?! My head is stuck to my pillow and sleeping bag!" she shouted in fright to the other girls. They had gathered all around Glenda, looking down at her in total confusion.

Jackie Lynn and Long Wolf shooed the girls away from Glenda and knelt down beside her. Jackie Lynn tried to calm the girl by talking to her in a soothing voice. Long Wolf tried to free Glenda's hair without pulling it out or hurting the girl.

Long Wolf worked for several moments before he could free her. Glenda crawled from her sleeping bag. She was still in a traumatized daze. She was helped to her feet by both Long Wolf and Jackie Lynn.

"Jackie Lynn, will you please take Glenda upstairs and call her parents? I want to talk to the other girls," Long Wolf told her, looking directly at Katie Rose.

Katie Rose met his questioning stare with scared, perplexed eyes. *What happened to Glenda? Who would have done such a thing?*

The deliberation no sooner crossed Katie Rose's mind than she turned to look at Callie. *Callie was angry with Glenda for making fun of her. Did she get even with her by sticking her hair down with something?* Katie Rose did not want to believe that her friend had done such a spiteful thing. Nonetheless, Callie was the most logical candidate.

"Alright, girls, I need to know who did this to Glenda," Long Wolf insisted in a strict voice. His sweeping gaze was studying them all now. He held up the empty bottle of glue. "Pranks sometimes occur at sleepovers, but this one takes things much too far. You all need to understand that what happened here hurt Glenda, and it was very wrong. This isn't a harmless prank. This is serious. It is likely that Glenda will have to have most of her hair cut off."

Some of the girls gasped. They exchanged horrified looks and passed a hand through their own hair. Katie Rose glanced at Callie again and was dismayed to see tears streaming down her face. *Is she feeling guilty?*

"Uncle Long Wolf," Callie addressed Katie Rose's father with affection. "We didn't mean to do anything to hurt anyone. It was only a prank. We thought it would wash out. Didn't we, Katie Rose?"

Katie Rose spun her head to glare at Callie. *What in the world is she saying? I didn't have anything to do with this!*

Callie flung her arm around Katie Rose's shoulder. She pulled Katie Rose close against her side. Callie lowered her head upon Katie Rose's shoulder and began to sob. Katie Rose stared down at her in complete bewilderment.

After several moments, Callie raised her head. She looked straight at Long Wolf once more and wailed with remorse, "We're very sorry. Aren't we, Katie Rose? We would never have done what we did if we had known it would hurt Glenda."

"Katherine Rose, did you plan this along with Callie?" Long Wolf asked. His somber eyes seemed to be burning holes right through her.

Katie Rose glanced at Callie's pleading eyes once again. She had serious misgivings about what she was about to do. Regardless, in a voice barely above a whisper, Katie Rose began to lie, "Yes, daddy, I did. I'm sorry. It was supposed to be funny. It wasn't supposed to hurt anyone. I didn't know Callie was going to use so much glue."

Callie gave Katie Rose's shoulders a tiny grateful squeeze. *I shouldn't lie to my daddy, but what else can I do. If I say I had nothing to do with this, after the show Callie has put on, I'll look like I'm lying to save my own butt. I might as well share her punishment. I'll find out later why Callie did such a terrible thing, and let her know I don't approve.*

"I'm extremely disappointed in both you girls," Long Wolf professed. There was a deep, disapproving frown on his face.

Tears stung Katie Rose's eyes. She hated disappointing her daddy more than anything. *Callie will owe me big for this lie!*

"Sorry, daddy," she stated, choking back a sob.

Jackie Lynn called from the top of the stairs, "Long Wolf, Glenda's parents are on their way."

"We'll be right up," he replied to his wife.

Then Long Wolf turned his attention to the girls once more. "Katherine Rose, Callista, you will come with me. You both need to apologize to Glenda and her parents. I'll figure out what punishment best fits your actions. You other girls can come up as well. We have some donuts and juice for breakfast if you would like."

Katie Rose and Callie started for the stairs with heavy hearts. Long Wolf positioned himself directly in back of them. The rest of the girls followed.

None of the girls were in the least bit hungry. They were anxious about what could have happened to them instead of

Glenda. They were all ready to go home. The girls never wanted to come to Katie Rose's house for a sleepover again. This had never happened at any of their other friend's houses when they had stayed over.

When Glenda's parents arrived, Long Wolf lined the girls up in front of Glenda and them. Callie pleaded for forgiveness with tears running down her face. She stuck to her well-planned story that Katie Rose had come up with the idea, but she had been the one to put the glue in Glenda's hair. She assured them that they had meant no harm.

Callie added on purpose, "I had no idea that you would have to have all of your hair cut off, Glenda. I feel so terrible!"

"My hair.... cut off?!!" Glenda exclaimed. She clutched at the dry brittle threads again before looking from one parent to the other. "Is it true?!" she asked them in despair. Big tears flowed down her fat cheeks once more.

"We don't know yet what we'll have to do for sure," her mother said, glaring at both Callie and Katie Rose. "Your father and I are going to take you home now. We'll call our salon and get an appointment first thing."

Long Wolf and Jackie Lynn followed the trio to their front door. Long Wolf assured Glenda's father that he would pay for any expenses pertaining to Glenda's hair. He apologized one final time for both the girl's actions.

"I can't believe the girls did this to her," Jackie Lynn shared with concern as they turned from the door. "It's so unlike Katie Rose to come up with something like this."

"It certainly is," Long Wolf agreed with obvious dismay. "She will have to be punished."

In the back of his mind, Long Wolf had grave doubts that Katie Rose had come up with the idea for this prank. He had to wonder if Callie had not engineered the whole thing. However, for whatever reason, Katie Rose had decided to accept part of the blame. Consequently, she would be punished for the deed as well. He was not finished questioning his daughter, however.

Long Wolf and Jackie Lynn made their way back to the kitchen. They were very unhappy with what had transpiring in their home. Long Wolf sent Katie Rose to her room. He instructed Callie to go and sit in the living room while they called her parents.

Long Wolf hated punishing Katie Rose. *Especially for something I'm not even convinced she's done.*

Jackie Lynn called Mary Julia and Jonathan. She told them what had occurred. Long Wolf offered to start taking the other girls home.

Long Wolf could tell that the other girls were all very upset by what had happened and were ready to go home. The donuts and juice had gone untouched. Long Wolf directed all of the girls to go downstairs and gather their things. He informed them that he would meet them out by the minivan.

After Long Wolf had left and Callie was sure she was alone, she allowed herself to smile. She could not believe how well her plan had worked. She had managed to get her revenge on Glenda. Callie did not even care that she would be punished.

She was certain that her punishment would not be all that bad anyway. Callie knew how to work her mommy too well. It would also work to her advantage that Katie Rose had taken part of the blame. Her mommy would most likely defend her actions by saying that Katie Rose had talked her into doing what she had.

*Regardless, whatever the punishment, it will be worth it.*

Callie refused to be made fun of by anyone. She sat and waited for her parents' arrival. Callie forced herself to think of sad things, so she would be able to cry on command when her mom and dad arrived.

# Chapter 9

# *Confrontations*

Katie Rose could not help but stare. Callie had emerged from the bathroom, after taking a shower, and she did not have on a stitch of clothes. Callie had never been bashful around Katie Rose, but now, Katie Rose wished her friend were a little more modest.

*We're thirteen. We're not little girls anymore. At least Callie isn't.*

Callie looked every bit a woman. She had long, slender legs, which neared her to Mason's six foot height. Callie dwarfed poor Katie Rose. She was barely even five foot tall.

Callie also had a tiny waist, and breasts that looked surreal because they were so large. Katie Rose glanced down with self-consciousness at the two *mosquito bites* that made up her bust line. *I can still wear my training bra. But Callie is as big as her mom on top. Or maybe even bigger. And all of that hair down below! I hardly have any of that either.* Katie Rose was glad she had taken her shower first and that her body was covered by clothing.

"Don't worry, Katie Rose, you'll get some too," Callie said.

She had noticed Katie Rose's stare. Katie Rose became bashful. She lowered her eyes and studied her lap with discomfort.

"You have to remember that you only started your period this year. I started mine over a year ago, and I had already started to develop a little before that." Over the past two years, Callie had gone from a training bra to a *'boulder holder'* – her nickname for her bra.

Katie Rose raised her eyes to look at Callie once more. She was relieved that the girl had put on some bikini underwear

64

and was shielding her enormous breasts with a bra. There was a slight smile on her friend's face.

*Callie's proud of what she's got*, Katie Rose concluded. *A little too proud for her own good. Especially when it comes to the boys.*

This year, as many of the boys began to go through puberty, Callie was all at once incredibly popular with them. Instead of discouraging their attention, Callie promoted it with blatancy. It was not the fact that boys were attracted to Callie that bothered Katie Rose. What disturbed Katie Rose was the way Callie used her body to tease these boys. It worried Katie Rose a lot. It especially bothered her when Callie flirted with Mason.

Callie was not her sister, or more importantly Mason's, but Callie teasing him in this manor did not seem right. Katie Rose could tell that Mason felt ill at ease with it as well. He countered by often meeting Callie's come-ons with rather hateful barbs.

Mason pretended to be totally disinterested in Callie. Nevertheless, Katie Rose often caught him studying Callie when he was sure she was not looking. Katie Rose was glad that Mason was not at home. This way there would be no chance of an uncomfortable encounter between her brother and her best friend today.

* * * *

*Man! Life doesn't get much better than this!* Mason was happily thinking, as he pulled his father's pickup truck into the driveway of his home.

He was on top of the world. He was finally sixteen! He had his driver's license. He was tall – six foot – dark – he had his father's Indian coloring – and handsome – thick, shiny, black hair; sensitive, golden brown eyes; sparkling white teeth; and muscular chest, arms and legs, from playing sports.

Mason had his first real girlfriend, a pretty, blue eyed, Irish, redhead named Rebecca. He was part of a band, Savage Pride, for which he wrote songs, played electric guitar and did backup vocals. Mason even had a job.

Mason's father had hired him to work with his construction crew for the summer, and Mason loved it. His dad had taken him to his construction sites as a visitor many times as a child. Now, he was proud to be working amongst grown men and learning the ropes of the building trade. Mason was getting home from a hard day's work, but he felt thoroughly energized.

Mason was looking forward to calling Rebecca and planning their weekend. He sprang from the truck and bounded toward the front door. He was eager to have the house all to himself for awhile. *Mom and dad haven't gotten home from work yet, and Katie Rose is still at the YMCA summer program.*

Mason headed to the kitchen first. He poured himself a tall glass of ice water and guzzled it down in seconds. He always developed quite a thirst each day working and perspiring in the heat. Mason vacated the kitchen, grabbed hold of the bottom of his soiled and sweaty tank T-shirt, and hoisted it over his head.

*It will feel great to take a shower.*

Mason began to climb the stairs two at a time. His sweaty T-shirt was wadded in his hand. When he reached the landing at the top, Mason took a second to slip out of his work pants. He picked them up and wrapped them haphazardly around the dirty T-shirt.

Mason stepped inside his bedroom, and he removed his last piece of clothing – white Fruit of the Loom briefs. He threw all of the dirty clothes down the laundry chute inside his closet. Then he headed to the door of the adjoining bathroom, the one sandwiched between his and Katie Rose's bedroom.

*Today, I have the house and the bathroom all to myself,* he mused with contentment.

But Mason's indulgence lasted only mere seconds. As he bolted into the bathroom, he came face to face with Callie. She was standing in front of the mirror in only her bra and panties.

"Shit!" he cursed, jumping from the shock of finding someone else in the house. Mason instantly endeavored to cover his nakedness with both hands. "What the hell are you doing here?!" he demanded to know.

Mason scrambled backwards into his bedroom. Without hesitation, he slammed the door. He turned and sprinted over to his chest of drawers.

Mason was retrieving a pair of underwear when he was amazed to hear the door opening. He turned his head to find Callie standing inside his room. She was grinning widely with amusement at his mortified face. She did not seem self-conscious at all about only being in her underwear.

"Gosh, Mason! Is that a banana in your hand, or are you happy to see me?" she teased, laughing heartily.

"Get out of my room, Callie!" Mason shouted.

He immediately slid his underwear the rest of the way up his legs, shielding his nakedness from Callie's uninvited view. He also turned his head away from her so he would not be tempted to look at her mostly naked body.

"Callie!" Katie Rose called as she entered the bathroom from her side. "What are you doing?! You aren't even dressed. Mason's right. You shouldn't be in his room."

"At least I have my essentials covered. That's more than I could say for Mason. He barged in the bathroom, without knocking, stark naked," Callie shared with a snicker. She turned slightly toward Katie Rose, but Callie still did not leave Mason's bedroom.

"I wasn't expecting anyone to be here," Mason explained in exasperation. "What are the two of you doing here anyway? Aren't you both still supposed to be at the Y?"

"We went to the Water Park today, and we got back early. Since we didn't want to sit around the Y for another hour, I called mom and she gave us permission to walk home together," Katie Rose shared. She grabbed Callie by the upper arm and rather forcefully persuaded her back into the bathroom. "You're not supposed to be home yet either, are you? Did you get off work early?"

"A little," he admitted. "And speaking of work…I'm tired and I'm dirty and I'd love to take a shower right now. So could the two of you scram from the bathroom? Is that asking too much?"

Katie Rose did not get a chance to answer. Mary Julia's voice startled both girls. "Callie! What's going on here?!" she asked with alarm.

Mary Julia was standing in the other bathroom doorway. She was glaring at her half clothed daughter. She could not see Mason, but she had heard his voice. It had come from his bedroom.

"Mom, what are you doing here?" Callie nervously inquired.

67

Callie hurried toward her, so that her mother could not come any farther into the bathroom. She certainly did not want her mom to look into Mason's room. Callie did not want her to discover that he was also only half dressed. It was bad enough that she was not properly attired.

"Jackie Lynn told me she had given the two of you permission to walk home and that I could pick you up here. So I left work as soon as I could to check on you. It appears it is a good thing that I did. What on earth is going on here?! Why are you standing in the doorway to Mason's bedroom without your clothes on?!"

"Mason and I were having passionate sex, and we thought it would be a riot to have Katie Rose watch!" Callie sassed with a foul-mouth. Mary Julia's mouth fell open and her eyes became watery.

Callie rushed on, "Good gosh, mom! Would you get a grip?! I took a shower. I didn't know Mason was home, so I didn't lock the bathroom door. He came home and headed for the shower himself, only to about have a heart attack when he found me in the bathroom. Now, can we get out of here, so Mason can come in and take a shower?"

Mary Julia snatched Callie's arm. She painfully sunk her fingernails into her tender skin. Mary Julia pulled Callie from the bathroom and into Katie Rose's bedroom. She slammed the door behind them, leaving Katie Rose in the bathroom.

Mary Julia slung Callie toward the bed. She ordered with sternness, "Finish getting dressed, young lady, and then I am taking you home! I won't stand for one more word of sass talk from you! Don't even think about it, or I will ground you for a month! Do I make myself clear?!"

It was rare for Callie to see her mother get so angry, so Callie realized she meant business. She politely replied, "Yes, ma'am."

Callie scurried over to her backpack. She hoisted the backpack onto the bed. She pulled out her clean clothes and started to dress.

Katie Rose was still standing in the bathroom with bewilderment. Mason had taken a seat on the end of his bed in defeat. He figured he might as well stay put until Mary Julia carted Callie away.

*I hope Mary Julia does lay into Callie about this. My coming in on Callie was all an innocent mistake, but the way she flaunted herself in front of me wasn't. Her mom needs to get control of her before Callie gets into some real trouble with a guy.*

Katie Rose heard Mary Julia call her name. Her insides tensed as she opened the door with trepidation. Then she made her way out of the bathroom as well.

"Yes," she answered with apprehension as she entered her bedroom. Katie Rose closed the bathroom door. She wanted to give Mason some well-deserved privacy.

"Callie and I are leaving now, but I would like to speak to your mother when she gets home. Will you please tell her to call me?"

"Of course," she agreed. Katie Rose nodded her head to further demonstrate her conformity. "Callie, I'll see you tomorrow?"

"See ya," Callie replied in a hushed voice.

She threw her backpack over her shoulder and started out of the room ahead of her mother. Callie dreaded going home now. She would most likely have to endure a long speech from her mother about the dangers of men.

*If she only had a clue how much I'd like to become familiar with those dangers. I'd love nothing more than to learn about them from Mason. I'll get him alone one of these days without Katie Rose or my mom or anyone else to come between us. Then we'll see what happens.*

Callie and Mary Julia were making their way out the front door when they came face-to-face with Jackie Lynn. "Mary Julia, is everything alright?" she questioned, noting the grave expression on both Callie and Mary Julia's faces.

"No, everything is not alright!" Mary Julia staunchly maintained.

Callie rolled her eyes, but chose not to voice her opinion. Mary Julia had caught a glimpse of Callie's deliberate reaction. She chastised her daughter, "Don't give me that ridiculous look, little girl!"

"Mom, can I go wait in the car?" Callie asked.

Her mother was going to have a longwinded conversation with Jackie Lynn. Callie did not wish to listen to her irrational tirade. She would hear quite enough when they got home.

"Yes, that's fine," Mary Julia replied to Callie. The girl hustled away.

"Can we go inside? I need to talk with you," Mary Julia asked Jackie Lynn.

"Of course," Jackie Lynn agreed. She wondered what had transpired between the girls *this time* to upset Mary Julia so much.

Mary Julia turned and started back through the open front door. Jackie Lynn closely followed her. Both women headed into the living room.

Mary Julia sat down on the sofa, but she only sat on the edge of the cushion. Her purse was still on her shoulder. Her arms were crossed in defiance under her breasts, and her face held a deep frown.

Jackie Lynn sat her purse and briefcase down beside the recliner across from Mary Julia. She had a seat in this chair, placing both her arms tensely against the arms of the chair. She was bracing herself for whatever would come next. This was not going to be a pleasant conversation between two old friends. Mary Julia plainly had an axe to grind.

"So what's up?" Jackie Lynn dared to inquire. The sooner they began their conversation, the sooner they could finish it. She was tired from a busy day at work and Jackie Lynn wanted to get dinner started before Long Wolf got home.

"*What's up* is your son purposely barged into the bathroom on my daughter today. Callie was just getting out of the shower," Mary Julia blurted out.

"Ma..Mason? What on earth are you talking about, Mary Julia?!" Jackie Lynn stuttered in exasperation. "Where in the world did you come up with this crazy notion?!"

Jackie Lynn had noticed Long Wolf's truck in the driveway. She had been surprised to find that Mason was home. *He's supposed to still be at work.*

"Evidently Mason came home early, and he came into the bathroom on my Callista. Thank heavens she at least had on her bra and panties. But when I came in on them, he was talking to both Katie Rose and Callie like nothing was amiss. Callista still looks at Mason as a big brother figure and trusts him implicitly, or she wouldn't have been standing there in her underwear in front of him."

70

"Let me get this straight," Jackie Lynn emphasized. "Mason was standing in the bathroom, with Callie partially clothed, casually talking to his sister and Callie?"

"Well, of course not!" Mary Julia was quick to clarify. "No, he had retreated to his room. Callie and Katie Rose were standing in the open doorway to his bedroom though. Callie still wasn't properly attired for him to be conversing with the girls. Mason should have shut his bedroom door and given Callie the proper privacy she needed. I'm sorry to have to say it, Jackie Lynn, but I believe Mason was getting his jollies out of staring at Callie in her underwear. She has the body of a woman now, even if she is still an innocent girl."

"Or maybe it was the other way around and your daughter is not as innocent as you may think. Maybe it was Callie who was getting her...to quote you...*jollies* out of teasing Mason by standing there in her underwear where he could see her," Jackie Lynn accused.

Jackie Lynn had overheard her children talking from time to time, and she knew that Callie sometimes teased Mason inappropriately. Jackie Lynn figured it was a harmless phase the girl was going through. However, she refused to sit silently and allow Mary Julia to accuse her son of being distasteful. Mary Julia needed to be informed about her own daughter's iniquitous behavior.

"Don't you even think about turning this thing around and blaming Callie! I won't stand for it, Jackie Lynn!" Mary Julia shouted.

She sprang to her feet. Mary Julia advanced forward a few steps and shook her finger in her friend's face. "I won't be like my mother and give a man the benefit of the doubt over my own daughter. I'll always stand by Callie. I'll stand by her and I'll protect her! She'll never have to suffer at the hands of men like I did. Never! Do you hear me?!"

"Yes, Mary Julia, I hear you," Jackie Lynn calmly replied. "It would be impossible for me not to hear you. You're screaming in my face." *I need to calm her down. It's time we had a long-awaited talk about all this.*

"I'm sorry if it sounded like I was attacking Callie. That's not what I'm trying to do. Would you please sit back down and let's talk about all this? I've put this off for years, but it's time I told you what's on my mind."

"What do you mean you've put this off for years? You've put what off? Has something happened that you haven't told me? It doesn't involve Callie does it?" Mary Julia interrogated, sounding frantic. She was still hovering over Jackie Lynn with nervousness.

"Mary Julia, will you please sit back down and calm yourself. I'm not harboring knowledge about some terrible act. Nothing has happened to Callie. That's what you're thinking. You're imagining that she's been molested or raped by someone, maybe Long Wolf or Mason, despite all your best efforts to protect her. You distrust every man around your daughter, even her own father, don't you?"

Mary Julia retreated to the sofa and lowered herself into a sitting position again. She bowed her head and was silent for a moment. When she raised her head back up, Mary Julia stared at Jackie Lynn with pitifully sad eyes.

She confessed, "Yes, I do distrust *every* man around my daughter. What else do you expect? Who would have ever thought that the two men I trusted most in the world would have betrayed me? Certainly not *my* mother! She trusted my father alone with me when I was small, and I was molested. Then years later, when I was the age Callie is now, she trusted my stepfather. I was repeatedly raped. How can you possibly expect me to take this chance with my precious Callista? I won't! She has to be kept safe! Can't you understand?" she pleaded, tears beginning to form in her eyes.

Jackie Lynn rose from her recliner and went to sit on the couch beside Mary Julia. She dropped a consoling arm around Mary Julia's shoulders. Jackie Lynn admitted in a quiet, sympathetic voice, "Mary Julia, my heart still breaks for the pain you suffered. Your father and your stepfather should both burn in hell as far as I'm concerned. But, not all men are like them. I know this is hard for you to believe, but it's true."

"So how exactly am I supposed to know who is a *good* guy and who is a *bad* guy?" Mary Julia questioned, tears running down her cheeks. "My daddy and my stepfather didn't have labels on their foreheads that said 'molester' and 'rapist'. They were average guys. My daddy was very affectionate with me, like Long

Wolf is with Katie Rose. How do you know he isn't taking it a step further with her when you aren't watching? He's always made me nervous around Katie Rose because he is so touchy. And some men don't abuse their own child but will abuse other people's children. How can you possibly guarantee me that he isn't one of those men?"

"Who can guarantee that anyone is truly who they appear to be? You've known me forever, but how do you know that you can really trust me? Women abuse children too. How do you know I don't have a secret dark side? Or Flora for that matter? Anyone could be a monster in disguise. But you have to trust some people. You can't go through life suspecting everyone of being evil. Basically, most people are good," Jackie Lynn professed. She gave Mary Julia's body a reassuring squeeze.

"Not only would Long Wolf never harm either Katie Rose or Callie, but he would kill any man who even tried." Jackie Lynn knew this from the bottom of her heart, and she believed the same about Jonathan.

"Well, I'm sorry, but I disagree with you. You and Flora are two of the few people I do trust, but most men have a dark side. Look at what happened to Flora. Jonathan's father was prince charming until he started beating her. Thank God she got out of that situation alive. She was lucky. I won't count on dumb luck to keep Callie safe. I intend to keep a sharp eye on any men who are involved in my daughter's life."

"You always have kept a sharp eye on her, Mary Julia. The problem is, in doing so, you have isolated her from all the good men in her life, even Jonathan. Children need their fathers too. Don't you ever worry how Jonathan's lack of affection toward Callie affects her?"

"No, because I've seen to it that Callie received plenty of affection from me. Jonathan can be there for Callie without touching and kissing," Mary Julia justified. "She's much too old for such nonsense anyway. She's blossomed into a young woman. The focus of my concern is not on her relationship with Jonathan anymore. The boys who are becoming young men, such as Mason, are who I fear I need to be worried about now. Jonathan knows his grounds, and he will not overstep them."

"The key word here is *fear*, Mary Julia," Jackie Lynn pointed out. "You're overcome by fear, and I can understand why, considering all you endured as a child. But you need to learn to trust the men in your and Callie's life as well. Have you thought about talking to a professional about all this? It helped you once before, remember?"

"I should go and see a shrink? No! This doesn't have to do with me. It has to do with Callie. I can't be *cured* of loving my daughter. I wouldn't want to be. This conversation is getting ridiculous! Callie is waiting for me in the car. It's time I go," Mary Julia stated. She abruptly slid forward on the sofa, disengaging herself from Jackie Lynn's arm, and sprang to her feet.

"Mary Julia, please think about what I've said. I'm not saying these things to hurt you. I love you and Callie. You know that," Jackie Lynn asserted. She also stood and began running after her fleeing friend.

*I've struck a nerve. That's why she is trying to escape,* Jackie Lynn recognized.

Erratic thoughts raced through Mary Julia's brain as she ran toward the front door. *I've got to get out of here! Jackie Lynn doesn't understand. I'm sure it's impossible for her to. I'll never let anyone talk me out of protecting my daughter. I won't have some doctor trying to say I'm paranoid. God only knows what would happen if they decided I needed to be confined somewhere like before. Who would be there for Callie? I'm doing what I must for my daughter!*

Mary Julia flung the front door open and rushed from the house without uttering so much as a goodbye to her friend. Jackie Lynn stopped in the doorway and called to her, "Be careful going home. I'll see you at work tomorrow."

*Maybe we can talk more at lunch,* she wished but did not verbalize.

Before climbing in the car, Mary Julia did turn at the last second and at least wave goodbye to her friend. She uttered no words though. Jackie Lynn could tell that Mary Julia was shaken, and she felt badly about this.

Jackie Lynn hated bringing her friend's painful past to the present again. However, she was relieved that she had broached the subject of Mary Julia's overwhelming fears toward men. Jackie Lynn only hoped that now her friend would seek the help she so desperately needed. Mary Julia needed to come to grips with her devastating fears once and for all.

*Mary Julia doesn't grasp that she is creating a whole other monster in her daughter.*

\* \* \* \*

Jackie Lynn decided to go upstairs and check on the children. *Mason's bound to be embarrassed about what transpired between him and Callie. I wonder what Katie Rose thinks of all this. I want to find out from her once and for all whether Callie is teasing Mason. Mary Julia is right about one thing. Her daughter has blossomed into an attractive young woman. Callie does* not *need to be teasing boys with her body. She could get into some real trouble.*

Jackie Lynn found that Mason's bedroom door was closed. Katie Rose's door was open, so she decided to go talk to her daughter first. Jackie Lynn stepped into the open doorway.

Katie Rose was lying atop her fully made bed. Her hands were cupped behind her head. She was staring at the ceiling with woe.

"Katie Rose," Jackie Lynn called in a soft voice. Her daughter appeared to be so deeply engrossed in thought that Jackie Lynn hated to startle her.

"Hi, mom," Katie Rose answered. She turned her head to look at her mother. Katie Rose's eyes looked troubled.

"Is something wrong, honey?" Jackie Lynn asked with concern, as she approached the bed.

"Yeah," Katie Rose admitted. She scrambled to sit on the side of the bed.

Jackie Lynn took a seat beside her daughter. "What is it, sweetie?"

"I'm sorry, mom," she began strangely. Jackie Lynn was distressed to see tears standing in her daughter's eyes. "I came downstairs a little while ago. I overheard some of your conversation with Mary Julia. I…I heard her talking about what her dad and her stepfather had done to her when she was a little girl. God, mom! What she said was horrible! Was she really molested by her own dad and raped by her stepfather?"

"Yes, honey, she was," Jackie Lynn told her the truth. She hugged the girl to her side and kissed Katie Rose on her temple.

75

Jackie Lynn was proud of her daughter for being so caring. "I'm sorry you had to hear that."

"I feel bad for her, mom," Katie Rose whined.

Tears began running down her face. Some of Katie Rose's sorrow was due to guilt. Secretly, she had always somewhat feared Callie's mother. Oftentimes, Katie Rose did not even like the woman.

"Shh, baby. It's okay. I know. I feel badly for her too," Jackie Lynn confessed. She stroked her daughter's back, trying to console her. "Any decent person would feel bad about what happened to Mary Julia. Her father and stepfather were very sick people. When you do something so awful to a child, it affects that person their whole life. That's why Mary Julia is so overprotective of Callie. Can you understand that?"

"Yes," Katie affirmed, nodding her head. "I do understand now, mom. Callie doesn't know what happened to her mother, does she?"

"No, honey," her mother replied. "I'm certain she doesn't."

This wasn't something Mary Julia would share with Callie.

"Don't you think she should know? Don't you think someone should tell her about what happened to her mom to make her this way," Katie Rose dared to ask.

"I don't know," Jackie Lynn confessed. "That's not up to you or me to decide. That's up to Mary Julia. If you are this upset by the news, how do you think Callie would feel? Maybe Mary Julia will choose to tell her one day, but I'm not sure now is the time. You and Callie share everything, but this is something you are going to have to keep between the two of us. What you overheard was private information. Do you understand?"

Katie Rose was silent for a few moments as she mulled over what her mother had said. *Learning what had happened to Mary Julia might hurt Callie.* Katie Rose had not thought about things in this manor. She would never intentionally do anything to hurt her best friend. She had only been thinking that it would help Callie to understand her mother better and not simply think she was crazy. *Like she calls her all the time.*

"I understand, mom," Katie Rose replied in a somber voice. "I won't tell Callie anything. I promise. I would never want to hurt her."

"That's my girl," Jackie Lynn praised. She pulling Katie Rose into a tight, yet gentle embrace and held her for a few moments.

Jackie Lynn wanted to talk to Katie Rose about what had transpired between Callie and Mason. She decided to let this pass. Her daughter had been through enough without having to endure an interrogation about her friend. *I'll wait and talk to Mason a little later and get his take on it instead.*

"Hey, why don't you come downstairs and help me start supper? I'm fixing tacos tonight. You can help me doctor them up right for the hungry men in this family. What do you say?" Jackie Lynn suggested with a somewhat silly, welcoming grin. She was trying to dispel Katie Rose's gloomy mood.

"Sure," Katie Rose agreed with an obliging smile.

She wanted to concentrate on something else. Katie Rose would never forget the terrible truths she had learned about Mary Julia. Nevertheless, her mom always made simple tasks fun. So Katie Rose was eager to go and help her.

The two rose to their feet and headed out of the room side by side. Jackie Lynn began conversing about the girls' day at the Water Park. She was attempting to lead the subject far away from Mary Julia's troubles.

# Chapter 10

# *Wild Thing*

Throughout the summer, Callie's behavior became even more outrageous. She flirted insatiably with every boy who paid her the slightest bit of attention. Callie even flirted with the boys who chose not to give her attention, such as Mason.

Callie seemed to relish tormenting each and every one of the young men in their summer program at the YMCA. One week she would pair with one guy. The next week she was on to another boy.

One of the more sensitive guys confided to Katie Rose that his feelings had been crushed. He had been tossed aside by the beautiful Callie. Two more aggressive boys got into a fistfight over her friend one day and were banished from the program for a month. Callie showed no remorse that they had gotten into trouble because of her. Quite the contrary, she seemed to find their jealous brawl amusing.

Katie Rose, on the other hand, was anything but amused by her friend's disturbing conduct. She tried on more than one occasion to broach the subject with Callie, but Callie repeatedly put her off. It was obvious that Callie did not intend to change her behavior in any way.

Nothing Katie Rose, or anyone else, could say could convince Callie otherwise. She was having far too much fun. Not to mention the fact that Callie relished, at last, having attention from the male species. Attention she had never gotten from her father.

\* \* \* \*

Flora and Kenny were planning to have a party at their house to celebrate the Fourth of July. Mason's band had been invited to provide the music for this festivity. They were not being paid to play, but it still was their first real 'gig'. Mason was thrilled that his band was being given this opportunity to perform.

They were practicing at Ralph's house one Friday evening, in his open garage, when Katie Rose and Callie paid them a visit. Normally, Mason would have been surprised to see the girls. Ralph lived a few streets over.

Nevertheless, Mason knew, from talking to his sister, that Callie had taken to walking all the streets around their neighborhood. Actually, she was not just out walking. Callie was searching the streets for young men, older than the usual guys from their summer camp.

"She stops and flirts with them any chance she gets," his sister revealed. Katie Rose also shared that she was worried about Callie. Mason could understand why.

*The girl has one hell of a body, and she isn't bashful about showing it off.* Tonight, Callie was wearing a skimpy, bright red, low cut halter-top. This shirt accentuated her ample cleavage and showed off her tanned, flat stomach. Callie also had on denim shorts, which barely covered the curves of her buttocks.

*Any normal guy couldn't help but notice her. Notice her and...shit...stop it, Mason,* he secretly chastised himself. *Callie should not be running around the streets dressed like that. She's still a kid. Even if she does look every inch the grown up woman. Wonder how she got out of the house dressed that way. Mary Julia would shit if she knew.*

Mason looked away from Callie. All the other guys in the band were transfixed by the girl. Their tongues were nearly hanging out with saliva streaming down their chins.

"What's up, *girls?*" Mason spoke, interrupting his friends' silent scrutiny.

"We came over to watch you guys practice," Callie admitted. She gave Mason a lovely, inviting smile.

"Well, you've wasted your time then. We don't want any audience until show time. The best thing you can do is head back to the house," Mason suggested in a stern voice. There was no trace of a smile on his face. "I doubt your mom would approve of you wandering around the neighborhood this close to dark anyway," he rather meanly added. Mason was trying to remind his friends that Callie was still a child.

"Now wait a second, Mason," he was disturbed to hear Ralph warn. "Last time I checked, this was *my* house. So I'd say that means I should have the right to say who stays and who goes. I see nothing wrong with us having an audience to practice in front of before the party. After all, these ladies have walked a good distance to hear us play. I'd say the least we can do is let them stay for a song or two. As for it getting dark, they can always ride back to the house with you in your truck after practice. What do the rest of you guys think? Would it bother you to have these ladies watch us?"

"No!" "Not at all!" "No problem!" the other three answered with eagerness, almost in unison.

"Guess it's settled then," Ralph concluded, vacating his seat at the drums.

He walked over to the side of his garage. Ralph pulled down two, folded, wooden chairs from a peg on the wall. He set them up and even took the time to wipe the dust off them with a rag.

Ralph gallantly motioned for the girls to have a seat. A wide grin showcased the rather unattractive, large gap separating Ralph's front teeth. Katie Rose sat down in one of the chairs, but Callie approached Ralph instead.

"Thank you, Ralph. You are *so* sweet!" she praised in a whiny, syrupy voice.

Callie placed a hand on each of his shoulders. She pulled the boy closer. Callie had to lean down a little, since Ralph was a few inches shorter than her. She swung her head sideways and kissed him directly on his mouth.

Callie let her soft, full, hot lips linger there for a few moments. When Callie released Ralph from her embrace, he chuckled with nervousness. His face had turned almost as red as the hair on his head.

Callie eyed Mason with a smug smile. She backed away from his friend and had a seat. Callie's actions infuriated Mason. This was made obvious to everyone there by the fiery glare he was giving the girl.

"Ralph, are we going to practice some time this century?" Mason barked at his shell-shocked friend.

Ralph was still standing a few feet away from the girls. He was gazing at Callie with a silly lopsided grin. Since he was rather homely, Ralph was not accustomed to being made over by pretty girls such as Callie. Her kiss put him in an overjoyed, stupefied daze.

"Come on, Ralph!" Mason growled with impatience.

At length, Ralph began to walk away from the lovely Callie. Her kiss still had his body tingling with excitement. Looking back as he was moving forward, however, proved to be more than he could handle.

Ralph stumbled over his own feet and almost fell flat on his face. He managed to right himself at the last second. With mortification, Ralph made his way back to the drums. He took a safe seat behind them.

"If you are through making an ass of yourself over some *little girls*, then maybe we can get back to work!" Mason chastised. He had emphasized the words *little girls*, because he wanted Callie to note his observation.

"Little girl, my ass!" Ralph mumbled. He added in almost a whisper, "You better buy some eyeglasses, buddy. That is one, mighty shapely, *little girl*. Although the one beside her may still have the body of a little girl," Ralph added with a rude laugh.

Ralph was muttering something, but Mason chose to ignore him. He could tell by the sad expression on Katie Rose's face she was not at all happy to be there. Mason only wanted to get back to playing and pretend that Callie was not even there.

Mason also wanted to pretend that she had not come on to one his friends. Katie Rose was right to be concerned about this girl. Mason intended to tell Callie exactly what he thought of her behavior when he took the girls home in his truck later.

* * * *

An hour later, the guys wrapped up their practice session. They were playing a combination of new pop songs, oldies that Flora and the other adults would like, and even a few of the songs that Mason had written. It was almost 9:30, and it was now dark outside.

Mason knew his mother was probably beginning to worry about the girls. They were not supposed to be out after dark, and he was certain she did not have a clue where they were. His mom did not keep constant tabs on Katie Rose the way Mary Julia did with Callie.

That was the main reason Callie liked to come over and hang out with his sister so much. Mason whisked out his cell phone. He phoned his mom and reported that the girls were over at Ralph's with him. Mason told his mother that he would be bringing them home in a few minutes.

"I've got to get these two little girls home," he explained to the guys when he had ended the call with his mom. She had been glad to hear from him. She knew the girls had gone out walking, but they were usually home well before dark.

"Right, we have to go," Callie eagerly agreed.

She sprang to her feet and hurried over to Mason's side. Callie had begun to get a little nervous. She noticed it was already getting dark and so near 9:30.

Her mother was supposed to pick her up around 10:00, and Callie still had to change back into the clothes she had worn over to Katie Rose's house. She also needed to wash off the makeup she had applied. Callie was also looking forward to the ride back to the house in Mason's truck.

*I'll get to sit right beside Mason.*

"You sure you need to rush off?" Ralph questioned. He scurried over to stand on the other side of Callie.

"Yeah," Mason snapped. *The sooner I get Callie out of here, the better.*

Ralph was staring at Callie like a lovesick puppy, and the other guys had gathered around as well. Mason picked up his guitar and handed it to Katie Rose. Then he grabbed his amps and said to the girls, "Let's make tracks." As he turned, he made a farewell gesture to his friends.

"See you guys later," he said.

"It was nice having you for an audience. Come back any time," Ralph told Callie. He kept pace with her as she headed to the truck with Mason.

Katie Rose followed right on their heels. Mason opened the driver's side door and stowed his amps in the space behind the front seat. He had to reach around Callie to get his guitar from his sister.

Mason rudely told Callie to move. Callie sprinted around the truck, with Ralph in tow. Ralph raced ahead and opened the passenger door for her to climb into the cab. Callie scooted to the middle of the bench seat. She intended to sit as close to Mason as she could.

"Excuse me," Katie Rose politely said to Ralph.

Ralph was blocking her entrance to the truck. He was standing in the open doorway, still staring intently at Callie. Ralph moved aside, and Katie Rose climbed inside the truck too.

"Bye. Come back soon," Ralph said. He almost sounded as if he was begging.

Mason climbed into the truck, and Callie whispered in Katie Rose's ear, "Close the door." She did not even say a word of goodbye to poor Ralph.

"Bye, Ralph," Katie Rose replied.

Then she closed the passenger door. Katie Rose felt sorry for the guy. Ralph was another casualty in Callie's cruel game of 'lead em' on, then leave em'.

Mason slammed his door shut with a force that shook the entire truck. He started the engine, and he turned his head to look behind him as he began backing out of Ralph's driveway. As Mason turned back toward the front, he could not help but catch a glimpse of Callie's breasts.

It seemed her tiny halter-top almost pushed more naked flesh out than it covered. Mason also became aware that Callie shapely thigh was pressing against his thigh. Fighting his rising desires, he gave Callie a push so as to have a little space to breathe.

Mason focused his gaze out the windshield. He applied a frustrated death grip on the steering wheel with both hands, and he pressed his foot down on the accelerator. *The faster I get us home the better!*

Mason was attempting to make himself concentrate on anything other than the *arousing* girl who was sitting beside him. Mason speeded down the road towards the safe haven of home. Callie began gushing, "Mason, you guys sounded great tonight! You're good enough to be a professional band!"

She dropped an arm around his shoulders, and Callie placed her other hand on Mason's thigh. She also laid her head upon his broad shoulder. It was more than Mason could stand.

He spun the steering wheel to the right, with recklessness. Mason sent the truck spiraling and bouncing into a nearby, church, parking lot. Callie's head sprang upright again, and Katie Rose grabbed the dash in momentary panic.

Katie Rose squealed, "Mason!"

He stomped down hard on the brake, bringing the truck to a screeching halt. Mason slammed the truck into park and shut off the ignition. He jerked his door open and leaped from the vehicle.

Mason stuck his head back inside the truck, and he hissed with anger, "Alright, that's it!"

Mason's fiery eyes were focussed directly on Callie's face. "Since you don't know how to behave, then you can either switch places with Katie Rose or you can ride in the back of the truck. I've had it with you tonight, Callie! First, you come on to Ralph; then treat him like a nobody when he responds to you. Now, you think you can make a move on me and get away with it. You're out of control!"

"*I'm* out of control?!" she challenged. "I'm not the one who nearly wrecked his truck and who is screaming in someone's face for no reason. What did I do that's so bad anyway? I wasn't coming on to Ralph. I gave him a little kiss to thank him for being so nice to Katie Rose and me. What's wrong with that? As for making a move on you, I was only complimenting you on your band. Why is that so terrible?"

"Come on, Callie! Save the crappy innocent act for your mother. She falls for it on a regular basis. You're talking to Mason here. I've known you since you were born, and I've seen the little games you play. You need to understand that you aren't going to play them with me and get away with it anymore. Now out of my truck!" he ordered.

"Come on, Callie. I'll switch places with you," Katie Rose offered.

Katie Rose opened her door. She could not blame her brother for blowing up at Callie. She knew her friend all too well, and Callie had been playing games with Mason for a long time now.

Callie did not want to switch places with Katie Rose. However, Mason could be very stubborn, and it was growing later and later by the minute. Callie needed to get back to their house and prepare for her mother's arrival.

She certainly did not want to incur her mother's wrath by allowing her to catch her dressed like this. Something like this could provide her mom with the excuse she needed for not allowing her to go to Katie Rose's house anymore. *It wouldn't be wise to push my mom any further.*

Something weird had transpired between her mother and Jackie Lynn anyway. All at once, Callie's mom had begun to avoid visiting with her longtime friend. Mary Julia had already become reluctant about letting Callie spend time with Katie Rose lately. Callie's mom had gone so far as to suggest that Callie spend more time with *her* instead of always running to Katie Rose's house to hang out.

"Oh all right! We'll switch places," Callie begrudgingly agreed.

Katie Rose had already vacated the truck, so Callie slid her body toward the open passenger door and climbed out. Once they were all settled back inside the truck, Mason set off again. The rest of the drive home was quiet, each of them lost in their own thoughts. Mason was still trying to curb his anger and frustration.

*Why does Callie have to behave the way she does? First she comes on to poor Ralph and then me. And the way she dresses! If Callie keeps carrying on like she is, some guy is certain to use it to his advantage. Surely she doesn't want to be one of those girls who are having sex at thirteen.* Mason was not even pursuing this with Rebecca yet, who was his age.

Katie Rose was worrying about what Callie might do to retaliate against Mason for pushing her aside and ordering her around. *Oh, Callie! Why do you have to torment Mason so?* She hardly ever saw her brother get as angry as he had tonight. She had been anxious that Mason was going to make Callie walk home alone in the dark if she refused to do as he told her.

Callie *was* scheming revenge against Mason. *So he thinks he can be mean to me and push me aside, does he? Well, fine! There are plenty of other guys who want me! I showed Mason an example tonight with Ralph. I'll continue to show him. I'll make him see. Mason will be sorry. Eventually he'll either come around to doing things my way or he'll miss out!*

In actuality, Callie was hurt by Mason's rejection. She could not fathom why she could easily lure every other boy under her spell.  They all seemed to fall all over themselves for her, but not Mason.

# Chapter 11

# *The Trick*

Mason loved his Aunt Flora very much, and the feeling was mutual. She and Kenny had always welcomed him and Katie Rose into their home. Now, Flora and Kenny had asked his band to play at their Fourth of July party. This meant a great deal to Mason.

Flora had always encouraged his love of music and praised his songwriting efforts. She was the only adult in his life that truly made him feel that his dream of becoming a professional musician could someday come true. Mason's parents – his father in particular – had far different dreams for his future.

Long Wolf had made it clear that he expected Mason to take over as president of Greathouse Construction one day. Mason loved working with the construction crew, but he could not begin to fathom running the whole company. The thought of sitting in meetings day in and day out, in some stuffy office, did not even remotely appeal to Mason.

He was glad his father was making him work his way up from the bottom. Mason was planning on taking his time climbing the rungs of the Greathouse Construction ladder. In the meantime, Mason intended to do what he loved – making music.

\* \* \* \*

Mason, Rebecca and the members of his band arrived at Flora and Kenny's house a half-hour before the Fourth of July party was to officially begin. He wanted to get all the instruments set up and tuned beforehand. Flora greeted Mason in her usual manor, with a welcoming hug and an affectionate kiss on his cheek. Mason returned her hug without embarrassment, even though his friends were standing all around them.

Flora released Mason from her embrace. She gave the three other teenage boys a sweeping glance. Then Flora's eyes came to attentively rest on the young woman at Mason's side.

Flora noted the girl's pretty, light blue eyes; long, wavy, dark auburn hair; and petite, attractive figure. Flora also approved of the young woman's choice of outfit. She had on a feminine, sleeveless, sky blue, light cotton blouse, medium length beige shorts and a pair of tan sandals. The sky blue blouse perfectly complimented the color of the girl's eyes.

"So why don't you introduce your old aunt to your friends, Mason?" Flora prodded with a happy smile.

"Oh, sure," he replied and proceeded to introduce his friends one by one.

Mason started with the members of his band. Each politely shook Flora's hand, told her it was nice to meet her, and thanked her for inviting them. Mason purposely left Rebecca until last.

Flora was dying to meet his girlfriend, and Mason was devilishly enjoying making her wait as long as possible. "Oh....and this," he started, placing his arm around Rebecca's shoulder. "This is....who are you again? Oh, yeah...this is my girlfriend, Rebecca. Rebecca, I'd like for you to meet my *not so old* Aunt Flora."

"Hi, Flora. It's very nice to meet you. I've heard so many wonderful things about you," Rebecca said with an attractive, genuine smile. She extended her hand out to Flora.

Flora shook the girl's hand with delight. She had heard a great deal about Mason's girlfriend from Jackie Lynn, but this was the first occasion she had gotten to meet the girl. She was glad Mason had decided to bring Rebecca along to the party.

"It's nice to finally meet you also, Rebecca. But don't let Mason fill your pretty head with stories about us old folks. Come on in and make yourself at home," Flora said.

She turned her attention back to Mason then. Flora teased, "Thanks so much for that long, drawn out introduction, Mason. I'll remember this when it comes time to purchase your Christmas present this year. I may have to buy you a bag of switches."

"Yeah, right. I'll believe that when I see it," Mason replied without a trace of worry.

He knew Flora was only teasing. The wide, toothy grin Mason gave her showed he was enjoying their easy banter. "If you did get me switches, I would love them anyway, because they came from my favorite aunt."

"Okay. Enough with the buttering up. Be on your way," Flora said with a conclusive chuckle. She could barely resist the urge to reach out and swat Mason on the behind. However, she did not want to risk embarrassing him in front of his friends or his girlfriend. "Kenny is out back waiting for you. He'll show you guys where to set up and give you a hand if needed."

"Alright," Mason agreed with eagerness. "See you in a little while. I hope you enjoy hearing us play."

"I'm sure I will," she assured him. "I'm looking forward to it."

Mason gave her one, final, grateful smile before he, Rebecca and his friends started away. Flora also smiled. She was contemplating what a cute couple Mason and Rebecca made.

Flora was glad to see Mason enjoying his youth. She was also looking forward to hearing his band play. Flora loved this young man as if he was her own son. She wanted only the best for Mason. She hoped that she and Kenny would continue to share in Mason and Katie Rose's lives for a long time to come.

* * * *

Mary Julia, Jonathan and Callie were the next to arrive. Flora momentarily studied Callie's formfitting T-shirt, short shorts, and leather, high-heeled sandals with silent disapproval. Then she greeted the trio with welcoming hugs.

No matter how hard she had tried, Flora had never developed the same connection with Callie as she had with Jackie Lynn's children. Much of this was due to the fact that Mary Julia had scarcely allowed Callie to spend one-on-one time with her and Kenny. Another reason was that Flora believed Callie to be somewhat of a spoiled brat.

Flora had heard many stories from Jackie Lynn, Mason and even Katie Rose over the years of Callie's distasteful shenanigans. Mary Julia's lenience in dealing with Callie's poor behavior was reprehensible. However, like Jackie Lynn, Flora had learned that Mary Julia could not be reasoned with when it came to issues regarding her daughter.

Flora had noticed the serious strain in Jackie Lynn and Mary Julia's relationship. She realized this was due to the fact that Jackie Lynn had accused Mary Julia of being much too overprotective of Callie. Flora believed Jackie Lynn was right, but she decided not to take sides.

Instead, Flora worked as a constant intermediary between these two women. She hoped the two would not take up any issues with one another today. Flora wanted today to be a relaxing enjoyable time for all.

\* \* \* \*

Two couples that were close friends of Kenny's arrived next. Jackie Lynn, Long Wolf and Katie Rose arrived shortly thereafter. Katie Rose looked darling. She had on a pale green skorts' set, with matching canvas slip-ons. Flora squeezed her into a tight, approving hug, and she told Katie Rose how cute she looked.

As the last of the partygoers strolled in, Flora made speedy introductions amongst everyone. Jackie Lynn helped her gather up the dishes she and the other women had brought and take them to her kitchen. Long Wolf and Katie Rose led their new acquaintances out into Flora's backyard.

"Is Mary Julia here yet?" Jackie Lynn asked when she and Flora were alone in the kitchen.

"Yes. She went out back with Jonathan and Callie," Flora freely volunteered.

"Doesn't that figure?" Jackie Lynn stated with sarcasm. "After all, Callie can't be left alone with all those males, now can she?"

"Jackie Lynn, can you please drop this for today?" Flora pleaded. "This is supposed to be a party, right? No fighting, okay?"

"There will be no fighting, Flora," Jackie Lynn promised. "It's obvious Mary Julia doesn't want to change, and I'm tired of beating my head against a wall. So whatever she does today, I won't say a word. Satisfied?"

"Very. Now why don't we go out back and join the others and try to enjoy this beautiful day. I'm so looking forward to hearing Mason's band play," Flora declared with noted excitement.

Flora took a gentle grasp on Jackie Lynn's arm. She led her out of the house with eagerness.

\* \* \* \*

Jonathan and Kenny were standing by the grill on the deck, drinking a Bud Light and making friendly conversation. Mary Julia was sitting in a lawn chair by the side of the pool, sipping a Diet Pepsi. Kenny had also offered her a beer, but she had settled on a soft drink instead.

*No alcohol! I need to keep my mind clear so I can focus on Callie. There are too many boys around today and I see how they are looking at her. I'll watch them! I'll watch them closely!* Mindful of this silent resolution, Mary Julia's eyes were fixated on her daughter like a hawk stalking its prey.

Callie and Rebecca were sitting on the other side of the pool, dangling their feet in the water and engaging in girl talk. Katie Rose had joined the two of them. *As long as she stays with the girls, everything will be fine*, Mary Julia silently concluded. She relaxed a little.

Katie Rose was amazed to find Callie getting along so well with Rebecca. Behind the girl's back, Callie called Rebecca all kinds of unkind names. *Callie does this because she is jealous of her being Mason's girlfriend. She wishes Mason was interested in her in this way instead.*

Katie Rose had her suspicions that Callie's sudden friendliness toward the girl was not real. She hoped Callie was not up to something mean. Katie Rose liked Rebecca. She did not wish to see her fall prey to one of Callie's evil tricks.

"So are we going to swim?" Callie asked the girls. "Did you bring a bathing suit, Rebecca? Did Mason tell you about the pool? Or was he only thinking about his band job? I'm surprised he even invited you to the party. He won't even remember you are here once he starts playing. He gets pretty intense, doesn't he Katie Rose?"

"I know," Rebecca answered before Katie Rose had a chance. "But he did remember to tell me to bring a bathing suit.

91

He even promised me one dance. And I like hanging out with you girls, since I don't have any little sisters. So this should be a fun party."

"Yeah, us *girls*. With any luck, it should be a party to remember," Callie strangely stated with an ugly grin on her face.

Katie Rose did not like the phony smile Callie gave Rebecca. *She* is *planning something. I've got to get Callie alone and try to figure out what she has up her sleeve and try to talk her out of it. Rebecca is a nice person and doesn't deserve any of Callie's crap.*

"So why don't we go and get changed into our swimsuits before Mason and the band start playing?" Katie Rose inquired.

"That sounds like a good idea," Rebecca was quick to concur. "I'd love to swim, but I don't want to be inside changing when Mason starts playing. I want to be here to cheer him on. After all, what are girlfriends for?"

*I could think of a few other things*, Callie unchastely reflected.

"Well, let's do it then," Callie promoted. "There's a changing room right off to the side of the deck, so we don't even have to go inside the house. I'll go first, since I can be back out in a flash. All I have to do is peel off my T-shirt and shorts. I have my bathing suit on under my clothes." Callie's eyes twinkling with mischief.

"That's a smart idea. I wish I had thought to do that," Rebecca praised. "My bathing suit is in a bag with Mason's swimming trunks. It's over by the guitar cases. I'll see if I can get Mason's attention and tell him what we are doing. That way he'll be sure to wait until we get back to start playing," she stated with confidence.

Rebecca's self-assurance made Callie hate her even more. *Who does she think she is that Mason will hold up playing for* her? *She's no one special! What in the world does Mason see in her anyway? I've got twice the body she does, and she looks like an Irish Setter with all that long red hair.*

Rebecca rose to her feet and started toward Mason. She waved a hand at him to gain his attention. Callie also scrambled to her feet. Her eyes were rooted on Mason as Rebecca approached him.

Callie watched as Mason put his guitar down to focus all his attention on Rebecca. He placed his arm around her shoulders and smiled as she shared her plans with him. Then Mason nodded his agreement.

Katie Rose got up too, scrutinizing Callie. She could tell by the tight stretch of her friend's lips and the fiery look in her eyes that Callie was furious. *Oh, Lord! I hope she doesn't try to drown Rebecca!*

A few seconds later, Rebecca rejoined the girls with her swimsuit in hand. "It's all set!" she shared with a wide, happy grin. "Mason said he wouldn't dare start until I got back. Let's hurry and get changed. I don't want to keep him waiting."

"No, we wouldn't want to do that," Callie agreed with a pretend smile. "Let's go. I'll show you where the changing room is."

"Thanks," she chirped and rushed along at Callie's heels.

Katie Rose scurried along behind the other two girls. She did not have a clue what Callie had up her sleeve, but she was certain she had to be planning something.

*Maybe if I keep a close eye on Callie, I can somehow stop whatever it is she is planning to do to Rebecca.*

\* \* \* \*

As promised, Callie was in and out of the dressing room in a few short minutes. The hot pink, string bikini she emerged in left little to the imagination. The bikini top covered only half her breasts and squeezed the parts that were not covered into voluptuous curving mounds of exposed flesh. Likewise, the bottom of the suit barely covered her buttocks and was rather obscenely cut in the front.

Katie Rose was not shocked by Callie's choice of bathing suits. However, she was stunned that she would dare to wear something so skimpy in front of her mother. Normally, Callie only attempted such boldness in secrecy behind her mom's back.

*I'm going to enjoy watching Mary Julia's reaction*, Katie Rose mused. A small smile appeared on Katie Rose's face.

Rebecca, on the other hand, was appalled by Callie's choice of bathing suits. Her mouth stood ajar. Her eyes were large with wonder, and they fleetingly scanned Callie's nakedness.

"Is…is that *all* you are going to wear?" she dared to ask.

"Of course," Callie answered without hesitation. "It's a bikini. What's the big deal?"

"Umm," Rebecca stuttered. "It's so skimpy! I couldn't wear something like that. I'd be too embarrassed."

"Yes, I suppose you might. You can't help it that God didn't bless you with the body I have. You know what they say, 'If you've got it, flaunt it'. And I've certainly got it," Callie proudly boasted. She placed her hands on her hips and proudly thrust her bust out even more.

"Geez, Callie! Cut it out!" Katie Rose pleaded. She gave her friend a slight shove.

"Oh, come on, you guys! I'm only kidding!" Callie insisted with a mischievous grin.

"About wearing that *thing*?" Rebecca inquired with hopefulness, staring Callie down once more.

"No. Not hardly!" Callie stubbornly assured. "I mean I was teasing about the body comments. I see nothing wrong with my bathing suit. I'm not shy like some girls."

"Obviously not!" Rebecca stated with apparent distaste.

"I tell you what. Since my suit makes you so uncomfortable, Rebecca, I'll put something over it until we get to the pool. Katie Rose, why don't you go ahead and change? When you get inside, hand me that short, terrycloth robe that is hanging in the closet. Do you mind?" Callie asked. "You know where it is, don't you?"

"Yes," Katie Rose agreed.

Katie Rose was wondering why Callie was being so amiable. It was not like Callie to give in to anyone. Callie especially did not submit to someone she did not like, such as Rebecca.

*Of course, it certainly does serve her purpose to cover up that tiny thing she is wearing. Her mom is going to go ballistic when she sees it!*

Katie Rose went into the changing room. She changed into her swimsuit, a modest, but attractive tankini. She gathered up her clothes. Then Katie Rose opened the small closet to her right and pulled out the robe that Callie had requested.

"Callie, here you go," Katie Rose said with a smile as she handed her friend the robe.

"Thank you oh so much!" Callie said, a little too eagerly. She took the robe from Katie Rose's outstretched hand and slid it on immediately. "Alright, Rebecca, get on in there and get changed. Mason and the band are warming up, so I'd say they will want to begin playing soon. We don't want to hold them up."

"No, we don't," she agreed and rushed forward into the room.

"Katie Rose, why don't you go and tell Mason we're almost finished changing, and we'll be ready in a second? I'll wait here for Rebecca," Callie suggested.

"Rebecca should be out in a minute or two. Why do I need to go and tell Mason anything? He'll see all of us in a few minutes if we both wait here for Rebecca. Right?" Katie Rose argued. The sense that Callie was up to something was too strong to ignore.

"What exactly is your problem?" Callie challenged.

There was a spark of anger showing in Callie's eyes. She did not like to be countered by Katie Rose and was not accustomed to her doing so. She raised her voice almost to a yell and began to rant, "I was only thinking about Mason. This is his first real band job in case you've forgotten! And he has to be anxious to start playing. He probably doesn't need the added stress of wondering where his girlfriend is or how much longer she might be. But do you even care? Or are you even thinking about him? Obviously not! Just forget I said anything, alright? We'll both wait here for Rebecca, and to heck with your brother! Or maybe I should go let him know what is taking so long. At least then he'll know someone cares"

"Okay. Okay. I'll go, alright?" Katie Rose conceded at last, throwing her hands up in easy surrender.

She had to admit that what Callie was saying did make sense. Mason was both excited and nervous about his first band job, and Katie Rose wanted everything to be perfect for him. Katie Rose was also not anxious to incur the perilous 'wrath of Callie', which could ruin the day for everyone if Callie so chose.

"I'll see *both* you and Rebecca in a second," she stressed as she started away.

"Of course, you will," Callie staunchly assured her. "We'll be right there as soon as Rebecca finishes changing. Now scoot!"

Katie Rose studied Callie's face for only a second more before she turned and hurried up the steps onto the deck. Callie remained rooted in the same spot, until she was certain her friend was not going to return. It seemed a very long couple of seconds.

When Callie was satisfied that she was alone with Rebecca, she stepped forward. She extracted a key from the pocket of the robe, and Callie placed it into the small keyhole on the dressing room door. She turned the lock.

Callie stepped back with a wide, satisfied, evil grin. She knew that Rebecca had no way of opening the door. The outside lock could only be unlocked with the key. *The key that I have.*

"Bye bye, Rebecca. See ya later. Much later!" Callie stated in an inaudible whisper under her breath. She dropped the key back into her pocket and raced away.

# Chapter 12

# *The Band*

Katie Rose sat on the side of the pool, by the concrete steps leading into the shallow end. She was waiting for the others girls to return before she entered the pool. She watched as Callie climbed the top step to the deck.

Callie striped the robe from her body and hung it on the railing. She held her head high and began strutting across the deck with pride. She was headed straight toward Mason and the band.

*She looks like a model on a runway,* Katie Rose could not help but notice with envy. *Where is Rebecca?* Katie Rose glanced with expectation back across the deck toward the stairs.

"Holy, shit! Would you look at that?! Tell me that isn't absolutely mouth-watering?" Mason heard Ralph exclaim in a low voice.

Mason had been looking down at his guitar. He turned to glance at his friend to see what he was mouthing off about. All his friends had stopped tuning their instruments and were gaping at something just past him. Mason turned back around, and he found Callie standing in front of him.

"Rebecca asked me to tell you to go ahead and start playing. She doesn't want to hold the band up," he heard Callie say. "She said she would be out shortly to listen to you guys and cheer you on."

Mason found himself thinking *'Rebecca who?'* His eyes were automatically riveted to Callie's tempting flesh, and his brain temporarily turned his mush. Mason forced himself to look Callie in the face, and he attempted to focus again.

Mason finally barked, "What in the world is taking Rebecca so long?"

"Girl stuff I guess," Callie answered with a shrug and a pretty, confident smile.

Callie hastened forward. She possessively locked her arms around Mason's neck. She leaned her head forward, and she secured her lips upon Mason's.

Callie had only intended to give Mason a brief kiss. However, she had not anticipated that Mason's lips would actually respond. Dazed and confused, Mason not only accepted Callie's kiss but readily reciprocated.

Excited butterflies began to flutter in Callie's stomach. Mason, at long last, managed to pull back. Callie was a little out of breath as she declared, "Just a little kiss for luck!" She swiveled and scurried away before Mason had time to say anything else.

"Hey, Callie. I'd love one of those good luck kisses too," Ralph called after her.

Callie ignored him and continued her retreat. As Callie looked about her, she caught a glimpse of her mother's horrified face. "Callista Roberts!" she heard her mom angrily shout and saw her rushing toward her.

Mason doubled up his fists and turned toward Ralph with a look of complete disgust – not only with his friend but also at himself. He was angry about the way his lips had unintentionally responded to Callie's teasing. He was embarrassed by what he had done in front of all these people.

Callie darted over to the diving board, arched her body, bounced into the air, and dove headfirst into the cool, refreshing water.

"I've died and gone to heaven. Did you see the way she bounces when she runs?" Ralph stated with crudeness.

"Shut up," Mason growled under his breath. He gave Ralph one, final, fiery, disapproving look. "Let's play," Mason commanded.

Mason turned back toward the guests. He announced in a professional manor, "Ladies and Gentlemen, the name of the band is Savage Pride. We hope you'll like what you hear." He immediately cued the band, and they launched into the first song on their planned agenda, *Fun Fun Fun* by the Beach Boys.

\* \* \* \*

Long Wolf's attention was instantaneously diverted from Callie, and the scenario unfolding with her, to his son and his band. He had not known the name of his son's band. He hated the name his son had chosen.

"Where in the world did he come up with that?" Long Wolf said half to himself.

"Where did he come up with what?" Jackie Lynn, who was sitting right beside him, asked.

She barely glanced at her husband. Jackie Lynn was attentively watching and listening to her son with pride. She was also trying to ignore the scene that was certain to unfold between Mary Julia and Callie. Long Wolf was a welcome distraction.

*I promised Flora there would be no fights between Mary Julia and me today, and I intend to keep that promise. I'll focus entirely on Mason, and everything will be fine.*

"Where did he come up with that name for his band?" Long Wolf replied to Jackie Lynn's inquiry. "Savage Pride. It sounds as if he is making fun of his Indian heritage. I'm not sure I like that at all."

"Oh, honey," she said. Jackie Lynn reached to squeeze Long Wolf's hand. "I'm sure that wasn't Mason's intention at all. He is proud of his Indian heritage. I'm sure the name Savage Pride was meant to reflect just that. Don't take it so personally. Listen to how good they sound. You should be proud that your son has such talent and not sweat the small stuff."

*Our Indian heritage has nothing to do with being a savage and it is definitely not 'small stuff'. I'll talk to Mason about this. This is one more reason not to like this music hobby of his.* Long Wolf decided.

However, as he listened to Mason sing and his band play, Long Wolf did have to admit that he was proud of his son. His hope was that Mason would embrace the Greathouse Construction business with as much passion and determination as he did this music business. If Mason did this, his son would go far and live the life Long Wolf dreamed for him.

\* \* \* \*

99

"Mary Julia, wait," Jonathan said.

He stepped into his wife's path. Jonathan also had placed his hands firmly on each of her shoulders. "Don't cause a scene. The band has started to play. Why don't you come sit with me and listen to the music? Okay?"

"But, Jonathan," she began to protest in a loud, panicked voice, "Didn't you see how your daughter is dressed? Didn't you see how she just behaved? Of course you did! All the men did! She kissed Mason right on the mouth in front of everyone. I've got to put a stop to this. She needs to go inside and put some clothes on. Now! Everyone is staring at her."

"Maybe they were. But now they are all looking at Mason and the band. You'll call more attention to Callie if you start a screaming scene. And you're likely to ruin things for Mason. Please come and sit down. Let's enjoy the band and at the same time, without causing any disturbance, we can still keep an eye on Callie. When the band takes a break, you can calmly go and talk to her. Please listen to me." *Just this once*, Jonathan was thinking.

"Please don't draw any more attention to our daughter right now," he pleaded.

It was rare to find Jonathan standing up to his wife. He held tightly to Mary Julia's shoulders. He was determined to make sure his wife did not make a scene with their daughter and disrupt the party for everyone.

\* \* \* \*

Callie had swum the length of the pool to the shallow end and came to stand by the concrete steps descending into the pool. Katie Rose was still sitting at the top of the stairs with her feet dangling in the water, but she was purposely not watching her friend. She was angry with Callie for the way she had behaved.

Callie had an enormous crush on Mason, but Katie Rose thought it was horrible the way she had waltzed up in front of everyone and kissed him. She was glad it had not disrupted Mason getting the band started. It obviously had not, because her brother and his band had her mesmerized. They sounded great and her heart was overflowing with happiness for his success. Katie Rose adored her brother and was thrilled to see that he was pursuing his dream of becoming a musician.

Callie turned her head and was amazed to see her father taking her mother by her arm and leading her back to her chair. *What's up with that?* She was grateful for the reprieve from one of her mother's tantrums, even though she knew the wrath of her mother was yet to come.

Sitting down on the second step at Katie Rose's feet, Callie gushed, "They sound great, don't they?"

"Yes they do," Katie agreed with excitement. She barely gave her friend a glance.

The girls watched and listened to the band. They barely moved they were so transfixed. When Mason launched into one of the love songs he had written and composed, Callie got tears in her eyes.

*Oh, Mason! I love you so much! You should be singing that song to me! Only me!* Her heart seemed to be abounding with love for this handsome young man. *Mason will feel that way about me soon. I know it!* Callie's imagination was now running berserk. *After all, he did kiss me back today for the first time!*

\* \* \* \*

Mason's small audience applauded. They cheered, and couples even danced in front of them. Mason was so thrilled by their avid response that he almost hated for the band to stop playing. None the less, they had been singing and playing for forty-five minutes straight, and it was time for them to take a short break.

Mason took his guitar from around his neck and placed it on its stand. He praised his friends, "Great job, guys!" With a wide smile, he turned and gave each one of them a high five.

"So are you going to go and talk to your biggest, and *hands down* prettiest, admirer now?" Ralph asked. He looked past Mason to study Callie's beautiful body again as she stood and came up the pool steps. "Maybe she'll give you another good luck kiss for our next set."

"In case you've forgotten, Ralph, I have a girlfriend," Mason grumbled his response.

*Where* is *Rebecca?* He scanned the backyard and saw no sign of her anywhere.

Mason realized, for the first time, that he had not remembered seeing Rebecca at all during his first set. But, then again, he had not exactly been looking for her. He had been concentrating solely on his music and its flawless execution.

*Did she see Callie kiss me? Did she notice that I kissed her back? Surely not. But where could she be?*

"Well, why don't you go and find your girlfriend then. Me and the guys will keep your little groupie occupied," Ralph offered.

"Callista!" Mason heard Mary Julia's shrill voice calling. He saw the woman making a beeline for her daughter.

*Good! That will eliminate the groupie problem.*

"Be my guest if there is anything left of her when her mom gets done with her," Mason said with a knowing smile and started away from his friends.

Mary Julia grabbed Callie by the arm and said, "Come with me, young lady!" She began dragging her toward the sliding glass doors leading into the house. "You have some explaining to do about that…that…thing you are wearing."

Callie knew better than to protest, so she allowed herself to be led away. *If I don't cause a scene, maybe when she is through screaming at me, I can come back out and watch Mason sing some more.*

Mason hurried over to Katie Rose. Katie Rose threw her arms around her brother and exclaimed, "You sounded fantastic! I'm so proud of you!"

"Thanks," he replied, as he drew back from her.

Mason was about to ask Katie Rose if she knew where Rebecca was when he was besieged by everyone there. First, Flora and Kenny sang him high praises. Then, Jonathan, and a few other couples that Mason did not even know, congratulated him on a job well done. And finally, his mom and dad approached him. They too offered words of esteemed congratulations and praise. He momentarily forgot all about Rebecca again.

# Chapter 13

# *Realization*

Mary Julia and Callie were scarcely inside Flora's house before Mary Julia started her inquisition. "Where did you get that *thing* you have on?" she growled. Mary Julia painfully squeezed Callie's arms and began shaking her.

"Let go! You're hurting me!" Callie pleaded. She tried fruitlessly to squirm free from her mom's death grip. "It's only a bikini, mother. Everyone wears them," Callie sassed. Tears of pain had welled up in her eyes.

"Don't get smart with me, young lady!" her mom warned. Mary Julia shook her index finger in her daughter's face, while still staunchly holding on to the other arm. "I know what it is called. What I don't know is where you got it, and more importantly, why are you wearing such a thing??!" Mary Julia continued her tirade. She was oblivious to the hurt she was inflicting upon her daughter.

"I bought it with my allowance money one day when Katie Rose and I were shopping at the mall. Why shouldn't I be wearing it? Katie Rose said it was cute. She talked me into buying it," Callie said, feigning innocence. Tears now freely streamed down her cheeks.

*Naturally, Katie Rose would say something like that to Callie. Then she dressed in a modest tankini and was probably sitting back laughing as all the men stared at Callie in that string she is wearing.*

"Well, Katie Rose was sadly mistaken. She shouldn't have goaded you into buying something like this. You see what she is wearing today, don't you? She isn't showing herself off like you are. You have allowed her to make a fool of you, Callie. I'm sure

103

Katie Rose is jealous of your body, and this was her way of trying to embarrass you. She isn't much of a friend to you."

"Katie Rose is a great friend," Callie defended. "I'm sure she didn't talk me into buying this suit to embarrass me. You're wrong, mother."

"Regardless of whatever Katie Rose's motives may have been, you can't go back out in that tiny thing. You're much too young to understand what goes through a man's mind when he sees a young girl dressed the way that you are."

Mary Julia looked down into Callie's face. She noticed the tear streaks on each of Callie's pink cheeks. Guilt overcame Mary Julia, and she released her daughter.

Mary Julia dropped her hands to her sides. Callie crossed her arms across her chest and began stroking where her mother's hands had been squeezing with such viciousness. Mary Julia caught a momentary glimpse of the deep red marks and scratches her fingers and nails had left on each of her daughter's arms.

It was heart wrenching to see. She had only been trying to protect the girl, yet she had hurt Callie in the process. It was almost more than Mary Julia could bear.

"Oh, Callie, please forgive me," she wailed, her own eyes filling with tears.

Mary Julia awkwardly embraced the girl without giving her a chance to uncross her arms. "Mommy didn't mean to hurt you. I would never hurt you. I never want anyone to hurt you."

Mary Julia began to sob, and she was causing Callie even more discomfort. Mary Julia was crushing her arms in between the two of them. "I love you so much. You know that....right?"

"Mary Julia? Is everything alright?" Jonathan asked with concern as he approached the two of them. He had expected to find his wife and daughter embroiled in a heated argument. He had not expected to find them both in tears.

"Daddy," Callie chirped in a small childlike voice. Her eyes were pleading with him to do something – *anything* – to help. Her mother was squeezing her so tightly she could barely breathe.

"Mary Julia," Jonathan addressed her again. He placed his hands on both her shoulders and carefully attempted to dislodge her from their daughter. "Come on, sweetheart, let Callie go. Are you trying to squeeze her to death? What's going on here?"

Mary Julia relaxed her arms and pushed Callie from her grasp. "Oh, God!" she exclaimed as Callie backed away from her in fear. "What is wrong with me! Callie, are you okay?!"

Callie nodded with uncertainty, and she was watchful to keep her distance. Her guarded eyes studied her mother and seemed to implore her father to continue interceding.

"Callie, why don't you go back outside? Your mother and I need a second alone," Jonathan instructed.

"No!" Mary Julia protested with urgency. "She can't go back outside. She won't be safe! Not dressed like that! Not with all those men around! We have to protect her, Jonathan. You have to help me!"

"I'm going to help you," Jonathan assured her. "If you don't want Callie to go out, then Callie can wait right here. You and I will go into one of the other rooms and talk. You'll wait for us here, right, Callie?"

"Sure," she agreed in a timid voice.

"You promise you'll stay right here?" Mary Julia almost begged.

"Yes, I promise," she said.

Callie knew she was lying. *I have to get back outside. Mason is probably looking for Rebecca by now. I need to go rescue her before they discover what I've done.*

"Let's go. We'll talk with Callie again in a minute," Jonathan prodded in a calm voice. He took gentle hold of Mary Julia's arm and began leading her away.

Callie waited with baited breath until her parents were out of sight. Then she turned and strode with haste toward the doors leading out onto the deck. As she approached the sliding doors, she came face to face with Mason. He had just slid the door open and was rushing into the kitchen. Katie Rose was right on his heels.

"Callie, have you seen Rebecca?" he asked with some alarm. "She isn't anywhere out back, and I don't remember seeing her during the band's first set."

"I'm sure you don't remember seeing her. You were entirely focused on your music. You guys sounded so wonderful!" Callie praised with glee. She had a wide smile on her face, and she was fighting the strongest urge to hug and kiss Mason again.

*I don't have time right now. I have to get outside and let Rebecca out.*

"So did you see her watching the band play?" Katie Rose chimed in.

"No. But I'm sure she was. She wouldn't have missed seeing Mason and the band play for anything," Callie tried to convincingly convey. "I'll bet she's in this house somewhere. I heard someone downstairs. Maybe she needed to use the bathroom and someone pointed her to the one down there. Kenny or Flora maybe? Did you ask them? Anyway, there are three bathrooms in this house, and there happen to be three of us. Why don't we split up and see if we can find her. Mason, you check the one upstairs. Katie Rose you take the one off the living room, and I'll check the one downstairs. We'll meet back here in the kitchen."

*I have to come back in here anyway and wait for my mother and father to finish with me.* "Well, let's not stand around here looking at one another. Let's go!" Callie half ordered.

"It makes sense. Where else could she be?" Mason said to Katie Rose as they raced away in different directions.

"See you guys in a few minutes," Callie said and started in the opposite direction toward the basement door. Her friends had barely disappeared from the room before she dashed over to the sliding glass doors. Callie slid them open and was out onto the deck in a flash.

"Is everything alright, Callie?" she heard Flora say and looked up to see her approaching.

*Oh Great!* Callie did not want to be held up by yet another person.

"Everything is fine," she answered with impatience. She further explained, "I have to go and get my clothes. Mom wants me to put my T-shirt back on over my swimsuit. I'll be right back."

Callie barely gave Flora a glance before she continued to race away in the direction of the changing room. She reached the steps going down off the deck, snatching her robe from the railing. She threw the robe over an arm and descended the stairs.

When Callie was sure she was completely out of the sight of everyone, she reached in the pocket of the robe and took out the key. She stepped up to the dressing room door and quietly turned the lock. Callie dropped the key back into the pocket of the robe and began to knock on the door.

"Rebecca?" she called in a soft voice.

Callie was dismayed when she got no answer. She knocked again, a little bit harder this time, and called her name a slight bit louder. There was still total silence.

Callie panicked now that perhaps someone else had discovered Rebecca and let her out – *but how without the key?* She hurried forward and turned the knob, opening the door. Callie's mouth dropped open and her eyes grew large when she found Rebecca lying on the floor.

*Oh my God! What have I done? Have I killed her?! Did she suffocate in there or something!* Callie's distraught mind concocted.

"Rebecca! Rebecca, are you okay?!" she shrieked as she darted into the room.

Tossing the robe from her arms, she dropped to her knees beside the girl and began frantically shaking her. "Rebecca, wake up! It's okay. Come on, wake up!" Callie was even more alarmed when Rebecca did not respond.

*I've got to go and get help! Daddy! Daddy's a doctor! He'll know what to do!*

She sprang to her feet and began running out of the room, around the corner, and up the steps. At the top of the stairs, Callie nearly collided with Ralph before she could stop her momentum.

"Hey, beautiful! I saw you come out of the house, and I came to find you so…"

"Ralph, get out of my way!" Callie shouted. She shoved him from her path. "I haven't got time for you right now!"

"Okay, no problem. Maybe later," Ralph called after her as she broke into a run once more. *Umm Umm Umm! I sure do love to watch that body of yours when you run!*

Flying across the deck, Callie narrowly escaped slamming headfirst into the glass doors leading into the house. She flung her arms out in front of her to break her slide. She struggled for a second with the latch on the door. Then Callie sent it crashing open. She was lucky the glass did not shatter.

"Callie, what's wrong?" Mason asked with concern as she almost stormed directly into him. He had just entered the kitchen, and Katie Rose was coming down the hall behind him. Callie's face was white as a ghost and she was shaking.

"Re...Rebecca!" she stammered, gasping for breath. Her adrenaline pumping, Callie reached out and roughly pushed Mason out of her way.

Staggering for balance, he barely missed stepping on Katie Rose's toes. As Callie continued her determined dash, Mason called out, "What about Rebecca, Callie? Has something happened to her?!"

Her only response was, "I need my daddy! He can help her! He has to be able to help her!"

\* \* \* \*

Mary Julia was sobbing, shaking, and pounding on her husband's shoulders with her fists. "Let go of me, Jonathan!" she demanded. "How...how can you dare say that I'm overreacting?! My carefree life as a child ended when I was Callie's age because a man violated me. I won't let it happen to Callie! I won't!! I won't, do you hear me?!" she screeched.

"Mary Julia, I.... Is that Callie?" he said, thinking he heard his daughter's voice.

"Oh my God, Jonathan! Yes, it's Callie! And she is calling for *you*?! What could be wrong?!"

Jonathan had no idea, but he had a dreadful sense something must be genuinely wrong. It was rare for Callie to call out for him instead of Mary Julia.

Jonathan released his wife, spun around, and had the bedroom door open in a flash. As he stepped out into the hall, Mary Julia right behind him, Callie nearly mowed them both down.

"Daddy!" she panted with relief, tears beginning to pool in her eyes. Callie clutched one of his arms, and she persisted with urgency, "You...You've got to come with me. Quick! Rebecca needs your help!"

"What's happened to Rebecca?" he asked with distress. He allowed himself to be whisked down the hall, his panic-stricken daughter leading the way.

Jonathan had never seen Callie this upset over another person. Tears were freely flowing down her cheeks. He feared that something terrible must have happened.

"Callie, what's happened?!" Mary Julia echoed, hastening along behind them.

"That's what I would like to know too," Mason told them as he met them halfway across the living room. "Where is Rebecca? What's wrong?!"

"She...she's in the changing room," Callie abruptly shared, stifling a terrified sob. *If I've killed Rebecca, I didn't mean to. I only wanted to get her away from you for a little while. So I could have you all to myself.*

"Something terrible is wrong with her. I don't know what, but Rebecca is laying there and won't wake up. We've got to hurry!" Callie urged again. She broke into a jog once more and drug her father along beside her.

"What?!" Mason questioned. He stood frozen for a second before he too began running in the direction of the door.

"Mason, what's wrong?!" Katie Rose asked with concern as they all ran past her in the kitchen.

"I don't know. Something is wrong with Rebecca," he curtly answered as he flew past her and through the open glass doors.

*Oh, God! Surely this doesn't have anything to do with Callie,* Katie Rose guiltily found herself considering. She rushed from the house as well.

"Katie Rose, where are you all running to? What's wrong?!" Flora asked with worry, stepping directly into her path.

"I'm not sure. Callie says something has happened to Rebecca," she answered, anxious to be on her way.

"Oh my goodness!" Flora exclaimed.

As she twirled around to search for her husband, Katie Rose sped on her way. Flora spotted Kenny out in the yard talking to Long Wolf, Jackie Lynn and another couple. She called out to him in a loud voice. "Kenny! Kenny, can you come here please?!"

Kenny heard the urgency in his wife's voice and saw her motioning for him to come to her. He excused himself from Long Wolf and Jackie Lynn and headed at once in Flora's direction. Long Wolf and Jackie Lynn exchanged confused looks but remained where they were. They had confidence that Kenny could handle whatever small emergency had arisen.

\* \* \* \*

Rebecca was slow to rise, staring all around her with incomprehension. She was dizzy; she felt sick to her stomach; and she could not quite remember where she was. She also became aware that her deodorant must have failed her, as she got a faint whiff of strong body odor.

It was then that it all began to come back to her. The door was open now, and Rebecca could not understand how this could be. She was certain she had been trapped in this room.

Rebecca had shouted and beat her shoulder against the door repeatedly. All of her efforts had been for naught. All she had accomplished was becoming hoarse, sweating profusely and making her shoulder sore.

All at once, there had seemed to be no oxygen in the room. Rebecca had not been able to breathe. She had been certain that the walls were beginning to close in on her. Rebecca had collapsed in the middle of the floor, crying and rocking herself to and fro in terror.

She had heard the band playing and knew no one could possibly hear her. *No one is ever coming to let me out!* Rebecca had been horrifyingly convinced. Then the music had seemed to get farther and farther away and she could barely hear it as everything had gone black.

Now, she stared in awe at the open door before her. *Who could have opened it?* Rebecca had staggered to a standing position on wobbly, unsure legs when Callie and Jonathan came into view.

"Rebecca!" Callie exclaimed with utmost relief. She was so glad to see that the girl was still alive that she nearly raced forward and hugged her.

"You!" Rebecca strangely snapped. She stumbled forward out of the room toward Callie with her arms stretched out in front of her like a zombie. Rebecca wanted to strangle the girl.

"You locked me in here! Didn't you?!" she accused, glaring hatefully at the younger girl.

Mason pushed past Callie and Jonathan and pulled Rebecca into a protective, warm embrace. "Rebecca, we were looking everywhere for you. Are you okay?"

Callie's concern for the girl was quick to turn to disgust as she watched Mason protectively kissing her clammy temple. "Mason, give her some air!" Callie demanded, pulling tenaciously at his arm. "Dad, will you tell him to leave her alone? Shouldn't

110

you exam her? What in the world is that *smell*?!" she cruelly added.

Rebecca self-consciously pushed herself out of Mason's arms and backed away from him several steps. "I...I'm okay," she stuttered in assurance, wiping tears from her cheeks. "I was locked in that room. Why don't you ask Callie what she knows about this? She's the one who locked the door," Rebecca insisted. Her eyes were blazing with fury at Callie.

"Callie, what is she talking about?" Mason inquired. He was giving Callie a hard stare.

"How should I know what she is talking about, Mason?!" Callie fired back. "Rebecca must be delirious! She was unconscious when I found her. Maybe she hit her head or something. Daddy, shouldn't you take her inside and exam her?!"

Katie Rose was fixedly studying Callie also. She did not want to believe that Callie had done what Rebecca was accusing her of, but she had strong suspicions that she had. After all, her feeling that Callie had been up to something had been overwhelming earlier.

*Callie wanted me to leave when Rebecca went in to change. Now, she is the one to find Rebecca in the dressing room. Is this merely a coincidence or is this because Callie locked Rebecca in there? Oh, please don't let it be true!* Katie Rose prayed for her friend.

"Jonathan, what's wrong here?" Kenny interrupted as he raced toward all of them. Flora stopped and stood beside Mary Julia and Katie Rose, looking on with concern.

"I'll tell you what's wrong," Rebecca snapped. "That little..." *I won't say the name I'm thinking.* "....Callie...locked me in your changing room," she accused again.

"This is bullshit!" Callie shouted.

Her eyes were giving Rebecca a piercing, fiery glare, and she had an enraged frown on her face. "I'm the one who found you on the floor of that room. I'm the one that ran and got my dad to help you. How dare you accuse me of locking you in there! I ought to knock you back down on that floor!" Callie snarled.

She took a few, threatening steps forward with both her fists clenched. With lightening speed, Jonathan reached out and grabbed one of Callie's arms. "Girls, let's calm down here," he addressed both Callie and Rebecca in an authoritative voice.

"Callie, Rebecca doesn't need this from you right now. Rebecca, you should come into the house, sit in the air conditioning for awhile, and get something to drink. You may have a slight case of heat exhaustion. I'd like to give you a little examination, if you don't mind, to make sure everything is okay. I'm a doctor."

"Okay," Rebecca agreed, nodding her head. She had been taught to respect adults. *Unlike Callie evidently. I can't believe she used that kind of language in front of everyone.*

"I need to get my clothes first though. I'd like to change out of this swimsuit and freshen up a little," Rebecca stated in a quiet voice. Her eyes were downcast, and her face was turning red with shame. *I'd like to kill that little brat for what she has done to me!*

"That's fine," Jonathan consented. "Callie, will you please gather up her clothes and follow us back into the house?"

"Oh, alright," she grudgingly complied. Callie rushed into the dressing room to begin gathering Rebecca's clothing. She certainly did not want Mason to volunteer.

*I can't believe the way Mason was kissing her temple.* She needed to keep the two of them apart. *If Rebecca goes inside, maybe she'll shut up and stop accusing me of locking her in that room.*

"I'll go tell the guys that the gig is over," Mason stated. "Then I'll come sit with you inside," he told Rebecca, giving her a slight, reassuring squeeze.

"No!" Callie protested without thinking.

She scrambled out of the changing room with Rebecca's clothes haphazardly in her hands. Rebecca's padded bra and pink underwear were visibly on top. Rebecca shot her a scathing look.

Then Rebecca turned to Mason and said, "I'll second that 'no'. You have a job to finish. I already feel stupid enough about all this. Please don't make me feel guilty as well because I've screwed up your first gig. You have to stay out here. I'll be fine."

"Are you sure?" Mason questioned. "I hate to leave you all alone."

"I won't leave her alone until I'm sure she is alright," Jonathan tried to reassure the young man.

"See, I'll be fine," Rebecca reiterated, giving Mason a slight smile. "I'll still get to hear you play your second set. I'm sure I can hear the music in the house. The first set I was kind of out of it," she truthfully stated, giving Callie another dirty look. *What a mean little girl!* "Why don't you go and get the band started back up?"

"Okay," Mason agreed, giving Rebecca the sweetest kiss on the cheek. "I'll come and get you when we're finished. Maybe you can come back out then. If not, we can head on home if you want."

Jonathan led Rebecca away in a slow gait, and Mason raced off to get the band started. Only Callie, Mary Julia and Flora went into the house with Jonathan and Rebecca.

Jonathan walked Rebecca all the way to the bathroom with Callie, Mary Julia and Flora in tow. "Thanks for bringing the clothes," Jonathan said to Callie as he took them from her arms and handed them to Rebecca. Flora went into the bathroom with Rebecca to make sure she had everything she needed to freshen up.

When Flora emerged, she was astonished to hear Jonathan ask, "Flora, could you do us a favor and go back out with Callie and keep an eye on her? As soon as I'm through tending to Rebecca, Mary Julia and I need to finish an important conversation we were having. Callie, we'll talk to you later. You don't mind watching her for us, do you Flora?"

"No, of course not," Flora agreed with haste. She caught merely a glimpse of Mary Julia's stunned expression.

"What?!" Mary Julia began to protest. "No!"

"Yes!" Jonathan stubbornly argued.

"Jonathan, have you lost your mind?!" Mary Julia questioned with alarm.

"No, I'm speaking my mind for the first time in years," he proclaimed with obstinacy. "Flora, Callie, would you mind leaving us alone?"

"Of course not," Flora said again. She took a gentle hold on Callie's arm and begin to lead her away.

"Flora, wait!" Mary Julia pleaded in desperation, starting after them.

"Mary Julia, you can trust me. Stay here with your husband. It's obvious this is important to Jonathan. I'll keep Callie in line. I promise. I won't let her out of my sight," Flora assured her friend.

"Thanks, Flora," Jonathan said and took his wife by the arm. "Come on, Mary Julia. Leave them be. It will all be fine."

Flora nodded her agreement, and she and Callie started away again. Callie was bewildered, but she was also grateful for the way her father was unexpectedly behaving. *Maybe the trauma with Rebecca has brought out the man in him.*

Mary Julia watched helplessly as Flora led her daughter from the room.

# Chapter 14

# *Accusations*

Jonathan settled Rebecca on the sofa in the living room. He instructed her to slowly drink several glasses of cool water. Then he led Mary Julia into the bedroom, so they would be behind closed doors again to talk.

"What is this all about, Jonathan?" Mary Julia asked with irritation. She began to nervously pace back and forth. "Can't we talk later? We need to see to Callie right now. She needs to change clothes. She also needs to be reprimanded for her crass behavior earlier. Callie needs to understand that she can not go around kissing young men, like she did Mason earlier. If you brought me in here to tell me again that I'm overreacting, I won't hear of it! I know what's best for *my* daughter!"

"Well, first off, she is not only *your* daughter. She happens to be my child too. Although, I'm sorry to say that today was the first time I have ever felt useful in her life. You've all but pushed me out of her life, and I've stood by and let you do it. But that ends today. Things have got to change, Mary Julia."

"What things?" Mary Julia questioned with anxiousness. She stopped her pacing, defiantly crossed her arms, and studied her husband with a fierce stare.

"For one thing, our daughter is growing up. And I don't just mean physically. You are going to have to stop trying to control every aspect of her life. You can't keep flying off the handle every time she tries to show a little independence. The two of you are going to keep coming to standoffs like you did today, and you are going to end up hurting Callie if you don't get a grip."

"Okay, maybe I was a little out of control today. But you are acting like what Callie did is absolutely nothing to be concerned about. How can you even begin to think that? You're a man, for god's sake! Don't tell me you didn't know what was going through all those boys' minds while Callie was parading around dressed as she is. Not to mention what everyone thought when she kissed Mason. Callie can't help that she has blossomed into a young woman at such an early age – any more than I could. But I can hear what would be said if anything bad were to happen to her. They would say Callie had it coming. That she asked for it. Just like my stepdad accused me of doing. And Callie probably has no idea how she comes across either," Mary Julia stated with a horrified look on her face.

"Things were different when you were Callie's age. I'm sure you were naïve about how your body affected men, but I'm just as certain that our daughter is not. She purposely dressed the way she did to attract the attention of one specific young man. The same young man she kissed, oblivious to everyone else who was watching. Our daughter has it bad for Mason Greathouse, and because he still basically sees her as a little girl, she is going out of her way to show him that she is becoming a woman. I'd say this is all pretty normal behavior for a girl Callie's age who has her first major crush."

"Yes, and what if Mason decides to act as is normal for his age? What's to keep him from taking advantage of Callie? Even though Mason isn't a grown man yet, he is old enough to ruin the rest of Callie's life if he so chooses. I can't take that chance, Jonathan! Not with Mason or any other boy or man! I have to keep Callie safe at all costs, and if that infringes on her being *normal*, then so be it! At least she'll have a chance to lead a happy, *normal* life later on. She'll never have to suffer like I did," Mary Julia staunchly maintained. She began to rub her arms as cold chills ran up and down her spine.

"Don't you think that every parent would like to keep their child in a protective bubble, safe from all harm?" Jonathan questioned, closing the gap between them. He pulled Mary Julia into a gentle sympathetic embrace. "I'm sorry that your mother did not try to protect you, and that you were hurt so badly by the men she brought into your life. But you can't continue to suffocate Callie because of this. You have become overbearing towards her.

That is why she does some of the things she does. You need help, Mary Julia. You need to talk to a professional about all your fears regarding Callie."

"So now I'm crazy! Is that it?! I am making Callie act and do the things she does?" Mary Julia snapped. She aggressively pushed herself out of Jonathan's arms. "If anyone is crazy, Jonathan, it is you! You are nuts if you believe that I am going to turn Callie loose to do as she pleases, because it's *normal* for her. And you are crazy as hell if you think I'm going to sit back and stop trying to protect her!"

"I'm not suggesting that you simply turn Callie loose to do as she pleases. I'm also not saying you should turn your back on her and not try to protect her from harm. What I am trying to say is that there are better ways of doing both these things than the way you have been."

"Who the hell do you think you are to criticize me?!" Mary Julia shouted. Her face was locked in a hideous, infuriated grimace now. "What makes you an expert on raising children all of the sudden?!"

"I'm far from being an expert at raising children, Mary Julia. I'll be the first to admit that. But I am certain that what you are doing is wrong and can lead to nothing but pain for all of us. You can't keep obsessively watching her every move, and you can't start doing physical harm to Callie to keep her in line. She will never give into you being in control. Callie will push you farther and farther away by doing exactly what you don't want her to. It's got to end before Callie does something she will truly regret. The only way you are going to be able to change the way you interact with our daughter is for you to seek help from a professional. That's doesn't mean you are crazy, Mary Julia. It means you need a little help. We all need help now and then, and it's well past time that you got some for yourself. I should have pushed this issue long ago."

"*You* should have pushed this issue?!" Mary Julia parroted. Her mouth was set in a deep ugly frown. "Who do you think you are all of the sudden?! Callie may be your child, but I certainly am not! If you think you can start ordering me around and telling me what to do, then you are sadly mistaken, Jonathan. I know what's best for my daughter! You, and certainly not some shrink, can't tell me otherwise!"

"You know what? You are right. I have no right to order you around. That's not the way I meant to come across," he seemed to surrender, but then added, "I'm so frustrated with the way things are, Mary Julia. Frustrated and tired. I need for things to change. I'm trying to tell you that we can't keep going on this way. I'm begging you to help change things. I'm trying to tell you that if things stay the way they are, our marriage may not survive much longer. Is that what you want? Do you want to throw away all the years we've had together? Or are you willing to fight for us – you and I – you, me and Callie as a family. Please tell me you will fight for us, Mary Julia?!" Jonathan began to plead, with sad eyes.

"Good Lord, Jonathan! Where is all this coming from? Is it because you are turning fifty in a few months? Is this some sort of midlife crisis? It sounds as if you are the one who should be seeking professional help," Mary Julia accused, feeling panicked.

"No, Mary Julia. This isn't about me roaring off in some bright red sport's car with a younger woman my side, if that's what you are thinking," Jonathan said in exasperation, shaking his head in disbelief. "It does have to do with the way we are growing apart though. There is more and more distance between us all the time. Pretty soon I'm afraid we won't be able to bridge the gap. I don't want that to happen. Do you?"

"You're talking about sex, aren't you?" Mary Julia conjectured. "We used to be intimate quite frequently. But lately, you haven't seemed interested, and to be honest, I haven't pursued it either. I've been so tied up with Callie that I'm exhausted a lot of the time. But, Jonathan just because it's been awhile since we've made love doesn't mean I don't still want you. I'm sorry. I forgot how important sex is to a man. I promise I'll make it up to you. There won't be distance between us anymore," she promised.

Mary Julia bridged the gap between them. She slipped her arms around Jonathan's neck and drew in for a kiss. Mary Julia was more than a little shocked when he rejected her kiss. Jonathan swung his head back and pushed apart from her once more.

"No!" he protested. "Sex isn't going to solve anything. That isn't the problem. You've always used it as a solution, and God help me, I've let you. But not anymore!"

"So if you don't want sex from me, then you must be getting it somewhere else. There is another woman, isn't there,

Jonathan?!" Mary Julia demanded to know. Frustrated tears sprang into her eyes.

"Yes, there is another woman who is coming between us. A much, much younger woman," Mary Julia was disgusted to hear him admit. "It's our daughter," Jonathan was quick to add.

Jonathan caught a glimpse of the look of horror in Mary Julia's eyes. He understood exactly what she was thinking, so he immediately clarified, "Not sexually. I would *never* do something like that to my own daughter! Callie comes between us because she is all you can focus on. It leaves little room in your life for me and the space keeps getting smaller and smaller all the time. I'll eventually be crowded out altogether. So I'll ask you again, is that what you want? Do you want to tear this family apart?"

"My God, Jonathan, are you actually jealous of your own daughter? You resent the time I spend with her. That's what this is about, isn't it?" Mary Julia continued to argue.

"I feel sorry for our daughter, not jealous. Who in their right mind would envy someone who is constantly being scrutinized and berated for every little thing they do?" Jonathan assured her.

Then with pleading eyes, he implored, "Mary Julia, please stop twisting things around. For the last time, I am not having a midlife crisis; I am not having an affair; and this isn't about me being jealous of the time you spend with Callie. This isn't about *me* at all! This is about you. You and a past that you let control our life now. It's time you put that past where it belongs, and that's behind you. You've got to stop letting it haunt you. You got to stop it from destroying all our lives. Listen to me, Mary Julia. Please hear what I'm saying. I'm tired of sitting on the sidelines in our marriage, and I'm especially tired of sitting on the sidelines of my daughter's life. Callie is almost grown. This is my last chance to be a father to her, and I'm going to take it. I'd like to share this with you, as I have so many other things over the years. But if you refuse to seek help and things aren't going to change, then I will be forced to leave. If I get a legal separation, the court is bound to grant me visitation time with Callie. Then I will have the one-on-one time I need with her at last. I'll get to know my daughter and share in her life before she becomes a grown woman. I need this, Mary Julia, and if you love me, you will make this possible with the two of us staying together. I will be there for you. I will stand by you no matter what or how long it takes. Tell me you will get help!"

Mary Julia stared at Jonathan in stunned silence for a minute. She seemed to be oblivious to the tears that were freely streaming down her face now. When she spoke, she asked in a small quivering voice, "Do you have any idea what you are asking me, Jonathan? You are asking me to choose between you and Callie. How can you do this? You say if I love *you*, I need to do such and such. I say if you love *me*, you wouldn't even ask such a thing."

Mary Julia paused, and then she added between sobs, "You...you don't lo..love mmm...me anymore, do you, Jonathan?"

"Mary Julia, you have things so backwards that it is pitiful," Jonathan stated.

He was fighting the urge to go to Mary Julia. He wanted to pull her into his arms and try to comfort her. It was tearing Jonathan apart to watch her crying so piteously.

Jonathan hated that he was the cause of Mary Julia's pain, but he could see no alternative. Things could not continue as they had been. "You are the only woman I have ever loved, and I still love you now, Mary Julia. That's why I want so badly for you to fight for us now – by getting the help you need. I'm the one who has had to choose between *you* and Callie for years. And so far, it has been you I've chosen. Now, it's Callie's turn. She needs me. She needs to know she has a father in her life too. But she could have both a mother and father sharing her life if you'll stop fighting me on this. Please say that you will. I'll be there every step of the way, like I always have been, if you'll agree to get help."

*Agree to get help?! I know what this means. He wants me to be institutionalized again – like I was all those years ago – for all those months. Why does Jonathan want to be alone with Callie for months on end? I want to believe that he only wants to bond with his daughter, but I can't take that chance! I'm not crazy! I love my daughter above all else. Even above my love for Jonathan. I won't be separated from her. Not for anyone! Not even Jonathan!*

However, Mary Julia did not want Jonathan to leave them. *If he leaves me, Jonathan would get private visitation with Callie. Or worse, he might even get custody of her because of my past, and*

*I'd still be separated from Callie. I can't allow this to happen either.*

"If I promise to make an appointment with a psychologist, will you stop all this Jonathan?" Mary Julia desolately appealed. "Will you promise you'll stay?" she begged.

Mary Julia closed the gap between them, and she gathered Jonathan in an insecure embrace. "Please, Jonathan! I don't know how I would survive without you!" she proclaimed. Mary Julia collapsed against him, sobbing uncontrollably.

"I don't want to live my life without you either, Mary Julia," Jonathan told her. He stroked the back of her head and squeezed her into a tight reassuring embrace. "If you'll make this first step, I'm sure things can get better. I won't leave you. I'll be right here helping you along the way. I promise."

"I'll do it. I'll do whatever it takes to keep my family together." *To keep my daughter* safe *with me.* "You'll see, Jonathan. Things will change. Why don't we go out and spend some time together as a family now? I promise not to obsess over Callie."

"Are you sure you are up to that after all this? You must be exhausted from the stress of it all. We could get Callie and go home."

"No, no! I'm alright!" Mary Julia was adamant to profess.

"Okay. You go into the bathroom and freshen up, wipe away those tears. I'll wait right here for you. Then we'll go outside together," Jonathan told her. He gave Mary Julia a kiss on the forehead and a slight smile. "You're doing the right thing, Mary Julia. You'll see."

"I am," she staunchly maintained. *I'll always do what's right for Callie. I'll always keep her safe. No psychologist will ever change that.*

\* \* \* \*

Mason and his band had finished their final song, and he was receiving congratulations and words of praise once more from everyone. He planned to go into the house and check on Rebecca the first chance he got. Mason hated that she had had such an awful day, and he hated to think of Rebecca off all by herself now.

Long Wolf approached Mason and told him that he and Jackie Lynn had gone inside to check on Rebecca. Jackie Lynn had decided to stay with the girl in case she needed something. Mason was glad to hear this. He told his father that he was going into the house to spend some one-on-one time with Rebecca for the rest of the party.

Callie and Katie Rose had been sitting by the side of the pool again listening to the band play. Now, Callie hopped to her feet to make her way through the crowd to give Mason her congratulations. *And maybe another kiss!* But Katie Rose stepped into her path.

"We need to talk," she told Callie in a determined voice.

"Okay," Callie agreed. She was still looking longingly over Katie Rose's shoulder at Mason. "We'll talk right after I've given Mason my congratulations."

"We'll talk *now!*" Katie Rose dictated. Her eyes were very serious.

"What's up with you?" Callie questioned. She was puzzled by the girl's strange behavior.

"This," Katie Rose answered. She spread her hand open in front of Callie's face. The small key to the changing room rested in the palm of her hand.

"What's that?" Callie feigned ignorance.

*Damn! Mason is making his way toward the house. He's going in to see Rebecca. I need to stop him.* "Can you get out of my way and stop playing games?!" Callie snapped.

Callie attempted to push Katie Rose from her path, but Katie Rose moved back into Callie's footpath. "I'm not the one playing games. You locked Rebecca in the changing room because you didn't want her spending time with Mason. It's true, so don't try to pretend that you don't know what I'm talking about! You should be ashamed of yourself, Callie!"

*Damn! Where did Katie Rose get that key?! Is she going to tell everyone what she suspects?*

Callie watched with helplessness as Mason entered the house. *I'll have to forget about Mason for now. I need to calm Katie Rose down before she shouts to everyone what I've done.*

Roughly taking Katie Rose by the arm, Callie began to drag her across the deck, away from everyone else. "Okay, you want to talk. Let's talk! How are you so sure I locked Rebecca in that room?" she asked in a quiet voice.

"Because I found this key in the pocket of your robe. The robe you specifically asked me to hand you after you were alone in the changing room. The key always hangs right inside the door of the changing room, and you knew that. If it had been hanging there, like it was supposed to be, then Rebecca could have let herself out. Isn't it funny that it landed in the pocket of *your* robe – the same robe you took back to the changing room with you when you went to let Rebecca out, about an hour after you left her there? I had a feeling you were up to something all along. And I felt it even more strongly when you asked me to leave you alone with Rebecca while she was changing. You locked her in that room, Callie. I know it! I want you to admit it to me!"

Callie stopped by the steps leading off the deck and released Katie Rose's arm. "Just because the key normally hangs in the changing room, but happened to be in that robe instead, doesn't prove anything. That doesn't mean I put it there. It could have been there all along."

"Cut the crap, Callie!" Katie Rose uncharacteristically spat out. "This is me you are talking to. Not your mom! I know you. I've been used by you, to cover your butt, way too many times not to know how you operate. So don't stand there and try to lie to me! I'll march right off and tell everyone what I know, if you don't start being honest with me right this second! Do you hear me?!"

*Yes, I hear you! So will everyone else if I don't calm you down and lower your voice.*

"What exactly happens if I 'fess up to what you are accusing me of?" Callie asked. "Are you going to run off and tattle on me to my parents? What do you want from me anyway?"

"What would be the purpose in me running off and telling your parents? You'd find some way to turn it around, and your mom would let you off the hook. This isn't about you getting in trouble with them. This is about you being honest for once. What you did was wrong. Rebecca is a nice person. She didn't deserve what you did to her. You need to go and apologize to her."

*Yeah, right. Like I'm going to do that.* "Look, I'm genuinely sorry about what happened to Rebecca. But I'm getting tired of being blamed for it because I found her. You should be thanking me for helping Rebecca and not accusing me of locking her up. You're the one who should be ashamed!" she chastised, her eyes blazing with anger. "Now I'm going back to the party! If you want to spread your ridiculous version of what you think happened, then go right ahead! You have no real proof of anything! You like Rebecca, but you are supposed to be my best friend. You better start acting like it if you want to continue to be my friend at all!" Callie warned with fury.

Without another word or waiting for a reply, she spun on her heel and raced away. She left Katie Rose standing there all alone. Katie Rose stared on in confusion.

Callie was guilty of locking Rebecca in the changing room. But Callie was right; Katie Rose did not have any concrete proof. Callie was a master of squirming out of tight situations.

Katie Rose was not interested in tattling on Callie anyway. She had only wanted to get her friend to realize, and admit, that she was wrong. At least Callie had seemed genuinely worried when she found Rebecca, and she brought her help right away. Hopefully this was a saving grace for her dear friend.

*Maybe finding Rebecca the way she did scared Callie enough to make her think twice next time*, Katie Rose earnestly hoped. She walked off in defeat to go back and enjoy the party. However, she and Callie had little to say to each other for the rest of the day.

# Chapter 15

# *The Movie*

After the Fourth of July, the rest of the summer seemed to fly past. True to character for both of them, Callie continued to flirt insatiably with Mason every chance she got, and Mason continued to largely ignore her. Callie still overcompensated for this ongoing rejection by openly flirting with every other boy she came into contact with. She especially seemed to enjoy leading on poor Ralph.

The weekend before they were supposed to be going back to school, and into the eighth grade, Callie asked Katie Rose to spend Saturday night at her house. Katie Rose was glad to be going there, because Callie still generally came to her house most of the time. When Callie visited her house, it was hard for Katie Rose to keep the girl from wandering the streets in search of boys to flirt with. This was not as likely to happen at Callie's house, where Mary Julia kept too close an eye on her. Katie Rose was looking forward to spending the time with Callie.

*Maybe it will be like old times*, she hopefully longed. *Just Callie and I spending one-on-one time together.*

Katie Rose had just finished eating dinner with Callie and her family when she was surprised to hear Callie ask, "Mom, can Katie Rose and I go to a movie tonight? The name of the movie is The Diary. It's rated PG, and it's at the $1.50 movie theatre. I have $3.00, so I can treat. It starts at 8:00, so we won't be out late. Can we go, please?"

Callie had said nothing to Katie Rose about wanting to see a movie tonight. She could not even remember seeing previews for the movie Callie wanted them to see. Fortunately, Katie Rose liked going to the movies though, so she was game to go along with her friend's plan.

"I had kind of hoped that you girls would be hanging out here tonight," Mary Julia stated. *So I could keep my eye on you.*

Mary Julia caught Jonathan's eye; she added with haste, "But I don't see a problem with the two of you going to the movies, if that is what you would like to do." *It will give me a chance to seduce my husband and keep him happy.*

Ever since their exhaustive fight on the Fourth of July, Mary Julia had been going out of her way to make sure Jonathan was happy, especially sexually. She had even visited a counselor a few times since then. She had not taken much of the counselor's advice, but she was still trying to give Jonathan the solid impression that she was trying.

"Thanks, mom," Callie said with a grateful smile. "Dad, you don't mind dropping us off, do you?"

It had become obvious to Callie that her father was all of the sudden trying to share part of her life. Callie had craved his presence for so long that she was happy to have him do just about anything with her. She also did not want her mother hovering over them tonight.

*It would be just like my mom to follow us inside and make sure we are safely seated in the theater before she leaves. That is, if she didn't decide to stay at the last minute.*

"Of course I don't mind dropping the two of you off!" Jonathan agreed with eagerness. He had a happy grin on his face.

Jonathan was, at long last, feeling as if he was being allowed to be part of his daughter's life. Dropping her and a friend off at the movies was a small part, but he was excited to be able to do it.

Mary Julia remained silent, since she could tell how delighted Jonathan appeared to be. *Callie has a friend with her. There can be no harm in letting him have this time with our daughter.*

"Well, that's all settled then," Mary Julia said. She gave them a smile of her own. "Why don't you girls come in the kitchen with me now and help me with the dishes? Then I'll give you the money for the show, some popcorn and drinks."

"Sounds good! Thanks, mom!" Callie proclaimed, hopping up from the table.

Katie Rose slid her chair back and also got up from the table. She and Callie helped Mary Julia gather the dishes. *Yeah! So far so good!* Callie was thinking with elation. She, her mother and Katie Rose vacated the room with swiftness, dishes in hand.

\* \* \* \*

In the car, on the way to the movie theatre, Jonathan allowed Callie to tune in and listen to whatever radio stations the girls enjoyed. Then he attempted to make light conversation with the girls by asking them about popular teen idols, their favorite music, and television shows. He was enjoying talking and laughing with them so much that he hated it when he pulled the car up in front of the theater.

Jonathan put the car in park, and he pulled Callie into a tight embrace. *I love you!* It felt wonderful to be able to hold his daughter in his arms.

"You girls enjoy the movie. I'll be back in a few hours to pick you both up," Jonathan said with a friendly smile when he freed his daughter from his arms.

Callie had hated for her daddy to release her. *He hugged me!*

"Bye, daddy," she said in a quiet voice as she slid out of the car. Callie was so touched that her father had actually had physical contact with her that tears threatened. "We'll be waiting right here for you after the movie. Thanks for bringing us."

"It was my pleasure," he stated. A silly grin was still on Jonathan's face as he pulled away and left the girls behind.

*I finally have my daughter in my life*, Jonathan pleasingly accepted.

\* \* \* \*

The girls entered the bright, bustling, crowded theater lobby. However, instead of getting in the long line to buy their tickets, Callie told Katie Rose that she needed to go to the bathroom. So the girls fought their way through hordes of people and went into the women's restroom. Once inside, Katie Rose headed to the only available stall, but Callie stopped at the mirrors.

When Katie Rose came back out to wash her hands, she was dismayed to find her friend applying makeup.

"Oh, good grief, Callie! What's the point in putting on makeup? We're going to be in a dark movie theater. The guys aren't going to be able to see you anyway," Katie Rose pointed out with some exasperation. Callie had a one-track mind lately, and the one track was *boys, boys, boys.*

"That doesn't matter," Callie replied. She plentifully stroked blush across her cheeks. "It makes me feel good to wear makeup. You should try it, Katie Rose. Why don't you let me put some on you?"

"I don't think so. Not tonight anyway," Katie Rose rather shyly told her. She backed away a slight bit. Not only did she not want Callie to put makeup on her, but Katie Rose did not want to needlessly block one of the sinks. There were other ladies in the restroom with them, and they were coming up to wash their hands.

Katie Rose had discussed wearing makeup with her mother, and Jackie Lynn said she would rather she wait until she was in high school to start wearing it. *That would be far soon enough.* Katie Rose was still pretty shy around guys anyway, so she did not want to do something that might call more attention to her.

"Suit yourself," Callie mumbled. She vigorously applied mascara to her pretty, long eyelashes. She finished by coloring her full lips with a bright red shade of lipstick.

*All this to be noticed by the guys while she walks across the movie lobby!* "Can we go buy our tickets now?" Katie Rose asked with obvious irritation, her eyes boring into Callie. She noticed other women glancing at Callie as they momentarily stood at the sinks on each side of her, washing their hands and quickly freshening their makeup. Katie Rose was anxious to leave the bathroom. It was crowded, and she and Callie were taking up space.

Callie all but ignored Katie Rose's question. Instead, she busied herself with quickly styling her long, blond, wavy hair. She lowered her head and vigorously fluffed it out with her fingers. She set it with a small travel size bottle of hairspray.

Lastly, Callie sprayed perfume on her neck and wrists. Callie stashed her makeup, hairspray and perfume back in her large purse. Katie Rose watched as Callie began unbuttoning her blouse.

She was shocked when Callie peeled away the short sleeve blouse to uncover a form fitting red tank top. Callie neatly rolled her blouse up and stashed it inside her purse too.

Callie glanced at her watch then, and she stated, "Okay, let's get this show on the road."

Katie Rose shook her head in disbelief at all Callie had done. *It will definitely be quite a show!*

Callie turned and strolled out of the bathroom. Katie Rose followed with reluctance. *I hope Callie doesn't try to flirt with strange guys in the lobby. We're likely to miss our movie.*

Katie Rose was even more concerned about this as Callie stopped in the middle of the lobby and stood watching the door. "The ticket counter is over there," Katie Rose pointed. "See. Where the long line is." She was persistently pulling on Callie's arm.

"In a minute," Callie promised, seeming distracted. She pulled loose from Katie Rose grip.

*Oh, there he is*, Callie thought with a smile and raised a hand to wave. Katie Rose looked toward the door and was distressed to see Ralph coming into the theater.

"What's Ralph doing here?" she asked her friend with suspicion.

He was taking quick strides right toward them with a huge grin spread across his face. He was by himself. Ralph was also dressed rather nicely. He had on a navy polo shirt, which complimented his blue eyes and red hair. Ralph had neatly tucked the shirt into a belted pair of beige slacks. He had brown loafers on his feet.

"Hi, Ralph," Callie greeted with an attractive happy smile.

"Hello to you, pretty lady," he enthusiastically replied.

Ralph proceeded to pull Callie into a tight, welcoming hug. The guy was so excited that Callie could feel his heart throbbing against her body. He held her for several seconds, stroking her back before he pulled back.

"You look great!" he proclaimed as he surveyed her face and body.

"How do *I* look?" Katie Rose spoke up. *He hasn't even noticed that I'm here.*

"Oh, hi, kid," Ralph replied, giving Katie Rose an affectionate shove. Then he refocused all his attention on Callie. "Have you girls gotten your tickets yet?"

"No, not yet. Maybe we were waiting for you. Wouldn't you like to buy them for *all* of us?" Callie prodded with a playful chuckle, flirtatiously squeezing Ralph's arm.

"Sure I will," he agreed with eagerness. "I'll even buy you some popcorn and a soft drink if you would like."

"Both of us?" Callie asked, glancing sideways at Katie Rose.

"Sure," Ralph agreed again. "I'll get each of us a soda and I'll get a big tub of popcorn that we can all share. Would that work?"

"Sounds great!" Callie chirped and flashed him another brilliant smile.

"Well, okay then. I'll be back in a second with the tickets. Don't take off with some other guy while I'm gone." He said, only half teasing.

"I'll be right here waiting only for you," Callie assured him with yet one more award winning smile and a bat of her eyelashes. "See you in a second."

Ralph nearly stumbled over his own feet as he started away. He was still looking behind him at Callie. *It's hard to take my eyes off her. I can't believe she's here with* me*! Mason's crazy when he calls that one a little girl!* Ralph turned his head and hurried away. He did not want to be gone for a second longer than necessary.

"So…it seems that Ralph is joining us in our movie," Katie Rose stated with a disapproving frown. "Is that why you asked me over tonight, Callie? To be a decoy so you could meet Ralph at the movie theater?"

"No, of course not!" Callie tried to assure her. "We are getting a free movie, popcorn and coke from Ralph, so don't start complaining. I'll buy you something with the money my mother gave me for the show and food the next time we go to the mall. So we both win all around."

"So you say," Katie Rose stated with sarcasm. Her mouth was stretched in a tight, annoyed line. "You win maybe. That is, if lying and using people is considered winning."

"Come on, Katie Rose, don't get all mad. We'll still have a good time, even if Ralph is along. You'll see," Callie tried to placate. "We're best friends," she declared with a smile, placing her arm around her shoulders and giving her an affectionate squeeze. "Best friends cover for one another all the time."

*I sure must be the greatest best friend in the whole wide world then. Because I've covered for Callie more times than I care to count,* Katie Rose sadly mused. She said nothing more.

# Chapter 16

# *Lessons*

Katie Rose, Callie and Ralph all exited the bright lobby, walked down a dimly lit hallway, and turned the corner into the theatre that their movie would play in. There was a slide show of advertisements and movie puzzles alternately flashing up on the screen. There was soft rock music playing on the speakers. Katie Rose automatically went down an aisle of seats near the front. She and Callie always sat up close.

"Hey, kid," Ralph called out to her. "You can sit there if you want, but Callie and I are going to sit in the back row," he informed her and continued down the side.

"Come on, Katie Rose," Callie encouraged. She paused for a second to make sure Katie Rose would follow.

"We always sit down here," Katie Rose said under her breath. Katie Rose had an irritated grimace on her face, but she fell into pace beside Callie.

"Ralph likes to sit in the back row. And he has the popcorn, so we go where he goes," Callie tried to justify. Callie grabbed Katie Rose by the arm and pulled her along with persistence.

*It's obvious that whatever Ralph says goes, and I'm along for the ride!* With intense annoyance, Katie Rose allowed herself to be led away to their new destination.

\* \* \* \*

The lights went down and the movie began. Ralph slipped his arm around Callie's shoulders, and he pulled her a little closer.

About a half-hour into the movie, Ralph appeared to be snuggling his face into Callie's neck.

Callie was sitting between Katie Rose and Ralph. She was holding the tub of popcorn, so Katie Rose could not help but notice Callie and Ralph. It was not until Katie Rose heard Ralph's lips smack that she grasped what Ralph was actually doing – kissing her friend's neck.

"Callie, can I have a kiss? Pretty please?" Katie Rose heard Ralph beg in a quiet voice. Katie Rose watched as Ralph puckered up his lips in longing anticipation. She had already watched Ralph kiss her friend several times on the cheek.

*Geez, Callie! Tell the guy to get a grip! Not only shouldn't you give him a kiss, but he needs to stops kissing all over you like that!* Katie Rose was thinking in disgust.

"Here, Katie Rose," she heard Callie whisper as she handed her the popcorn. "You can have the rest of this. Ralph and I are done with it."

*Then why don't you dump the rest of it over Ralph's head?* Katie Rose was concocting with uncustomary meanness. *Better yet, use your soft drink, and cool him down some!*

A few minutes later, Katie Rose was astonished to watch Callie put her arms around Ralph's neck and pull in for a long, drawn out kiss. When Callie and Ralph parted, several minutes later, they were both out of breath.

*They are panting like animals.* Katie Rose looked around her in embarrassment to see if anyone else was noticing what her friend was doing. She was thankful that everyone still seemed to be engrossed in the movie. All Katie Rose could focus on was the drama that was unfolding beside her. *I've got to do something to stop this!*

"Here, Callie, pass this back to Ralph," Katie Rose instructed in a voice which was loud enough to be heard. She plopped the bucket of popcorn back in her friend's lap.

"What…?!" Callie uttered out loud and jumped in alarm. She had been absorbed in her adult play with Ralph.

Someone a few rows up turned and attempted to quiet them with a loud and defining, "Shhhh!"

Ralph reached over and took the bucket from Callie's lap and placed it on the floor between them. "Next time, why don't you leave the kid at home?" he asked Callie in an annoyed whisper.

*Because I can't.*

Katie Rose was the ticket to almost all of Callie's freedom. The distraction with the popcorn had been deliberate on Katie Rose's part though. Katie Rose had wanted to stop what had been happening with Ralph.

*Oh, well! I have to take the good with the bad*, Callie realized.

Callie slid up in her seat and appeared to be focusing on the movie once again. Katie Rose could feel Ralph's eyes glaring at her on occasion. But he too attempted to watch a little more of the show.

*I did it!* Katie Rose decided with triumph. *Maybe now they will stop all that nonsense for good, and watch the movie like we came here for in the first place.*

* * * *

Katie Rose's victory was short lived, however. Shortly after she had begun to concentrate on the movie plot again, about fifteen minutes, she heard a noise beside her. Katie Rose glanced over to discover Callie and Ralph wrapped in a tight embrace with their mouths greedily feeding off one another.

Callie and Ralph, concluding one kiss, only seemed to rush instantaneously into the next one. They almost looked like two monsters that were trying to devour one another. Katie Rose could even hear Ralph begin to slightly moan.

*Oh God! What do I do now!* Katie Rose was certain everyone else in the theatre must be aware of what Callie and Ralph were doing. She was embarrassed to even be sitting beside them. About that time, she was relieved to see Callie pull back.

"Wait, Ralph," Callie gasped in a barely audible voice. "I need to catch my breath." Callie was feeling dizzy. She sat back against her chair, closed her eyes and attempted to take normal breaths.

Callie nearly hyperventilated a few seconds later, when a hand cupped over one of her breasts and began to slightly squeeze. "Oh, Callie!" Callie heard Ralph wail and felt his hot breath as he began kissing the side of her neck.

"Cut it out, Ralph!" Katie Rose snarled with loathing. She reached across Callie to completely empty the ice from her soft drink directly into his lap.

"Yowl!" Ralph howled in a loud voice. He broke all contact with Callie as he sprang to his feet and shook the ice from his lap. "You little....!"

"Shhhh!!" several people warned again. They were growing perturbed with the noise from these children now.

"I think we should leave," Callie announced in a determined whisper, rising to her feet as well.

She felt like all the eyes in the theatre were on them now, and Callie was still shaken from Ralph trying to grope her. She had not anticipated this. She had only wanted to kiss.

"That's an extremely good idea!" Katie Rose was quick to agree, also standing. "This movie has been ruined anyway!" she added under her breath.

"You can say that again," Ralph grumbled with fury.

Ralph staggered out behind the two girls. He self-consciously crossed his hands and held them in front of the icy wet spot on the front of his jeans. He was also shielding the slight swelling that still remained in this region, despite the uninvited *cold shower* Katie Rose had given him.

* * * *

They emerged from the theatre, and Ralph pointed toward the nearby men's restroom. He dashed in that direction. Ralph looked back over his shoulder and said, "I'll be back in a second, Callie. Will you please wait for me?"

Callie gave him a slight smile and nodded.

"Callie, I want to leave! Now!" Katie Rose demanded as soon as Ralph had disappeared into the bathroom. "I can't believe what you did with Ralph in there!"

"Shhh!" Callie cautioned with a finger to her lips.

Callie was self-consciously glancing all around them. She was shocked when she saw Mason and Rebecca coming down the hall toward them. *Mason?* Callie said to herself in disbelief.

Katie Rose followed Callie's attentive gaze and turned to see her brother and Rebecca coming toward them. "Mason," she said with relief and started toward them.

"Hi, Katie Rose," Rebecca said with a friendly smile. "Looks like Mason and I weren't the only ones to decide on a movie tonight. What are you girls here to see?" *I hope it isn't the same movie as Mason and I. Not that I would mind having Katie Rose along. But I can't stand that other brat. I still can't believe how she got away with locking me in that room.*

The smile disappeared from Rebecca's face. She glared rather hatefully at Callie for a few minutes. Rebecca also noted, with disapproval, Callie's formfitting tank top and the fact that she was wearing a lot of makeup.

"We *were* seeing The Diary," Katie Rose answered, shooting Callie an irate glance.

"What do you mean *were*?" Mason questioned. He noticed the agitation in his sister's voice and caught the angry glare she had given Callie.

"She means that's the movie we just finished seeing," Callie helpfully added. She dared to walk up to Katie Rose and place her arm around her shoulder. "I treated Katie Rose, my best friend in the whole world, to a movie tonight. It let out a second ago."

"No, Callie, you know very well that it was Ralph who treated us both to the movie," Katie Rose revealed. She shoved Callie's arm from her shoulder.

*I'm not playing your game, Callie! Not after you used me like you did tonight!* Katie Rose decided. She was fighting to keep angry tears from springing to her eyes. Katie Rose's feelings were very hurt.

"*Ralph*?" Mason asked with confusion. He had no more said the name then he saw his friend coming out of the restroom down the hall. "Katie Rose, what is up?" Mason questioned. He could tell his sister was tremendously upset.

*Why was Ralph seeing a movie with my sister? This has to have something to do with Callie. What has she done now?*

"Do you want to tell Mason what's up, Callie? Or should I?" Katie Rose uncharacteristically challenged with unveiled hostility.

"Katie Rose, I don't know what you are making such a big deal out of," Callie was fast to downplay. Callie flashed Mason an easygoing smile, and she explained, "I asked Ralph to join us for a movie, and he bought all our tickets." Callie turned back to Katie Rose, and she said, "There, I told Mason. Are you happy now?"

"Hey, guys," Ralph greeted with a cordial grin as he walked up beside Callie and casually placed an arm around her shoulder.

He was glad he had managed to dry out the front of his jeans with the hot air from the hand dryer in the bathroom. "Must be date night at the $1.50 theatre tonight. Hey, maybe you could treat your little sister to a movie with you and Rebecca. We cut our movie a little short because it wasn't very good. The kid is disappointed. I could drive Callie home. What do you say, pal?" Ralph asked with a mischievous wink.

Mason was studying both Ralph and Callie. He noticed how Callie was dressed and also noted that she was wearing makeup. He weighed the way Ralph had his arm around Callie's shoulder and thought about his words, 'Must be date night at the $1.50 theatre tonight'.

*Shit! He's on a date with Callie. She drug Katie Rose along so she could pull this off. No wonder my sister is upset.*

"Ralph, the two of us need to have a little talk," Mason said in a stern voice.

"Mason, our movie starts in fifteen minutes," Rebecca reminded him. She did not want their night together spoiled by him getting mixed up in Callie's problems.

Mason reached in his back pocket and took out his wallet. He handed Rebecca a ten dollar bill, and he asked, "Why don't you go and buy us some popcorn and drinks? My talk with Ralph won't take long. I'll join you in our theatre in a few minutes. Okay?"

"Alright," Rebecca agreed with some reluctance. *At least I won't have to stand here and try to make small talk with Callie. She would probably say something out of line, and I might strangle the life out of her!*

"See you in a little bit," Rebecca said as she hurried away.

"Okay," Mason agreed. He turned his attention to his sister then and asked, "Katie Rose, do you have your cell phone with you?"

"Sure," she answered. "Why?"

"I want you to call Callie's mom while I am talking to Ralph and tell her that you and Callie are ready to be picked up. Alright?"

"I'd rather call mom or dad and tell them to pick me up. I was supposed to spend the night with Callie, but I've decided I don't want to," Katie Rose confessed.

She glanced at Callie with clear hurt in her eyes. "Callie can call her own mom or dad. She has her cell phone with her too."

"Callie doesn't need to," Ralph chimed in again. "I already said I would take her home. So that's all solved."

Callie hesitantly nodded her agreement. She did not want to ride home with Ralph, but she did not want Mason to know this.

"Whatever," Katie Rose stated through gritted teeth.

She was shaking her head in exasperation. Katie Rose turned and started away toward the door. She reached in her purse to extract her cell phone.

"Katie Rose, wait!" Callie called after her. She propelled herself from Ralph's arm and rushed after her friend. "I'll be back, Ralph. Have your talk with Mason."

*Perfect! I'm glad Katie Rose raced off like that. She's upset and needs me, her best friend, to be with her. This will give me the perfect excuse for leaving with her instead of going with Ralph.*

"Mason, your little sister is a pain in the ass," Ralph stated with annoyance. He was tired of Katie Rose interfering with his plans for Callie tonight.

Ralph was shaken when Mason grabbed him by his shirt collar and hoisted him off his feet. Ralph was short and skinny, and Mason was tall and well-built. Ralph feared that Mason could do him some real physical harm.

"What's up, man?!" Ralph uttered in fear as Mason shoved him backward toward the wall.

"That's what I would like to know," Mason growled as Ralph's back impacted the wall with a slight thud. "Who do you think you are to call my sister names?! And what do you think you are planning with Callie, Ralph? Have you lost you mind?! She's a kid!"

"Kid hell!" Ralph argued. He was struggling to free himself from Mason's determined grasp. "Why don't you go and buy some glasses, buddy?! You sure as hell need them! Callie may be a few years younger than we are, but she is far from being a kid. She's got the body of a woman, and if you had been kissed by her like I was tonight, you sure would never call her a kid again," Ralph stated with a reminiscent smile.

"You jerk! Were you making out with Callie with my sister right beside you?! What is wrong with you?!" Mason growled.

He tightened his grip on Ralph's neck before he abruptly released him. Mason was so angry at this moment that he was afraid he would strangle the life out of Ralph if he continued to have any contact with him.

"I can't help it that Callie brought your sister along. Callie sure wasn't worried that Katie Rose was sitting right beside her though. She's wild, man! She initiated the whole thing, and I almost had trouble keeping up with her. So you can stop all this 'she's a little kid' crap!" Ralph insisted.

In a quieter voice, he added with slight remorse, "I am sorry that your sister was there, and I didn't mean to be calling her names. Katie Rose *is* still a little kid. She proved that tonight. I was frustrated that she kept coming between Callie and me on purpose. Next time, I'll make sure that Callie and I are alone."

"Dream on, you idiot," Mason stated with a mocking grin. "I can guarantee you that Callie's mother is not going to let her date you. Not now and probably not ever. And Katie Rose knows that she was being used tonight, so Callie won't be able to use her for a cover next time. So it will be a cold day in hell before you and Callie will be getting together again." For once, Mason was glad that Mary Julia was so strict with Callie.

Ralph opened his mouth and started to say something in rebuttal, but he thought better of it. "Shouldn't you be joining Rebecca for your movie?" Ralph asked instead.

"Yes, and I will. First, I'm going to make sure the girls have called someone to pick them up. You *aren't* driving Callie home, Ralph. Your fun time with her tonight has ended. Got that?"

Ralph wanted to argue in the worst way, but he recognized it would be best not to. He could tell that his friend was determined to separate Callie and him. When Mason set his mind on something, it was fruitless to try and change it.

"Fine," Ralph agreed with resentment. "Can I at least go and say goodbye to Callie? Or is that off limits too?"

"Goodbye would be a good thing for you to say to Callie, Ralph," Mason declared with a serious expression on his face. "Let's go. I don't want to keep Rebecca waiting any longer than I have to."

Ralph fell into pace beside Mason as they set off toward the front of the lobby in search of the girls. There was no more conversation between the two of them. Mason was deeply lost in thought. He was torn between being angry and being understanding with his friend.

On the one hand, Mason still wanted to view Callie as a helpless kid who needed his protection. After all, she was his sister's age, and they had all grown up together. However, on the other hand, Mason could not deny that Callie had matured more than Katie Rose had.

Mason also could not deny that he had noticed how shapely Callie's body had become. How could he not, when she purposely showcased it in tight clothes every chance she got?

Then there was Ralph to consider. His friend was not the best looking buy in the world, and he was awkward around girls their own age. Girls their age tended to avoid Ralph. How could Mason expect Ralph to avoid the temptation of Callie, a pretty young girl who was coming on to *him*?

*Does Callie have any idea what she could be getting herself into? What if she does? Do I have a right to interfere?* The image of Callie and Ralph being together bothered Mason a great deal. *This is because I view Callie as another little sister.*

However, the stirring Callie aroused in Mason every now and then – *like when I responded to her kiss on the Fourth of July* – was anything but brotherly.

*It's okay if Ralph is attracted to Callie. It's even okay if I'm occasionally attracted to her. Oh Lord, I* am *attracted to her!* This revelation deeply disturbed Mason.

*Regardless, that still doesn't change the fact that Callie is only thirteen years old. Her age still makes her a kid, even if she doesn't look or act like it. I have to remember this! That makes her off limits to both Ralph...and to me. She is off limits, Mason!* He reasserted to himself. *Why in the world am I even thinking like this?! I need to focus here! All I need to concentrate on right now is making sure that the girls get a safe ride home. Then I can go and spend time solely with my girlfriend and put all of this Callie nonsense out of my head for good. Nonsense! Pure nonsense! That's all these thoughts about Callie are!* Mason tried to force himself to believe this. However, for the first time in his life, there was an uninvited, nagging doubt lingering in Mason's mind.

# Chapter 17

# *The Separation*

Over the next two years, Jonathan began spending more and more time with Callie. Mary Julia attempted to willingly allow this, but each time Callie would leave to go someplace alone with Jonathan, Mary Julia would be gripped by such a devastating panic that she would almost hyperventilate.

Mary Julia did not want to be mistrustful of Jonathan, but she could not help herself. Jonathan and Callie were becoming closer, which should have only been normal. Callie was his daughter, after all.

Mary Julia came through the front doorway one day and heard laughter coming from the kitchen. She made her way to the kitchen, and she came up behind her husband and her daughter. Callie and Jonathan were sitting side-by-side, *very close to one another...much too close!*

Jonathan and Callie were both bent over a puzzle that they were putting together. Their close proximity to one another was enough to make Mary Julia feel uneasy, but Jonathan also had an arm draped around Callie's shoulder. He was rubbing her arm.

*They look like two kids on a date!* Mary Julia found herself observing. She could almost envision Jonathan kissing Callie on the lips next. The picture in her mind almost caused Mary Julia to gag.

"What.... what's going on here?!" she shrieked in a loud voice before she could stop herself.

Jonathan and Callie both jumped in alarm. They looked up at Mary Julia in bewilderment as she came around the table and stood in front of them.

"Jonathan, what do you think you are doing?" she demanded to know and stared at him with disgusted, piercing eyes.

Jonathan followed Mary Julia's gaze. He saw that she was looking at where his arm rested. Jonathan pulled his arm from his daughter's shoulder and leaned back in his chair. He was disappointed by what his wife's accusing eyes were inferring.

"We are doing a puzzle together, mom," Callie answered for her father.

"Jonathan, can we talk?" Mary Julia inquired.

"Yes. We should," he replied. He slid his chair back and stood up.

"Oh, come on, dad. You were going to help me with this. Can't the talk wait, mom?" Callie complained in a whine.

She hated that her mother was once again taking her dad away from her. Callie had enjoyed having Jonathan's full attention and having him touch her. *The way other dads do with their daughters.* Her dad was at last being affectionate with her.

"This won't take long," Jonathan tried to assure his daughter. "I'll be back. You keep working on that while I'm gone." Jonathan completely unnerved Mary Julia as he bent down and kissed Callie on the cheek.

Callie giggled like a much smaller child and smiled from ear to ear. "Okay, daddy," she answered in a little girl's voice. "I'll be waiting right here for you. Hurry back, okay?"

"You betcha," Jonathan promised, returning her smile.

It made Jonathan so happy to see Callie take such joy from receiving little forms of affection from him. *She'd been starved for it*, he concluded with regret.

Jonathan had been trying to remedy this, little by little, over time. *Mary Julia is going to have to accept this. I won't be separated from my daughter any longer. But it's obvious that the counseling that Mary Julia has undertaken has done little to help her trust me.*

Mary Julia had been seeing a therapist once a month for almost two years now. However, whenever Jonathan spent time alone with Callie, he could still strongly perceive that his wife was not comfortable with this. Mary Julia especially hated it when he showed any form of physical affection with Callie. *Such as having my arm around her today.*

Jonathan had broached the subject that Mary Julia possibly needed even more therapy sessions. Mary Julia had become defensive and threatened to stop going altogether. Jonathan had figured that Mary Julia getting some help was better than none at all. However, the distrustful, appalled look Mary Julia had given Jonathan today had him wondering anew if any progress at all had been made in her therapy.

Jonathan followed Mary Julia out of the kitchen, down the hallway and into their bedroom. After he had entered, she walked over and shut the door behind him. Mary Julia approached Jonathan, unfastened his belt, and reached to place one of her hands down the front of his jeans.

Jonathan was flabbergasted by her strange actions. "What are you doing?" he questioned.

Jonathan grabbed Mary Julia's hand before she slipped it into his underwear. They had not come into the bedroom for romance. Their daughter was waiting for him in the kitchen. Callie could come looking for him at any time, and Mary Julia had not even locked the door.

"I'm seeing if you have an erection," Mary Julia crudely answered with a serious, almost fanatical look on her face.

It took a few seconds for the full impact of what Mary Julia was suggesting to register with Jonathan. "Please tell me that you aren't implying that I have a boner because I was spending some time with our daughter," he almost pleaded with Mary Julia.

"You weren't just spending time with Callie. You were fondling her," Mary Julia spat out her outrageous accusation.

"For God sakes, Mary Julia! Enough is enough! I was spending some quality time with Callie and showing her a little affection. I was not molesting her! You need help!"

"You'd like me to think so, wouldn't you? You'd like to have me locked away again in some hospital. Then you'd have Callie all to yourself. Well, it's not going to happen, Jonathan! It's not! I won't let you hurt her! I won't!" Mary Julia began to rant.

She started pummeling her fists against Jonathan's chest. He reached and grabbed Mary Julia's arms. Shaking her, Jonathan demanded, "Calm down, Mary Julia! I'm not trying to hurt Callie! I love her just like you love her. I only want to spend time with her. I want to be allowed to be a father to her. I'm sorry you were

144

so hurt by your own father so long ago, but I'm not him. I would never hurt Callie."

"No you won't," she agreed, pulling away from him.

Mary Julia began to cry, and she headed over to the dresser. She began jerking open drawers and flinging clothes out in the floor – Jonathan's clothes. He watched Mary Julia with bafflement. *What in the world is she doing?*

Mary Julia went to the closet, pulled a suitcase out of the top, and tossed it on the bed. Jonathan no longer had to speculate what her intentions might be. *Oh my God! Mary Julia is going to ask me to leave!! No, she is actually throwing me out!*

"You threatened to leave unless I let you spend time with Callie, so I backed off. Now you want me to stand by and watch you touch her inappropriately and treat her like she's your girlfriend. I won't do it. You will not hurt Callie. You need to leave! I don't want you in this house anymore, Jonathan!"

"Mary Julia, I'm pleading with you not to do this," he said in a soft, level voice. Jonathan walked a few steps in her direction. "You are going to tear apart our marriage and what little family life we have left. Is that what you want?"

"I only want Callie to be safe. She is my number one concern," Mary Julia declared. She backed farther away from Jonathan. "I don't trust you, Jonathan. I don't even know if I love you anymore."

Mary Julia's words hit Jonathan like a ton of bricks. They hurt him far worse than the pounding of her fists. They wounded him, because they were indisputably true.

*Mary Julia does not trust me. She never will. Not when it comes to Callie. She's gone to counseling, and it has not helped. I don't want to leave, but I don't want to live this way anymore. And if Mary Julia no longer loves me then what is the use anyway?*

Jonathan began picking up articles of his clothing from the floor with dejection. He started placing them in the suitcase on the bed. Mary Julia continued to watch him and softly cried. *I should take back what I said*, she discerned.

However, Mary Julia could not make herself do so. *This is for the best. Jonathan can't sue for custody unless we get a divorce, and maybe I can keep that from happening. I'll do what I can to keep Callie safe, including destroying my marriage – if that's what it takes. I won't be like my mom. I'll put Callie first.*

## Chapter 18

# *The Arousal*

After her father left, Callie ran off to her bedroom to have a good cry. She was not there long before she decided she wanted to get out of the house in the worse way. She also wanted to confide in a friend about all this.

Without calling Katie Rose first, Callie packed a small overnight bag. She asked her mother if she could go to Katie Rose's house to spend the night, and surprisingly, her mother did not object. Mary Julia actually wanted some time alone. She drove Callie to Katie Rose's house and dropped her off. Mary Julia assumed that Katie Rose was expecting her.

Mason was watching television in the den when he heard the doorbell ring. He meandered down the hall and through the living room. When he looked out the window, he was surprised to find Callie standing on the porch. *What is Callie doing here? Katie Rose isn't home.* Mason hesitated for a moment before he opened the door.

"Hi, Mason. Could you get Katie Rose for me, please?" Callie politely asked.

"Katie Rose isn't home. My mom took her shopping to buy her a birthday present," Mason answered. *And so Katie Rose could buy yours*, Mason knew but, of course, did not share. Both girls would turn fifteen next month.

Mason was eyeballing the small suitcase Callie was holding. He also noticed that Callie face looked a little flushed, her eyes a bit bloodshot, and her clothes and hair were disheveled. *That's strange.*

Callie stared at Mason in silence for several long moments. She had a befuddled look on her face. It was as if Mason had not spoken in English.

"She...Katie Rose is not home?" Callie questioned. Her bottom lip was quivering, and her eyes were welling with tears.

"No, she isn't," Mason was blunt to confirm. Then he fired several questions. "Callie, what's up? Is something wrong? What's with the suitcase?" *What's with your weird appearance?*

"Oh, Mason," she wailed. Callie dropped her suitcase and threw her arms around him. She began to disconsolately weep.

*What on earth!* Mason was wary to put his arms around Callie in comfort. *Is she playing some sort of game? Has she turned on the waterworks to try and get me to put my arms around her?*

Over the years, Mason had observed Callie playing on her tearful emotions an overabundance of times. "Callie," he called.

Mason took a rough grasp on her arms, and he pushed Callie back from him a bit. "What's the matter?" *If there really is something wrong, then you need to tell me. Otherwise, cut the crap!*

Callie turned and lowered herself to the step beside her suitcase. She put her hands to her face, dropped her head into her lap, and continued to compellingly sob.

*Something truly is wrong! She isn't faking!* Mason concluded with alarm.

He had never seen Callie so genuinely upset. Mason dropped to a sitting position beside the girl. He threw a consoling arm around Callie's shoulders and pulled her close to his side.

"Tell me, Callie. Tell me, what's wrong. I want to help if I can. But you have to tell me."

Callie raised her head and removed her hands from her face. She looked toward Mason. Tears still rolled down Callie's face. She began to rather incoherently mutter, "You... you... can... can't help, Mason. No..one..ca..can!"

Mason had never felt so helpless in his life. Callie usually irritated him, but his heart was breaking for her now. Mason wanted to do something – *anything* – to ease Callie's pain.

"Callie," he said in a soft voice. Mason stroked the tears from her cheeks with gentle fingers. "Maybe I can help, or maybe

I can't. But why don't you let me be the judge of that? Won't you at least tell me what's got you so rattled, so I can try?"

Callie turned into Mason's body. She wrapped her arms around his shoulders, and she laid her head upon his shoulder. Callie whispered, "Can you hold me, Mason? Please?"

"Okay," Mason agreed without hesitation. He held Callie against him and affectionately massaged her back.

Callie did need to be held. Mason's strong arms and warm body were soothing to her. All Callie wanted from him was comfort at this moment. For once, she was not playing any games with Mason. It was completely new for both of them.

Mason continued to hold Callie and stroke her back and neck for several minutes longer. When her body ceased to shudder, he guessed that Callie might have stopped crying. Mason eased her back a little to see if he was correct. Callie lifted her head off Mason's shoulder and stared at him with bloodshot eyes. A few tears still escaped and made their way down her tear-streaked face, but the worst seemed to have passed.

"Better now?" Mason questioned with a slight, hopeful grin. He was still caressing her back.

"Yes," Callie answered in a small voice. She forced a smile, and she added, "Thanks, Mason."

"I didn't do much," he downplayed. "Why don't you come inside with me? I could get you something cold to drink. Then maybe we could talk, if you feel like it. It'll only be the two of us. My dad is at a business dinner. If you don't feel like talking, then you can make yourself at home and wait here for Katie Rose. What do you say?"

Mason was being so sweet, and he was focusing all of his attention solely on her. Callie was awestruck. She did not want her time with Mason to end.

However, Callie did not want to do something to turn Mason off again either. Anymore, he did everything in his power to avoid her. "Are you sure it's okay?" she questioned.

"I wouldn't ask you if it wasn't," Mason responded.

He arose and helped Callie to her feet beside him. Mason picked up her suitcase, opened the front door and courteously held it open for her. Callie walked through the open door. Mason directed her into the living room.

"Can I get you something to drink?" Mason offered.

"No thanks," Callie declined. "Could we sit and talk?"

Mason had never seen Callie like this. She was not at all herself. Mason was worried because Callie was not being pushy and lewd. Her odd behavior concerned him a great deal.

Mason took a gentle grasp of Callie's arm. He led her to the sofa, and he lowered them both to a sitting position, side by side. "If you are ready to talk, then I am ready to listen," he stated with maturity, closely studying her.

Callie stared into Mason's handsome, chocolate brown eyes and felt something deep within her stir. She had the most overwhelming urge to pin Mason into a tight embrace, lock her mouth upon his, and kiss him over and over. *I know how to really kiss now, Mason. This wouldn't be a little girl's kiss like you've gotten from me in the past.*

Ralph had been the first guy to kiss her like a woman, but Callie had practiced lots since then with other guys. She was dying to demonstrate to Mason right now, but she thought better of it. *If I come on to him, he'll run. He always does. I need to cool it! I have Mason's full attention. I need to be satisfied with this for now.*

Callie could tell that Mason was waiting for her to say something. She was having an awful time getting the conversation started. She was not used to having serious discussions with guys. Usually, the full extent of her conversation with a guy was to flirt, or to otherwise lead them on in some way.

"Do you want me to leave you alone?" Mason broke the awkward silence by questioning. It was obvious that he was making Callie terribly uncomfortable. That was the last thing Mason wanted to do. "You came over here to talk to Katie Rose. I'm a poor substitute for a girl's best friend. I was only trying to help."

"No, Mason! Please don't go!" Callie protested. She reached to grab his arm. "It's hard to talk about, that's all."

As Callie said this, she realized that this was true. It was hard to talk about how her father had left her mother and her. Merely the thought of it made her want to cry again.

Mason noticed the change in Callie's facial expression. *Oh, Lord! She looks like she might start to cry again!*

"Hey, it's okay," Mason tried to console. He placed a reassuring arm around Callie's shoulders. "I'm not abandoning you. I didn't want you to feel pushed to talk. That's all."

"Oh, Mason, you've been so wonderful," Callie proclaimed. She laid her head over on his shoulder for a few seconds. "I'm sorry about all this nonsense."

Callie raised her head back up and wiped away a few more fresh tears. She could not seem to control her emotions today. This was definitely a first for her. Callie gave him a strained smile and choked back any remaining tears.

*Talk, damn it! Stop crying! This is bound to be getting old!* "My dad left my mom today," she blurted out all at once.

"What?" Mason asked in confusion. He studied Callie's face with a hard stare. "What do you mean your dad left your mom?"

Mason found this hard to accept. Callie must be mistaken. After all, her parents had been married forever, as had his own. He could not imagine them separating now.

"I mean…he packed his bags and left," Callie reasserted with the saddest expression. "He's gone, Mason. He said he and mom are going to try and 'work it out', but I'm afraid they are going to get a divorce. My world is falling apart."

Callie lost control again. Her shoulders started to shake and the tears started to spring plentifully from her eyes once more. "Damn!" she cursed out loud. She was trying to rein her wayward emotions back in.

"Shhh. It's okay," she heard Mason saying.

Callie's body began to shudder in other ways as Mason warmly kissed her forehead. "I'm so sorry, Callie," he commiserated.

Mason could understand Callie's fears. Many of his friends' parents were divorced. He could only imagine how awful he would feel if his parents split up.

Mason gave Callie a reassuring squeeze and began to stroke her back again. He was unhappy about the devastated state Callie was in, but he was pleased to see that Callie's family meant so much to her. Oftentimes, she had given him the impression that no one mattered to her.

Several moments later, Callie raised her head from Mason's chest. He gazed into her watery eyes with compassion. He had the wildest urge to kiss away all Callie's tears.

Mason reined in his foolish impulses. He drew in to plant a rather playful, affectionate kiss on the tip of Callie's nose instead. Callie allowed him to kiss her nose, but she brought her face level with his.

They gazed into one another eyes for several moments. Then Mason planted a kiss on Callie's lips. He could taste the salt from Callie's tears. Mason's innocent kiss deepened in an unplanned hungry exploration.

*The girl certainly knows how to kiss.*

Several, delightful minutes passed before Mason managed to gain control of his senses. He separated first his mouth and then the rest of his body from Callie. He had practically been lying on top of her.

*Good Lord! What was I thinking!* Mason scooted farther away from Callie. *Not only was what I did wrong – I have a girlfriend, and I was taking advantage of a vulnerable girl – but my dad could have walked in on us. He could be home at any time.*

"Callie, I'm sorry," Mason apologized. He was studying the stunned expression on her face. "I don't know what got into me."

Callie had no idea what had *gotten into* Mason either, but she had liked it. Her heart was beating so hard that she feared she might hyperventilate.

"Why don't I go and get us both something cold to drink?" he offered as he stood.

*I could use something cold! Maybe I should dump it over my head. Or maybe between my legs.*

Callie merely nodded. She could not seem to get her vocal cords to work. Mason had struck her dumb with passion.

"I'll be back," Mason said. He started away as hurriedly as he could. His pants were tight in the front, so this retarded his movement a slight bit.

\* \* \* \*

Mason stood in front of the open refrigerator for several minutes. He allowed the cool air to wash over him. He reached inside and pulled out two cans of soft drink, sitting on the counter. He opened one of the cabinets and reached up to extract two glasses. Mason did get the chance to turn around.

Two arms tenderly enclosed his waist. Callie slid her breasts up against him, and she started seductively kissing the back of Mason's neck. Quivers of forbidden desire surged all throughout Mason's body. His legs grew weak.

"Callie," he addressed in a husky voice.

Mason grabbed hold of her arms to release them from his waist. He turned from the counter only to find himself face to face with the alluring girl. Their lips were inches away from one another again.

"You have to stop," Mason half begged. He noticed Callie's hot breath on his face. She was driving him wild with desire.

"I don't want to stop," Callie stated. She placed her arms securely around Mason's neck and leaned in to lock her lips to his again.

*Shit! I should stop this!* Mason mind registered in protest. Nevertheless, his mouth and his body were not listening. They responded with eagerness to Callie's hot, needful lips once again.

They paused for a second, several minutes later, to catch their breath. Callie moaned in a rasping voice, "Oh, Mason."

She took one of his hands into her own. Mason was taken aback when Callie guided it toward one of her breasts. "Do you want to touch me?" she asked, being naughty.

Mason's hand trembled and his breath caught in his throat. Callie placed his hand on top of her supple, warm breast. The magnificent feel of her stimulated erect nipple, through her shirt and bra, triggered Mason to jerk his hand back in shock. *What in the hell am I'm doing!*

Callie gave him a sweet smile and asked rather breathlessly, "Would you like to try that again?"

She reached out to clasp his hand once more, but Mason rather roughly pushed Callie's hand away. He placed his hands on both her shoulders and mulishly pushed the two of them apart. Mason scrambled away from the counter so Callie could not pin him in again.

"This has got to stop!" he declared. "You need to get a grip, Callie!" *So do I! I can't believe I lost control like that!*

"Damn it, Mason!" Callie swore with frustration.

Mason's consistent rejection hurt her. Callie had at last managed to get past his irritating defenses, but Mason had rebuffed her advances again anyway. "Sometimes I wonder about you, Mason! None of the other guys I've been with have ever pushed me away. I usually have to fight them off! So why do you always push me away?! You're not gay. I can see that from here," she pointed out with lewdness.

Callie was staring at the front of Mason's pants with an evil grin. There was still a significant bulge there. "Shit, Callie. Why do you always have to be so crude?" Mason chastised with a disapproving grimace.

With a watchful eye fixed on Callie, he walked back over toward the counter. Mason reached to the side of the girl. He snatched up one of the soft drinks he had sat on the counter.

Mason backed up several steps to distance himself from Callie before he popped opened the can of soda. He took several, long swallows. Mason lowered the cold can, and he held it low. Mason rested the cold can lightly against the front of his jeans.

"I could make it feel better than that old can," Callie seductively taunted. Her grin widened, and her eyes sparkled with mischief.

"You know what, Callie? You are going to tease the wrong guy one of these days, say something like that, and wind up getting yourself raped," Mason bluntly pointed out. "Is that what you want?"

"Is that all you think I am is a tease?" Callie asked, slightly changing the subject.

"Well, since you are only fourteen years old, then I'm hoping that all you are doing is teasing. But who knows, maybe you *are* already having sex. Is that what you are trying to tell me, Callie? Are you sleeping around?" Mason questioned with disgust. He genuinely did not want the answer to be yes.

*It's because she is too young*, he tried to convince himself.

However, Mason did not like the thought of Callie having sex with anyone, regardless of her age. *No one but me.* Mason shuddered with forbidden reflection. *My mind is messed up because of what happened between the two of us. That's all! That has to be all it is!*

"Am I sleeping around?!" Callie indignantly repeated in a raised voice. "First you call me a tease! And now you are calling me a slut! Is that what you think?! Well, you know what you are, Mason?! You're a stupid asshole! And you know what, asshole?! It's none of your damn business who I *might* or *might not* be sleeping with! You got that?!"

"Oh, yeah. I got that loud and clear," Mason replied with an annoyed frown. "But for the record, I wasn't calling you anything. I was only trying to help you, but it's obvious I am wasting my breath, as usual. So you act any way you want to, and let happen what may. See if I care! I'm out of here. You can wait in the living room, by yourself, for Katie Rose if you want to."

Mason headed past her. *I need to get out of here and finish clearing my head,* he wisely decided. He took long strides toward the back door.

"Fine. Leave then! I don't need you to be here with me! You're no fun anyway! You're a weirdo, Mason! Damn you!" Callie shouted with bitterness. The only response Mason gave Callie was a finalizing slam of the back door. He escaped outside with relief.

As if Callie expected Mason to come back in, she stared at the back door for several more moments. Callie was so exasperated she felt like crying again. *Why does it always have to end this way between the two of us? Why do I always manage to drive Mason away? Damn! If I hadn't pushed today, then maybe he would still be here. Maybe he would still be kissing me. Maybe he would have touched me all on his own. I can't believe he accused me of sleeping around. Why doesn't he realize that he's the only guy I want to be with? First, my dad abandons me and now, Mason leaves me too. And Katie Rose isn't even home. What a horrible day! I can't stay here. I might as well go home. Maybe my mom will at least need me. No one else seems to.*

Callie meandered back into the living room and gathered her purse and small overnight bag. She proceeded to the front door and vacated the house with sadness. Callie lived a few miles away, so she would have been wise to call her mom to pick her back up.

However, Callie concluded, *The long walk might do me good. It'll give me a little time to settle down.* She headed to the sidewalk. She began the long, slow trek home, lost in despondent and deep meditation.

# Chapter 19

# *The Betrayal*

Nearly an hour later, Callie arrived at her house. She was surprised to discover an unfamiliar automobile in the driveway, a nice black SUV. *I wonder who's here*, she was thinking, as she dug in her purse for her house key.

Callie did not recognize the automobile. *Unless Flora and Kenny have bought a new truck.* She did not see them often enough to keep up with what they might be driving.

Callie entered the house and rounded the corner into the living room. She was dismayed to find that the room was empty. Callie had assumed her mother would be entertaining the visitor in the living room. She sat her overnight bag and purse down by the sofa.

*They must be in the kitchen*, she logically concluded. Callie was thinking more than ever that it must be her *Grandma* Flora. It made perfect sense; after all, she was one of her mother's oldest and dearest friends. *Maybe Flora can help. After all, she was my dad's stepmom at one time. Maybe she can talk some sense into my dad and get him to come home.*

Callie strolled across the room and into the kitchen, only to find this room empty as well. *What the heck?* she questioned with bewilderment.

She walked across the kitchen and looked out onto the back patio, but it also was unoccupied. Callie walked over to the basement door and opened it, but all was dark down the stairway. *Maybe whoever it is went out with mom in her car*, she reasoned.

Callie strutted across the kitchen to the door leading into the garage. She pulled back the short curtain. Her mother's car was still parked in the garage.

All at once, Callie began to be afraid. *Who could be in the driveway? Where are they? And where is my mother? The only rooms I didn't look in are the bathroom and the bedrooms.*

All of the sudden, Callie heard someone crying. Or was it more of a constant moaning? *They must be in the bedroom. It must be Grandma Flora, and she is trying to comfort my mom. Shit! I guess I shouldn't have left! I'll go and let my mom know I'm home now. That'll make her feel better. And maybe Flora can work on my daddy and get him to come home too. Then everything might be okay again. It has to be!*

Callie hurried out of the kitchen and down the hallway, toward her parents' bedroom. It was the farthest room at the end of the hallway. The door was closed.

This was another sign that someone was in that room. Her mom always left the door open during the day. As Callie drew closer, she heard more muffled moaning.

As she reached the door, she recognized her mother's voice exclaiming, "Oh, God! Oh!"

Callie rapped on the door and simultaneously opened it, without waiting for permission to enter. She wanted to get to her mother and help her in any way that she could. Callie rushed into the room and stopped with a horrified jolt as she saw the unthinkable.

Her mother was gaping at her in shamed shock. She was scrambling to disentangle her naked body from some unknown man's equally nude body. They had been having sex, and Callie had interrupted them. *My mother is cheating on my father. No wonder my dad left!*

Tears clouded Callie's eyes, and she spun and ran from the room. She could hear her mother shouting her name over and over as she sped down the hall. Callie dashed into the living room, snatched up her purse, and raced for the front door.

*I have to get out of here!*

Callie had no idea where she was going. *I have to be anywhere but in this house!* She could not stand to be in her mother's presence right now.

Callie did not know if she could ever stand to be in this woman's presence again. *She's destroyed our home! She's destroyed my life!* Callie darted from the house.

\* \* \* \*

Mary Julia leaped out of the bed. She mumbled a few words of apology to her male playmate. She threw a robe over her naked body, and she sprinted through her house.

Mary Julia was in pursuit of Callie, but there was no sign of her daughter. The front door was standing wide open. "Callie!" Mary Julia screamed as she flew through the open front door and out onto the front porch.

She ran down the front porch steps, into the driveway and toward the sidewalk. Mary Julia frantically searched the neighborhood for some sign of her precious child, but she did not see Callie anywhere.

"Oh, God! What have I done?!" she wailed. "Callie! Callie, come back! I didn't mean…I'm sorry! I'm so sorry!" Mary Julia cried in anguish. It took all of Mary Julia's remaining strength not to collapse in the middle of the sidewalk.

Mary Julia was devastated that her daughter had caught her in the act of cheating on her husband. *What was Callie doing here? She was supposed to be spending the night with Katie Rose. How could this have happened? How could any of this have happened? Why did I call that man here? Why was I so foolish as to resort to using sex to deal with my problems again?*

*I need to find Callie. I have to try and explain things to her as best I can.* Mary Julia turned to make her way back inside the house. *I need to get some clothes on and get into my car and drive around the neighborhood until I find my daughter. I'll find her. I have to! I have to set things straight as much as I can!*

\* \* \* \*

Callie slowed her jog to a fast walk after several minutes. After running out of the house, she had make a sharp turn. She had run through her backyard, hopped over her back fence, ran across their neighbor's backyard and out their front gate. Callie had jogged up that street a little ways. Then she had darted through some stranger's front gate and backyard and jumped yet another fence.

Callie was attempting to put as much distance as she could between her mother and her. She figured her mom would come looking for her, and she wanted to make herself difficult, if not impossible, to find. It would be easier very soon to hide. The sun was beginning to set, so it would be dark soon.

*Where am I going to go?* Callie was tempted to head back to Katie Rose's house. *No, because mom will call there looking for me.* Jackie Lynn would turn her over to her mother. *I have to think of somewhere else. But where?*

Callie had never felt so lost and alone in her life. Tears began to cloud Callie's vision again, and she choked back a sob. *How can this all be happening?* she grappled. Callie angrily swiping her tears away. It was all so unfair and heartbreaking.

Callie heard loud music all at once, and she stepped off into the grass. A car full of teenagers roared down the street toward her. Normally, Callie would have stopped to inquisitively check out who was in the car. She was too lost in her agony to even think about it right now. However, the car decelerated and stopped right beside her.

"Callie, is that you?" she heard a somewhat familiar female voice ask.

She turned her head to find Glenda staring out the front passenger window at her. Callie had not seen this girl since they had graduated from grade school last year. Glenda had gone on to public high school and not to a Catholic high school like Callie and Katie Rose. Glenda had not had much to do with either Callie or Katie Rose after the glue incident at Katie Rose's sleepover several years ago. Callie was astonished she was taking the time to talk to her now.

"What's up, girl?" Glenda inquired with a silly smile on her face.

"Not much," Callie mumbled, glancing away. She was in no mood to make small talk; especially with a girl she did not even consider a friend.

"Have you got any cash on you?" Glenda peculiarly asked.

"Yes. I have a few dollars. Why?" Callie cross-examined with suspicion.

"Well, me and my friends are out cruising. We are going to go to the park and party for a while. If you want to chip in a few bucks for some party supplies, you can hop in and come along. What do you say? Want to party with us?" Glenda invited.

The driver, an older man, looked over at Callie with a wide smile and added, "Come on. You look bored. You won't be bored with us. I promise. I know where we can get some really good shit."

*Good shit? What is he talking about?* Callie puzzled over for a few minutes. *Does it matter? They are offering me a ride to the park. I can get even farther away from home. From there, maybe I can find a place to crash tonight. Maybe I can make friendly with Glenda again and spend the night with her.*

"Okay. Sounds good by me!" Callie agreed. Another girl opened one of the rear doors for her, and Callie eagerly climbed inside. The car sped away down the road.

* * * *

Callie soon discovered what the 'good shit' was. It was not the first time she had ever watched someone smoke marijuana before. It was not even the first time it had ever been offered to her. But, it was the first time she had ever chipped in to purchase it. She could not believe how naive she had been.

At first, Callie declined smoking any of the drug. She was passed a bottle of alcohol instead. Callie again hesitated.

Glenda began to coax with persistence, "Come on, Callie! Are you here to party with us or not? Don't be a party popper. You aren't chicken, are you?"

"No, I'm not afraid," Callie met the challenge. *What could a little drink hurt?*

Callie took the bottle from Glenda's outstretched hand. She put it to her mouth and took a small swig. She almost instantly began to snort and cough as the hot liquid burned her throat and nostrils.

"Hey, guys. Would you lookie here? It looks like we have a virgin amongst us," Glenda taunted with a mocking snicker. "So you've never drank before, huh, Callie? Bet you've never smoked weed before either. Who would have figured? I never pegged you as such a goodie goodie. You may not want to hang out with us, after all. Maybe you should run along."

Glenda took the marijuana cigarette that was being passed. She inhaled a long hit from it. Then she held it out to Callie. Callie stared at the marijuana cigarette and nervously considered her options.

*If I say no to doing drugs and drinking with them, then they might send me away. Then where do I go? Wander the park? Hitch a ride with some stranger? A ride to where? I can't go home!*

Callie took the cigarette. She stuck it in her mouth and deeply inhaled. *No one cares about me anyway. So why shouldn't I drink and do drugs.* The smoke burned Callie's throat and lungs and made her want to cough again. Regardless, she took a second quick puff for good measure.

* * * *

Mason did not come back home until 10:00 p.m. He was relieved when he saw his mom's car in the driveway. This meant Katie Rose was also home. *Callie will have someone else to entertain her.*

Now, more than ever, Mason needed to keep his distance from this disturbing girl. Callie could be trouble for him. Mason could not allow Callie to push his buttons like she had earlier.

Mason unlocked the back door. He was about to push it open when his mom pulled it open. Mason's dad and Katie Rose also converged upon him as he came indoors.

They all asked Mason the same erratic question, "Have you seen Callie?"

Mason told them she had come to the house earlier looking for Katie Rose. "When I left, she was still in this house waiting for Katie Rose to return. What's up?"

"Mary Julia thinks that Callie may have run away from home," his mother explained. "They had a disagreement earlier, and Callie ran out the door. Now, Mary Julia cannot find her anywhere."

Jackie Lynn knew the whole, terrible story of why Callie had left. She had told her husband, but she was not about to share the gruesome details with her children. Mary Julia had enlightened Jackie Lynn about everything.

She had told her about Jonathan leaving. She had told Jackie Lynn about how she had reverted to her old, self-destructive ways. Worse of all, Mary Julia had informed Jackie Lynn that Callie had discovered her having sex with a man who was not her father.

"Does anyone know where Jonathan is? Have they told him that she is missing?" Mason asked. Jackie Lynn noticed the edge in his voice.

"Did Callie tell you about Jonathan leaving?" she questioned.

"Yes. She was extremely upset about it. I'd wager to say that is why she's split. Not over some little disagreement with her mom. Callie had a suitcase with her earlier. I think she was planning on spending the night with Katie Rose. Chances are Callie has gone to one of her other friends' houses," Mason prophesized with hope.

"Mary Julia has called all of Callie's other friends. Callie isn't with any of them. Since you were gone, we were in hopes that maybe she was with you somewhere. I guess, at this point, we are grasping at straws. Needless to say, Mary Julia is beside herself with worry," Jackie Lynn told him.

She was worried as well. Callie had been traumatized by all that had happened in her young life today. Jackie Lynn hoped and prayed that the girl had not gotten herself into some kind of trouble.

"Hopefully, Callie will turn up soon," she said to Mason as well as to herself. "I need to go and call Mary Julia. I need to tell her that you have no idea where Callie may be either." Jackie Lynn sped away toward the phone.

Mason was thinking about all that had transpired between Callie and him earlier. He commented, "I sure hope Callie turns up soon. That girl has absolutely no business out wandering the street by herself at night. She could get into all kinds of trouble."

Mason noticed his sister's anxious expression, so he was quick to add, "She'll be fine, Katie Rose. Callie is probably close to home. Knowing Callie, this is a ploy to scare everyone and get her father to come back home."

*Mason is most likely right*, Katie Rose hoped.

She could not believe that Jonathan had left Callie's mom. Katie Rose had no doubt that Callie would do just about anything to get her parents back together. Katie Rose could conceive that Callie's disappearance was orchestrated to try and bring about her parents' reconciliation.

*Surely she'll be home soon*, Katie Rose tried to convince herself. However, she could not help but be concerned about her friend. *I'll be happy when Mary Julia calls and says Callie is back home, safe where she belongs. Come on, Jonathan; go back home, so Callie will too.* Katie Rose prayed for her friend's safe return home.

* * * *

*What happened to the music that was playing?* Callie was wondering.

All was deadly quiet around her, except for the sound of crickets. The last thing Callie could remember was hearing the car's stereo playing loudly. She had been feeling the beat of the music more intensely than she ever had in her life.

Callie had been dancing in circles. She had been gazing up at the bright, parking lot lights and laughing. Callie had been so happy and carefree. She smiled serenely as she thought of it.

"Miss," she heard a deep male voice say. Someone began shaking Callie with persistence.

It was only then that Callie discovered that she was lying on her side on the ground. She opened her eyes, and in slow motion, Callie rolled over in the grass. A wave of nausea and acute dizziness overcame her.

The man shined a bright light down into her face, and Callie clenched her eyes shut. She placed her hands securely over her face. Callie was attempting to shield her eyeballs from the painful glare.

"Please stop!" she pleaded in a shaky voice.

"Sorry," the man said, and clicked the flashlight off. "Do you need help, miss? It's after midnight, and the park is closed to teenagers. Do you have a home to go to? If not, I'll have to take you to the station. You can't sleep here."

*Sleep? How could I have fallen asleep here? Where did everyone else go? And who is this man?*

Callie uncovered her eyes and struggled to rise to a sitting position. The movement of her body caused her head to throb with pain and another overpowering wave of nausea to overtake her. She gagged and bile rose in her throat.

"I think I'm going to..." she managed to utter. Then Callie hung her head to her side and vomitted on the grass. She retched for several minutes.

Callie was slow to raise her head. Her eyes were watering so badly that she could not see, and she was violently shaking. She wondered if she had been poisoned and was going to die.

"I'm really sick," Callie stated in a pitifully small voice. "Can you help me? Please?"

Callie heard a strange buzzing noise. Then she heard the man talking to someone else. "Dispatch, this is Sergeant O'Malley. I have a teenage girl I found sleeping in the park. Subject is vomiting profusely and is very disoriented. Please dispatch an ambulance?"

*The man who is standing over me is a policeman. Am I going to be arrested?*

Callie wanted to get to her feet and try to run away. However, every time she raised her head upright, everything spun, and she felt sick all over again. She was not going anywhere.

*Anywhere that is...but maybe to the hospital and then...to jail.*

The police officer hung his two-way radio back onto his belt. Then he told Callie, "Help will be here soon. In the meantime, you can start by giving me your name, and the name of someone I can call for you."

*Call for me?? Is he going to let me go?* Callie hopefully yearned. Right now, she wanted to go home, crawl in her bed, and be taken care of by her mother. Her mother always took care of her when she was sick.

*But my mom cheated on my dad, and she destroyed our home.* Callie remembered with heartbreak. *I'm not sure if I have a place to go home to anymore. But what else can I do? If I don't give this policeman my mom's name, then he may take me to jail.*

"My name is Callista Roberts," Callie told him in a quiet, hesitant voice. "My mother's name is Mary Julia Roberts. My phone number is 555-0304. Will you call my mom, please? I'm sure she is worried about me."

*I need my mommy! Please get her for me, quick!* Another wave of nausea and dizziness had Callie hanging her head to the side again and dry heaving in agony.

# Chapter 20

# *Confessions*

Callie had been violently sick, and her stomach had been pumped. She had spent the early morning hours in Juvenile Hall, like some criminal. As if all this was not punishment enough, her mother had grounded Callie indefinitely.

She felt more depressed than ever. The last place that Callie wanted to be right now was at home with her mother. Callie had desperately needed her mom when she had been in trouble, but she still had not forgiven her for what she had done to their family.

Consequently, Callie stayed in her room all day Saturday. She did not feel well anyway. Callie still had a splitting headache. The hospital had inserted a tube down her throat to pump her stomach, leaving her throat raw. Callie also still felt nauseated.

Callie was totally exhausted as well. She had not dared to close her eyes and sleep at Juvenile hall. The girls there had looked mean enough to tear her heart out, so Callie had kept a close eye out.

To compensate for her night from hell, Callie slept on and off all day Saturday. Her mother came and checked on her a few times. Mary Julia bought Callie lots of water to drink and aspirin. She said this would help with her hangover, so Callie took everything that her mother offered. She was restless Saturday night but got some sleep then as well.

Sunday morning, Callie meandered out of her room. She headed toward the kitchen. She was intent on fixing a big bowl of cereal for herself.

Thankfully, she was feeling much better. The headache remained, but at least she felt hungry again. Callie had eaten very little the day before.

She rounded the corner into the kitchen, and she spied her mother sitting at the kitchen table drinking a cup of coffee. As their eyes met, Mary Julia stated, "Oh, good, you're up. I was about to come and check on you. Are you feeling better this morning?"

"Yes," Callie bluntly replied. She averted her eyes. Callie set about gathering a cereal bowl, a spoon, some cereal and milk.

"Hungry?" She heard her mother ask.

"Yes," she curtly answered again. She busied herself with pouring the cereal and milk in the bowl. Callie placed the milk back into the refrigerator. Then she turned and slowly made her way over to the table. She had a seat across from her mother and began to eat in silence.

Her mother put a stop to the tranquility. "I left you alone yesterday, Callie, because you weren't up to listening. But today, I need to have a very serious talk with you. I need for you to listen carefully to what I have to say. Is that understood?"

Callie gave her mother a momentary, disinterested glance. She saw the determined look in her mom's eyes, so Callie nodded in agreement. Her mother began to talk. Callie continued to keep her eyes focused downward on her food. She was shoveling cereal into her mouth.

*What can my mom say? Nothing can even remotely excuse what I had caught her doing.* Regardless, Callie had no other option at this point but to listen. She half-heartedly gave her mom an ear.

Several moments later, however, Mary Julia had Callie's full, albeit stunned, attention. She had revealed to the girl that she had been molested by her father and raped by her stepfather. Callie dropped her spoon into her cereal bowl and stared at her mother in disbelief. Her mouth was gaping open.

"Wha...what did you say?" Callie cross-examined with uncertainty. *She must have said that to make sure I was paying attention. Surely it isn't true.* Callie could not comprehend that such terrible things could have happened to *her* mother.

"You heard me the first time. I can tell by your expression," Mary Julia responded. She had a very sad, faraway look in her eyes. "It hurts every time I have to talk about it. But I had to tell you. You have to understand that what happened to me as a child and a young adult…I was seven when my dad molested me and thirteen when my stepfather raped me…these things have shaped the way I have lived my life. It's made me do some very stupid and wrong things sometimes. When I met your father, I was recovering from a sexual addiction. I've had it under control for years – all the time I've been with your father – but when he left….well…I don't know how to make you understand this….but it made me feel ugly and unworthy again. That's the way I felt for years before I was institutionalized for my sexual addition and started to recover. What you saw Friday….me with that other man….is something you never should have seen. It was something I never should have done. But I had a relapse to an old addiction. I reverted back to my old way of dealing with things. Addicts do that sometimes. But know that it only happened that one time, and I won't allow it to happen again. I don't blame you if you don't believe this. I don't expect you to fully understand all this. But you needed to know. Maybe you will understand and trust me again someday. Understand, trust, and hopefully forgive me….in time. Now, speaking of addicts, we need to talk about what *you* did Friday night."

"I'm not addicted to anything, mother," Callie barked with irritability. "That was the first time I've ever done anything like that. What do you expect after what I caught you doing? I needed an escape. That's all."

Mary Julia had disclosed an awful bombshell about her past. But Callie was still upset with her mom. *Let her wonder whether I'll drink and do drugs again.*

"I hope it was the first time, Callie. More importantly, I hope it was the last. No, you may not be addicted to anything yet, but it comes all too easily if you allow it. Don't hide from your problems that way. Be it drugs, alcohol, or a sex addiction like I have, it's a horrible way to live, Callie. I know firsthand. I never wanted you to know. I've tried so hard to protect you, but I've failed," Mary Julia said.

Her voice became muffled as she stifled a sob. Tears clouded Mary Julia's vision. She lowered her head into her hands and wept.

167

Callie watched her mother and felt a strong tinge of guilt. She could not begin to imagine what it must be like to be molested by your father and worse, raped by your stepfather. Callie had seen movies about women who had been raped. She understood from this that women sometimes did some strange things afterward.

*My mom is a sex addict, because she was abused as a child,* Callie let sink in. The realization chilled and sickened her.

Callie rose from her chair. She went over to her mother. She wrapped her arms around her neck to console her.

Callie declared, "I'm sorry, mom. For what I did and for what happened to you when you were a kid. I didn't mean to hurt you. I won't drink or do drugs again. I promise. Please don't cry. It will be okay. It has to be."

Mary Julia wrapped her arms around Callie and squeezed her into a grateful embrace. "It will be okay, Callie. I promise you it will be."

Mary Julia continued to securely hug Callie. She began rocking her as if she was a baby.

* * * *

Later that day, Callie took refuge alone in her room. She decided to call Katie Rose. She was grateful that she still had phone privileges. After the emotional scene with her mother earlier, Callie needed to talk to a friend. Jackie Lynn answered the phone.

"Hi. May I talk to Katie Rose, please?" Callie politely asked.

"Yes you may. How are you today?" Jackie Lynn asked her.

"I'm much better, thank you," Callie answered.

Jackie Lynn had come to the hospital to support her mom. She had still been with her mother when they had picked Callie up from Juvenile Hall. Jackie Lynn was aware of everything that Callie had done.

"I'm sorry about everything," Callie added for good measure.

"I hope that you are, Callie. I also hope that you recognize how serious what you did was," Jackie Lynn lectured. "I'm glad that you are okay. How's your mom?"

"She's better too. We...we had a long talk today," she admitted in a quiet, meditative voice.

"I'm glad," Jackie Lynn commented.   She noted the pensive pause in Callie's last sentence.

*Mary Julia might have told Callie about her past.* It was what she had told Jackie Lynn she intended to do. It was a lot for a girl just shy of fifteen to comprehend and accept. Regardless, Jackie Lynn was glad that Mary Julia had shared the truth with her daughter.

*It might help Callie understand why her mother behaves so oddly at times.* "Well, let me get Katie Rose for you," Jackie Lynn ended their conversation by saying.

"Thank you," Callie replied. She waited for several long moments before her friend picked up the phone.

"What the hell were you thinking?!" Callie was astounded to hear Katie Rose uncharacteristically growl.

"Well, hello to you too," Callie replied with a nervous giggle. *It's obvious that Katie Rose's mom has shared all the details of what I did.*

"It's not funny, Callie," Katie Rose started to lecture. There was an angry edge still in her voice.

"I know. I know," Callie was prompt to assure her. "It was stupid. I was upset, so I did something very, very dumb. Believe me, I paid for it. You don't ever want to have to have your stomach pumped, and you don't ever want to be hauled down to Juvenile Hall. Trust me on that one, will you?"

"No problem there. I'll be glad to take your word for it. I don't have any desire to get drunk and do drugs. I sure would never want to be hauled down to Juvenile Hall either. But it served you right to have to go there," Katie Rose pointed out.

As she calmed down a little, Katie Rose added in a soft voice, "I'm sorry your dad left. I'd be upset if my parents split up too. I don't even like imagining it. Are you okay?"

"No. Not really. It turned out that my dad leaving was only the tip of the iceberg," Callie shared.

There was a moment of silence. Then Katie Rose was startled to hear Callie add, "I found my mom in bed with another man."

"You...you did what?!" Katie Rose asked. She was unable to fathom what she had heard. "You're kidding, right?!"

"Don't I wish," Callie admitted. "But, no, I'm not making some cruel joke. My mom did this. I had a hard time believing it too, so don't feel bad."

"So is that why your dad left, because your mom is having an affair? Are they going to get a divorce, so your mom can be with this other man?" Katie Rose questioned with insensitivity.

It dawned on Katie Rose, all at once, what she had done. She apologized, "I'm sorry, Callie. I shouldn't have asked that."

"That's okay. Those same thoughts ran through my mind, believe me. I was crushed. All I could do was run away. I ran away, and I tried to escape any way I could."

"I understand that, Callie. But you do realize that turning to alcohol and drugs isn't the answer, don't you?" Katie Rose questioned with fear.

If Callie's mom intended to leave her dad for another man, then Callie would have plenty of other stress. Katie Rose could not bear to think of her friend becoming addicted to alcohol and drugs to survive. "Please promise me that you won't go that route again, no matter what happens between your mom and dad. Okay?"

"Sure, why shouldn't I promise you? I've already had to promise my mom and your mom. Do you want to put Mason on the phone and I'll pledge it to him too? Your dad?" Callie inquired with a trace of sarcasm. "You all seem to think I'm some sort of addict because I screwed up this one time."

"No, I don't. Neither does my mom or your mom. But we are all worried about you. We all love you, Callie. If you can't handle that, it's too damn bad," Katie Rose professed. Her voice was quivering a little with emotion. It was not often that the girls told one another they loved each other, but Katie Rose felt Callie needed to hear it now.

"Potty mouth. Better watch those cuss words, or I'm going to have to tell your mother. That's two I've heard during this conversation. If I didn't know better, I'd think you were some sort of hood," Callie teased.

She was attempting to lighten things up a little. It did make Callie feel good to hear Katie Rose say she cared though. Callie knew this, but it was nice to hear now and then. Callie cared a great deal about Katie Rose as well.

"Okay, change the subject if you want," Katie Rose replied. "But know that I'll be watching you. I better not catch you drinking or doing drugs again, or I'll kick your butt. You got that?"

"Got it loud and clear," Callie answered. "And believe me; I'm not anxious to try either thing again. I've learned my lesson. Happy now? But if you want to hang out with me and keep an eye on me, then that's okay. You won't be able to do it for a while, though, because I'm not allowed out of the house anytime soon. That is, other than to go to counseling with my mom."

"Your mom is sending you to counseling?" Katie Rose hesitantly asked.

"Not exactly. She wants me to go along with her to a counselor, so I can better understand why she did what she did. You won't believe this, Katie Rose, but my mom told me terrible things about her childhood today. She said that she was molested by her father and raped by her stepfather. Can you believe that? Anyway, she claims that this turned her into a sex addict. She said she had her addiction under control for years, but my dad leaving caused her to slip up again. That's why she was with that man. She said she wouldn't be seeing him again. If I have anything to do with it, she sure won't. I'll be watching her. I guess what she told me is true, but it's hard to believe."

"It is true," Callie was flabbergasted to hear Katie Rose say with conviction. "At least the part about the abuse by her father and stepfather is. I heard my mom and her talking about it one day."

"You what?! What do you mean you heard them talking about this? Why didn't you tell me?!" she demanded to know. Callie raised herself to a sitting position on the side of the bed. She had been lying on her back.

"I wanted to tell you. I thought maybe it would help you understand why your mom is so overprotective of you. I know that's always driven you nuts. My mom made me promise that I wouldn't tell you. She said it was your mom's place to do that. I didn't want to tell you something that would hurt you or make your mom mad, so I kept it to myself," Katie Rose tried to explain. "I'm sorry, Callie. It's awful what happened to your mom, and I could see why it could have made her sick. It made me feel sick hearing about it. I hope she gets things back under control, and that your mom and dad get back together soon. I'm glad she told you. It's the only secret I've ever kept from you, and I'm glad I don't have to keep it anymore."

There was silence on Callie's end as she tried to process this new information. It seemed that everyone in the world had known about the terrible things her mom had gone through but her. Callie felt betrayed.

She could not believe that Katie Rose had not told her what she had heard. Callie had not thought that Katie Rose was capable of keeping secrets from her. Now, she knew differently. This fact hurt Callie more than a little. For the first time, she felt a distance between her and Katie Rose.

"Callie, please say something," Katie Rose interrupted her deep musings.

"I should go," Callie said. Her voice sounded distracted.

"Are you mad at me for not telling you about your mom?"

"Hell yes, I am!" she snapped. "It hurts that you would keep something that important from me. If you'll keep a secret about something big like that, what else aren't you telling me? I can't trust you now. That's really disappointing."

"I swear that I have never kept another secret from you, Callie. I couldn't tell you about your mom. I didn't know how to tell you, and I didn't want to hurt you," Katie Rose tried to clarify. "Please believe me, and please forgive me for hiding something from you. It won't happen again."

*Here is another person to forgive for hurting me. First, my mom asked my forgiveness and now, Katie Rose.* Callie felt overwhelmed by it all.

"I need to go," she gruffly announced. Callie jerked the receiver away from her ear.

"Callie, wait," she heard Katie Rose pleading. Callie dropped the receiver back in its cradle anyway, abruptly ending their phone conversation.

*God, my life sucks lately!* she concluded with despair. Callie laid back on the bed. It seemed the surprises kept coming one right after the other, and they were not good surprises. *Far from it! Everyone I love has hurt and betrayed me in some way. How do I deal with this?*

The phone started to ring. Callie figured it was Katie Rose calling back. She did not want to talk to her right now. *Damn it! Why doesn't she leave me alone? That's the least she could do!*

Callie finally snatched up the phone on the third ring. She was intent on giving her friend a furious earful. "What the hell do you want now?" Callie bellowed into the phone.

"Callie?" an unsure voice asked on the other end. It took Callie a few minutes to recognize the strange voice.

"Glenda?"

"Yeah, girlfriend. How are you? I called your house yesterday, and your mom said you weren't feeling well. Sorry we left you in the park Friday night, but you were major wasted. How'd you get home?"

"I got picked up by a cop, who first took me to the hospital, where they helpfully pumped my stomach. Then I got the pleasure of taking a trip to Juvenile Hall. Thanks a hell of a lot! What do you want now?!"

"Sorry," Glenda said with a snicker. "I'd say you had that coming. Call it retribution for ruining my hair when you put glue in it at the sleepover a few years ago. Why don't we call it even between us now? What do you say? After all, I was calling to invite you to join me and my friends at the park again tonight, if you would like."

"I don't think so," Callie rejected. "Even if I wanted to…and after the way Friday night turned out, I don't think I do…I have been grounded indefinitely by my mother."

"Been there, done that. Can't you sneak out your bedroom window or something?" Glenda suggested.

"Not interested," Callie stated with determination.

"Okay. Whatever," Glenda conceded. "We hang out pretty much every weekend. If you ever want to get together again, give me a call. It's a great little escape, and you seemed to enjoy yourself the other night."

The word *escape* held Callie's attention. That's what she wanted to do more than anything right now – *escape*. *Escape* from her dad leaving, *escape* from what her mom had done, *escape* from what she had learned about her mom's childhood, *escape* from her mother's overprotectiveness, and *escape* from her best friend's silent betrayal.

Before she had drunk and smoked too much, Callie had felt fantastic Friday night. *Couldn't I do a little less of both and still flee from all of my problems for awhile? Why should I keep my promise to my mom or especially Katie Rose? They've both hurt me.*

"What time are you going to the park tonight?" Callie found herself asking.

"What time do you normally go to bed?"

"To bed?" Callie repeated. She was wondering why Glenda was asking such a silly question.

"Have you ever snuck out before?"

"No," Callie honestly replied.

"Well, what you do is, you pretend to be going to bed for the night. You ruffle up your blankets and sheets. Stick one of your pillows under the covers, so it looks like someone's in your bed. This is in case your mom should open your bedroom door to check on you. Then you climb out the window. Don't forget to bring a few dollars with you. The party favors aren't free, you know. So what time and where do you want us to pick you up?"

"I'm supposed to be in bed by ten on a school night. I could turn in by 9:30. I could meet you on the corner of Winkler and Morris, by the stop sign, about five minutes later. Would that work, or is that too late?"

"No. We'll be there to pick you up. We'll hang around about twenty minutes. If you don't show, we'll figure you couldn't make it out. Otherwise, it's party in the park. Glad you changed your mind. You won't regret it," Glenda promised.

"I better not," Callie said in a slightly threatening way.

"See you later," Glenda said, concluding the conversation.

"See ya," Callie agreed and hung the phone up.

# Chapter 21

# *Disappointment*

Monday, at school, Katie Rose approached Callie at her locker. "Hey, Cal," she tried to affectionately greet.

Callie refused to even acknowledge Katie Rose's presence. Instead, she made a show of ignoring her outright. Callie kept her back to the girl. She finished gathering her books from her locker. She slammed the door shut, locked it, turned around, and walked right past Katie Rose. She did not give her a glance or utter one single word.

*I'll punish Katie Rose for not telling me about my mom. She'll know better than to ever keep anything from me again.* Callie was resigned.

Katie Rose stood where she was. She watched Callie walk away. *Man, she is still mad at me. I can't believe Callie won't even talk to me. We haven't **ever** not talked before. What can I do to fix this?*

Katie Rose and Callie had always been so close. She could not imagine her life without the girl in it. Katie Rose turned and headed toward her own locker. She was still focusing on Callie. *What can I do to save our friendship? Maybe I can somehow get Callie to talk to me at lunch. I've got to think of some way to settle things between us. I don't want to lose having her as my friend.*

\* \* \* \*

When Katie Rose entered the cafeteria for lunch that day, she found that Callie was not yet at their table. She had a seat with some of their other friends and awaited Callie's arrival. A few

175

moments later, Katie Rose saw Callie enter the cafeteria. However, instead of approaching their table, Callie walked away in a different direction.

"Where's Callie?" Barbara, one of the other girls at their table asked. She was looking at Callie's empty seat.

"She sat down at that table across the way," Katie Rose answered unhappily.

Katie Rose pointed toward where she had seen Callie go. "She's mad at me. So I guess she decided not to sit with any of us. I can't believe Callie is carrying this so far. She's not only snubbing me, but everyone else at this table too."

"She's been acting strange all day," Maria volunteered. Maria and Callie had all the same classes together, unlike Katie Rose and her. "She hasn't had a lot to say to any of her usual friends. She's started talking to Julie and her group. I guess Callie's decided to hang out with 'em as well, since she's having lunch with them. They're roughnecks. I don't like them. Whether she is mad at you or not, Callie shouldn't be hanging out with Julie and her friends. She could get into some real trouble with that gang."

"Yeah, I agree," Barbara chimed in. "They are partiers. I've heard they drink and do drugs. Callie's not into any of that. So why would she want to hang out with them?"

*Is Callie* into *the party scene?* Her friend had gotten into quite a mess the past weekend, so Katie Rose had ample reason to be concerned. *Or is that what Callie wants? Is she purposely hanging out with those girls so that I will worry about her?* Katie Rose knew all too well how her friend operated. She had no doubt that Callie might be trying to upset her by hanging out with the wrong crowd.

"She is hanging out with them to upset me," she verbalized to the rest of her friends.

"What happened between the two of you to piss Callie off so much?" Gina, one of the other girls at their table inquired.

"I kept something from her that I shouldn't have," Katie Rose admitted. *I shouldn't have listened to my mom. I should have told Callie about her mom when I learned about it so long ago.*

"Secrets aren't a good thing to have between best friends," Cassie, another of the girls at the table, pointed out.

Her comment only served to make Katie Rose feel a bit worse. *I didn't want to keep a secret from Callie. I only kept things from her because I was afraid of hurting her. But now I've done that anyway.*

The girls began to debate amongst themselves the issue of keeping secrets. Katie Rose silently finished her lunch. *I'll call Callie tonight and somehow get her to talk to me again. I'll tell her how wrong I was and how sorry I am. In time, Callie will forgive me. She has to. I can't lose my best friend.*

\* \* \* \*

Katie Rose was unusually quiet at supper that night. She always had something about her day to share with her family, but this evening, Callie preoccupied her mind. So, Katie Rose remained still. This did not go unnoticed by her family.

"Why are you so quiet tonight, squirt?" Mason teased. He lightly poked Katie Rose with his elbow to rouse her from her deep, private meditation. "No exciting stories to tell about school today?"

"No," she rather curtly answered. She barely gave him a glance before she went about eating in silence once more.

"Is everything okay, sweetie?" her father asked next, studying her with concern. "Did everything go okay in school today?"

"School was fine," she answered without much enthusiasm. Katie Rose was still despondently staring down at the food upon her plate. *I need to finish eating, so I can go and call Callie*, she decided.

Katie Rose shoveled more food into her mouth. She did not have much appetite, but she was expected to eat. So she did.

"Are you feeling okay?" her mother added her worry.

"I'm *fine*," she assured all of them with an irritable edge to her voice.

Katie Rose merely wanted to be left alone right now. She loved her family, but she did not wish to talk about her falling out with Callie. *This is something I need to straighten out by myself. My mom would assure me that I was right to have kept the secret from Callie, but I'm not sure that she is right.*

Jackie Lynn and Long Wolf exchanged an uneasy glance. They were both convinced that something was amiss in their daughter's life. But they got the definite impression that Katie Rose did not wish to discuss whatever it was right now.

So, for the time being, Long Wolf diverted his focus from Katie Rose. He asked Mason how his day had gone. Mason took the cue and began talking about how his week had begun.

Katie Rose was relieved to be left alone for the moment. She practically inhaled her food. She rose from the table with her empty plate, glass in hand, and asked to be excused. Jackie Lynn nodded her approval.

Katie Rose escaped into the kitchen. She sat her dishes in the sink and turned to find herself face to face with her mother. Jackie Lynn had followed her daughter into the kitchen.

"I know that something is bothering you," she informed Katie Rose. "I can also tell that you don't want to talk about it. I want you to remember that your father and I are always here and ready to listen if you need us."

"I know, mom," Katie Rose declared. She was touched that her mom cared so much. "Thanks."

She had a strong urge to hug her mother, but Katie Rose stifled it. She feared that physical contact might cause her to break down and cry. Callie's rejection had Katie Rose's emotions on edge, and the last thing she wanted to do was start crying in her mother's presence.

*Then I would have to share things with my mom. She wouldn't let me alone until she knew what had me so upset.*

"I'm going to go to my room," she informed her mother and started past her.

"Okay. Just remember what I said," Jackie Lynn emphasized.

Katie Rose turned and nodded. She gave her mother a bittersweet smile, and then she scurried out of the room. *I'll go call Callie now and straighten things out with her. Then everything will be fine.*

\* \* \* \*

Katie Rose went directly to her room. She sat down on the side of her bed, picked up her cordless telephone, turned it on, and speed dialed number one. This was the number she had programmed for Callie. Callie's number had been programmed into Katie Rose's phone forever. After all, they normally talked to each other at least once a day.

Mary Julia answered the phone. "Hello."

"Hi. It's Katie Rose. May I speak to Callie, please?" she asked.

"I'm sorry, Katie Rose, but Callie's not home," Mary Julia relayed. "Her dad picked her up from school today. She is spending some time with him this evening. I'll tell her you called, and she may call you back if she doesn't get home too late."

"Okay," Katie Rose replied with disappointment. "Bye."

She listened as Mary Julia also said goodbye. Then Katie Rose turned her cordless phone off, ending the connection. Katie Rose was glad that Callie was getting to spend time with her dad, but she was disheartened that she had not gotten to speak with the girl. She hoped that Callie would call her back, but she had her doubts.

*Now, I will most likely have to wait until tomorrow to try and make amends with Callie.* Sad and lonely, Katie Rose lay back on her bed and dejectedly stared at the ceiling.

# Chapter 22

# *Conversations*

Jonathan enjoyed spending the afternoon and evening with his daughter. Mary Julia was not happy with this arrangement. However, she had agreed to it.

Mary Julia understood that Callie was not at all happy at home right now, due to the terrible thing that she had done. Plus, Mary Julia did not want Jonathan to file for divorce, so she realized she had to make some concessions.

Jonathan was temporarily staying in a hotel, trying to decide which direction his life was going to take. Tonight, Jonathan took Callie to a nearby restaurant. They ate dinner together, and he helped her with her homework.

Afterwards, since it was such a pleasant evening – temperature in the low seventies, balmy breeze, clear blue sky, and a beautiful sunset – Jonathan took Callie out to the park. They sat on a shaded bench, beside a concrete walking path. Pine, maple and dogwood trees were scattered on all sides of them. There was a small glistening pond within their view. Many fat ducks and geese happily waddled to and fro. Both children and adults also milled about on the grass by the pond, offering food to the fowl.

Jonathan wanted to have a talk with Callie. He was aware of everything that had been going on. Mary Julia had told him everything, so he wanted to frankly discuss all of the confusing occurrences with his daughter.

Jonathan hesitantly began by addressing the trouble that Callie had gotten into over the weekend. "So…your mother tells me that you had a rough weekend. Would you like to talk about it?"

"What's there to talk about?" Callie questioned rather flippantly.

*She's on the defense now*, Jonathan ascertained. *How do I get her to talk to me about this weekend?*

"From what I hear…there is quite a bit to talk about. Like you having your stomach pumped. Like you spending most of the night in Juvenile Hall. Does that refresh your memory a little?"

"I know what happened this weekend, dad. And I'm sure that mom made it sound ten times worse than what it was."

"She probably did, so why don't you tell me how it really went," he coaxed.

Callie had given him a bit of an 'in' in their discussion. Jonathan was glad to find this. He needed all the help he could get, since he felt so awkward about having a serious talk with his daughter. "I'd like to hear it from you, Callie."

Callie was unaccustomed to sitting down and talking with her father about her life. She did not know how to react to all of this. She was tired of being cross-examined about the weekend, but at the same time, Callie was happy to have her father's undivided attention. She did not wish to do anything to lose this, so she slowly began to tell her dad all about the weekend.

Jonathan remained silent, merely listening, until Callie was completely through. When she had finished relaying all of the details of her disconcerting weekend, Jonathan finally spoke again.

"Callie, I can understand why you turned to drugs and alcohol to cope. You had entirely too much dumped on you this weekend. First, I left your mom. Then…you…you…well…you caught your mom with another man. Your friends are probably telling you that the way to get by is by using drugs and drinking. But, Callie, even if I'm not living at home, I'm still here for you. What I'm trying to tell you is that I want you to lean on me instead. Okay? Can you at least try that?" he asked her.

"I understand now why you left mom, dad. I didn't know she was cheating on you. I can't believe she is doing that," Callie seemed to change the subject.

*I need to address Mary Julia's sexual addiction*, Jonathan was quick to conclude.

He diverted his attention from Callie for several moments. Jonathan absentmindedly watched some joggers run past and others strolling along the path in front of them. There was silence for several minutes as he tried to discern how to address this important issue with his daughter.

Callie took her father's silence for irritation. "I'm sorry, dad," she apologized. *I don't want you to stop talking to me.* "I shouldn't have brought up what mom did. I'm sure you don't want to think about that. Just forget I brought it up. I don't want you to be upset with me."

"I'm not upset with you, Callie," Jonathan was swift to assure her. "You're right when you say I don't want to think about what your mother did. It's hard for me to deal with, but I'm sure it's much, much worse for you. Your mother has an illness, Callie. She had it under control for many years, but the stress of our separation caused a relapse. She isn't having an affair. She is just using...sex...sex with another man...to cope."

"But it's so wrong...!" Callie began to protest.

"I'm not defending what your mother did, Callie," he interrupted her. "I'm just trying to explain it to you...as best I can. She told you about her sexual addiction, right?"

"Yes...she told me...it's just...it's still hard to accept," Callie admitted.

"I know, honey," Jonathan commiserated. Callie liked the fact that he had used a term of endearment with her. It was the first time her father had ever done this. It touched her deeply.

Jonathan pulled Callie close, and she laid her head over on his shoulder. He hugged her tightly and held her for a very long time. He had never loved her more.

His daughter seemed to have matured a great deal in the few short days he had been away. However, Jonathan wondered if this was a good thing. Callie had had far too much thrown on her all at one time.

"Dad," Callie spoke again at last. She raised her head off of his shoulder and was staring him directly in the eyes.

"Yes, honey?"

"I promise you that I won't drink or do drugs anymore. I'll lean on you."

Jonathan was relieved. "I'll be here for you," he pledged. *Callie will be okay*, Jonathan attempted to convince himself. *I'll be there for her, and I'll help her to be strong. She won't fall to the temptations of drugs and alcohol anymore. I'll see to that. She's a beautiful, smart young lady, and she deserves to have a bright future. I'll make sure that she does.*

They changed the subject then and began to talk about much lighter issues. Callie chattered on and on about everything under the sun – teen idols, music, clothes fashions. She never wanted her special time with her father to end. She had never felt as close to him as she did tonight.

\* \* \* \*

Jonathan brought Callie home about 9:30 p.m. She was supposed to be in bed by 10:00 p.m. on a school night. As Jonathan pulled into the driveway, Callie asked out of the blue, "Dad, why do I have to stay with mom? She obviously is screwed up. So why can't I stay with you? I could go in and pack right now."

"Callie, I'm staying in a hotel. This is your home," Jonathan pointed out. Then he hastily added, "Yes, granted your mother does have some problems, but she is working hard to overcome them. You are the light of her eye. I can't imagine what it would do to her if you left her."

"But *you* left. If you can't live with her, then why do I have to?" Callie argued. Then she hit very close to home when she questioned, "Can you ever forgive her for having sex with another man?"

It was a question that was already haunting Jonathan. Mary Julia had an addiction, and his abandonment had pushed her over the edge. Nonetheless, it was still hard for Jonathan to accept that she had been with another man. It was still a betrayal to him, and he was not certain how he was going to deal with it.

"You *can't* forgive her, can you?" Callie pursued.

"I honestly don't know, Callie," Jonathan responded at last. "That is something between your mother and me."

"No, it isn't just between you and my mom. It affects me too. You forget that I am the one who *saw* her with *him*. I can't get it out of my head. I think about it every time I look at her. Do you have an idea how terrible that is? If you do, then you won't make me stay here. I don't care if you are staying in a hotel. I'd rather live there than in this house with *her*. I can't forgive mom. I don't know how."

"I honestly don't know how either, Callie," Jonathan sadly and truthfully confessed. "But I still love your mother, and I know you do too. We can't give up on her. Your mother told me that you were supposed to go to counseling with her. I am too. I'm hoping and praying that we will find some answers there. But, in the meantime, I can't take you away from home. You can come visit me, but you *cannot* come and live with me. I can't do that to your mom."

"So much for you always being there for me then!" Callie barked with anger. She opened her door and bolted out.

Jonathan shoved open his own door and stepped out of the car. "Callie," he called after her.

She was fleeing around the front of the car and up the sidewalk leading into the house. Callie scrambled in her purse for her house key. It turned out she did not need her key. Her mom opened the front door all at once. Callie sped past her mother into the house.

"Callie?" Mary Julia half questioned, as she watched her daughter rush past. She looked back outside to find Jonathan hurrying up the sidewalk toward her. "Jonathan, what happened? What's wrong with Callie? She looked as if she was about to burst into tears. What have you done to her?!"

He came to an abrupt halt a few feet away from Mary Julia. Jonathan stared at her in disbelief. He began to shout, "What have *I* done to her?! You are a real piece of work, do you know that?! *I* didn't do anything to Callie. Unlike *you*!! She didn't want to come home to *you*, and I made her. I'm a real monster, aren't I?!"

Jonathan's shouting and his words jolted Mary Julia back to her senses. She grasped how wrong she had been to accuse Jonathan of hurting Callie in any way. *I'm the only one who had done anything lately to hurt our daughter.* Overwhelming guilt swept over her.

"Jonathan, I am *so* very, very sorry," she professed, as tears came to her eyes. She was apologizing for much more than her latest miscommunication.

"Save it!" he snapped.

Jonathan clenched one of his hands into a fist in frustration. He raised his hand and shook it near Mary Julia's face in heated frustration. It almost appeared he meant to strike her.

When he saw the fear in Mary Julia's eyes, it made Jonathan even angrier.

*My God! Mary Julia thinks I'm going to hit her. Boy, am I tempted to make her fears come true!*

No sooner had the awful thought registered, then Jonathan reprimanded himself. *What in the hell am I doing? I need to get control of myself. I need to leave!*

He lowered his hand, unclenched his fist, and started to back away. "Just do me a favor, and go and see to our daughter. Can you do that?" Jonathan asked in a much calmer voice.

"Yes, of course," Mary Julia assured him. "I'm sorry," she said again in almost a whisper.

Mary Julia watched Jonathan turn and race away. She shut the door. She leaned against it, and Mary Julia allowed herself to cry with remorse for a long while.

*I'm destroying my life. I have got to get help before I lose everyone I love. I will! I won't allow my illness and fear to drive everyone I love away.*

Mary Julia pulled herself together as much as she possibly could. She went to check on Callie. When she opened her daughter's bedroom door, she found Callie was already in bed. She appeared to be sleeping.

*I'll have to talk to her tomorrow*, Mary Julia concluded. *Sleep well, sweetheart. Momma is going to make things better soon. I promise.*

185

# Chapter 23

# *Exposure*

The next day at school, Katie Rose waited near Callie's locker for a chance to confront her friend again. She waited and waited, but Callie never appeared. Katie Rose relinquished her post when the first bell rang. She had to head to her homeroom, so she would not be marked tardy.

*I wonder where Callie could be. I hate that we aren't talking. I don't even know for sure if her dad brought her home last night. Callie could even be sick. I guess I'll have to wait and try to call her again tonight. I have to get through to her. This rift between us is driving me bananas.*

\* \* \* \*

Callie arrived at school only a few minutes before the second bell rang. She narrowly escaped being marked tardy. Callie had had a terrible time getting started this morning. She was still draggy. She had taken two Motrin, but still had a terrible headache. *I drank too much again last night*, she now accepted with regret.

After Callie ran away from her dad last night, she went to her room. She took a few moments to carefully camouflage her bed. Callie arranged several pillows, her blanket and bedspread so that it looked as if she was in it.

Then she escaped the house by climbing out her bedroom window. Callie had done the same thing the previous night, when she had met up with Glenda. However, last night, she had not hooked up with Glenda.

186

Callie went to Julie's house instead. Julie had mentioned that she all but had the house to herself most nights. Her dad often passed out drunk, and her mother had left them when Julie was only a baby. Callie was glad to find that this was indeed the case last night.

Julie had been happy to see her. She had been watching television and drinking a beer alone when Callie arrived. Julie's father was passed out on the couch. Several beer cans sat on the table and laid tossed on the floor around him.

Julie led Callie to the kitchen. She took a six-pack out of the refrigerator, and she directed Callie out onto the back deck. Before Callie realized it, she drank five of the six beers. Julie drank the other one.

When Julie offered Callie a cigarette, Callie declined. But she asked Julie if she had any weed to smoke instead. Julie shook her head 'no'.

"I'm all out," she told Callie. "But I do know who you can buy some from though, if you are interested."

Callie indicated that she was, so Julie asked if she could meet her after school the next day. Callie readily agreed to do so.

She left shortly thereafter. Callie wobbled home in a drunken haze. Luckily, Julie only lived a street over.

Callie struggled to climb back into her bedroom through the window. She came close to clumsily falling on her face. Then, when Callie brought the window closed, she misjudged the distance. She ended up bringing it closed with a slam.

She froze in place and frantically waited to hear some sign of her mom moving about. She was thankful when all remained silent. *Thank heavens, mom is a deep sleeper.*

Callie quietly scrambled over to her bed and began reorganizing the bedding. She pulled the pillows out from under the blanket and comforter. Callie placed them back at the top of the bed where they belonged.

She wearily shoved back her comforter and blanket. Then she fell into bed, sliding between the chilly sheets with relief. Callie was out like a light within minutes.

It had seemed only a short while before her alarm was screaming at her. The clock seemed to be inside her head, pounding. Callie's arm flew out and shut off the alarm.

The movements made her feel nauseated. Callie lowered her head back to the pillow. She lay very still until the wave of nausea – *thankfully* – passed.

Several minutes later, Callie almost managed to go back to sleep. However, her mother opened her bedroom door. "Callie, it's time to get up, sweetie," she announced, in a much too loud and chipper voice.

Callie lethargically rolled onto her side to face her mother. She opened her eyes, and she had been blinded by an offending – *much too bright* – light from the hall. Callie groaned and shielded her eyes with her hands in stunned response.

"Callie, are you feeling alright?" Mary Julia inquired with some concern, stepping inside her bedroom.

"I'm fine," she grumbled.

Callie forced herself into a gradual sitting position. She kept both her hands planted on the bed at both her sides to steady herself. The room was spinning, and Callie felt sick to her stomach.

Her eyes were still, for the most part, shut, but Callie lowered her head to try to escape *that damn light. It's killing my eyes! And Oh, God! My head is killing me!*

She compelled her legs to stand, and she turned her back on her mother. Callie pretended to need something across the room. She meandered even further away from her mother. Another strong wave of nausea overtook Callie, but she somehow managed to fight it off.

"Callie, honey, you slept in your clothes??" her mother questioned, as she got a good look at her daughter.

*Shit! I didn't even think to change last night when I came back in. How could I have been so stupid?! Because I was loaded. That's why.*

"I was upset, so I went straight to bed when I got home last night," Callie tried to rectify in haste. "I fell asleep with my clothes on. What's the big, damn deal, *mother*?" she asked. She sounded very cross.

Callie leaned against the side of her closet for support. She acted as if to she was searching for a clean blouse to wear to school. Half turning, Callie barked, "I'm late, mom. I don't have time to talk, right now. Okay?"

"Alright," Mary Julia conceded. "But we *will* talk, Callie," she clarified with determination. "If not this morning, then this evening. Now hurry up and get ready, so you won't be late to school."

Mary Julia left then. Callie backed up and took a seat on the end of her bed with relief. She went into the bathroom and threw up before she managed to take a shower and dress for school that day.

Callie blamed being late as to why she had not eaten any breakfast. Her mother made her take pop tarts and a glass of milk with her in the car. Callie managed to choke down one on the pop tarts and drink most of her milk to satisfy her mom.

When they arrived at school, at last, Callie hopped out of the car with barely a word to her mother. *She's just late*, Mary Julia tried to convince herself.

However, Mary Julia understood that there was more to her daughter's hasty departure. *She doesn't want anything to do with me.*

As she drove away, Mary Julia made a firm resolve that she would find some way to make things right between Callie and her again. *No matter what it takes.*

\* \* \* \*

Katie Rose rushed to leave the school when the final bell rang. She wanted to get outside. Katie Rose wanted to confront Callie before she got into the car with her dad and was off again. Jonathan always picked her up at school, and this custom had not changed.

Katie Rose had plenty of time to talk to Callie, because Mason had baseball practice. So she would be hanging around the school for a bit before she got her ride home. Katie Rose had not realized that Callie was even at school, until she saw her come into the cafeteria at lunch.

Callie had sat with Julie and her friends again that day. *I have got to get this* thing *between us settled*, Katie Rose was determined. *I can't stand the silent treatment that Callie is giving me…well…actually giving all of her usual friends. It's got to stop.*

Katie Rose waited by the front doors to the school. She stood in the grass at the bottom of the steps, persistently scanning the faces of all the fleeing students. Katie Rose watched and watched.

The crowd grew fewer and fewer, but she never saw Callie come out of the school. *Where could she be? Could Callie have somehow known I would be waiting for her and went out another way to avoid me?*

After a few more minutes, Katie Rose decided that Callie was not coming out. *Not out this door anyway.* Disappointed once more, she turned and headed away. Katie Rose walked along the sidewalk that ran around the side of the school. She was headed toward the baseball field. She scanned the parking lot across the way.

Katie Rose saw Jonathan's car. He appeared to still be waiting for her as well. *Could Callie still be inside the school for some reason?*

It suddenly dawned on Katie Rose that Callie might have gotten a detention for being late. After all, she had not seen her that morning. And she had waited by the lockers until the first bell. Receiving a late detention meant a student had to stay after school for fifteen minutes.

*That has to be it!* she concluded with renewed hope. Katie Rose glanced at her watch. She saw that almost ten minutes had passed since school the final bell rang.

*If I wait five more minutes, then I ought to be able to catch Callie*, she schemed.

Katie Rose raced toward the annex building around the back of the school. That was where students served detentions. She planned to wait nearby and detain Callie as she came out. As she approached the annex, however, Katie Rose caught a glimpse of her friend. Callie stepped out a slight bit from behind the annex building. Then she circled and went back behind the building.

*Callie must have already gotten out of detention, but what is she doing behind that building?* Katie Rose brooded. She rushed in that direction, instead of to the front of the building. She passed by the windows that ran along the side of the annex. The building was dark and empty. *Either detention let out early, or there was no one serving detention today*, she deduced.

Callie stuck her nose out from behind the building again. Katie Rose was sickened to discover that her friend was holding a joint in her hand. Callie did not notice Katie Rose. She swiveled to head back behind the building. Callie raised the joint to her mouth to take another drag. Katie Rose startled her. She shouted in a loud, confrontational voice, "Callie, what in the hell are you doing?!"

Callie's head jerked in nervous response. She stared in disbelief, with wide stunned eyes, at Katie Rose. She promptly lowered the cigarette. Callie held it out in front of her, out of Katie Rose's sight. Julie was quick to take it from her. Julie scurried around the other side of the building.

She extinguished the marijuana cigarette and stuffed it safely under the corner of the building. If she and Callie got caught with drugs on school grounds, they would both be expelled. It was not something Julie was going to allow. It had not been her idea to smoke weed here. Callie was to blame for that.

*Katie Rose had better scram if she knows what's good for her. I'll beat* little miss goody two shoes *to a pulp before I will let her turn Callie and I in*, Julie decided with malice. She was clenching her fists.

Callie stepped out into the open. She blocked Katie Rose from going around the building. Callie could not allow Katie Rose to find Julie. For all Callie knew, Julie was still holding the joint.

"Katie Rose, what are *you* doing here?" Callie asked in a non-aggressive voice. She reached in her purse and pulled forth a small bottle of perfume. She sprayed it excessively on her neck and wrists. Then she walked closer to the girl.

With a slight smile, Callie added, "I'm sorry I didn't return your call last night. I got in late and went straight to bed. My mom didn't tell me until this morning that you had called. What did you want?" Callie was attempting to direct her friend's attention away from what she had discovered her doing.

Katie Rose was not to be dissuaded. She was determined to find out what was going on with her treasured friend. "Why are you using drugs again, Callie?" Katie Rose interrogated. Her eyes were serious, and there was no trace of a smile on Katie Rose's face. She was deeply concerned about her dear friend. *Callie actually uses drugs.* Katie Rose had now seen it with her own eyes, and there was no denying it.

"Answer me, Callie!" she demanded. "What is going on with you?"

"Nothing is going on with me," Callie tried to assure Katie Rose. She started to nonchalantly walk past her.

With lightening speed, Katie Rose reached out and grabbed hold of Callie's upper arm. She squeezed tightly as she commanded, "Don't give me that crap, Callie! I saw what you were doing. I smelled it. Spraying on strong perfume isn't going to fool me! Where'd you stash it? Did you throw it on the ground in back of that building? Why don't we go and find out?!"

Katie Rose started moving in that direction. She was persuasively pulling Callie along with her. Callie struggled to free herself from Katie Rose's ironclad grip.

"Let go of me!" she adamantly insisted. Katie Rose had Callie stumbling backwards. "What is wrong with you?! You're hurting me!"

"You're hurting yourself by doing drugs," Katie Rose maintained.

She continued to drag Callie forward. Katie Rose was determined to find Callie's marijuana. She wanted to make her friend confess to what she had been doing.

"Callie. Katie Rose. What's going on here?" Callie was shocked to hear her dad call.

She looked over Katie Rose's shoulder to find him approaching them. *Shit! I hope he didn't hear what Katie Rose said about me doing drugs.*

"I should tell your dad what I saw you doing," Katie Rose half whispered to Callie. With great reluctance, she released her.

"If you do, I swear I will never talk to you again. Our friendship will permanently be *over*. Is that what you want?" Callie threatened in a low growl. Her angry eyes were boring into Katie Rose's.

Callie's warning was not being issued in vain. Katie Rose understood that. Callie would never talk to her again if she said anything to Jonathan. The mere thought of it greatly upset Katie Rose.

"What are you girls fighting over?" Jonathan asked. He drew to within a few feet of them. "Callie, I've been waiting for you. What are you doing back here? I would have never found you if I hadn't seen Katie Rose headed this direction. I was going to catch up to her and ask her if she had seen you. I was getting worried."

Callie turned her attention to her father and replied, "I'm sorry, dad. I was late for school this morning, so I had to serve detention for fifteen minutes in that building."

Callie pointed toward the annex beside them. Then she continued, "I was on my way to the car when Katie Rose waylaid me. She's upset because I haven't been talking to her. But we've worked things out, and everything will be okay between us again. Right, Katie Rose?"

Callie threw an arm around the girl's shoulders and pulled her close. Katie Rose stared into Callie's bloodshot eyes. Those same eyes were now pleading with Katie Rose not to say anything to her father. *What should I do?* Katie Rose struggled. *What would help Callie more? If I tell her dad, I end our friendship. If I stay quiet, I'll remain Callie's friend. If we stay friends, then I can closely watch Callie. Or maybe I won't have to say a word. Maybe Jonathan will notice her eyes and realize what she has been doing.*

"Everything's fine," Katie Rose spoke up at last.

She looked toward Jonathan and flashed him a slight, unconvincing smile. It was all Katie Rose could muster. Her mind was still too troubled by Callie. *Look close at Callie, Jonathan. Notice her bloodshot eyes. Notice the smell that's in the air. It isn't just Callie's strong perfume. You need to realize what she has been up to.*

"Are you sure everything's okay?" Jonathan verified. He sensed there was something greater going on between the girls. This made him uneasy.

"I'm sure," Katie Rose assured him with more conviction than she actually felt. "Callie, I'll hear from you later. Right?" she questioned the girl. There was a strong hint of intimidation in Katie Rose's question, and in her eyes.

"Of course," Callie assured her with a fake smile. She gave Katie Rose a slight squeeze. "You're *still* my best friend." Callie released Katie Rose then. "Are you ready to go, dad?" she asked. Callie eagerly started toward him. "Talk to you later, Katie Rose," Callie stressed once more as she joined her father's side.

"Katie Rose, do you have a ride home?" Jonathan asked before they started away.

"Yes. I have to wait on Mason. He has baseball practice. It's okay though. I'll do homework while I'm waiting," she explained to Jonathan.

"Okay. But, if you'd rather go home now, I could give you a ride," he offered with kindness.

"Thanks. But I'm fine," she replied, studying Callie.

If her friend had given her any encouragement, Katie Rose would have gone with them. But, quite the opposite, Callie seemed to be evasive. She was staring at the ground, rather than looking Katie Rose's way.

*Callie is still frightened that I might say something to give her away. Have I made the right choice to remain silent?* Yes. *Because I don't have much other choice right now. I need to stay friends with Callie. I've got to find another way to help her, other than squealing to her parents.*

"I'll see you guys later," Katie Rose said.

"Okay. Bye," Both Jonathan and Callie responded.

Katie Rose watched them turn to leave. She started away in the opposite direction. She went behind the annex and searched the ground for the evidence. Katie Rose saw no sign of it. *Callie must have thrown it over in the grass somewhere.*

She considered searching some more but decided not to. *What purpose would it serve? I don't want to be carrying marijuana around anyway. It would be my luck that I would get caught with it, and they would believe it was mine. I'm not getting suspended or expelled for something I had no part of.*

Katie Rose started away toward the baseball field to do her homework – *if I can concentrate* – and wait for Mason. Safely out of sight, from the side of the annex, Julie watched Katie Rose walking away. She was very relieved that Katie Rose was finally going away.

Julie slyly made her escape in the opposite direction. She purposely left the marijuana cigarette safely stowed under the corner of the building. *If Callie wants to dig it back out tomorrow, then she can. I'm outta here!*

# Chapter 24

# *The Secret*

Mason's practice lasted about an hour. During this time, Katie Rose managed to finish all of her homework. Katie Rose was quiet during the short drive home.

Her mind was still heavily preoccupied by the situation with Callie. Mason did not give Katie Rose's silence a lot of notice. He was tired from a hard practice, and he longed to get home and take a revitalizing shower.

When they got home, Mason went to his room to get out of his sweaty clothes and shower. Katie Rose also went to her bedroom. She had a seat on the side of her bed and stared at the telephone in painful confusion.

*Who can I talk to about what is going on with Callie? Who can I trust not to say anything?* All at once, Katie Rose thought of her Aunt Flora. *Hasn't Flora always told Mason and me that we could always talk to her about anything? But would she keep a secret if I asked her to?*

Katie Rose was not at all certain of the answer to her musing. She needed to talk to someone about what was going on. However, that *someone* could not be her mom or dad.

*Mom would for sure tell Mary Julia. Dad would try to talk me into telling Mary Julia or Jonathan, and if I didn't, he would tell one of them. Flora is an adult friend. What could it hurt to see if she would keep a secret for me? If she tells me that she can't, then I'll have to keep it to myself until I can figure out what I must do to help Callie.*

Katie Rose picked up the phone and dialed Flora's number. *Please keep my secret, Flora. I need some advice from an adult.*

*An adult I can trust.* Katie Rose listened as Flora's telephone began to ring.

A moment later, Flora answered the phone. "Hi, Aunt Flora," Katie Rose greeted her with affection.

"Well, hello, Katie Rose," Flora happily replied. "How is one of my favorite young ladies doing today?"

"Um...well... I could be doing a lot better," Katie Rose hesitantly began. Her voice was quivering a bit.

"Katie Rose, is something wrong, sweetheart?" Flora asked with a hint of concern.

"Yes," she admitted. Katie Rose nervously chewed on her bottom lip. "Aunt Flora, if I tell you something, will you promise me you will keep it between just you and me?"

"Between just you and I? Is this something you don't want your parents to know?" Flora questioned.

"Yes," Katie Rose truthfully disclosed. "It's something I can't tell them right now, Aunt Flora. But I need to talk to someone about it. You told Mason and me you would always be there if we needed to talk."

"I'm always here to listen, sweetie," Flora assured her. "But...I can't promise you that I will keep something from your parents, most especially your mom. There aren't any secrets between Jackie Lynn and I, Katie Rose."

"Oh," she responded with disappointment. "Okay, then." Katie Rose replied.

There were several moments of silence. Then Flora heard Katie Rose sob.

*Katie Rose is crying. Why?* "Katie Rose, honey, please tell me what is wrong." Flora pleaded with her.

She was worried now. All kinds of scary thoughts ran through Flora's head as to what might be wrong. The most important thing, at this moment, was finding out what had Katie Rose so upset.

Flora assured her, "I promise I'll keep your secret, okay? Talk to me, Katie Rose. Please."

"You....you won't tell...tell...my mom or my...my dad?" Katie Rose verified between sobs.

"I promise I won't tell another soul," Flora pledged. "Whatever you tell me will be our secret...just between the two of us, like you asked. Now will you please tell me what's the matter?

I love you, honey, and it breaks my heart to hear you cry. Tell your Aunt Flora. You can trust me, Katie Rose. You know that, right?"

There were another few minutes of silence. Katie Rose was struggling to compose herself. Flora heard her blowing her nose.

Katie Rose finally began to reveal, "Aunt Flora, it's Callie."

"Callie? What's she's done this time?!" Flora snapped with exasperation.

*I should not be accusing the girl of wrongdoing right off the bat, but Callie has been trouble incarnate recently.* Both Mary Julia and Jackie Lynn had told Flora about the mess Callie had been in of late.

"She…Callie is still doing drugs, Aunt Flora. I caught her smoking weed today," Katie Rose disclosed. It felt good to be able to share this with someone else.

"Oh, isn't that grand!" Flora stated with sarcasm. "I was afraid that Mary Julia was being a little too optimistic in regards to Callie. Callie supposedly promised her mom that she would not drink or do drugs again. Mary Julia believed her. I guess that promise meant nothing to Callie. Where did you catch her doing drugs again, Katie Rose?"

"After classes let out today at school," she conveyed. "Callie was behind the annex building. She lied to her dad. Callie told him she had detention, and that's what held her up. But I saw her smoking weed, Aunt Flora. I threatened to tell her dad, but Callie said if I did, she would never talk to me again. She means it, Aunt Flora. I don't want to lose having Callie as a friend. What should I do?"

Flora was silent for a moment. She was ingesting all that Katie Rose had revealed. Flora was also trying to ascertain what she should advice the young girl to do. *Callie was being bold to smoke marijuana at school. The girl might genuinely be developing a serious problem.*

Callie obviously seemed to be using the drug as a coping mechanism. This was Callie's way of dealing with all the hurtful things that were happening in her life right now. *If this is the case, what if Callie is offered a more serious drug, like crack cocaine? Would she use that as well?*

Flora was fearful that she might. Callie was not likely to lose her life with marijuana use. But with harder drugs, it was a possibility.

"Katie Rose, Callie could get into some serious trouble doing drugs. You do realize this, don't you?"

"Of course!" Katie Rose was quick to agree. "That's why I'm so worried about her."

"Me too, honey," Flora agreed. "This is too big of an issue to remain silent about. Your silence could enable Callie to hurt herself. That's the last thing you want to happen. In this case, Katie Rose, if you want to be a true friend to Callie, it may mean you will have to tell on her. It would be for Callie's own safety. Do you understand what I'm telling you, sweetheart?"

"Yes, I understand. You are saying the same thing my mom or dad would have. But, Aunt Flora, if I tell, Callie will *never* talk to me again. She will no longer be my friend, and what purpose would that serve? Neither Mary Julia nor Jonathan can get her to stop using drugs anyway. They are part of the reason Callie is using drugs in the first place. When Callie makes up her mind to do something, it's nearly impossible to stop her. What are her parents going to do? Ground her for the rest of her life? Take Callie out of school? That's probably what it would take. Are they going to have someone at Callie's house to watch her constantly? Otherwise, Callie would most likely have friends come over to bring her drugs. If I stay her friend, then I can at least keep an eye on Callie. I can try to find some way to convince her to stop. I don't want to end my friendship with her. I need for you to help me find some other way to help Callie – Other than squealing on her to her parents. Can you do that, Aunt Flora? Please??"

"I don't know, Katie Rose," Flora truthfully replied. "You are only fourteen years old...."

"I'll be fifteen in less than a month," Katie Rose interrupted Flora to point out. Her voice was very serious. Katie Rose was trying to sound mature.

*Oh yes, and fifteen is* most certainly *a grown woman.* "Okay, so you are almost fifteen," Flora corrected. "That's still pretty young to take all this on by yourself. You want to help your friend, but Katie Rose, what concerns me is what if you can't help Callie? How are you going to feel if Callie gets herself into trouble or gets deeper into drugs and alcohol? I *personally* would feel terrible. I would wonder if I should have told Callie's parents and if they could have done something, which I didn't, to stop her. It also worries me that she might drag you down with her. Or Callie may try to use you as a scapegoat if she gets into another mess."

Flora was aware that this fear disturbed Jackie Lynn as well. "How far are you prepared to go to remain Callie's friend? Do you intend to take the fall for her if she gets into trouble?"

*You have in the past.* Flora knew, but did not point out.

"I don't know how I will feel if Callie doesn't stop, gets worse, or gets into trouble," Katie Rose lamented with honesty. "But I do know that Callie has never gotten along with her mom. She was just beginning to get close to her dad, but now he has left. So how do you expect her parents to help her, Aunt Flora? I don't see how they can. They can only make things worse. If that's the case, then I may be the only one who *can* help Callie. I can't turn my back on her. But, no, I will not let Callie pull me down. And I *won't* take the fall for her if she doesn't straighten herself out. I can promise you that."

*What more can I say?* It dawned on Flora, all at once, that both girls were very much like their mothers. Both were extremely headstrong. *Katie Rose will have her work cut out for her if she has decided to go head to head with Callie.*

Unfortunately, Callie was turning out to be like her mother in self-destructive ways as well. Mary Julia had used sex to escape, and Callie had turned to drugs. *What can I do to help? Katie Rose has her mind set that she isn't going to confess about her friend's drug use. She isn't going to tell her parents or Callie's parents. I could go behind Katie Rose's back and break my confidence to her. But is that something I should do? Katie Rose would never trust me again; and would it help Callie in the long run? Mary Julia and Jonathan certainly do have enough issues of their own to deal with. They don't need more concerns added to their plates. On the other hand, what if something happens to Callie? If Mary Julia and/or Jonathan find out that I knew Callie was still using drugs and I didn't tell them...whew...I don't even want to think about that one!*

"Aunt Flora? Are you still there?" Katie Rose asked. Several moments of silence had passed.

"Yes, honey, I am still here," Flora responded. "I was deep in thought over all we have discussed. What path to advise you to take is even confusing for me," she confessed.

"I only see one path, and that's to try and help Callie by myself," Katie Rose reinforced with sadness. "I needed to talk to someone I could trust about all this. I *can* trust you, can't I, Aunt Flora? You *won't* tell anyone what we talked about, will you?"

*Time to decide one way or another, Flora.* There were another few hushed moments before Flora said, "No, Katie Rose, I won't tell anyone about our conversation. Not even Kenny. I promised you, and I intend to keep that promise. But I need for you to do something for me. Okay?"

"Anything," Katie Rose was eager to pledge.

"You need to stay in touch with me. I want you to keep me informed about how things are going with Callie. Call me at least once a week. As long as I determine that things aren't getting too out of hand, then I will let you go at this alone. But if Callie in any way threatens you, or she is threatening herself, then I reserve the right to reconsider keeping our secret. But I will tell you if I intend to tell anyone else. Is this understood?"

"Yes, Aunt Flora. Thank you so much," Katie Rose gushed. "I love you."

"I love you too, sweetie, and I'm glad you called to talk to me about this. I'll be talking to you."

"Bye. Talk to you soon," Katie Rose concluded the call by saying.

Flora lowered the receiver back into its cradle. She wearily sat back. *Am I doing the right thing? Will I regret this decision? How am I going to keep this all to myself?*

She bowed her head, closed her eyes, and took a second to fervently pray for both Katie Rose and Callie. She also prayed for strength to keep this secret, and she prayed that she was *indeed* doing the right thing.

# Chapter 25

# *New Friend*

Callie had her mom's credit card, and she was on a mission. She vitally needed to get a prom dress. *Since I took my mom's credit card without asking, she won't even know about the dress until her credit card bill comes in.*

Mason's senior prom was only a week away, and Callie was supposed to be going with Ralph. *Thankfully*, she was no longer being grounded by her mother. Julie had already volunteered her house for Callie to get dressed, fix her hair, and do her makeup.

Julie was even going to keep the dress for her, since Callie's mom had no idea she was even going to the prom. Callie had already gotten permission from her mom to go to a sleepover with her new friends next weekend. Julie had promised to back her up on this lie should her mom happen to call. All her bases covered.

Callie was exceedingly excited about the prospect of going to the senior prom. *I can even put up with having to spend time with goofy Ralph. It'll be worth it to be able to hang out with Mason and his friends. I'll find a way to dance with Mason. He's more attracted to me than Rebecca. Why wouldn't he be!*

Callie's Grandma, Flora, was unexpectedly supposed to pick her up and have dinner with her. *I bet she wants to play like she's my real grandmother, instead of only my mom's good friend. I'm sure Flora wants to lecture me on the dangers of drinking and drugs. I'll pretend to listen and* of course, *agree.*

After dinner, pursuant to Mary Julia's approval, Flora had agreed to pick up Julie. She was supposed to be dropping both girls off at the mall. Flora had inquired if Katie Rose was also going along. Callie had tersely informed Flora that she was not. "We are getting together tomorrow night."

Flora found this very odd. *I wonder why Katie Rose is being left out. She and Callie usually do everything together. I'm anxious to meet this Julie. Maybe there is a reason that Callie does not want Katie Rose hanging out with this new girl. Is Julie the one who is getting Callie drugs? I've got to try and find out while I'm having dinner with Callie.*

\* \* \* \*

Flora and Callie were seated at their table at Cornucopia Restaurant. Cornucopia provided casual dining in a cultured environment. The restaurant was dimly lit. The tables were all covered by white, linen tablecloths and the silverware was wrapped in linen napkins. The plates were china and the beverage glasses crystal. There was a small tea lamp candle, in beveled glass, burning in the center of each table. Soft, instrumental, piano music played in the background.

Flora and Callie had no sooner been seated than a waiter took their drink orders. Flora ordered water and Callie ordered iced tea. Both drinks were sitting in front of them now. They had sent their waiter away, several minutes ago, with their dinner orders. This was Flora's opportunity to start on her important crusade for answers. She did not waste any time.

"So, Callie, tell me; how is everything going? I know, from talking with your mom, that all of you are going to counseling. And now you have a new friend...Julie, right? It seems as if your life is getting better."

*Oh, Lord! Not another counseling session! Question...question...after boring question!* Callie's mind moaned.

With a feigned smile, she replied, "Yeah. Everything is going fine."

Noting Flora's invasive stare, Callie averted her lying eyes. She stared down at the table instead. *I figured this was going to be an interrogation or a lecture. Wonder how long it will take her to warn me about the dangers of drinking and drugs? Boring!*

"I'm happy to hear you say that everything is going well, Callie, honey," Flora commented. She reached to affectionately pat one of the girl's hands. "I'm also pleased that you agreed to have dinner with me this afternoon. It's been a long time since just the two of us have done anything together."

Callie looked up from the table. She intently studied Flora's smiling face. She had to acknowledge that it had indeed been a long time since *just* her and Grandma Flora had spent time together. Most times, Katie Rose and/or Mason had been along. Callie did have to admit that it felt nice to be singled out by Flora for a change. "I'm glad you invited me to have dinner with you, grandma," she stated with fondness.

"Me too, sweetie," Flora gushed. She gave Callie's hand a slight, assuring squeeze before she released it. Flora sat back in her chair. "So tell me all about what's going on in your life now. Tell me about school, about your new friend Julie, about any special boys that might be pursuing my beautiful granddaughter. I want to hear it all, Callie." Flora encouraged with a wide, enthusiastic grin.

Callie was mystified. *This dinner was merely going to be a boring lecture, from yet another adult, but Grandma Flora only seems to be interested in talking and spending time alone with me.* This made Callie feel special. It had been awhile since anyone had made her feel this way.

*But should I trust this? Everyone else in my life that* supposedly *cares about me has let me down. Can I trust that Flora won't as well?*

Flora took note of the distressed look on the girl's face. "Callie, honey, is everything okay? Why are you so quiet all the sudden? Did I say something to upset you?" She questioned with concern.

"No. I'm fine, grandma," Callie declared with a slight smile. "It's just...well...with my mom and dad still separated...I...I don't have too many people caring what is going on in my life right now," she admitted. "It means a lot that you do."

"Always, honey," Flora pledged. She reached to pat Callie's hand once more. "I love you, Callie. I'm sorry that it's been so long since we've spent time together like this. We need to change that, okay? How about we plan on getting together once a week from now on? How would that be? Think you can squeeze your old grandma into your schedule?"

"I'll sure give it my best shot," Callie agreed without hesitation, her grin widening.

"Okay. That's all settled then. Now, why don't you bring me up to date on your life? Any special guys I should know about?"

Callie was amazed to find that she was totally relaxing. As the waiter came back with their dinner orders – Callie had ordered prime rib with steak fries and Flora had ordered roasted chicken breast with a vegetable medley of carrots, cauliflower and broccoli – Callie began telling Flora all about her life. It felt nice to be able to talk to someone and have them truly listen and be interested.

Her Grandma Flora was coming across as an older friend. She was not coming across as some judgmental adult, like all the other adults in Callie's life. Every other adult only seemed to want to give Callie a sermon about how she should be living her life.

After conversing some more and sharing a meal, Callie felt so comfortable talking to Flora that she dared to ask, "Grandma Flora, if I tell you something, will you promise not to tell my mom and dad?"

*More secrets!* However, Flora was eager to hear what Callie might have to say. *Maybe she's about to confide something important. Like about her drinking or smoking marijuana. Callie needs to believe that she can trust me to keep her secrets.*

Flora stopped eating and she sat her fork and knife down on the side of her plate. She made full eye contact with Callie and attempted to assure her, "I can keep a secret, Callie. You can tell me anything. I promise that I won't tell your mom or dad. Now, what is it that you want to share?"

"I have a date to the senior prom next weekend," she confessed with a somewhat wicked smile. Callie's eyes were sparkling with mischief. "That's why Julie and I are going to the mall tonight. She is going to help me pick out a dress."

"And obviously neither your mom nor your dad know that you are going to the prom," Flora stated rather matter-of-factly.

"No, they don't," Callie confessed, taking a drink of her iced tea. The waiter had just refilled both of their drinks for the third time. He was swift to refresh them each time he saw the glass was half full.

Her eyes were closely studying Flora. The smile on Callie's face had disappeared. Her eyes had become serious.

*Callie's on guard now. This is a test. She is waiting to see if I will lecture her or go back on my word and threaten to tell Mary Julia or Jonathan what she plans to do.* Flora concluded.

She casually picked her fork and knife back up and took another bite of food. She looked down at her plate as she chewed up a bite of chicken. She looked back up at Callie as she lifted her glass and washed her food down with some water. Then Flora stunned Callie by asking with nonchalance, "So who is the lucky guy?" She had a wide smile on her face too, as if she approved of Callie's wayward actions. "Are you secretly dating a senior, Callie? Have you been holding out on me?" she further insinuated.

"No," Callie was quick to contradict. "I'm not dating a senior. I'm not dating anyone. There have been several boys in my class who have asked me out, but I'm not interested in any of them. I like to string them along and make them think I am. Mason is the only guy I would truly be interested in dating. But, as you know, he is connected to the hip with Rebecca right now. So, I'm going to the prom with his friend Ralph." She paused and then unexpectedly added, "Mason *is* attracted to me though. This is a fact. We...we kind of made out in his kitchen not too long ago."

"You...you what?" Flora asked with some shock. She almost choked on her food. She took another large swig of her water. "When?" Flora had a hard time believing that this had occurred.

Flora did not doubt that Mason was attracted to Callie. She had seen this with her own eyes on various occasions. Nevertheless, Mason had always fought this attraction.

*He's always believed that Callie was too young for him. Has Callie managed to break down his defenses? If so, how?*

"Relax, Gran. Nothing much happened. Mason pushed me away as usual. So, I went and got drunk and high. The next thing I knew I was in the hospital having my stomach pumped. Real fun night!"

"That was the same day that you found your mom with another man, right?" Flora hesitantly interrogated.

"Yeah. I don't want to talk about that," Callie asserted with haste. She averted her eyes and picked at the food she had left on her plate. Flora could tell that the mere mention of this incident had upset Callie.

"Okay. That's fine," Flora conceded. The last thing that she wished to accomplish was shutting down their dialogue. Flora was more than willing to sidestep any difficult issues that Callie wished to avoid.

*She's brought up the drug and alcohol issue. How do I talk to her about this without sounding preachy?* "Callie, before I got out of college, there was a lot of partying that was going on. So I know all about drinking and doing drugs," Flora acknowledged, eating some more of her vegetable medley.

"You did drugs, grandma?" Callie asked, her eyes wide with wonder. She absentmindedly dropped her fork on the corner of her plate. Some people at surrounding tables looked over to see what had caused the small disturbance in the hushed restaurant. Flora jumped a little, but Callie did not even seem to notice the clatter it had made. She was transfixed by what her Grandma Flora had alluded to doing. She could not even begin to imagine her Grandma Flora doing drugs. "No way!"

"Yes...I did experiment some," Flora confessed. "I also used to drink. Quite a lot as a matter of fact."

"Did you get drunk?" Callie inquired with marvel.

"Yes. On occasion," Flora admitted.

"I'm sorry, Gran," Callie said with a chuckle. "But I can't picture you drunk and stoned. It doesn't compute."

"No. Not now. Because it's something I decided to stop doing a long time ago, Callie. It's hard to make that stand though. Especially when it seems like all of your friends are drinking and doing drugs. It's even harder when you are young, like you are, with parents who have problems of their own. Drinking and doing drugs can become an escape, can't it? Isn't that what you were trying to do that night you had to have your stomach pumped? Weren't you only trying to escape?"

The amused smile that Callie's face had been donning disappeared. Her eyes grew solemn. *Is this where the lecture comes in?* Callie stared at her Grandma Flora's face. She remained silent.

Flora noted the change in Callie's demeanor immediately. The last thing she wanted to do was put the girl on the defense. "I'm sorry, Callie, honey," she apologized. Then she went on to add, "I didn't mean to sound as if I was interrogating you. I'm sure every other adult in your life has already done that. All I was trying to say is that I can understand why things got out of hand that night. I could even understand if you told me that you've used drugs and drank since then. If I was your age and had all the crazy stuff going on in my life that you do, I'd probably be tempted to do the same thing."

"So are you telling me that it would be okay if I was still drinking and doing drugs?" Callie questioned with obvious doubt in her eyes.

*So how do you answer that one, Flora?* Once more, she took the time to leisurely consume some more food and water before she replied. "I'm not telling you anything. I'm merely saying that I don't intend to judge you. Adults have judged your actions enough. I want to be here for you...no matter what you might or might not do. I'm not here to tell you what is right or wrong; that's your parents' job. I only want to...well... quite frankly, I'd like to be your friend. What do you say, Callie? Would you like to have me as your friend?"

"Have you as my *friend*? Let me get this straight," Callie began to clarify, quickly chewing up the last of her steak. "You say you don't intend to judge me. So does that mean you won't lecture me, and you won't go running to my mom and dad if I tell you something they should know?"

"Yes. That's right," Flora agreed. "I won't break your confidence...no matter what. You can talk to me about anything, Callie, and I promise to keep it just between the two of us. You can fully trust me with all your secrets."

"Why?" Callie questioned with skepticism.

"Why what?"

"Why do you all the sudden want to be my friend? Why would you keep things from my parents for me? Why should I trust you?" Callie scrutinized.

"That's fairly simple to answer," Flora said with a smile. "I want to be your friend because you are a beautiful, interesting young woman. And more importantly, because I love you. As far as keeping things from your parents, that isn't something I like to do. Nevertheless, I will. Why? Because you aren't comfortable talking to your parents right now, but you still need an ear. I want to be that ear for you, Callie. As far as trust goes, why do you feel that you can't trust me?"

"It's not that I don't trust you," Callie confessed, pushing her nearly empty plate off to the side. There were still some French fries left. "It's just...well...everyone I trusted has let me down. I guess I wonder if you will too."

"Everyone...meaning your parents and Katie Rose?"

"Yes. Do you know what happened with Katie Rose? Did she tell you?"

"No, she did not tell me what happened. She did mention that you had made new friends and that the two of you weren't spending as much time together. I kind of figured, considering how close the two of you have always been, that there had been some type of falling out. Do you want to talk about it? As I said, I'm more than willing to listen," she reiterated. Flora placed the last of her vegetable medley in her mouth. Then she too pushed her plate aside.

"Maybe another time," Callie told her with a dismissive smile.

"Another time? Does that mean we'll be getting together again next week for dinner?" Flora probed. The waiter returned to fill their glasses one last time, leave their check on the table, and to clear away their dishes. The two ladies hardly acknowledged his presence. The were entirely focused on one another.

Callie laughed then. "You're serious about this friend thing, aren't you?"

"*Very* serious!" Flora stressed. "So what do you say, Callie?" she inquired. Flora offered her hand for a confirming handshake.

"Yes. I could use another friend," Callie agreed. She took Flora's hand and shook it in confirmation.

Flora stood. She pulled Callie to her feet and engulfed her in a tight, affirming embrace. "It's good to have you for a friend, Callie. I look forward to us spending more time together. For now though, it's about time we left to go and pick up Julie. The time slipped away. We've been in this restaurant for nearly two hours."

Callie nodded her agreement. She was slow to separate from her grandma's hug. Flora glanced at the check and pulled some money from her change purse – enough to cover the food, plus a nice tip. She laid the cash on the table on top of the check. The two meandered away from the table toward the door. Callie affectionately put her arm around Flora's shoulder, and Flora wrapped hers around Callie as well.

Flora pulled the girl close to her side. The two headed to the restroom before they exited the restaurant. Flora had never felt closer to Callie, nor had Callie to Flora. *I intend to keep it this way*, Flora resolved. *I'll become Callie's friend, and I'll help her. I may not have gotten all the answers that I wanted yet, but I will in time. You're going to be okay, Callie. I'll see to that.*

# Chapter 26

# *The Prom*

"Wow!" Julie commented with awe. She was appraising Callie with a careful eye from head to toe. "You look like a movie star who's on her way to one of those big award shows. You look spectacular, Callie. You really do. I'm jealous!"

"Thanks, Julie. I couldn't have done it without you," Callie acknowledged with gratitude. She flashed Julie a wide appreciative smile and gave her a slight, grateful hug.

Callie did look breathtakingly beautiful. She was wearing a long, form-fitting, strapless, periwinkle, formal gown. The dress complimented her stunning blue eyes.

As Callie turned to show off the soft chiffon, the gown flowed gently and made her look as if she was an angel. The dress also complimented all of the luscious curves of Callie's body. She had finished her wardrobe by slipping silver sandals with delicate straps upon her feet.

Callie had painstakingly swept her long, blond hair up off her neck. She had left only a few curls dangling down just past her shoulders and had also carefully freed a few wisps of hair to loosely frame her innocent, but beautiful, face. She had set her hair with a sparkling hairspray, which left it gleaming with shine.

Callie's makeup was flawless. She had lightly applied foundation to her entire face and modestly stroked blush on both cheekbones. She had colored her lips with a pretty pink lipstick. She had painted her fingernails and toenails with an almost identical color.

Last but not least, Callie had set her concentration solely on her eyes. She had used a black eye pencil to outline just above her eyelashes, had applied a periwinkle shade of eye shadow, and had finished by generously applying mascara to her long curled eyelashes. The perfect combination of eye makeup and the coloring of the dress made her eyes look absolutely magnificent. It was impossible not to notice them.

No one would have guessed that Callie was not quite fifteen years old. Most anyone would have thought her to be at least eighteen.

"Well, Ralph is supposed to be here in about fifteen minutes. Do you want another beer before he gets here?" Julie offered.

"Nah. I better not," Callie replied. She was tempted to drink another can, but she had already had two. Callie also did not want to mess up her lipstick or chance spilling any beer on her dress.

Callie and Julie went into the living room. They stood looking out the front window. Ralph thought he was coming to Callie's house to pick her up.

He had no idea that Callie's parents did not have the faintest clue that Callie was going to the prom. Callie's plan, when she saw Ralph pull into the driveway, was to be out the front door before he possibly had any chance of coming inside. Callie had planned everything right down to the minutest detail.

*Everything is going to be absolutely perfect!* she was determined. *There is no way Mason won't notice me tonight. I'll take him away from Rebecca. I have to. The two of us are meant to be together.*

* * * *

Ralph had barely climbed from his car when he saw Callie step out of the house. She quickly closed the door behind her. Ralph stared at her with breathless admiration.

*Jesus, Ralph! How'd you ever get so lucky! Is that really Callie, or a picturesque illusion?! She's so lovely that she doesn't look real!*

"Well, are you going to stand there all evening with your mouth hanging open, Ralph?" Callie asked after several moments had passed. She was secretly pleased by his goggle-mouthed expression. Callie only hoped that Mason would be as dazed by her.

"Um…it's just…" Ralph began to mumble as he ambled toward her. "Good Lord, Callie! You look amazing! I won't be able to take my eyes off of you. Who would want to?"

"Thanks, Ralph," she said with a dazzling smile that made his legs weak. "You look nice too."

Ralph genuinely did look nice. He was wearing a striking black tuxedo, and he had had his nappy red hair cut close to his scalp. He looked neat and tidy, but Ralph still could not be described as handsome.

This did not matter to Callie tonight though. After all, Ralph was merely a means to an end for her. And that end was Mason.

"I…I have something for you," Ralph stuttered.

He held out the corsage he had brought for her. It had tiny white roses with the edges delicately tipped in periwinkle. The corsage was nestled in iridescent ribbons that perfectly reflected the color of Callie's dress.

Ralph took a gentle hold on Callie's arm. He slid the wrist corsage with care over her hand. "Do you want to go back inside? Don't your parents want to take pictures of you? Of the two of us together? My parents will want copies."

"Um…no," Callie unexpectedly answered. She placed a restraining hand against Ralph's chest. "Actually my parents aren't even home."

"You're kidding me, right?!" Ralph stated with apparent surprise. He glanced from Callie to the closed door.

"Nope," Callie tersely replied. "Can we go, Ralph? You're taking *me* to the prom, not my parents; right?!" she pointed out.

She sounded a little irritable. Callie did not wait for Ralph's response. She had pushed him aside and was making her way down the steps.

*Geez! Callie's parents sure must be strange*, Ralph could not help but conclude.

He hurried with Callie along the sidewalk toward the car. His parents were going to be upset. They had wanted him to bring Callie back to the house, so they could take pictures of the two of them together. Ralph had assured them that he would ask Callie's parents for copies of the pictures he was sure they would take.

*Don't girls' mothers always take loads of pictures of them before dances? Oh well, evidently Callie's didn't.*

Ralph rushed to the passenger side of the car and swung open the car door for Callie. He watched as she climbed inside. Then he courteously closed the door behind her. Callie looked like a princess, so Ralph intended to treat her like one.

*Who cares about having dumb pictures taken? I get to spend time alone with my beautiful princess now!* Ralph noted with excitement. He climbed into the car with Callie, and the two of them set off.

\* \* \* \*

The senior prom was being held in the Crystal Ballroom at the Hyatt. Ralph debonairly offered Callie's his arm. They strolled through the hotel corridor toward the ballroom.

People were watching them. They were mostly looking at Callie. Ralph held his head high. It made Ralph feel proud to know he was her escort.

*If I never have another date in my life, I'll never forget tonight and the fact that Callie came to the prom with me.*

As they came to the closed double doors of the ballroom, Ralph looked at Callie with a wide gleeful smile. He inquired with noted admiration, "Ready to make our grand entrance, princess?"

"Why certainly, sir," Callie answered in kind. There was a dazzling, eager smile on her face.

Ralph gazed with longing at Callie's beautiful, happy face for a few long moments. His heart began to race. He hated to open the door and take her inside the ballroom. Ralph liked having Callie all to himself.

"Ralph, you are going to take me inside, aren't you?" Callie inquired with anxiousness. This put an abrupt end to Ralph's obsessive thoughts.

"Oh, yeah…of course," he stammered.

Ralph reached out for one of the door handles. He pushed the handle and swept the large door open with eagerness. Ralph stood back a step and watched as Callie sashayed through the open doorway. He dashed after her to once again join her side.

# ILLUSIONS

\* \* \* \*

"Wow! It sure looks great in here, doesn't it? They did a great job on the decorations," Ralph stated.

He was trying to make light conversation. The ballroom was ornately decorated throughout. There were colorful streamers, depicting the school colors, and other symbols of their high school and of the senior class.

Callie had not even noticed the decorations, though they were aplenty. She was centered on Mason. Their eyes had met and locked nearly as soon as she entered the room. She gave Mason the prettiest, inviting smile and headed in his direction. Ralph was totally forgotten. He struggled to keep up with Callie's speedy long-legged gait across the large ballroom floor.

Mason still had not been able to take his eyes off her, and this pleased Callie immensely. Ralph, however, was not at all pleased to discover what – *or rather who* – held Callie's rapt attention. Callie had always had an enormous crush on his friend. However, Mason was not the one that had asked Callie to the prom.

Not only had Ralph asked Callie to be his date, but she was here with him now. Ralph did not intend to let Callie forget this. Her infatuation with Mason was not going to spoil the evening. Ralph was determined of this.

As they drew to a stop directly in front of Mason and Rebecca, Ralph possessively circled Callie's waist with his arm. He pulled her in close to his side. With a wide, proud smile Ralph greeted, "Hi, Mason. Hi, Rebecca. How are you guys this *fine* evening?"

"We're great," Mason rather gruffly answered for both of them. There was not a trace of a smile on his face.

It was hard for Mason to force his eyes away from Callie. *She looks absolutely beautiful! Fourteen, Mason! Callie is lovely, but she is still only fourteen!* However, despite Mason's newfound conviction, his eyes still gravitated back to poring over Callie.

Callie's eyes returned his admiring stare. *Mason has always been so handsome! But in that tux, he's an absolute hunk! I'm more in love with him than ever.* Pains of longing clutched relentlessly at her rapidly beating heart.

Ralph did not mind that Mason could not take his eyes off of Callie. It only made him feel more fulfilled that Callie was with him. However, it did bother Ralph – *quite a bit* – that Callie was so smitten by Mason. He did not intend to share his precious Callie with anyone tonight. Ralph gave her a little squeeze to remind her that he was still there by her side.

"You look nice, Rebecca," Callie heard Ralph say.

"Thanks, Ralph. It's nice that *someone* is noticing," she replied rather harshly.

Mason did not even seem to detect it. Callie, however, did take her eyes off of Mason for a second. She wanted to check out her competition. Callie was met with a cold hard stare from Rebecca.

Callie had to admit that Rebecca did look somewhat attractive. Regardless, she did not feel even remotely threatened by Rebecca. For one thing, Rebecca was dressed much more modestly than Callie. She had chosen to wear an old fashioned, floor length, black evening gown, which was amply adorned with sequins.

Rebecca's gown somewhat complimented her modest bust line. However, its high neck and silky mid length sleeves managed to cover almost all of her freckled flesh. Rebecca had had her hair, nails and makeup professionally done. Her long, auburn hair was styled atop her head in a flattering French roll.

*Rebecca looks prettier than usual, but I look stunning*, Callie rather conceitedly concluded. An evil grin was playing at the corners of her mouth.

"You look great too, Mason," Callie dared to praise with bright, devilish eyes and a wide engaging smile.

"Thank you," he politely, yet curtly replied.

Rebecca was studying both Mason and Callie with noticeable disdain. *What a jerk! I'm standing right here beside him, and Mason's tongue is practically hanging out over another woman. Or actually, he's salivating over a trashy little girl, who is trying to act like a woman. Her body obviously is that of a woman though. It all comes down to sex! I'm glad I'm still a virgin and haven't gone all the way with Mason. That clearly would have been a huge mistake! He obviously doesn't care about me at all.*

Mason looked at Rebecca for the first time in several minutes. He said, "Well, I guess we should be taking a seat. The band is supposed to start playing in a few minutes."

"Fine," Rebecca tersely agreed.

Rebecca took a tight clutch on Mason's arm and led him away. She did not say a parting goodbye to either Ralph or Callie. With a sense of urgency, Rebecca pulled Mason toward an almost full table off to the side of the dance floor.

"I guess we should find a seat also," Ralph suggested with an encouraging smile. He began urging Callie away in the opposite direction.

*I want her as far away from Mason as I can get her.*

"R..Ralph," Callie opened her mouth to protest.

She was swept farther and farther away by Ralph. Callie watched over her shoulder and saw more and more distance being put between Mason and herself. "Where in the world are you taking us? Out in the hall?"

*I'd like to take us out of here altogether and up to a hotel room*, Ralph inappropriately planned. However, he continued to lead Callie to a table across the room. *We'll stay here at the prom for a while and have a few slow dances. Then...after...oh, I can hardly wait, my sweet, beautiful Callie, for what will come after.* Ralph's lewd thoughts were causing him to become overly aroused.

They approached the table he had intended to take them to. Ralph slid a chair out for Callie. He told her, "I'm going to go and get us some punch. Have a seat. Jay, Martin, this is Callie," he addressed two of the guys sitting at the table.

"Hi, Callie." They greeted almost in unison. There were silly, lopsided smiles on their faces, and both these guys were crudely surveying her body.

"Sit down, Callie. We'd be glad to have you join u..u..us," Jay stuttered and jolted as his prom date painfully kicked his ankle. *Ow! I guess she didn't like me checking Callie out!*

"Jay, why don't you go and get us some punch to drink as well," his girlfriend half ordered. "*You* especially could use something cold to drink."

"Okay," he was fast to agree. Jay did not wish to incite his date's wrath again.

Jay's ankle was already throbbing. He stumbled to a standing position as Callie begrudgingly sat down. Jay dared not look at Callie again, as he hobbled away at Ralph's side. The two guys made their way toward one of the refreshment tables.

"Man, how did an ugly mug like you get lucky enough to have a beauty like that come to the prom with *you*?" Jay candidly teased as he and Ralph joined a line to get some drinks.

"Oh, believe me, I know that I'm *very* lucky that she agreed to come to the prom with me," Ralph professed with a proud smile.

"So do you *also* intend to get lucky with her after this dumb dance is over?" Jay pried. "That's what prom night is really all about, isn't it?"

"Well, let's say I'm hopeful," Ralph stated with more assurance than he actually felt. A slight grin was on his face. *If I can kiss Callie and touch her a little, I'll be in heaven.*

"Want to make it a sure thing?" Jay strangely asked.

"Sure I would. But how do I do that?" Ralph questioned. A look of confusion was on his face now.

*Now, maybe if I was Mason...it would be a different story.*

"When the band has their first break, walk out to my car with me, and I'll show you," Jay secretively told him.

"Okay," Ralph agreed with slight uncertainty. Jay had peaked his curiosity.

They made their way up to the refreshment table then and proceeded to gather the drinks for themselves and their dates.

\* \* \* \*

The first several songs that the band played were fast ones. Hardly anyone danced. However, when the band launched into their first slow song, several couples took the floor. Ralph arose and asked Callie if she would like to dance.

Callie had spied Mason and Rebecca taking the floor, so she readily accepted Ralph's invitation. Ralph held out his hand, and Callie took a tight grasp of it. She leapt up from the table. Callie made a beeline across the floor, dragging Ralph along behind her.

*Geez, she is going to pull my arm out of socket!* "Hey, Callie, where's the fire?" he questioned. Ralph rushed to keep up with Callie as she darted in and out between couples. *Where in the world is she heading?* Ralph's uncertainty was only temporary.

Callie abruptly stopped her forward charge near Mason and Rebecca. She reached out one of her long arms and scooped Ralph into a tight embrace. He had not liked it that she had pulled him across the floor to be near Mason.

However, Ralph was quick to forget, and forgive, her when Callie began seductively kissing the side of his neck, as they swayed in an easy rhythm to the music. The close proximity of Callie's perfect body and the feel of her luscious lips touching his skin was arousing Ralph to the point of senselessness.

"Callie," he gasped, out of breath. With haste, Ralph began kissing her neck, the side of her face and the side of her mouth. Callie pulled away before he could make full contact with her lips. She was pleased when she saw that Mason was watching them with annoyed, disgusted eyes. He did not seem to be concentrating on Rebecca at all.

*Yes!*

Ralph could not help but notice where Callie's attention had strayed. *So her teasing is all merely a ploy to make Mason jealous again.* He was surprised to find he was angry. With force, he spun Callie around so that her back was to Mason. Ralph drew her close. He half demanded in a quiet growl, "Give me another kiss! On the lips this time!"

"Ralph, don't be a jerk!" Callie chastised through gritted teeth. She shoved away from him.

"Yeah, that's me! Just a dumb jerk!" he snapped, raising his voice. Ralph grabbed hold of the top of Callie's arm and began hauling her off the dance floor. *You won't play me for a fool!*

"Ralph, let go!" Callie demanded as she struggled to free herself from his ironclad clasp. "You're hurting me!"

"Too damn bad!" she was shocked to hear him snarl. "We are going to sit the rest of this dance out. And we will sit out all of them if you are dancing with me, *and kissing me*, to make Mason jealous. It stops now, Callie! You're here with me! Not Mason! I asked you! Not Mason! You will pay attention to me! Not Mason! Got it!"

Callie was flabbergasted, and more than a little upset, by Ralph's violent demeanor. She had used him before to make Mason jealous, and Ralph had not reacted in this hostile manner.

She was fast to decipher that she did not want to do anything to make him even angrier.

"I'm sorry, Ralph," Callie apologized in a quiet voice. "You're right; I am here with you. I'll start acting like it from now on. Now, could you please let go of my arm? You really *are* hurting me!"

Ralph gave Callie's arm one last, tight squeeze. Then he released it from his brutal grasp. "Head to our table and take a seat!" he barked. Ralph pointed to their table. It was only a short distance beyond.

Callie took a seat at the table and watched Ralph dejectedly plop in the chair beside her. He was giving her the meanest stare. She wondered if she had made a big mistake by agreeing to come to the prom with him.

*Damn! I can't let this idiot guy spoil everything for me. I need to find a way to get near Mason without Ralph knowing.*

## Chapter 27

# *Bad Judgment*

The band played several more slow songs during their first set, but Ralph and Callie did not dance again. Instead, Ralph possessively held Callie's hand and watched her like a hawk. He had a stern look on his face the whole time. Callie was uncomfortable and annoyed by Ralph's bizarre dictatorial behavior.

He was watching her closely, so she did nothing to arouse his fury. Callie merely sat there. She allowed Ralph to continue holding her hand, and she watched many others dance. Callie was relieved when the band announced they were taking their first break.

*Now maybe I can send Ralph away to get me another drink. Or maybe I'll go to the bathroom. Anything to get away from him for awhile!*

The thought had barely crossed Callie's mind when Jay announced in a quiet voice, "You know, I have cocktails in my car. Would anyone care to go out with me while the band has their break?" It was strange that he was looking directly at Ralph.

"Yeah, I'll go," Ralph agreed with eagerness, much to Callie's astonishment.

*I had no idea Ralph drank.*

He rose to his feet. Callie was relieved that Ralph, at long last, had released the death grip he had had on her hand. Ralph leaned over Callie's shoulder. He rather harshly warned, "I *will* be back. Don't cause any trouble while I'm gone."

A drink of alcohol sounded much too tempting to Callie right now. Regardless, she staunchly remained in her seat. "I'll be right here when you get back," she attempted to lie. Callie plastered a fake smile on her face.

*I seriously doubt that!* Ralph concluded, but did not verbalize. He turned and raced after Jay toward the exit doors.

\* \* \* \*

Callie waited with strained patience for several long moments. She wanted to make certain that Ralph was not going to come back right away. She arose and pretended to be heading toward the restrooms. Instead, Callie began making her way across the room and over to Mason's table.

He was sitting at the table alone. Her heart began to race with excitement. Mason had his back to her, so he did not notice her approach. *Wonder where Rebecca has gone? Who cares! Mason is alone. This is my chance to make my move!*

Callie sashayed forward toward Mason. She was in an eager rush. She reached out and touched Mason's shoulder to gain his attention. Callie was amazed to discover that her hand was slightly shaking. Mason felt Callie's trembling hand on his shoulder. He knew, without seeing, that it was Callie.

Mason turned to face her and was stunned once more by how beautiful Callie looked. *Beautiful and much older! But, it's all illusion. She's still the same little girl.* Mason stubbornly tried to reign in his overwhelming attraction and forbidden desires.

"Where's Ralph?" he asked in a gruff voice. Mason's eyes made a quick sweep of the room.

"He went outside with one of the guys at our table to drink. I've sworn off liquor, so I stayed behind. Where's Rebecca? Why'd she leave you here all by yourself?" *I wouldn't have! I wouldn't let you out of my sight if I were your date...as I should have been!*

"Rebecca went to the bathroom. She'll be back in just a second. Are you making up stories, or did Ralph really go outside to drink?" Mason questioned with skepticism. He found it hard to believe that Ralph was outside drinking. Mason had never seen him so much as touch any kind of alcoholic beverage.

"No, I'm not making up stories," Callie was swift to assure him. She sounded slightly irritable. "It's out of character for Ralph, but he is acting really strange tonight. He has me a little scared. Did you see the way he jerked me off the dance floor earlier? He may be jealous of you. He can see how attracted you are to me."

*So why on earth can't you?!*

"Or he is sick to death of being used by you," Mason correctly guessed. "You have absolutely no business being here tonight, Callie. So if Ralph is being mean to you, then you are only getting a little of what you have coming to you. You shouldn't play games with people. I keep telling you that, but you have yet to listen. So maybe if Ralph is nasty to you tonight, it will finally wise you up. Here's hoping."

"I'll second that," Callie heard Rebecca say as she slipped past her.

Mason stood and gallantly pulled out Rebecca's chair. Rebecca seated herself, and Mason pushed her chair back up to the table. "What happened, Callie? Did Ralph wise up and run out on you? No one in his or her right mind would blame him if he has. Just don't expect Mason to take up the slack now. He's here with me, and he wants nothing to do with you tonight. Right, Mason?" she verified.

Mason was a little taken aback by Rebecca's viciousness toward Callie. Nevertheless, he was glad to have her back by his side. It gave him added strength and a genuine reason to send Callie away.

"That pretty much sums things up," Callie was crushed to hear Mason assent. "If Ralph has run out on you or if he *really* is drinking, call your parents. Tell them you need a ride home, Callie. I'm sure they'd be more than happy to come and get you."

Mason sat down in a chair beside Rebecca. He dismissively turned away from Callie. He appeared to be focusing all his attention on Rebecca.

"Bye, Callie," Rebecca snarled with a satisfied smile. She raised a hand to mockingly wave goodbye to the girl.

Callie was so furious she wondered if steam was pouring out of her ears. She longed to grab Rebecca by the neck and strangle her until she was dead. Instead, she spun on her heels and practically jogged away from Mason and Rebecca. Hot, dejected tears began to burn Callie's eyes. She dashed into the bathroom to hide, and to nurse her wounded broken heart.

*What went wrong?* Callie disappeared into one of the stalls. She dropped her head into her lap and began to sob.

\* \* \* \*

Callie reemerged from the bathroom countless minutes later. She was not surprised to find Ralph waiting for her with impatience in the hallway by the bathrooms.

"It's about time you came out of there," he barked with notable irritation. "What took you so long?"

"I....I was...Ralph, could you please take me home? I'm not feeling well," Callie relayed.

She was not feeling well. Mason's rejection had broken not only Callie's heart, but it had seemed to crush her very spirit. She was miserably exhausted, and she had a monster headache. Callie's boundless tears had also ruined her flawless makeup. She was more than ready to leave the dance hall. She wanted to be dropped off at Julie's, so she could drink and smoke herself into oblivion and attempt to forget all about tonight.

*I need to somehow forget all about Mason too*, Callie resolved. She was embittered about being hurt over and over by his constant rejections. *I'm through with Mason once and for all.*

Ralph did not need to ask Callie what was wrong or why she wanted to leave. He had already talked to Rebecca and Mason. They had filled him in on Callie's latest encounter with them. It angered Ralph that Callie's tear-streaked cheeks and bloodshot eyes where courtesy of Mason's denial.

*She wants Mason – and only Mason! Coming to the prom with me was merely a ploy in Callie's game to get him. Or at least that's what she thought. She'll soon find out otherwise.*

"Look, this is my senior prom. I don't want to leave this soon. Jay has rented a room upstairs for a party afterwards, so I'll take you up there. You can rest for a while. You can even have a beer or a bourbon and coke to help you relax. Then maybe I'll get in at least one more dance before the night is over. What do you say?"

Callie wanted to say no, but she was tired. She did not feel like arguing or arousing Ralph's discontentment again. "Okay," she meekly agreed. Overly weary, Callie linked her arm to Ralph's. She leaned against him for support. "Can we go?"

"Sure," Ralph agreed. There was a smile oddly playing at the corners of his mouth. He eagerly led Callie away.

\* \* \* \*

Mason ran into Jay in the bathroom. He was still curious about what Ralph had been doing with him. As they washed their hands at side by side sinks, Mason pryingly questioned, "So Jay, I hear that you and Ralph were having cocktails a little while ago out in the parking lot. How'd you talk Ralph into drinking? I've never seen him indulge before, and we've been friends for years."

"Um...well, truth be told, Ralphie didn't go outside with me to drink. He went outside to get party favors for that hot little number he brought to the dance. I rented a room at this hotel for my girl and myself for later, and Ralph is using it now to be with Ms. Hottie. Lucky son of a gun! I was glad to help him out," Jay freely confessed with a wide, envious grin.

Mason took a second to let this alarming information entirely settle in. "Let me get this straight," he verified. "You're telling me that Ralph took Callie up to your hotel room to have sex with her. What party favors did he get from you? Alcohol? Drugs? He isn't planning on getting Callie drunk or stoned and taking advantage of her, is he?" Mason questioned with noticeable disbelief. Callie had told him that Ralph was behaving totally out of character tonight. *Should I have listened to her?!*

"Oh come on, man, get real," Jay said with an evil, cockeyed smile. "That little chick was asking for it big time. So anything Ralph is doing shouldn't come as any surprise to her. I only gave him something to move the process along a little easier."

"That chick...as you call her...is a fourteen year old girl! Ralph has no business having sex with her. That's statutory rape! How long have they been gone? What's the room number?!" Mason demanded to know. He was beginning to sound hysterical.

Mason bounded toward Jay and grabbed him tightly by the lapels of his tuxedo. "Tell me now, Jay! I'm not playing around! I'll pound you into the ground!"

"Okay! Okay!" Jay surrendered with haste.

Jay was small in frame. He realized that Mason could indeed 'pound him into the ground'. "I didn't realize the little looker was a friend of yours, and I sure as hell had no idea she was that young. She looks a lot older. Anyway, they've been gone about fifteen minutes. They're in room 605. I'd leave now if I were you, because I'm sure Ralph isn't planning on wasting any time."

Mason jerked his hands free of Jay. He swiveled on his heels and dashed out of the bathroom. *Crap, Callie! What mess have you gotten yourself into this time?!* Mason sprinted across the room toward the exit doors. He had gotten only a short distance when he almost collided with Rebecca.

"Whoa, Mason! Where are you running off to?" she inquired with dismay.

She had drinks in both hands, which she had barely managed to keep from spilling. Rebecca had been making her way back to their table with punch for both of them. She had thought Mason would already be there, having come from the bathroom. Rebecca had not expected to find him running across the room.

"Rebecca, I don't have time to explain right now," Mason curtly told her. "Callie is in trouble, and I've got to go and help her. I'll be back."

"Callie?!" Rebecca asked in disbelief.

Mason endeavored to go around Rebecca, but she placed herself in his path once more. "Mason, stop!" she half pleaded. "That little girl needs to learn that she can't play games all of the time with people and not get into trouble. You need to stop being so obsessed with trying to protect her. You fall hook, line and sinker for her schemes. You need to stay here with me. Let's enjoy the prom, and let Callie suffer the consequences of her actions once and for all. Please listen to me, Mason! Stop being foolish!" If both of Rebecca's hands had not been full, she would have reached to clutch Mason's arms.

"I can't ignore this, Rebecca. Go back to the table and wait for me," Mason barked.

He darted around Rebecca. Mason proceeded to leave her behind without concern. Rebecca almost felt like bursting into tears. *Well, I guess this tells me once and for all exactly where I stand with Mason. He doesn't care about me at all. He's in love with that terrible girl, but he won't admit it. Well, I'm tired of being second best. I'm done!*

Dejected, Rebecca headed back toward the table. She gathered her purse, and she headed to the lobby. Rebecca was going to call a taxi to take her home.

\* \* \* \*

Mason fidgeted with nervousness. He was bouncing from one foot to the other as he impatiently waited for the elevator to reach the sixth floor. Much to his dismay, the elevator stopped on every floor. People were exiting and entering the elevator as leisurely as possible.

At last, he reached the sixth floor. Mason sprang out of the elevator as soon as the doors opened. He searched the directory numbers on the wall with urgency. The arrow for room 605 was pointed left. Mason raced off in that direction.

When he located the room, Mason charged toward the door. He pounded loudly on the door with both fists and shouted, "Open up, Ralph! Open this goddamn door right now, or I'll call the cops! What you're doing is rape! Open the damn door! Now!"

Only a moment later, although it seemed much longer, Ralph sheepishly opened the door. His tuxedo jacket was missing. His ruffled white shirt was jostled and buttoned haphazardly, and his hair was messed up.

Mason grabbed Ralph in a death hold around the waist. He almost hoisted him off his feet. Mason shoved Ralph backwards into the hotel room.

"Mason...," Ralph began to protest. A powerful blow to his jaw silenced him at once. It also sent Ralph sprawling backwards across the floor in pain.

"You stupid fool!" Mason chastised.

It was then that Mason noticed Callie lying upon one of the beds. The top half of her dress had been pulled down, exposing her strapless bra. She appeared to be unconscious.

Mason grabbed Ralph by his shirt collar. He started hoisting him off the floor. "What did you do to Callie, you crazy bastard?! Did you knock her out? Did you rape her?! What kind of a monster are you?! I'm going to kill your ass!"

Ralph was spurting blood from where his teeth had cut the inside of his mouth. He began to plead, "Please, Mason, stop!

Callie needs help. She passed out, and I couldn't get her to wake up. You need to let me go, and go see what you can do for Callie. I didn't do anything to her – Other than kiss her a little and start undressing her. Then she passed out cold. That's all that happened. I swear."

Mason did not want to release Ralph. He wanted to pound him into the ground. But Callie's needs were much more important than taking his vengeance on Ralph at this time. Mason released Ralph with a fierce shove. Ralph almost went sprawling on his butt again.

Mason turned his entire attention to Callie. He went over to the bed and carefully lifted her to a sitting position. Mason slipped her gown back over the top half of her body. Then he began to lightly shake her.

"Callie. Callie, it's me, Mason. Are you okay?"

She showed not even the minutest sign of response. Mason felt for Callie's pulse. He was very relieved when he could still feel her heart beating. Callie appeared to be in a very, very deep sleep, almost coma like.

"What the hell did you give her, Ralph?" Mason demanded to know. His fierce, menacing stare made Ralph uneasy.

*Mason would gladly beat me to a pulp.* Ralph could still taste the blood from the cut on his mouth. He did not want to do anything to further incite Mason's wrath.

"I don't know for sure what it was," Ralph truthfully confessed. "I got something from Jay that was supposed to relax Callie. I didn't know she would totally pass out and not wake up. I wasn't going to rape her. I only wanted to fool around a little. She owed me at least that much after the way she played me tonight. You know this is true, Mason," he tried to justify.

"You are a sick bastard! That's exactly what I know. She's only a kid playing a game. If you didn't like what she was doing, then you should have taken her home. I can't even stand to look at you. I can't believe I considered the likes of you a friend," Mason raved.

He stood, and he carefully pulled Callie to her feet beside him. "Help me get some cold cloths in the bathroom. I'll see if that brings Callie around. If not, I'm going to call an ambulance."

*Shit!* Ralph thought, but did not verbalize. *If Callie is not revived and Mason calls an ambulance, I could get into real*

227

*trouble for what I've done. If Mason says that I tried to rape Callie, then I could even be prosecuted.* Ralph merely wanted to make his escape. *I need to get out of here!*

"Look, man," Ralph started to negotiate. He was sweating. He was so nervous. "Why don't you take Callie into the bathroom, and try the cold cloth routine? I'll run downstairs and find Jay. I'll get him to come clean about what he gave me to give her. If you have to call an ambulance, they will probably need to know exactly what is in Callie's system. You know?"

Mason was swift to determine that what Ralph had said was true. Regardless, he suspected that Ralph was trying to pull one over on him. Nonetheless, Mason did not have the leisure to try and figure out what other motives Ralph might have for leaving.

"Okay," he agreed with reluctance. "But hurry back."

"Sure," Ralph tried to convincingly agree. He dashed toward the door.

Once Ralph was on the other side of the door in the hallway, he broke into a jog toward the elevator. Ralph did not aim to go and talk to Jay, but he did have every intention of leaving the hotel as quickly as possible. Ralph hoped that Callie would be okay. He had not meant to harm her. However, if Callie had relaxed and freely offered him sex, Ralph surely would not have turned her down.

*That would have been a lot different from rape,* he generously reasoned. *Mason will handle things. Callie will be fine. No one besides Mason and Jay even knew I was with Callie in that room. Jay won't squeal, because he's the one that gave me the drug. I'm outta here!*

# Chapter 28

# *Emergency*

Mason hauled Callie's limp and deadweight body into the bathroom. He grabbed the shower curtain and hoisted it back out of his way. He lifted Callie off her feet and stood her in the bathtub.

Mason climbed into the tub beside Callie. He struggled to keep her upright while he bent to fully turn on the cold-water faucet. As Mason arose, he hastily pulled upward on the knob that turned on the shower. A steady, immediate stream of frigid water flooded down upon both their bodies.

Mason shuddered in response. The ice cold water soaked into his hair, tuxedo jacket and shirt. It also splashed onto his trousers and dress shoes. Mason maneuvered Callie under the strong, chilling spray. She was facing him. Callie's head hung lifelessly, and she still showed no sign of response.

"Shit, Callie! Come on! You've got to wake up!" Mason pleaded. He had never felt so useless.

Mason began alternately patting one side of Callie's face and then the other. She was not coming around. Mason was beginning to get very frightened now. He had fully expected that Callie would spring to life again once he got her under some chilling water. On the contrary, the icy deluge was not even remotely fazing her. *What the hell did Ralph give her?! My God, what if she* doesn't *wake up?! No! I can't think like that.*

"Come on, Callie," Mason shouted. He vigorously shook her back and forth under the water. It was then that Mason noticed Callie's eyelids slightly fluttering. He pulled her forward a little.

229

The water was now streaming down Callie's back instead of hitting her in the face.

"Callie, can you hear me?!" Mason demanded to know. He cupped her chin with his hand and held up her head. It was with some relief that Mason saw Callie's eyes flicker open. However, they swiftly closed again.

*Maybe she is coming around. Be patient, Mason!* "Callie!" he called again. Mason patted her cheeks once more, a little harder. "Come on, baby. Can you talk to me? Huh?"

"M…m…mason," she mumbled in a very quiet voice.

Mason could scarcely tell if Callie had actually spoken his name. *Or was it merely a hopeful illusion on my part.* "Yes, Callie. It's me. It's Mason. You are going to be fine, okay? Can you try and stay awake for me? Can you do that? Can you talk to me some more?" he fired questions at her in panic.

Callie had begun shivering. Mason stepped back to the end of the bathtub. He persuaded Callie forward out of the nippy water. She struggled to open her eyes and talk to Mason once more. However, Callie discovered that her body seemed to be paralyzed for the most part. Her head seemed as if it was not even connected to her body. It felt as if it was floating somewhere high above.

*Have I been drinking? Am I stoned? Why am I so cold? Why is it so dark? Why can't I open my eyes and move? Oh, I feel so sick! So tired!* Callie slumped against Mason again. "Help," she managed to murmur in a weak desperate voice. Then she passed out once more.

"Crap!" Mason cursed. Callie's body had gone completely inert again. *This isn't working! I've got to go and call an ambulance! Callie could be dying! Where the hell is Ralph?! I don't even know what he gave her! Damn it!!!*

Mason effortlessly scooped Callie into his arms and climbed out of the tub. He whisked her back into the other room. Water from her drenched hair, body and dress soaked into Mason's clothing and also trailed behind them. It made small puddles along their path on the carpet.

Mason carefully laid Callie on the bed where he had initially found her. She looked pitiful, like a drowned rat. The hairdo, makeup and dress that had been so beautiful were all in terrible disarray.

Mason snatched up the phone. He called the main desk and told them he needed an ambulance, "ASAP!" He was prompt to explain that there was a young lady unconscious in room 605. Mason elaborated that she had been given some unknown drug, and he could not revive her. The clerk said the hotel would dispatch a doctor to the room immediately if one was available. He also assured Mason that he would call for an ambulance right away.

"Okay. Make it quick!" Mason pleaded, and he hung up the phone.

Mason stood looking down at Callie. He felt helpless. *What more can I do?!* He placed two fingers on the side of Callie's neck and was extremely relieved when he still could feel a pulse. However, it seemed to be getting weaker. *Maybe I'm only imaging this. Let's hope this is the case.*

The only other thing Mason could think to do was walk Callie around the room. Yet, Mason had no clue whether this was the right thing to do or not. Regardless, he pulled Callie to her feet again, and he started walking around the room. *God, please help her!* he fearfully prayed. He walked Callie around in circles. Mason also called her name every now and then. Most of all, with impatience, he strained his ears for the sound that would be the most welcome – *an ambulance siren.*

* * * *

No doctor ever came to the room. However, paramedics did show up about ten minutes later – the longest ten minutes of Mason's young life. The paramedics worked with diligence on Callie. They were preparing her for transport to the nearest hospital.

A police officer also entered the room. He had several questions for Mason regarding what had transpired with Callie that evening. Mason relayed everything that he knew. The policeman listened in silence. He was careful to record all the facts in a little notebook he had brought.

Mason watched the paramedics rush Callie from the room. All he wished to do was go to the hospital with her. He wanted to make sure that she was going to be okay. The police officer also needed to head to the hospital to find out how the young lady fared.

If possible, he needed to question the young woman as to what had happened to her. He asked that Mason ride in the police car with him to the facility. Mason was more than happy to go along with the officer. He believed that he would get to the hospital faster this way.

"Can I call my parents?" Mason asked the policeman, as they hurried to vacate the hotel room. *And Callie's. They need to know what has happened also. Maybe mom or dad can take care of that. I'm not up to listening to Mary Julia, and I'm not even sure how to reach Jonathan.*

"I'll radio the station once we get to the car and have them call your parents," the police officer relayed. "It's best they meet us at the hospital."

"What about Callie's parents? Or at least Callie's mom? Can you have the station call them as well?" Mason inquired. He was racing down the hall, close to the policeman's side.

"Yes, of course," he assured Mason. "I'll get all the telephone numbers from you in the car."

That being said, the two practically jogged the rest of the way down the hall to the elevators. They had just leaped on the first available elevator, when Mason exclaimed,
"Oh, crap!" He slapped himself in the forehead in exasperation. "My girlfriend! She's downstairs at the prom. I need to let her know what is going on. If she doesn't want to leave, then maybe she can stay and catch a ride home with someone else. "Should I drive separately to the hospital?"

"No," the police officer was quick to answer. "I'll go into the prom with you to talk to your girlfriend. Then I'll escort you and the girl, or only you, to the hospital afterwards."

The officer did not say it to Mason, but he did not want to let him go off by himself. The policeman did not have a confirmed account of what had happened here tonight. Thus Mason was still a suspect for any wrongdoing that might have been done. The officer intended to keep Mason close by his side for the time being.

\* \* \* \*

Mason sat with restlessly beside the policeman in the Emergency room. He nervously cracked his knuckles and waited for some word on Callie. When he and the police officer had gone back into the prom, they had not been able to find Rebecca. One of her friends had told them that she had been upset and had left the prom.

Mason had been amazed to hear that Rebecca had left. He knew she had been irritated with him about going to help Callie, but he had not thought that she would run out on the prom. However, it had appeared that this was exactly what Rebecca had done. She was nowhere to be found, and her purse had been gone.

Mason had not been able to locate Ralph either. Mason figured that Ralph would not be stupid enough to go back down to the prom. Regardless, part of him had still been hopeful that Ralph would turn up there after all. If Mason had caught sight of Ralph, he would have dragged him out of the prom. He also would have made him confess to the police officer what he had done. *I wish I could have been so lucky.*

Mason was jolted back to the present when he saw Mary Julia race through the front doors of the hospital. She was heading directly toward the information desk. *Oh crap!* he began to fret. *I hope, when they send Mary Julia back out to the waiting room with us, she doesn't start some scene with me. She's bound to be hysterical and think that I did something to cause Callie to be here. Mary Julia always finds a reason to blame me when Callie has done something stupid. Which is quite a lot.*

About ten minutes later, Mason was still waiting for Mary Julia to reappear. He was watching for her with apprehension. He felt a sense of relief when, instead of seeing Mary Julia, he observed his mom, dad, and sister rushing into the hospital. They were headed toward the information desk too.

Mason sprang to his feet and shrieked in a slightly erratic voice, "Mom! Dad! Katie Rose!" Jackie Lynn, Long Wolf and Katie Rose all skidded to a halt and turned at the sound of Mason's voice.

Long Wolf touched Jackie Lynn's shoulders with a gentle hand and said to her, "Honey, you and Katie Rose go on up to the desk. See if you can find out anything about Callie's condition. I want to talk to Mason alone and see if I can find out exactly what transpired."

Jackie Lynn and Katie Rose both nodded their agreement and continued their forward charge toward the information desk. Long Wolf hurried in Mason's direction instead. As Mason watched his dad approach, he could see the worry and the questions in his eyes. However, before Mason or his father could get a word in edgewise, there was a bloodcurdling scream.

Both Mason and his father, and everyone else in the waiting room, looked up in alarm to see Mary Julia hurtling across the waiting room toward Mason. She ran up to Mason, grabbed him by the lapels of his tuxedo jacket, and began shaking him with insane vigor. "You little SOB!" she began to shout. "Who the hell do you think you are?! I've always known you were up to no good where my daughter was concerned. I've seen the way you always gawk at her. The disgusting way you undress her with your eyes! You are scum! Do you hear me?! Scum!"

Mary Julia drew back her hand. She was about to slap Mason hard across the side of his face, when the police officer abruptly seized her arm. "Ma'am!" the policeman addressed in a deep, authoritative voice.

With controlled strength, he forced Mary Julia away from Mason. The officer placed his body between the two of them, as a much needed barrier. "I'm Officer Williams. I'm here to investigate what happened to your daughter. You need to calm down. Assaulting this young man is not the right way to proceed," he shared his wisdom.

"This monster tried to rape my sweet, innocent girl!" Mary Julia accused with disgust. "I'm pressing charges! I demand that you arrest him! Put the handcuffs on him! I want him arrested right now! Do you hear me?! What are you waiting for! You're a police officer, aren't you?! Isn't it your job to arrest people who commit crimes?! Well, do it then!"

Jackie Lynn and Katie Rose scurried to join Long Wolf's side. He met their eyes with a bleak, bewildered stare. *What?!* All their eyes seemed to question. *What on earth is going on here?! Where in the world is Mary Julia coming up with such utter nonsense?*

Mason was so startled by Mary Julia's unexpected, vicious attack that he was struck dumb for a second. He opened his mouth to speak but nothing came out. Fear registered in his mind for the first time. He looked into the foreboding face of Officer Williams, who was looming nearby. *What if, God forbid, Callie doesn't wake up? How can I prove that I was only in the room with her to help her? That I didn't do anything to harm her? Ralph and Jay sure aren't going to come forward and confess any wrongdoing. Shit, Callie, what have you gotten me into this time?!*

Officer Williams glanced from Mary Julia's menacing stare to Mason's distressed and pale face. Then he told Mary Julia, "I need to gather all the facts before I can do anything here, ma'am. Now, why exactly are you accusing this young man of attempting to rape your daughter?"

"Because I talked to Dr. Harris. He told me that Callie was given a date rape drug. You can ask him yourself if you don't believe me. He's in the back treating my Callie and other emergency patients, but I'm sure they can call him out here. After all, this is a serious crime that we are talking about here," Mary Julia stated with certainty.

She glared with hate at Mason over the policeman's broad shoulder. Mary Julia wanted to strangle the life out of this young man and be done with it. "So are you going to do anything or not?" she further challenged.

"Yes, ma'am, I am," Officer Williams guaranteed her. He reached to take a gentle grasp on Mary Julia's arm. Officer Williams persuasively suggested, "Why don't you come with me and we will question the doctor some more about all this? I need to know more about your daughter's condition. When she is up to it, I need to question her as to what happened. Did the doctor give you any idea when she might be coming around?"

"He doesn't know for sure," Mary Julia stated with worry. Then she inquired, "You aren't going to leave *him* here alone are you?" She pointed an accusing finger at Mason once more.

"I'll take responsibility for my son," Long Wolf spoke up for the first time. He took another few steps toward Mason.

"That would be a first," Mary Julia declared. She gave Long Wolf a disgusted look. "Maybe if you had been taking responsibility for your son's actions all along, then he would not have tried to attack my daughter tonight. He's been stalking my pretty Callie ever since she started to blossom into a woman. I've warned you before. I warned Jonathan. None of you would listen, and now look what has happened."

Mary Julia turned her attention back to the policeman. She pointed toward Long Wolf and warned, "Officer, you can't trust this man. He will probably load Mason up in his car and leave as soon as we walk away. He could hide him from the authorities. You can't permit him to do this!"

"None of us are going anywhere," Long Wolf pledged. "Mason, Jackie Lynn, Katie Rose and me will be waiting here when you come back out. You have my word," he stated with sincerity. Long Wolf directed his steady gaze at Officer Williams. He knew it would do no good to reason with Mary Julia.

"Son, will you have a seat right there?" Officer Williams asked Mason. He pointed to the closest chair. "I need for you and your parents to wait here. I'd imagine your parents would like a little time to talk with you anyway."

Mason had an expression of alarm and uncertainty on his face. He lethargically took a seat where the officer had indicated. Long Wolf was swift to sit in the chair right next to him. Jackie Lynn and Katie Rose hastily took a seat in the two chairs facing Mason and Long Wolf.

"Ma'am, can we go and talk to the doctor now?" Officer Williams asked, once again turning his full attention to Mary Julia. "The sooner I gather all the facts, the sooner I can take action," he reminded her. "I can't do anything without all the facts, and I can't gather information sitting here in this waiting room. Why don't we give these folks some time alone?"

"Okay," Mary Julia begrudgingly approved.

She was not happy about leaving Mason and his family alone in the waiting room, but she was anxious to get Callie's confirmation of what happened. *That way the policeman can arrest Mason and take him away. I'll do everything in my power to see that they put Mason in jail and throw away the key.*

Mary Julia gave them all one, last, reproachful look. Then she and the officer started away. Jackie Lynn spoke up for the first time. She grilled, "Mason, what in the world is going on here?" There was a disturbed expression on her face.

"Callie got herself in over her head this time," Mason began in a quiet, defeated voice. His eyes were fixed on his shoes and not on his mom's face. He felt a little sick to his stomach. *What did the policeman mean when he said the sooner he could gather the facts the sooner he could take action? Is he going to arrest me? I may be in real trouble here! Shit! I didn't do anything! That is, but step in and help Callie. But what if she doesn't speak up and the police don't believe me?*

236

"What does that mean, son?" his father asked with concern. *What's he trying to say? Surely this can't be true? Mason wouldn't try to drug some girl...and...Callie is more than just* some *girl to him. He wouldn't do this! I know my son. He isn't capable of this!* "Mason, please speak up, son. Tell us what happened. We need to know," Long Wolf coaxed.

Mason looked up at his dad. He was made uneasy by the flicker of doubt he gleamed in his father's eyes. *Surely, he doesn't think I did this too!* Mason's stomach did more nervous flip-flops. *If my own family doesn't believe in me, then I'm sunk!*

"Callie got Ralph to take her to the prom," he began to relay. "She was flirting with him like she always does, kissing him and leading him on. She came over to me, and she said Ralph was acting strange. Callie said he was coming on a little strong, but I told her she deserved anything that she got. Then I found out from another guy that Ralph had, quote, 'taken Callie upstairs for a good time'. So I strangled the guy until he gave me the number of the hotel room. Then I went up to see if I could help Callie. She's a pain in the ass sometimes, but she is still only a kid. I didn't want to see her get hurt, or do something stupid. I found Callie partially undressed and unconscious on the bed. Ralph confessed to having given her something to 'relax her'. When I asked him what it was, he claimed he didn't know. He offered to go back down to the prom. Ralph was supposed to track down the guy who had given him the drug and find out what it was. I let him leave. Ralph never came back. So now the police and everyone think I did this. I only tried to help. That's all I did."

Mason's gaze swept from his father's eyes, to his mother's and even to Katie Rose's with desperation. He was diligently searching for some sign of reassurance that they all believed him.

"Why does Callie always do such stupid things?" Katie Rose lamented. She slapped her hands on the arms of the chair in irritation. She felt overwhelmingly guilty. She sheepishly lowered her eyes and stared at the floor. "I kept telling Callie that she was going to get into trouble. She's gotten even wilder since her mom and dad split. She's hanging out with a rough crowd now, and she drinks and does drugs with these kids. I caught her smoking marijuana once at school," Katie Rose admitted all at once in a quiet, distressed voice.

ILLUSIONS

*Callie needs help. I should have said something before now. Didn't Flora try and tell me this? She said Callie might end up getting hurt if I didn't speak up, but I wouldn't listen to her. I thought I could do more by keeping quiet and keeping an eye on Callie. I was wrong! I hope Callie will be alright. I hope she hasn't been raped. I'll feel terrible if something horrible has happened to her tonight.* Katie Rose was fighting to keep from crying.

"So that explains why she hasn't been hanging out as much with you lately," Jackie Lynn rather absently commented. *It all makes so much sense now. Now I understand what had been upsetting Katie Rose the last few weeks. This is why neither I nor Long Wolf could get her to talk about what was bothering her. Oh God! If Callie was drinking and smoking marijuana tonight and Ralph mixed this other drug with that, could it do serious damage? What if Callie slips into a coma, or what if when she gains consciousness, she can't remember what happened? What if she isn't able to clear Mason?*

"Katie Rose, why didn't you tell us that Callie was still doing drugs?" Long Wolf asked. He had directed his focus to his daughter now instead of his son.

Tears clouded Katie Rose's vision. She cautiously raised her head, and she saw a distorted view of her father's chastising, disappointed eyes. In between her regretful sobs, Katie Rose confessed, "She...Callie said...she said that she...that she would...would never...never speak to me again...if I...if I told. I...I thought I could...I could help her more...by...by staying her friend and...and watching what she did, than...by...by telling. I...I didn't want anything...anything bad to happen to her. I'm sorry, dad. Do you...do you think...she will be...be okay?"

"We have no way of knowing yet, sweetheart," Jackie Lynn answered. She put her arm around her daughter's shoulders and pulled her close to her body. Katie Rose laid her head on her mom's shoulder. She began to freely cry.

"Katie Rose, what happened to Callie tonight is not your fault. You feel guilty. You think that maybe you should have revealed what you saw Callie doing. Then, by some miracle, maybe Callie wouldn't have been where she was tonight. You are right in thinking that you should have revealed what Callie was doing. This issue was too big for you to have tried to take on by yourself. But, regardless, Callie has always been headstrong. If she had her mind set on going to Mason's prom with Ralph, then she probably would have found a way to do it. What we should hope and pray for is that she will not only come out of this okay, but that Callie will learn a lesson from what's happened to her tonight," Jackie Lynn preached. *And let's hope and pray that she clears Mason of any wrongdoing soon too.*

"Mom's right, squirt," Mason chimed in. "This is *not* your fault. You've been a good friend to Callie, Katie Rose. She's been out of control for some time now. If anyone is to blame, it is Mary Julia. She turns a blind eye to everything bad Callie does. She tries to pawn it off on someone else: Jonathan, me, you, mom, dad. You name it. I wish this would be a wake up call for Mary Julia tonight too. But I bet Callie will find a way to worm out of this too."

*I hope it isn't by blaming me. The whole reason she came to the prom tonight with Ralph was to flirt with me, and I rejected her come-ons. She may want to get even, and she has the perfect opportunity.*

"Do you know if Mary Julia called Jonathan about this?" Long Wolf directed his question to Jackie Lynn.

"I have no idea. I only called Mary Julia after the police called us. I didn't know how to get hold of Jonathan. Hard telling whether Mary Julia called him or not. Why?"

"Because he needs to be involved. As Mason said, I would hate for Callie to worm her way out of the consequences of this. Jonathan seems to be seeing things more clearly where Callie is concerned. I think that is some of the reason why he left Mary Julia, because he sees how her behavior is hurting Callie. Jonathan should be here as well," Long Wolf soundly reasoned.

Katie Rose blew her nose. Her mom had handed her a tissue from a box on a nearby table. "Jonathan is still staying at the Parkside Hotel," she enlightened them.

"Okay," Long Wolf said half to himself. He stood up. "I'm going to go to a pay phone and see if I can get in touch with Jonathan. Hopefully, I will be able to reach him, and he can come to the hospital and take an upper hand where Callie is concerned. It can't hurt to try. That girl needs all the help she can get. And Mason, whether I get hold of Jonathan and he helps us out with Callie or not, everything is going to be okay. We'll find a way out of this. I won't let you be blamed for something that you did not do. I'm proud of you for trying to help, son. You did the right thing. Even if it doesn't feel that way right now," Long Wolf declared. He bent to give Mason's shoulder a reassuring squeeze.

Long Wolf took a moment to also address his daughter's emotional distress. He put his hand under Katie Rose's chin, and he raised her head. Long Wolf looked her directly in her eyes, and he instructed, "Chin up, my beautiful Emerald Sea. Your heart was in the right place. You truly believed you were doing what was right to help Callie. We are *all* going to do everything we can to get Callie the help she needs now. Maybe after tonight, things will get better for Callie. We have to believe this. Let's not think the worst. Okay?"

Katie Rose merely nodded, a bittersweet smile on her face. Somehow her daddy always made things seem a little better. *I should have trusted him all along and told him what Callie was doing. Go, daddy, and get hold of Jonathan. Maybe he can help. Someone has to. Callie has to be alright, and she has to recognize that the things she does are hurting her and other people. She has to!*

# Chapter 29

# *Revelations*

Long Wolf was able to contact Jonathan, and Jonathan was grateful to him for having made the call. Mary Julia had *not* called him. He told Long Wolf he would be at the hospital as soon as he could get there. Jonathan also assured Long Wolf that he did not believe that Mason had attacked his daughter. "I've seen firsthand how my daughter behaves around your son and around other guys. She's had a major crush on Mason for ages now, and Callie uses other guys to try and make Mason jealous. I've been telling Mary Julia that sooner or later Callie was going to get into trouble. I guess it's finally happened. I wish I'd had the courage to stand up to Mary Julia sooner. Then maybe our daughter would be different than what she is today," he sadly confessed.

Jonathan was anxious to get to the hospital. Long Wolf ended their conversation, and then he returned to the waiting room. He sat with his family and shared the details of his phone conversation with Jonathan. Officer Williams came back into the waiting room with them.

"Is there any news?" Long Wolf questioned. He rose to his feet as if to shield his son.

"No," the policeman relayed, shaking his head. "The doctor said it will likely be hours before Callie comes around. She was given a pretty powerful sedative. The good news is they expect that she will be alright." *The bad news is she might not remember what happened to her. So her attacker might walk away from this without punishment*, Officer Williams knew, but did not share.

The policeman did not want to tip Mason off to this fact. He wished for this young man to worry. Then, if he was guilty of anything, the police had a chance, albeit a slim one, of getting a confession from him.

"Where's the girl's mother?" Long Wolf asked. He glanced about with apprehension. He was making certain that Mary Julia was not about to pounce on Mason again.

"I told her it would be best if she remained in the back with her daughter. I made it clear that I would not tolerate any further altercations between her and your son in this waiting room," Officer Williams answered. "I appreciate that she was upset about her daughter, but this is a hospital and not a war zone. They are supposed to send a nurse out to get me whenever the young lady regains consciousness."

"Thank you. I appreciate that," Long Wolf acknowledged with slight relief.

The policeman nodded in response. Officer Williams walked over and took a seat a few chairs over from Long Wolf and his family. He picked up a magazine from a nearby table, and he started thumbing through its pages. Long Wolf and his family were free to go home now if they wanted, but Officer Williams did not volunteer this information to them either.

If they asked him if they could leave, then he would have to grant them permission. However, if they did not ask, then he would just as soon they stuck around. This would make it so much easier to take Mason into custody, should the young lady regain consciousness and say that Mason had indeed been the young man that had attacked her.

* * * *

Callie did not awaken until 10:00 the next morning. Mary Julia had kept careful watch over her daughter for hours in the emergency room. The hospital had, at long last, decided to admit Callie and assigned her a room. Mary Julia was now fast asleep. She was curled up in an easy chair by Callie's bed. Mary Julia had not wished to sleep, because she had wanted to be awake when Callie regained consciousness. However, she had been too exhausted to continue to fight it any longer.

242

As Callie opened her eyes and looked about her in confusion, she spied her mother sleeping soundly in the chair beside her bed. Callie was about to call out for her mom and rouse her, when the door to her room opened. Callie was astounded to see her father enter. He was carrying a cup of coffee in his right hand.

"Callie," he addressed, a smile spreading across his face. Jonathan scurried toward the bed and sat his foam cup down on the bedside table. He reached out, with enormous relief, and he pulled his daughter into a tight affirming embrace. It felt good to be free to do so. "How are you doing, sweetheart?" Jonathan asked as he pulled back from her. He was perusing her dirty, perplexed face with a careful eye.

Heavy mascara was still smeared about her eyes and face. This made Callie look as if she had been in a fight – *a fight she had badly lost.* Callie's hair was also an unattractive, tangled mass. Jonathan's heart went out to her in sympathy.

"Daddy, where am I?" she asked in a small, childlike voice. Callie was still peering about the room in utmost bewilderment.

She glanced at her mother again and found she was still dead to the world. Neither Jonathan's nor Callie's voice had aroused Mary Julia. She looked as if she was the one who had been drugged, instead of Callie.

"Callie, you are in the hospital," Jonathan answered her with hesitance.

"Hospital?" she repeated in a still somewhat groggy voice. "Why? What happened? Is mom alright?" she asked with slight fear. Callie looked over at her mother once more.

"Yeah. Your mom is fine," Jonathan was quick to assure her. He slid her dainty hand into his and lightly squeezed it in reassurance. "You, on the other hand, had us all very worried for awhile. I'm glad you are awake. I'm also glad that you aren't hurt. Things could have been a lot worse, Callie. When you are back up to par, we need to have a long talk about what happened."

Callie was silent for a moment. She was diligently trying to recollect what had happened to put her in the hospital. As she tried to concentrate, Callie became aware that she had an awful headache. *Oh no! Did I go out and get stoned and drunk again, and I don't even remember doing it? Did they pump my stomach again?* She swallowed hard then. *No, I don't think they did that, because my throat isn't sore. I had a terrible sore throat when they did that. Why am I here?*

"What happened?" Callie mustered the courage to ask at last.

Jonathan glanced at Mary Julia's sleeping form. He gave brief consideration to waking her. *Should I ask her opinion about what to say to Callie?* Jonathan was swift to decide against such action. *No. Mary Julia didn't even bother to call me to tell me that our daughter was in the hospital. And she was not at all happy when I showed up at the hospital last night. She all but banished me to the waiting room. So why should I care what her opinion might be? I can handle this on my own. Callie is my daughter too, and I have a right to say what I want to her.*

"Well…" Jonathan began in a slow drawl. "Callie…it's like this. You were almost raped last night."

Callie mouth dropped open in shock. She questioned with disbelief, "Raped? Dad, are you crazy?! What are you talking about?"

Callie looked over at her mother again. *Is this some cockamamie story that mom invented for some reason?* This was the only logical explanation that Callie could come up with. *But why?*

"Mom," Callie called out all at once. When Mary Julia still did not stir, Callie cried a little louder and with more insistence, "Mom, wake up!"

Mary Julia's body shuddered in response. She abruptly opened her eyes. Callie's beautiful sapphire eyes were open and staring at her. Mary Julia gasped and with skepticism questioned, "Callie?" She also sprang to her feet.

If it had not been for Callie's bedrail, Mary Julia would have tumbled to the floor. Her legs were not quite awake yet, and they threatened to buckle under her. Mary Julia awkwardly lowered herself back to the edge of the chair. With a delighted smile on her face, she reached out one hand. Mary Julia lovingly touched her daughter's arm and began gushing, "How's mama's baby girl? Are you okay? I'm so glad you are awake."

Mary Julia did not so much as acknowledge Jonathan's presence. Jonathan was not sure if she was oblivious to him being there or if she was choosing to ignore him. He did not care one way or the other. Their daughter was the person who was important at this moment.

"I'm not a baby, mom. I hate it when you talk to me like that," Callie sassed. Her sass was a welcome hum to Mary Julia's ears. Her daughter sounded like her usual self. *Callie is going to be fine.*

"And what's this crap that dad is coming off with about me almost being raped?" Callie demanded to know, looking from one parent to another.

Mary Julia looked up and met Jonathan's eyes. Disapproval showed clearly in her eyes. She was not at all happy with Jonathan's words to Callie.

"Honey, I don't think you need to be worrying about that right now," she told Callie. Mary Julia forced herself to stand again. She reached down and patted Callie's arm. "The main thing is you are going to be fine. And Mason is going to be severely punished for what he did. All you have to do is tell the police everything. That is, when you are up to talking. You don't have to talk at all right now if you don't want to. You take your time, sugarplum. Justice will still be done. I'll see to that. I don't want you getting upset, so don't you fret about anything. Okay?"

"Mom, have you gone stark raving mad?" Callie probed with irritation.

She turned her head to look into Jonathan's face again. With trepidation, she recommended, "Dad, mom needs to be hauled away to the nuthouse this time. She's making all this up, or has imagined it. Mason *did not* try to rape me. Why in the world would she say something like that? She doesn't like him, but that is nuts! It really is, dad."

"Now….now, Callie," Mary Julia tried to soothe. She massaged her daughter's shoulders. "You need to calm down, sweetie. Jonathan, why don't you go and try to find Callie's doctor or a nurse? One of them should probably be in here. They should see that she is awake now. They should be informed that she is so confused," Mary Julia suggested. She also silently mouthed to Jonathan behind Callie's back, '*And the policeman. Get the policeman*'.

"I'm not confused," Callie continued to argue, growing angry. She shook herself free from her mother's grasp. She continued with stubbornness, "The only thing that is wrong with me is I have a killer headache. What did you do, mom? Hit me in the head with something, bring me to the hospital, and then make up this ridiculous story about Mason raping me. Please don't leave me alone with her dad! I don't think she is well. I'm serious!"

"Okay, honey," Jonathan also tried to pacify her.

Callie sat up more erect in bed and began sliding to the side of the bed closest to his dad. She looked as if she was going to jump out and flee the room. Jonathan was fast to place his hands on both of Callie's shoulders and tried to ease her back into the bed.

"Whoo, Callie! What are you doing, sweetheart? I don't think you are supposed to be getting up yet. Can you stay in bed and settle down a little bit? We need to talk a little more about what happened to you. You really were almost raped. Your mother is *not* crazy."

"Mason did *not* try to rape me, dad!" Callie adamantly professed. "He wouldn't do something like that."

"I know, honey," Jonathan acquiesced with haste, much to Mary Julia's dismay. "Mason only tried to help you. It was his friend Ralph who tried to rape you. You went to Mason's prom with Ralph, and he tried to take advantage of you. Do you remember anything about this?"

"Jonathan! Where are you getting such nonsense? From Mason? Don't put that scumbag liar's ideas into Callie's head," Mary Julia chastised.

She turned her attention back to Callie. Mary Julia instructed with care, "Don't feel like you have to defend Mason, honey. If he tried to hurt you, then he should be punished. Don't let him get away with trying to blame someone else."

Callie was silent for several moments. She was attempting to force her brain to recollect what had happened to her. She had a foggy memory of going to the prom. *Mason? What happened with Mason?* Callie tried to work through the haze in her brain. *Mason rejected me for Rebecca*, she recalled all at once. She felt a stab of pain again. She also vaguely recollected leaving the prom with Ralph. *Ralph took me up to one of the hotel rooms. I had had a drink with him...vodka...but only one drink.*

No matter how much harder she tried, this was the last thing Callie could remember. *Did Ralph really try to rape me?* Something bad had gone down between the two of them, or she would not be in the hospital. *Did Ralph hit me in the head with something?* Callie absently began running her fingers along her forehead and along the back and top of her skull. Her head was throbbing, but Callie could find no sign of physical injury.

"Callie, is your head hurting, sweetie?" Mary Julia disturbed her thoughts. "Jonathan, can't you please go and get her doctor or a nurse? Can't you see that Callie getting upset has her in pain? Maybe we weren't supposed to be talking to her about all this yet."

"Mom, why don't *you* go get my doctor or a nurse? I am fine here with dad," Callie unexpectedly demanded. "Could you please go now? My head does hurt. Please, mom."

Mary Julia did not want to leave Callie's side. For one thing, she did not trust Jonathan not to talk to her more about the attempted rape. However, Mary Julia did want to go and get the doctor or a nurse, and more importantly, she wanted to go and get the policeman. If Callie was covering for Mason, then maybe she and the police officer could get the truth out of her daughter somehow.

"Okay, baby, Mama will be right back," Mary Julia pledged. She moved toward the door then. Before Mary Julia opened the door and stepped outside, she made a final plea to Jonathan, "Jonathan, please do not get Callie agitated again while I'm gone."

With a sneer on his face, Jonathan nodded. He watched with relief as Mary Julia vacated the room. *Why does she always have to make everything so damn hard?*

The door had barely closed when Callie started to question, "What did Ralph do to me, dad....other than try and rape me? Did he knock me unconscious somehow? The last thing I remember was drinking something with him in one of the hotel rooms. Mason wasn't even there. How come he is being blamed?"

"Callie, maybe we had better wait until your mother and the doctor come back to talk about all this," Jonathan cautiously warned.

"Bullshit! I'm going to get more upset if I have to wait for *her* to come back. She is trying to twist the truth. Tell me what happened. Tell me why Mason is being blamed. Is he here at the hospital? He wasn't hurt too by Ralph was me. Tell me, dad. I need to know."

Jonathan caved easily, "Okay, honey." If he did not start to answer Callie's questions, she was likely to throw a fit. In this instance, Jonathan could not blame her. *Callie has a right to know what has happened to her.*

"Ralph gave you a drug with a big name that is also called a date rape drug. It is a sedative, basically a strong sleeping pill. So it caused you to pass out. Fortunately, Ralph got scared when you were so unresponsive, and he did not rape you. You were very lucky. Many other girls who are given this same drug are not as lucky as you. I hope you realize this, Callie."

"Ralph is scum, dad," Callie proclaimed, an angry edge to her voice. *He'll get his. I'll see to that. He'll be sorry he tried something so stupid.* "But what about Mason? Where does he come in to all this?" Callie continued her important crusade for answers.

"Mason found out what Ralph was up to. Evidently, the other boy who gave Ralph the drug…a Jay somebody…bragged to Mason about what Ralph was up to. Mason got the room number of where you were at, and he came to your rescue. He, Katie Rose, Jackie Lynn and Long Wolf all spent the night downstairs in the waiting room. They're still waiting to hear some word on you."

Jonathan paused to let all the information sink in that he had provided, thus far. Callie was studying him with calm and alertness. Since Jonathan had her undivided attention, he was prompt to add, "Mason did not have anything to do with trying to rape you, Callie. He and his family care about you a great deal. They are all good people. You should be ashamed of yourself for making them worry like they have been. For making us *all* worry. What Ralph tried to do to you was very wrong, Callie, but so were your actions that led up to this. You lied about where you were going. You led Ralph on, so he would take you to the prom. You did all this to try and make Mason jealous. This time it backfired in your face. Don't try to deny any of this, because it won't work with me. I'm on to your little games, and you are not going to get away with them anymore."

Callie did not care for the harsh, disciplining tone of her father's voice. She was not used to him coming across like this to her, and she did not know how she should react. Fortunately, Callie did not have to decide, because her mother reentered the room with her doctor, a nurse and a police officer.

"Well…well…look who's finally awake," the doctor said with a smile. He and the nurse approached Callie's bed.

The nurse, engaging in her standard, hospital-patient routine, stuck a thermometer under Callie's tongue and swiftly set about taking her blood pressure. The doctor patiently waited until the nurse was done, then he asked Callie, "So how are you feeling this morning, young lady?"

"I have one hell of a headache," Callie replied truthfully, not mincing any words.

"Yes. That's to be expected," the doctor told not only Callie, but her parents. "We'll get you some medicine for that."

The doctor wrote a note and gave it to the nurse, and she left the room. "Got ya' covered," he said with a grin and winked at Callie. He patted Callie on the leg. Then he said to Mary Julia, "She is going to be fine. We'll dismiss her in an hour or so. The nurse will be bringing back some pain pills for her headache. She'll give her two now, and then she'll give you a prescription for some more. You can give your daughter two more every fours hours. The headache should eventually subside."

"Thank you, doctor," Mary Julia purred. She was giving him a radiant smile, and she reached to pat his arm.

Jonathan watched Mary Julia with a hard stare. She was still grinning like an idiot at the doctor, and Mary Julia touched his arm for a moment longer than was necessary. *Is she on the make for this guy?* The jealous stir he felt was unnerving.

Mary Julia noticed Jonathan watching her. She also noted the serious expression on his face, but she did not take the time to investigate what he might be thinking. Instead, she directed the policeman to move toward Callie's bed. "Callie, this is Officer Williams. He has some questions for you. I need for you to honestly tell him what you remember about what happened to you. Okay?"

"No problem," Callie replied with a defensive edge to her voice.

She did not wait for the police officer to start to question her. Rather, Callie informed him, "You need to put out an arrest warrant for a guy named Ralph Conner. He forced me to go up to a hotel room with him and to drink alcohol," she stretched the truth a little. "The drink must have had some drug in it, because it paralyzed me. Then when I couldn't move, Ralph tried to rape me."

"Callie, is this something you actually remember happening, or are you only repeating what your dad has told you?" Mary Julia was fast to chime in. She gave Jonathan a dirty look.

*She wants Callie to blame Mason so badly. Mary Julia does not want to hear the truth*, Jonathan was swift to conclude with distaste.

"It's what I remember, mother," Callie professed. "Can you please go and arrest this guy?" she asked the policeman with wide innocent eyes. "He could be out there right now trying to hurt some other girl. I know where he lives. I can give you his address." *Ralph, you rotten scum! You are going to be so sorry!* she silently schemed.

The police officer verified again that Callie was certain that she had been coerced by Ralph Conner to go up to a hotel room and to drink an alcoholic beverage. Callie was prompt to reiterate that this was all true. She added again that Ralph had also tried to rape her. Then she gave the policeman Ralph's address.

Jonathan did not believe that Callie had been forced to leave with Ralph or to have a drink with him. Nevertheless, he did not say anything. Ralph Connor did deserve to be punished. *And so does Callie. I'll see to that somehow. Something needs to be done so that she realizes how serious what almost happened to her was.*

# Chapter 30

# *The Breakdown*

Mary Julia and Jonathan both followed the Officer Williams from the room. He promised that he would be paying Ralph Conner and his parents a visit. He told Jonathan and Mary Julia that Ralph would be extensively questioned about what had happened to Callie.

Officer Williams did not promise them anything further. It would depend on how their investigation turned out as to whether Ralph would be charged with attempted rape. Unlike Mason, they had not discovered Ralph with Callie, so it would make the case that much harder to prove. If Ralph was arrested, he would either be sent to juvenile services or to jail, depending on his age.

As the Officer Williams made his exit, Jonathan said to Mary Julia, "So…are you ready to go and apologize to Mason? If it hadn't been for him, then Callie might have been raped. At the very least, she would have woken up in that hotel room and had no idea where she was."

"I'm still not sure that Mason did not have something to do with this," Mary Julia was quick to dispute Jonathan. "How do we know that he did not help Ralph try to take advantage of Callie? Maybe they both panicked when they couldn't wake Callie. Callie would cover for Mason, because she has always had such a crush on him. She thinks the sun rises and falls in that boy."

"You know what, Mary Julia, I'm not going to argue with you about this. It wouldn't do any good. You're determined to think the worst of Mason. That way you don't have to see Callie for the way she is."

251

"What exactly is that supposed to mean?" she grilled with clear hostility. "In what way should I see Callie?"

"As a girl who is much too young to be going around trying to seduce boys the way she does. Her actions caught up with her last night, and it's past time that we did something to see that things change."

"My little girl is not some...some seductress. That's the way you men always see a beautiful girl. She can't help it that she is pretty. That doesn't give Ralph or anyone a license to try and rape my baby!" Mary Julia raised her voice in fierce opposition.

"You are absolutely right, Mary Julia. No man *ever* has a right to rape a woman. But neither should our daughter be allowed to put herself in situations where she could be taken advantage of."

"I've done everything I could to protect Callie since she was born, Jonathan. How dare you accuse me of not watching out for her! You don't know what you are talking about. You are attacking me because you feel guilty for not being in the house to watch over Callie. Well, that is your fault, not mine. You brought this all on yourself."

"I left because you asked me to, Mary Julia. But our relationship problems have to do with you still living in the past and letting your past affect our daughter. And you are still doing that. Your suspicions of Mason have nothing to do with the facts. The facts are that Callie has chased Mason for several years now. The facts are that Callie has tried to seduce that young man. The facts are that she has paraded around in front of him half dressed on too many occasions to count. It is also a fact that Callie showed up at Mason's prom last night with one of his friends to make him jealous. And what has Mason done during all this? He has repeatedly rejected Callie's come-ons. And why? Because he sees her as a young girl and because he doesn't want to see her get hurt. But yet, you attack him every chance you get. It's all such a shame, Mary Julia. You should be ashamed of what you have done."

"Don't you dare attack me, Jonathan," Mary Julia shouted, and charged toward him. In fury, she began to pound both his shoulders with fisted hands. "I didn't do anything wrong! Do you hear me! I didn't!" she began to strangely declare.

"Shhhhh, Mary Julia. We're in a hospital. Stop shouting. Quiet down," Jonathan demanded in a determined, yet controlled voice. He grabbed her by the shoulders and gave her a forceful push backwards, to cease her physical assault.

Mary Julia staggered backwards a few steps. Then she froze and looked over Jonathan's shoulder. Her face grew pale and she began to shout, "Oh no…no…no…no!" Mary Julia started to point.

Jonathan spun around, but he saw nothing or no one standing in the hall. "What, Mary Julia? What is it?" he asked with concern, reaching out his arms to her.

Mary Julia instantaneously backed away from Jonathan a few more feet. She continued to shriek and point down the hall. "Don't let him get me!" she shouted.

"Who?" Jonathan questioned in uncertainty.

"My stepfather. He's coming to get me. Make him stop!" Mary Julia pleaded in a pitiful voice. She lowered herself to the floor and began to curl up in a protective ball.

"Sir, can I help?" a caring nurse asked, as she approached with hesitation from the other direction down the hall.

"Yeah," Jonathan said in a quiet voice, motioning her over. "My wife is having some sort of mental breakdown. She was molested as a child, and she seems to be having some sort of flashback or something like that. Since you are a woman, then maybe she might respond to you. I don't think I can help her right now."

"What's her name?" the nurse inquired.

"Mary Julia."

The nurse cautiously lowered herself to a stooped position beside Mary Julia. "Mary Julia, it's okay," she tried to assure her in a soothing voice. "Can you hear me, honey?"

"No, Mama! It wasn't my fault! It wasn't my fault! I didn't mean to seduce him. I didn't mean to dress wrong. I wasn't parading around in front of him half dressed. It wasn't my fault! I didn't do anything wrong! Stop saying that I did!" Mary Julia began to pathetically whine.

"No, of course it wasn't your fault, sweetie" the nurse tried to play along.

However, Mary Julia only continued to say the same things over and over. She seemed to be growing more and more distressed. The nurse rose to her feet again in a hurry.

"I don't think I can help her, sir. I'll go and call psych. They have some excellent doctors that should be able help your wife." Jonathan was overcome with guilt. His words about Callie had locked Mary Julia into this terrible episode. 'Crap!' he said under his breath.

"Yes, would you please go and see if you can get my wife some help?" he addressed the nurse once more.

"Of course," she agreed, and scampered off down the hall toward the nearest nurse's station.

A few moments later, Jonathan was still watching Mary Julia with powerlessness. She continued to rock back and forth and whimper. He all of the sudden heard Jackie Lynn's voice ask in alarm, "Jonathan, what's wrong? Has something happened to Callie? Officer Williams told us that she was awake and had confessed that Ralph had tried to rape her. We asked if we could come back to visit Callie, and the nurse said it was fine."

"Yes, that is okay. Callie is fine," he assured her.

It was then that Jackie Lynn noticed Mary Julia sitting against the wall. "Mary Julia?" she said in a quiet voice.

Jonathan glanced over his shoulder. He saw that Long Wolf, Mason and Katie Rose were also all standing in the hall behind him. They were all staring with shock at Mary Julia's tormented form as well.

"Mary Julia is just…well…she is having some sort of bad spell. She seems to have regressed to when she was a little girl, being abused by her father or stepfather. I was trying to convince her that we needed to take a firmer hand in disciplining Callie, and I'm afraid I went too far. I said some things I shouldn't have. I don't know what to do now. A nurse has gone to get Mary Julia some help."

Jackie Lynn walked past Jonathan and began lowering herself toward Mary Julia. However, when she reached out to touch her friend, Mary Julia shrieked in terror and scooted back several more feet.

"No, Mama!" she protested in a screech. "Leave me alone! I wasn't parading around half dressed and trying to seduce anybody. Really I wasn't! I didn't do anything wrong! Please don't blame me!"

"Mary Julia, it's me, Jackie Lynn. It's not your mama," Jackie Lynn tried in vain to convey to her long time friend. Mary

Julia showed no sign of response. Instead, she curled more tightly into a ball and covered her head with her arms. Jackie Lynn turned her head and gave Jonathan a distraught look. She did not have a clue what she could do to help Mary Julia either. She had never seen her friend in this dreadful state.

Two male orderlies and a female doctor rushed toward Mary Julia. With gentle hands, they urged Jackie Lynn away from Mary Julia. She stood and stepped back beside Jonathan in slow step. Long Wolf came over behind her and placed his hands on Jackie Lynn's shoulders, in a gesture of support. They all watched helplessly as the doctor evaluated Mary Julia. A few moments later, the doctor arose, and turned around. She looked directly at Jonathan and inquired, "Are you her husband?"

He nodded.

"I'm Doctor Benson," she introduced herself. She reached to shake Jonathan's hand.

"I'm Jonathan Roberts, and that is my wife Mary Julia," he told the doctor. "How bad is she? Is she going to snap out of this in a minute?" he probed in frightened ignorance.

"I would say that this is highly unlikely, Mr. Roberts," the doctor communicated with frankness. "Your wife appears to have had some sort of mental break. As to how serious, I cannot tell you at this moment. What I would advise is that we take her down to the mental health ward and admit her for a full evaluation. Then we can give you an idea of when she might, as you say, 'snap out of this'."

"How long would you need to keep her?" Jonathan continued to question.

"I have no way of knowing," the doctor answered honestly. "The first thing I need to get from you is a full mental history. Has she ever had a spell like this before?"

"No," he answered with haste. "She was hospitalized once, years ago, for a sexual addiction. She only recently had a relapse, due to trouble in our relationship. Her sexual addiction was caused by her being sexually abused when she was a girl. My daughter was almost raped last night, and we were arguing about this right before she collapsed. Something I said triggered this state," he confessed with utmost guilt.

"It's more likely that whatever you said was merely the straw that broke the camel's back," the doctor tried to console.

"Anyway, we need to move her out of the hallway. Can I instruct the orderlies to fully sedate her and take her to the mental health ward?"

Jonathan agreed with reluctance. They all were sad to watch as Mary Julia was sedated and the orderlies placed her on a gurney and wheeled her away. The doctor told Jonathan that he would have to sign papers for his wife's admittance. He would also have to fill out a written medical and mental history on her.

Jonathan asked Jackie Lynn if she would come with him. She knew more about when Mary Julia had been in the hospital before, since it had been before he and Mary Julia had married. Long Wolf said that he would also go along. His wife was upset about Mary Julia, and he wanted to be there to support her in any way that he could.

"Hey, if you guys want to go in and visit with Callie for awhile, feel free," Jonathan said to Mason and Katie Rose before they started away.

"We'll meet you both either in Callie's room or back in the waiting room out front," Long Wolf told them.

"Okay," Mason and Katie Rose both agreed almost in unison.

"Why don't you go on in and visit with Callie?" Mason asked Katie Rose when they were alone in the hallway outside Callie's room. "I'll wait out here for you."

"Geez, should I tell her about her mother?" Katie Rose debated, gnawing on her bottom lip in nervousness.

"No. Jonathan should do that. I'd let Callie know that you're glad she is okay. I'd leave everything else to Jonathan...including strangling her. You feel like doing that because she was so stupid, right? I do too. I'd go a little easy on her right now though."

"You sure you don't want to come in with me, and help keep me under control?" Katie Rose questioned, a slight amused smile on her face. Mason knew her well. Katie Rose loved her big brother so much. She hated all Callie constantly put him through.

Mason looked exhausted. None of them had gotten much sleep in the waiting room last night. Mason had been especially worried. Katie Rose fully understood why. Callie could have easily lied and made it appear that Mason had been the guy who had tried to hurt her. Katie Rose was relieved that her friend had at least had the decency to clear Mason of any wrongdoing.

"Nah, I'm sure you will be fine. I'll be out here if you need me for anything," he assured her.

"Okay. Chicken," Katie Rose teased her brother a little.

She took a deep breath, then turned, opened the door, and made her way into Callie's hospital room. Mason watched the door close behind Katie Rose. Then he meandered toward two chairs he had spotted at the end of the hallway. If he sat there, he would still be able to keep an eye out should Katie Rose come out in the hallway and need him for any reason. Yet, he could still get off of his feet. Mason was extremely tired.

While his parents and Katie Rose had catnapped all through the night, he had been awake. He had been contemplating his immediate future, which he had prayed did not include jail time for something he had not done.

His dad had also made it plainly known that he expected Mason to work at Greathouse Construction during the summer after he graduated. However, Long Wolf did not want Mason to work construction this summer. He wanted his son to get dressed up in suit and tie and come into the office with him. He wanted Mason to begin to learn the ropes on how construction deals were negotiated and closed.

Mason, on the other hand, had been looking forward to working construction again that summer. The mere thought of being dressed up in monkey suits all day and being trapped indoor made him feel supremely smothered. He wanted no part of this.

Mason had expressed his dismay to his father. He had made it clear that he wished to focus most of his energy on his music that summer. Long Wolf had given him a stern look and persuasively argued, "Mason, you need to start concentrating on your future after your graduation. It's time to start being a man. You need to start learning the ins and outs of the construction business. The sooner you get involved, the sooner you will be able to work hand-in-hand with me. And then one day, you can take over command of the company. As I did from my dad. You can hang out with your friends and play music in your spare time."

His dad did not appreciate what his music meant to him. Long Wolf did not grasp what a natural high it was for his son when he wrote a song. Or when Mason played it with the band and listened to people clapping for them. He did not understand Mason's dream of becoming a professional songwriter. In Long Wolf's mind, this was merely a fantasy life that existed in a boy's mind. Yet, with Mason's graduation, Long Wolf intended to consider Mason a man. His son now needed to put aside his boyish dreams and start accepting adult responsibility. There was no way Mason could convince Long Wolf otherwise.

Accordingly, before the incident with Callie tonight, Mason had not been looking forward to his upcoming summer. Now, he felt as if his free time and his music time may have been wrecked as well. His friendship with Ralph was now undisputedly ended. Mason no longer wanted anything to do with this guy. So, he had not only lost a long time friend, but the drummer in his band. Before he could begin to set up band jobs, Mason would have to find another drummer. The drummer would then have to learn his music and songs.

Then there was Rebecca. She had baled on him at the prom last night, and Mason innately sensed that this was the end for their relationship as well. Unfortunately, part of him felt a little relieved. Mason was weary of their constant fights over silly issues and of Rebecca's almost complete lack of affection toward him.

Lastly, there was Callie. During the summer, Callie always found some way to chase after him, and after tonight, Mason truly was not up to that. He was drained from fighting off Callie's advances and from watching her get hurt in the process. He would have felt terrible if Ralph had succeeded in raping her last night. It would not have been his fault, but Mason still would have felt awful. Callie had only been with Ralph in the first place to flirt with him. Mason had been attracted to Callie at the prom the night before. Callie's beauty had almost taken his breath away, and it was not the first time he had been drawn to her.

*Why else would I have kissed her in my kitchen not long ago?* After the far from innocent kisses they had shared, regardless of how hard he had tried, Mason had been unable to continue to see Callie only as a little girl. In fact, when he could persuade Rebecca to make out with him, Mason had sometimes found himself thinking about Callie. These forbidden thoughts had filled him with guilt.

*No wonder I have been so cross with Rebecca.* Some of Mason's discord with Rebecca had nothing to do with her. All at once, Mason felt overwhelmingly trapped by his own life circumstances. Thus, he had come to a careful, planned decision last night. He had determined that he needed to get away from everyone for awhile. He had only been hoping, and fervently praying, that this did not include going to jail. What Mason actually had in mind was going away to college a little early.

Mason had already discussed, with his parents, going away to college in the fall. Last night, he had concluded that he might like to start college in the summer instead. This would mean that he would have only a month and a half after graduation before he would be living several miles away from home, in a dorm on the college campus. The thought was very inviting and even comforting to him right now.

Mason assumed his dad would be fine with this decision. *After all, wouldn't this mean I was taking adult responsibility for my life a little sooner?* Nevertheless, Mason was not sure that his mom and Katie Rose were going to happy about this at all. Mason would greatly miss them both, but he needed to get away and begin his new life early. He would go to school in the summer, fall and winter. This would give him plenty of time away to clear his head. During his many sleepless hours the previous night, this was what Mason had resolved to do.

*This will work. It has to. After I basically spend a year away, I'll hopefully meet some other girl or girls. Maybe I'll have another special girlfriend within the year. Callie can move on and meet some boy or boys her own age, and maybe she'll settle down a little. Here's hoping anyway. Then things will be as they should be. It will all work out. It will. It has to. Things need to change from the way they are now.*

# Chapter 31

# *The Farewell*

Ralph caved under the pressure of being questioned by the police. He confessed to giving Callie a drugged drink. He gave them Jay's name, and he told them that he had gotten the drug from him.

Ralph swore that he had only given the drug to Callie to relax her a little. He insisted that he had never intended to hurt Callie in any way. He emphasized that he had *most certainly, under no circumstances* ever intended to rape Callie.

Ralph's family attorney worked a plea bargain for him. He convinced Ralph to plead guilty to attempted rape. The sentence would be anywhere from one to five years, but his attorney was confidence that Ralph would serve little or no time. After all, Ralph had no prior convictions.

The judge sentenced Ralph to thirty days in jail, with five years of probation to follow. He sternly warned Ralph that he did not want to see him again, or he would get a nasty taste of what prison life was all about. Callie was enraged that Ralph had not had to serve any prison time.

She was also furious when she found out that Mason intended to go away to college in a short while. Callie had found out about Mason from her Grandma Flora. She had not found out from Katie Rose. Callie refused to talk to Katie Rose or have anything to do with her. She was very angry with Katie Rose for revealing her drug use to everyone.

Callie was miserable. Her mom was locked away in some mental institution. Her dad was watching her every move now. And as if this was not bad enough, the love of her life was going away. *Mason will hardly ever be home.* Callie was very depressed.

\* \* \* \*

The morning that Mason left for college everyone in the house was quiet. No one was in a talkative mood. Apprehensiveness, worry and sadness all took the place of conversation.

Katie Rose found it hard to believe that her brother was leaving. He had not even taken his stuff out to his truck yet, but she missed Mason already. She did not want him to go away to college, but Mason had made it quite clear that this was what he needed to do. Consequently, Katie Rose had to accept that her brother was moving out, at least for a few years.

Long Wolf would miss his son. *But what Mason is doing is a good thing. My son is getting an early start on his college education, and Mason setting out on his own will make more of a man out of him.*

Jackie Lynn was not at all happy about her baby boy leaving the nest. She wished Mason had decided to attend college at a nearby university. She wanted him to still be living at home while he went to classes. However, Mason had insisted that going away to college and living in a dorm was something that he absolutely had to do. This had seemed to be vital to her son, so Jackie Lynn had put aside her selfish desires and gave Mason her full support. Regardless, she was going to miss him dreadfully.

\* \* \* \*

They all walked out to the truck with Mason, each carrying something. They handed him items, one by one, to place in the bed of the truck or behind the seat. After Mason had finished packing the truck, he took a little time with each family member before climbing into the vehicle and heading out on his way.

Long Wolf was the first to say goodbye to Mason. He both gave his son a hug and shook his hand, a demonstrative sign that he deemed Mason a grown man now. While he still had a firm grasp of Mason's hand, Long Wolf said to him, "We all love you, son.

Drive safe. Call us when you get there. And know that you can call us at any time if you need anything."

"Does that include money?" Mason teased. He was attempting to lighten the somber mood a little.

"Yes, if the money is needed for tuition or books or anything else school related," Long Wolf assured him with a smile. "Take care, son," he instructed, concluding his goodbye. Long Wolf released Mason's hand and stepped back so his wife or daughter could approach.

Katie Rose came up to him next. She placed her arms upon Mason's shoulders and hugged him securely. She held on to him for several long moments before she spoke even a word. When she pulled back, Mason could see that Katie Rose had tears standing in her eyes.

"Hey, don't cry, squirt," he half ordered. "It's not like you'll never see me again. I'll be home from time to time."

"It won't be the same as having you here," Katie Rose stated her true feelings. She was fighting back a sob.

"Geez....you'd think you would be glad to be rid of me," he attempted to kid with her. Mason hated it when his little sister got upset. It tugged at his heartstrings.

"I'm not," she admitted with candor. "I wish you weren't going."

"I know, but this is something I need to do. We've already talked about this," Mason began to explain once more.

"I know," Katie Rose agreed.

She was struggling to keep her composure. Katie Rose had not meant to get so emotional. She did not want Mason to leave feeling bad. "I'm going to miss you. That's all."

"Well....truth be told, I'll miss your pestering little butt too," Mason taunted with a devilish grin.

"Pestering, huh?" Katie Rose asked with a slight chuckle. *He's trying to cheer me up.* Katie Rose pushed up on her toes and gave Mason a warm kiss on the cheek. "I love you. You better call me a lot. How's that for pestering?"

"Great. And I will call," he promised with a lopsided grin.

Katie Rose stepped back then, and his mother hurried toward him. Jackie Lynn framed Mason's face with both her hands, and she gave him a tender peck on the lips.

"I love you from the bottom of my heart. You may be moving out, but you will always be my little boy. Do you understand this?" The question was rhetorical, so Mason did not attempt to interrupt his mother to answer. As expected, Jackie Lynn continued, "If you get up to that college dorm and you decide that you don't like it there, then I want you to know that you are free to come home at any time. Is that understood?"

"Yes, mom. I know," Mason did reply this time. *But I won't be back home. I'll be fine in the dorm.*

"Okay. And as your father already said, you can call us at *any* time if you need *anything*. Anything at all. Now don't forget to call when you get there. If you don't, you will get to see me again a lot sooner than you've expected, because I *will* hop in our car and follow you to college. This isn't something you want to see happen."

"No, you are right. It isn't," he admitted with a slightly embarrassed chuckle. "I'll be fine, mom. You'll see. But, yes, I promise that I will call you as soon as I get to the dorm. Give me a little leeway though. If I'm a few hours late, because of a wreck or construction on the freeway, I don't want to look up in traffic and see you barreling along to catch up with me. Alright?"

"Deal," she agreed with a forced smile. Jackie Lynn grabbed her son. She pulled him into a tight embrace, and she held him for a long while. Mason was beginning to wonder if his mother intended to ever release him. When Jackie Lynn pulled back, she instructed, sounding like a typical mother, "Be careful and be good."

"I will," Mason promised her, and he gave his mother one last kiss on the cheek.

# Chapter 32

# *College Days*

"Hey, Mase, aren't you going over to the frat party at Alpha Beta House?" Josh, his roommate asked.

He was toweling his sandy blond hair. Pieces of wet hair were sticking up everywhere. Water was still pearled on Josh's bare chest and back, and a towel was securely tucked around his waist. He had just gotten out of the shower.

Mason was sitting at his desk on his side of the room. He was attempting to read a chapter in one of his books. "No. I've got a lot of reading to do, and I still need to finish up an essay for one of my classes," Mason shared. He barely gave Josh a disinterested glance.

"Man, what the hell is the matter with you?" Josh demanded to know.

He charged toward Mason with annoyance. Josh ripped the book loose from his hands. He snapped the book closed, and he threw it with a thump facedown on Mason's desk.

"Books, reading and writing? Or girls, beer and the possibility of getting laid? Guess what your choice should be? You've been here for almost a month now, and you still act like your mommy and daddy are watching your every move. It's time for you to get out and live a little, buddy. You should at least make an appearance at this party. Reading and writing will still be waiting for you when you get back."

Mason did have to admit that he was more than a little bored. He was not into the party scene, and he was not much of a drinker. But the chance to meet a female did sound appealing to

264

him. He had not heard from Rebecca since he had left her at their prom. Mason had tried repeatedly to call and apologize, but Rebecca had refused to take his calls. It was for the best that they had broken up, but it still hurt a little.

"So are you going to go and get cleaned up or not?" Josh continued to urge.

"Okay, already!" Mason barked, but gave his roommate a slight smile. "I'll at least go and check it out. Will that make you happy?"

"You won't be sorry, Mase. Alpha Beta throws some awesome parties. You'll see. And the girls are very, very friendly, if you know what I mean!"

"Okay, okay! I'm sold. I'm going to go and take a shower now," Mason told him. He got up from his desk, grabbed a clean pair of underwear and a towel out of a drawer, and headed for the door. The bathroom, that the entire floor shared, was at the end of the hallway. He sprinted off in that direction now.

\* \* \* \*

Mason had been at Alpha Beta House for less than fifteen minutes. A tall, nicely endowed, blonde female approached *him*. She was dressed in a formfitting, low-cut, V-neck T-shirt, which proudly emphasized her ample cleavage. She also had on very short shorts, which showcased her round bottom and pretty, long, sleek legs.

*She reminds me a little of Callie*, Mason found himself thinking with a mixture of excitement and disgust. *I moved away from home to get away from that little temptress. And now what happens? Callie pops into my mind with nearly the first female I come in contact with. What's that all about? Forget Callie. Focus on this sweet little thing in front of you.*

\* \* \* \*

They talked; they danced; they drank a little beer together. Mason discovered that this fine lady's name was Belinda, and she was a few years older than he was. Mason was extremely attracted to Belinda, and she seemed to be very attracted to him as well.

Belinda suggested that the two of them leave the party. She wanted to go someplace much more private. She shared with Mason that she lived in an apartment just off campus. Mason enthusiastically agreed to leave the party with Belinda.

They left the party and started across campus. Mason slipped Belinda's hand into his. They strolled hand-in-hand the rest of the way to her apartment.

They were fortunate that it was summer, and the nights were warm. There was a soft breeze, which caressed their skin. The weather was perfect for a nice walk. The bright light from the almost full moon, which illuminated their path, seemed to be in their favor as well.

Belinda's small, one bedroom apartment was just on the outskirts of the campus. As they strolled across the campus grounds, she briefly explained to Mason that she had once lived in a dorm. This had been about three years ago when she had first started college. Belinda went on to elaborate that she had been caught with a guy in her room late one night. She confessed to Mason that she had been kicked out of the dorm. Her parents had blamed her roommate's bad influence for her wayward judgment.

Belinda told Mason that her parents had rented her small apartment for her so that she could continue her education. Belinda shared with Mason that she had been living in this apartment alone ever since and was happy here.

She unlocked the door, switched on a light, and hastily ushered Mason inside. Belinda turned from Mason to shut the door and lock it. Mason made his way down the narrow hall. He stood just inside a room that looked to be a combination of the entire living quarters. Mason peered at his surroundings, and he discovered the apartment was indeed quite small.

There was a compact stand-in kitchen area at the end of the hall with a small stove, refrigerator and microwave. Connected to the side of this area was a long counter that had three stools beside it. This clearly replaced having a kitchen table. If you turned to face the opposite direction, you were looking at the tiny living room area, with a couch, table and lamp. A television and a small stereo system stood in the corner on what looked to be plastic milk crates.

Directly to the rear of the living room area, Mason was amazed to see Belinda's queen-sized bed. The bedroom was not partitioned off. There was only one door that led off from the bedroom space. Mason guessed that this must be the bathroom. He noted that his dorm room was larger than this apartment. *But at least Belinda doesn't have to share this space with anyone, like I do at the dorm.*

"This is nice," Mason told Belinda.

"Have a seat on the couch," Belinda told him. "Do you want anything to drink? I have beer or soft drinks."

"No thanks," Mason answered. He had not even finished the one beer he had been drinking at the party. He was not much of a drinker.

Mason had a seat on the couch. *It's facing away from that bed which is directly behind me. I'm sure Belinda didn't invite me to her apartment for anything like that anyway. After all, we barely know each other. We'll sit here on the couch, talk, and get to know each other a little more. Hopefully, she'll feel comfortable enough with me to let me kiss her good night. Man, would I like to kiss her! She's gorgeous!*

Belinda bent down and leaned across Mason. She was reaching for the lamp on the side table by the couch. An unbelievable view of Belinda's appealing, ample cleavage was placed before Mason's eyes. His heart sped up a little more with excitement. *I should look away.* This was the right thing to do, but Mason could not make himself do so. Instead, he thoroughly enjoyed his brief revealing glance, noting Belinda's supple looking, pink nipples.

Belinda turned the switch on the lamp a few times. She set it on a low-light setting. As she straightened back up and walked away from him, Mason watched Belinda's hips invitingly sway from side to side. He also observed her cute, well-rounded little bottom. Belinda's shorts barely cleared each cheek and seemed to give her attractive derrière more emphasis than was necessary.

*Maybe I* should *ask for something to drink after all!* He deliberated with slight panic. Mason noted that his body had begun to respond to all of the delightful, enticing views. Being alone with Belinda in this apartment – *and knowing that big bed is right behind us* – was not helping matters at all.

Mason tried to rein in his desires. However, Belinda was not helping him. She switched off the bright light overhead – the one she had turned on when they had first walked in the door.

Belinda sauntered over to her stereo and put in a CD. The soft sound of a sensual love song began to fill the room. Then she came back and had a seat hip-to-hip with Mason the couch.

"You know, Mason, I think you are very handsome," she told him. Belinda began running her fingers through his thick, black hair. She also pleasantly massaged the back of his skull.

"Well, Belinda, I think you are a very pretty lady," Mason said with an appealing smile, showcasing his nice white, straight teeth. He raised his arm, slipped it around her shoulders, and squeezed her a little tighter to his side.

Mason was surprised to find that he was a little nervous. He wanted to kiss Belinda in the worst way, but the only other female he had ever kissed – *other than Callie* – had been Rebecca. Belinda was a beautiful, older woman, who he was sure had been kissed many times. Belinda most likely had been with older guys. Mason feared his kisses might pale in comparison.

Mason did not have to worry about this for long. Belinda wasted no time taking matters into her own hands. She slid her arms around Mason's neck, drew in close and began to kiss his lips with tenderness. After only a few moments, however, Belinda's kisses became much more aggressive and demanding. Mason opened his mouth a slight bit and allowed Belinda to intertwine her fiery, persistent tongue with his. *This woman certainly knows how to kiss!*

Mason lost himself in dizzying pleasure. He had dated Rebecca for over two years, and their kissing had never been this passionate. The closest he had ever come to this was when he and Callie had kissed in his kitchen. But Callie had only been a little girl playing at being a woman. *Belinda was all woman!*

Belinda did not have to take Mason's hand and place it on her breasts as Callie had. He willingly moved his hands to fondle her breasts. He grew even more excited when he felt her erect nipples underneath the thin cotton fabric of her T-shirt. *I don't think she has on a bra.* No sooner had this pleasant thought registered than Mason's body responded aptly with a familiar throbbing against his shorts.

"Mason, wait," Belinda said in an almost breathless whisper. She pulled back a little from him.

*Here it comes. She's going to tell me we need to slow down and cool things off. She doesn't want to go too far too fast.*

*I'm way too familiar with this from Rebecca.* Mason loathly stopped what he had been doing. *I'll need to take a cold shower in her bathroom before I'll be able to walk home! Or maybe she has an icepack I can slip into my pants?*

He watched as Belinda stood up. *She's either going to escape to the kitchen to get us something cold to drink, or disappear into the bathroom.*

Instead, Belinda shocked Mason when she reached down and took a firm grasp on one of his hands. "Why don't we get a little more comfortable?" Mason was astonished to hear her ask.

He nearly leaped to his feet beside Belinda. He freely allowed her to lead him around the couch and over to the bed. *Am I dreaming?! If so, I don't want to wake up!* They stopped and stood right beside the bed.      Belinda began to persistently kiss him again, and Mason returned her sultry, passionate kisses. Waves of tremendous desire were rocking his body from head to toe. He had never experienced anything as magnificent as this.

Mason began to tremble as Belinda's soft, able hands undid his belt. She unbuttoned his khaki shorts, pulled his T-shirt loose and hoisted it up his chest and over his head. Belinda had a wicked, inviting smile on her face as she said, "Guess it's your turn to be able to take something off of me now."

Belinda raised her arms in the air and Mason shuddered again. He readily placed his hands on each of her sides, just above her hips, and took hold of her T-shirt. He slipped Belinda's shirt upward, revealing her flat belly. Mason paused for a few moments. He was expecting that Belinda would make him stop before he went any further.

Belinda did not protest, so Mason eagerly pulled the T-shirt the rest of the way up and off of her body. Belinda's lovely, large, full breasts were fully exposed to him. Mason was paralyzed for a few moments by the stunning picturesque image of Belinda's naked upper body. *What a beautiful sight!* He sighed. Mason took his time gazing at Belinda's exquisite breasts and tempting erect nipples. He tried to catch his breath.

Mason's heart was beating so forcefully that he feared he might have a heart attack, or even pass out. His shorts were much too tight just below his waist. Mason wanted to kiss and caress Belinda's bare breasts, but he truly did not know how much more enticement his body could endure. Mason was trying to keep from losing control.

"My turn again," he heard Belinda say with a conniving giggle.

Mason's legs began to shake as he felt Belinda's fingers nimbly unzip his shorts. She placed a hand on each side of his waist and began to tug his shorts downward. As Mason's shorts slid down his legs and hit the floor, his erection was made prominent. With fear, he began to wonder if he would fall as well. His legs felt like jelly.

His eyes were transfixed as Belinda unzipped her own shorts. She sent them sailing to the floor where his had haphazardly been left. With relief, he watched Belinda lower herself to a sitting position on the side of the bed. Mason immediately sat down beside her. He was severely struggling to maintain control over his body. He felt as if he could loose the battle at any time. *Good Lord, we're nearly naked. How far is Belinda going to allow this to go? I don't know how much more I can stand!*

Belinda pushed her legs off the floor. She slid herself up to rest in the center of the bed. Mason was impatient to be able to kiss and touch Belinda again, so he swung his own legs off the floor and slid over beside her again.

"Well, what have we got here?" Mason heard her ask. He saw that her eyes were staring at the significant bulge in his underwear.

Mason was not at all prepared for what came next. Belinda reached to cup his erection through his briefs. Unfortunately, it was more than he could withstand. His body automatically stiffened in response. *Oh no!* No!! Mason's mind was screaming, but his body was no longer listening to any of his commands.

Mason experienced the glorious release that his lower half had been demanding for some time now. His entire body was rocketed by the fierce intensity of this accidental, forceful eruption. As soon as his body ceased betraying him, Mason stared at Belinda's wet hand and the saturated front of his underwear with mortification. *Oh, just give me a giant hole in the floor, because I need to crawl in it right now!*

"I am *so* sorry," Mason managed to utter several long moments later. He slid back a little in the bed and despondently laid his head against the headboard. *You'll never know how sorry I truly am!* He was attempting to decide how he could escape this apartment with some *small* degree of dignity.

"Hey, it's okay," Belinda began to console him. "This was all my fault. I came on way too strong. I overwhelmed you. It will be okay."

Mason watched as she climbed from the bed. Then he looked away. He could not stand to stare at this beautiful, half naked woman whom he had *forever* blown his chance to be intimate with. *Where is Belinda going? Is she going in the bathroom? I need to go in there and clean up a little. Then I need to leave. I can't believe I let this happen. What a dipshit!*

"Mason, please don't feel bad," Belinda pleaded with him. "It's no big deal. Really it isn't. You lay there and relax for a minute. I'll be right back. You wait right there for me, please."

*Like I have a choice.* He sure could not slip his shorts back on and make his escape until he cleaned up a little. *Hurry and go in the bathroom and wash your hands, so I can get in there, get cleaned up and get out of here. She has no idea how awkward this is for me, or she would have let me go first.*

"I'll be right here," he curtly responded, staring absently at the ceiling. Mason lay there and listened to the water running for several moments in the bathroom. *What in the world is she doing in there, taking a shower? Come on, Belinda, I need to get cleaned up and be on my way. It's been fun, and it could have been a lot more fun, but I blew things, or rather my overly responsive body did!*

Belinda came out a moment later. Mason was relieved to see that she had covered her nakedness with a long, silky, black robe. He started to sit up in the bed, but she held up a hand in protest and said, "No, slide down and lay your head on a pillow. I'm going to help you freshen up."

It was then that Mason noticed the washcloth she had in one hand and the towel she had draped over her arm. *What is Belinda talking about? She can't mean that she intends to wash me! Not* there!

Belinda did not give Mason the option or the time to mull over what his next action might be. Instead, she climbed back in bed with him and was softly rubbing his chest. She persuaded him with gentleness to lay his head back on the pillow. She tenderly kissed Mason's lips and assured him once more that everything would soon be okay.

"Trust me, Mason. What happened won't be a problem for long. It actually will work in our favor."

He had absolutely no idea what nonsense Belinda was uttering, but he did know that she was being very soothing. Mason decided to relax for a few moments and enjoy it. The intense orgasm he had experienced had left him rather spent.

Mason planned to get up and get cleaned up in a minute. He had no idea what Belinda was planning to do with the washcloth and towel. Maybe he was supposed to take these from her, so that when he got up, he did not make a mess on the floor on his way to the bathroom. It was nice of her to bring these to him. He did not want to make this *thing* any worse than it had already been.

Belinda continued to rub Mason's chest and kiss his lips, neck, shoulder blades and chest for several more minutes. She wanted to make certain that Mason was thoroughly relaxed. Actually, Mason was almost in a light slumber. Belinda carefully slipped her hand, with the warm, wet washcloth in it, down to the edge of Mason's briefs. Mason's head sprang up off the pillow, and he gaped at Belinda in amazement. However, before he could protest, she kissed his lips again and whispered into his ear, "Just give me a minute and everything will be fine."

Belinda began to slide Mason's briefs down, little by little. She used the still warm washcloth to wipe away the little mess that had occurred from his accident. She was speaking so softly as she gave Mason instructions for each next move, "Raise your hips a little; now lay still a minute; okay, raise your leg."

Belinda's warm smooth hands moved over Mason's lower body. She removed his briefs, and with skill, Belinda wiped away any memory of what had previously happened. The glorious feel of Belinda's gentle fingers massaging and stroking his manhood had Mason both bewildered, flabbergasted and...*am I getting excited again*? Mason did not believe that this could be possible.

"Aw...our friend down here likes this," Belinda said and gave him a wide, satisfied smile.

She wrapped her hand around his hardening shaft and began to move it up and down. Belinda was stroking him with tender fingers. She began to dry off Mason's lower body with the soft towel. First she dried the inside of his legs, and then Belinda moved to Mason's testicles. She caressed them smoothly over and over until they were also dry.

Belinda turned and proceeded to reposition herself so that she was straddling Mason's legs. She crawled upward over Mason's body. Belinda took his manhood into her hands again and began to fondle him a few more times in the soft towel.

When she was satisfied that Mason was cleaned up, Belinda crawled to the foot of the bed. She wrapped his briefs and the washcloth in the used towel. Belinda climbed out of bed. She turned to face Mason, not a shy bone in her body, and instructed, "Hold that thought...or should I say that magnificent erection?" Then Belinda escaped into the bathroom again.

Mason was staring at himself as if he did not recognize the lower portion of his body. He had no idea that he could respond like this again so fast. *Oh my gosh! I'm now totally naked in this woman's bed and I'm aroused again. I can't believe this is happening. This must be a dream; please God, don't let me wake up yet!*

Mason heard Belinda coming back out of the bathroom. As she approached the side of the bed, she untied her robe, slid it over her shoulders, and let it fall to the floor. She had no clothes on underneath. It was evident that she had taken off her panties in the bathroom.

*This is going to happen! I'm not dreaming. We are going to have sex!* Mason concluded with renewed optimism and impatience.

As Belinda crawled back into bed with him, Mason decided to completely submit to her will. He was eager to do anything that she might ask of him at this moment. Mason wanted to please Belinda as much as she was supremely pleasing him. She was making all of his dreams come true.

# Chapter 33

# *Flight*

Mary Julia had been sequestered at the hospital, so Flora began making a concerted effort to check in often on Jonathan and Callie. After all, Callie's secret was out in the open now, so Jonathan now knew that his daughter was using drugs and running with a wild crowd of kids. Callie was no longer having anything to do with Katie Rose, since she had revealed her secret at the hospital. Flora wanted to stay on a friendly basis with the girl and thus help to keep an eye on her, at least as much as she could.

Flora continued to take Callie out to dinner on a regular basis and to talk to her as if they were two adult friends. Flora figured that the time she spent with Callie also gave Jonathan a needed break from the girl. After all, fatherhood was being thrown on him all at once. Mary Julia had never allowed him much of a father role in Callie's life before.

Flora was over visiting with Callie and Jonathan one evening when her cell phone unexpectedly rang. She figured it was Kenny calling to say he was back in town. He had gone to visit his sister, who was in the hospital. She lived in another state, a five-hour drive away. Kenny had spent the night at a hotel near the hospital the night before.

Flora had wanted to go with her husband, but she was a judge now, and she was presiding over a big trial this whole week. Kenny was always understanding of her career. He had assured Flora that it was no big deal. However, Flora hated being parted from him and not being by his side to support him.

"What?...No...I don't think I understood you. You said...NO...who is this?! That can't be right!" Flora sounded frantic.

She stood and paced in front of the coffee table, arguing with some unknown person on her phone. Jonathan was not sure that he liked Flora's demeanor at all. Whoever she was talking to was saying something very upsetting to her.

"Oh, dear God! No!" Flora began chanting. She broke into tears.

"Flora, what is it?" Jonathan asked, as he rose to his feet also.

"Kenny...they said...they said that...K...Ken...Kenny is dead!" she managed to mumble, almost incoherently, through her tears and sobs.

Jonathan reached and took the phone out of Flora's hand. After talking to the person on the other end of the connection for a few moments, he determined that it was a policeman from a city about an hour away. According to this policeman, there had been a terrible pile up on the freeway and Kenny's car had been crushed by a semi. He had died instantly.

"Thank you for calling," Jonathan said rather numbly to the officer on the other end of the receiver. "We will call you back about the arrangements."

Jonathan ended the call and held out his arms to Flora. She fell into them, bawling her eyes out. "Flora, I am so sorry," was all Jonathan could say to her. He held her tightly and allowed his heart to break a little for his dear friend's agonizing loss.

\* \* \* \*

In the months following Kenny's death, Jonathan and Flora began spending quite a bit of time together. Instead of her checking in on Jonathan and Callie, Jonathan began inviting Flora to have dinner with them rather often. A few times, he even took her out to dinner. Jonathan was Flora's sounding board for her overwhelming grief about Kenny's death. Flora was Jonathan's sounding board about Mary Julia's continued illness and Callie's uncontrollable tirades. Jonathan had pulled in the reins on his daughter. He kept a much closer watch over who Callie was hanging out with and what she might be doing. Jonathan and Flora had always been good friends, but they seemed to grow even closer now.

\* \* \* \*

One evening, after a particularly bad argument between Jonathan and Callie – He had gotten her report card that day, and she was flunking every class – Callie had stormed out of the house in an angry huff. Flora had been approaching their front door, and Callie had almost knocked Flora off the porch.

Jonathan threw his hands up in the air. He went back into the house with Flora following closely at his heels, "I don't know what to do with Callie, Flora. She is out of control. She seems angry at the world. The doctors tell me that Mary Julia is getting better, but how will she deal with Callie being like this if they release her from the hospital? And do I stay here with Mary Julia and try and help her with Callie, or do I move back out? Lord knows, Mary Julia and I haven't even begun to look into the problems in our marriage. I'm almost at my rope's end."

"I feel so badly for you, Jonathan," Flora commiserated. "I wish I could answer your questions for you, but I can't. All I can tell you is I'll be here for all of you in any way that I can."

"Like you always have been," Jonathan said with a strained smile. "I'm sorry to be unloading on you like this, Flora. You have enough on your own plate to deal with. I know you miss Kenny."

"I do, and I always will, but it helps to involve myself in other people's problems. It gets my mind off being alone," Flora confessed.

"You're never alone. You'll always have me, Jackie Lynn and even Mary Julia – as much as she can be there for you. You have to remember that."

"I do," she tried to reassure him. "It still helps to be here and try to help you."

They sat down on the couch together. "And it is greatly appreciated," Jonathan told Flora. He took her hands into his own. "You are a very special woman, Flora. I don't understand why God took Kenny away from you. You deserve a good man to be by your side."

"Thanks, Jonathan. I don't fully understand it yet either, but I guess in time God's plan will come to light. I have to believe that," she said. However, tears came to her eyes.

"I'm sorry, Flora. I didn't mean to upset you," Jonathan apologized. He pulled her into a tight embrace and began tenderly patting her back.

*She smells nice.* He could not help but notice.

What happened next was nothing that Jonathan had planned. Their mutual neediness had bonded Flora and Jonathan closer together, and this now manifested itself as physical attraction. Jonathan had always been true to Mary Julia, and he was still faithful to her. However, desire overcame his logic, and before he thought about what he was doing, Jonathan brought his lips to meet Flora's.

She certainly had not meant to respond. Nonetheless, Jonathan's warm embrace and his needful lips had Flora's mind betraying her. She began to heartily respond to his kiss before she could stop herself.

The loud scream instantaneously brought them back to their senses. Mary Julia stood in the entranceway to the living room, gaping at them in horror. Jackie Lynn was standing right behind her. She had an equally horrified look on her face. *What is going on here?!*

As Callie was coming back in the front door, she heard her mother's voice. *But it can't be. She is still in that mental hospital.*

"Oh my God, one of my best friends and my husband! I can't believe this!" Mary Julia was ranting.

Callie made her way a little farther down the hall with hesitation. She was shocked to find Jackie Lynn and – *yes* – her mother standing there. *What is she doing here? And what is she talking about?*

Callie quietly crept up behind Jackie Lynn, and then she could see her father and Flora sitting very near each other on the couch. They both had stunned and guilty expressions on their faces. *What did they do?*

"You whore!" Mary Julia swore at Flora and began charging toward her. Jonathan stood and caught both of Mary Julia's arms as she violently swung her fists toward Flora. Flora was still numbly sitting on the couch. She looked like the person who was catatonic now.

"Mary Julia, it isn't what you think," Jonathan was trying to reason with her. "I was only trying to comfort Flora. We were talking about Kenny and she got upset."

"Yeah, you were trying to comfort her alright. You were comforting one another with your mouths and tongues. Tell me, if Jackie Lynn hadn't brought me home for a visit, would you have moved this *comfort* into the bedroom? I had Jackie Lynn bring me home to surprise you. But I guess the surprise is on me!"

Callie could not believe what she was hearing. *My dad and Flora? Is that why she has been coming around so much lately? Is that why she started spending all the extra time with me all of the sudden? I can't trust anyone. All of the adults and even friends, like Katie Rose, have let me down.*

Callie felt overwhelmed by all of the betrayal she had seen in her young life. "You bitch! Who do you think you are coming into my house and sleeping with my dad?!" she shouted.

Callie startled Jackie Lynn as she raced around the back of her. Jackie Lynn had not realized that Callie was even there. Jonathan was also astounded to see his daughter running across the room toward him and Mary Julia and Flora. He released his hold on his wife and instead grabbed his daughter.

"Let me go!" Callie demanded as she fiercely struggled against Jonathan's strong grasp. "Stop trying to defend your lover. I'm sorry, mom. I didn't know. I wondered why Flora was hanging around so much."

"N...no," Flora was saying and shaking her head from side to side. "Nothing like that is happening. Please believe me."

No one was listening to her, especially Callie. She had made up her mind that her dad and Flora were now having an affair and nothing Flora could say now would convince her any differently.

"Callie, my baby, Mama is so sorry," Mary Julia was cooing in Callie's ear. She was trying to rub the back of Callie's head. "You shouldn't have to see this. Mama should have been here."

"Stop talking to me like that!" Callie turned her rage on Mary Julia now. "I'm not a baby. When are you going to realize that?"

"Callie, you will always be Mama's baby," Mary Julia continued to declare.

Callie managed to break free from Jonathan's confining arms. "Leave me alone! All of you!" Callie shouted. She cupped her hands to her ears to try and shut out Mary Julia's annoying baby talk.

Callie ran from the room and down the hall to her bedroom. She slammed and locked her door. *I can't take this anymore! I don't want to end up a nutcase like my mom. If I stay here with these people, that is exactly what is going to happen.*

Callie opened her closet and pulled out a little travel case. She threw some clothes and a few other essentials inside. Then she went over to her bedroom window, quietly raised it, and made her escape.

*I don't know where I'll go. But I'll find somewhere. I can't live here anymore. I won't let them make me crazy like they all are.*

\* \* \* \*

Callie went to Julie's house. She had hidden there nearly a week before Julie's father discovered her. Julie had been away at school and her dad was supposed to have still been at work. However, he came home early that day and caught Callie taking a shower.

Callie screamed with terror, at the top of her lungs, when he jerked the shower curtain back and exposed her. Immediately, she attempted to cover her nakedness with her arms and hands. She stood there in astonishment.

Callie naively expected that Julie's dad would turn his back in decency or perhaps even dash from the room in embarrassment. Quite the contrary, this man stood there leering at her with indecency. As he leaned over to turn off the shower, Callie moved back as far as she could until her back was against the cold, wet, tile wall. The whole time she still struggled to impossibly shield her nude body.

"Well, who have we got here?" he asked in a slurred voice.

His breath smelled nasty with the heavy scent of strong liquor. Callie could have guessed that he was drunk. *Why else would he be in here?* This did not come as any big shock to Callie. Julie's dad was always drunk. Most of the time she had spent in

279

this house, he had been passed out on the couch from alcohol consumption.

"I...I'm a friend of Julie's," Callie nervously answered.

She awkwardly stood facing him with one leg crossed in front of the other. Callie used her arms and hands to block what little she could from this man's uninvited intense examination. Callie wanted, in the worse way, to reach out and pull the shower curtain from his hands and fully hide her nudity. She did not like the way that Julie's dad seemed to be inspecting her naked body with evil looking eyes.

After what seemed to be a lifetime, he spoke again. "And where is Julie?" he questioned her. He was glancing from side to side, as if he expected his daughter to spring forth from somewhere at any moment.

"Um.....I'm not sure; she's somewhere in the house," Callie had lied. "Julie!" she shouted.

Callie did not want to tell him that Julie was still at school. The reality had dawned on her that she was alone in the house with this man. Callie was petrified. She foolishly thought that she might be sparred some ugly scene with Julie's dad if she could convince him that Julie was also someplace in the house. Callie had been rather relieved when Julie's dad had stumbled backward towards the door. *Maybe he is finally going to leave*, she assumed.

However, her heart began to race in trepidation when she watched him pull the bathroom door shut and lock it. *Oh my god, what is he doing?!* With only a second to spare, Callie reached out and grabbed the shower curtain. She wrapped it as much as possible around her glistening wet body. Julie's dad approached her again with an unsteady step. Callie stood there shivering in the tub, trying to determine what she could do to defend herself. *I'm trapped! What can I do!*

"Now don't get all shy on me, little beauty," Julie's dad said with a wicked smile. He disgustingly reached down to hold his male member. He reached out with his other hand to grab hold of the shower curtain. He intended to pull it from Callie's body. Callie released it.

In doing this, she caught Julie's dad by surprise. He had expected resistance from Callie with the shower curtain. The loose shower curtain caused him to stagger backwards. He looked over to catch hold of the wall.

This gave Callie the chance she had been praying for. With all of her adrenaline pumping, she pushed outward with all the force she could muster. She hit this man's chest with both her open palms. Julie's dad was so intoxicated that Callie's unexpected compelling thrust easily sent him sprawling away from her. His feet went out from under him, and he had plunged backwards. His head struck the corner of the sink with a thud, and he crumpled the rest of the way to the floor and lay very still.

Callie stared at him for only a moment in alarm. *Oh dear God, have I killed him!?* Then she intelligently grasped that she needed to get out of that room while she could – *in case he isn't dead.*

Callie climbed out of the tub and rushed over to the door. Her fingers were trembling, as she unlocked the door and hurried out of the room. She raced down the hall to Julie's room. She pulled the door closed behind her and locked it. Callie proceeded, at breakneck speed, to throw on her clothes and shoes. She grabbed her purse and her suitcase, with what was left in it. She opened the window and leaped out. As soon as her feet had hit the ground, Callie started to run as fast as she could.

She wanted to get as far away from this place as possible. She could no longer depend on Julie to hide her anymore. *Julie's alcoholic dad is a pervert and drinks himself into oblivion day after day. Julie's mom left shortly after she was born to pursue some acting career, never to return. Then there's my mom and dad, they both sleep around, and my mom is confirmed mentally ill; she is basically crazy. I'm not sure which is worse. Everybody's parents must be screwed up in some way*, Callie cynically concluded. Callie had no idea where she might be running. All she knew for sure, once again, was that she had to get away and that she could only depend upon herself.

# Chapter 34

## *Sweet Sixteen*

Today was Katie Rose's sixteenth birthday. It should have been a very exciting and happy day for her. Instead, she was feeling a bit disoriented. The reason for her turmoil was the fact that both Mason and Callie were missing from her life.

Mason sent her a card. He even wrote a special note in it. 'Katie Rose, I hope your BIG 16 is a great one! I'm sorry I can't be there to help you celebrate. I have to be here for exams. College life gives you no breaks. ☹ Love and Miss Ya! Your big bro, Mason. ☺ '

He sent her a present – a bright red, women's, stretch, V-neck T-shirt with his college name printed on the front. She was wearing it. Mason also called and sang Happy Birthday to her, but this was far different from him actually being there. Katie Rose had missed him a great deal since he had gone away to college the year before. She missed him even more on this special day. It did not seem right to be celebrating her birthday – especially her *sweet sixteenth* – without Mason being there.

Then there was Callie. She and Callie had always celebrated their birthdays together. This was the first year that Katie Rose had this day all to herself. Ever since Callie ran away, Katie Rose had worried about what had become of her. Thoughts of Callie heavily preoccupied Katie Rose's mind today. She could not help but wonder if her friend was someplace safe celebrating her birthday as well.

Katie Rose's parents and Flora went out of their way to make her birthday extra special. They threw a big party for her and invited all her friends. The ceilings in the living room and dining room were decorated with many bright streamers of pink, blue, red and yellow, and Millar balloons with BIG 16 written on them had been strategically placed all throughout the house. In the middle of the dining room table was a large sheet cake. It had white icing and pink, blue, red and yellow Roses all around the corners. Written across the cake was 'Happy BIG 16, Katie Rose. We all love you!' There was also an icing drawing of a long, dark-haired lady, with green eyes, driving a red car.

"Is this a hint?" Katie Rose asked with a smile, pointing to the car, as she saw the cake for the first time. The room was now full of her friends.

Her parents merely returned her smile. Jackie Lynn lit fifteen small candles and the one, large, 16 candle in the center of the cake. Then Katie Rose's family and friends all boisterously sang 'Happy Birthday' to her. She opened up her friends' cards and gifts then and thanked each one with a wide smile and an appreciative embrace. Katie Rose received many nice gifts – clothes, CDs, DVDs and earrings – but Mason and Callie's presence would have been nicer.

After she read the last of the cards and unwrapped the last of the presents, Long Wolf stepped forward and handed her one final card and gift. "Your birthday present from your mom and I," Long Wolf said with a devious smile.

Katie Rose opened the card first. It was a sentimental card. She read it and then she gave both her mom and her dad a hug and kiss. Then she centered her attention on the present. She carefully tore away the shiny gold paper with 16's all over it. Then she lifted the lid off of the large box. Inside, she found another wrapped box.

"Oh, no," she said with a chuckle, eyeballing both her mom and dad's smiling faces. "What have you guys done to me? Was this Mason's idea?" *I wish he was here to see this. I wish Callie was too.*

Long Wolf and Jackie Lynn merely directed her to keep opening her present. Katie Rose opened two more boxes before she finally got to the last one. When she lifted the top off of this box, there was a note inside. The note said that she had already been enrolled in a driver's education course. Below the note was an envelope. Inside the envelope was a keychain with a remote and car keys attached.

"What do these go to?" Katie Rose asked with a wide, gleeful smile and sparking animated eyes.

"Um...." Long Wolf stalled. "Jackie Lynn, what are the keys for, honey?"

"Well...I would guess that they must go to some car."

"Oh, come on," Katie Rose half begged. "Where's the car?!"

"Why don't we go to the garage," Long Wolf suggested.

Katie Rose was sprinting in that direction before her parents scarcely had a chance to move. As she reached the door, leading from the kitchen into the garage, she jerked back the curtain. She began shrieking in excited screams and bounced up and down. Long Wolf, Jackie Lynn, Flora, and her friends were now gathered in the kitchen behind her.

"Well, are you just going to stand there screaming, or are you going to go and check it out?" Long Wolf asked with noted amusement.

"Is it really mine?!" Katie Rose asked. She looked amazed and extremely pleased.

"Yes, Emerald Sea, it is all yours. The only stipulation is you have to learn to drive it safely. I don't want any accidents."

He walked over and unlocked the door and opened it for her then. Katie Rose bounded through the doorway, down the two stairs, and over to the car – a bright red, shiny Mustang. She hit the button on the remote on her key ring, heard a beep, and heard the lock for the driver's door snap open. She pulled the door open and dove inside. As she slid down into the leather seat, she began shrieking with delight again.

"I take it you like it," Long Wolf said, bending to look inside at his daughter's ecstatic face.

"Oh, daddy, I love it!" she screeched, throwing her arms around his neck and giving him another kiss.

"I know you will take good care of it."

"I will! I will!" she promised.

Her mom came over next and Katie Rose also gave her a hug and a kiss and shared her utmost pleasure with the car. Then her friends all gathered around the car. Katie Rose heard many exclamations of 'Wow!' 'Sweet!' 'Too Nice!'. For the moment, she was very happy.

\* \* \* \*

Katie Rose had felt special and happy on her sixteenth birthday, but without Mason and Callie there, she also had not been able to help feeling a little sad and lost from time to time. Everything in her life seemed to be changing, and Katie Rose was not at all sure that she liked the changes.

Later, after all her friends left, Long Wolf caught Katie Rose by herself. She had a rather forlorn expression on her face. "Hey, Miss Sixteen, why the sad expression?" he asked as he hugged his daughter to his side and kissed her on her temple.

"I miss Mason and Callie. This birthday didn't seem right without them both here – especially Callie. I've never celebrated a birthday without her by my side," she freely shared with her father.

"Yeah, I know it's tough. And I know you worry about Callie. We all do. But things change as you reach adulthood, Katie Rose, and you are all growing up. You have a new car, and you'll have your license soon. You couldn't drive a car if you weren't growing up. I don't want you to be sad about changes in your life. It's just something that happens. You will probably have many birthdays that your brother and...or Callie won't be at from now on."

"Thanks a lot, dad," she said with a sarcastic chuckle. "That's makes me feel so much better."

"Well, one thing will never change. Your mom and I will always there for you," Long Wolf pledged and gave his daughter another slight embrace. "No more sad thoughts today, Emerald Sea. Okay?"

"Okay," she agreed, but Katie Rose still could not help mulling over the changes that were occurring in her life.

# Chapter 35

# *Innocence Lost*

Callie had been living with David for almost a year. David was thirty-five, which made him nineteen years older than Callie. He was a big man, over six feet tall and weighing over 200 pounds. With the weight training he did everyday, he was not afraid of anyone anywhere.

However, Callie had no fear of David. He treated her like she was a princess, bringing her bouquets of flowers and special little presents. David had introduced Callie to crack cocaine. He freely shared his stash of the drug with her quite frequently. Plus, David had unselfishly opened up his home to Callie when she had nowhere else to go. Callie had first encountered David in the park. This was on the day she had run away from Julie's house.

Callie had recognized David. He had been the man behind the wheel the night that Glenda had picked her up. That was the night Callie had passed out, had been taken to the hospital, and had had her stomach pumped.

David had recognized Callie as well. He apologized to her for having left her in the park that night. David asked Callie why she had stopped hanging out with Glenda. Callie explained that she and Glenda had never really been friends.

"I started partying with some friends at school instead," Callie explained.

After David heard that Callie was still into 'partying', he had been quick to offer her alcohol and drugs once more. Callie had been very tempted to partake. But she decided that she needed to keep her head clear. *I still need to decipher where I might go for the night*, Callie had been wisely thinking.

David next asked Callie if she would like to go to dinner with him. He told her that he had supposed to have been partying with friends, there in the park. "But they evidently stood me up." Callie had been a little hesitant to go with David, since she hardly knew him.

However, hunger overtook Callie's better judgment. She had not eaten since breakfast, and she had only had a granola bar then. Plus, she had very little cash in her purse and had not wished to spend anymore than necessary. So Callie agreed to go to dinner with David.

This turned out to be a good decision on her part after all. At dinner, David confided to Callie about how terrible his family life had been. He shared that he had run away from home when he was sixteen and had lived on his own since then. David made Callie feel relaxed. Thus she eventually admitted that she too had a very dysfunctional family, had run away from home, and had been living with a friend for the past week. Callie also disclosed that she was not sure where she would be staying tonight or subsequent nights to come.

Callie had been stunned when David extended the invitation to her that she stay at his place for a while. "I have plenty of room. I have a big comfortable couch you can crash on. I know what it is like to have screwy parents and to have to fend for yourself at a young age. I wouldn't have made it if I hadn't had help. Why don't you let me help you out, Callie? What alternative do you have? Are you going to sleep on the streets? Or do you plan to go back home? I can give you a roof over your head and some food to eat. I might even be able to help you find a job. You can show your crappy parents that you can stand on your own two feet. Then you can eventually get a place of your own. You'll never have to go back home."

Everything that David said sounded fantastic to Callie. However, she did not know him well at all, and she had to wonder what else he might want from her. *If I go with David to his apartment, will I be putting myself back in the line of danger again? Will he expect things from me like Julie's dad did?*

David seemed to sense her reluctance. He reached across the table, gently took her hand, and reassured her, "Callie, you will be completely safe at my apartment. I will look out for you. I'm not some kid or some dirty, horny, old man. I'm thirty-five years old. You can look at me like the big brother that you never had. I don't want anything from you. I only want to help. Please say that you will stay with me, at least for tonight. If you find you feel uncomfortable, then you can always leave. There are no strings attached. I don't want to see you on the street at night all by yourself. There are some real sickos out there."

David seemed so sincere that Callie decided to trust him. *After all, what other alternative do I have?* She concluded. Callie had not wanted to sleep on the streets, and she certainly did not want to go back home.

As far as Callie was concerned, she had no home with her mom and dad anymore. She did not care if she ever saw either one of them again. They had both broken her heart, and she wanted them out of her life forever.

Callie went with David to his apartment. She had been happy living there ever since, and David had not seemed to be in any hurry for her to leave anytime soon. Callie tried to find a job, but this had proved difficult. She had not graduated high school, and thus did not have her diploma. All of the places Callie checked with for jobs had turned her away.

Not only was Callie a dropout, but she also looked horrible. Her eyes were always bloodshot from the alcohol and drugs; her makeup had been slept in over and over again. She dressed like a tramp, with clothes that were too revealing.

Of course, David consoled Callie after each of these discouraging job incidents. He told her not get discouraged. David always assured Callie that something would soon come along.

In the meantime, he continued to supply Callie with plenty of drugs and alcohol, sweeping aside all her worries again and again. David was also very affectionate with Callie. He had taken over the role that her father had never been able to fill. David hugged and kissed Callie quite often. Callie felt warm, secure and even loved. She had craved affection like this for so long from her father. She absolutely ate it up from David. *David truly cares for me*, Callie truly believed.

She was willing to do anything that David asked of her, but he never asked for much. David merely cared for Callie and freely shared everything that he had, his home, his food, his alcohol, his drugs and even his love. Callie deeply cared for David, although she merely regarded him as a father substitute.

David was far from being the most handsome man in the world. He had a badly receding hairline, which left only one small tuft of sandy blond hair in the center of his skull. David would have otherwise been completely bald. David's pale blue eyes tended to look a little bulgy, and his large nose was a little crooked. To Callie, nevertheless, David looked fine. She adored him for his kindness to her, and Callie had been grateful to him for everything that he had done for her.

* * * *

Callie had smoked a little crack cocaine and was lying back on the bed, relishing the intense high that it gave her. David also smoked some of the drug. Then he lay down on the bed beside Callie. David gathered Callie in his big burly arms. He was planting sweet little kisses along her forehead and cheeks. Then he began to lightly kiss her lips. Since Callie was high, David's lips touching her skin felt extraordinary. She did not ever want him to stop. David lulled Callie's yielding body with more of his tender caresses.

Then he asked in his usual, quiet, low voice, "Callie, will you do something for me?"

She opened her eyes and gazed into David's with contentment. Callie said with a heavenly smile, "Sure, what? Anything."

"Will you take your clothes off? I want for the two of us to lay naked here in my bed."

Callie was astonished to hear this request coming from David. She chuckled a little and waited for him to say that he was only teasing. But, the seriousness in David's eyes told Callie otherwise.

David saw the wariness and confusion in Callie's eyes. He was swift to set out to alleviate all her worries, "It's okay, Callie. I won't do anything to you that you don't want me to. I only need to feel your skin next to mine. I want you to know what it's like to be able to lay together naked with a man that loves you. You trust me, don't you?"

"Of course I trust you," she told David with unwavering confidence.

"I'll leave the room while you undress, and you can slide under the covers and lay on your side away from the door. That way you won't see me naked. I'll slide into bed beside you. How does that sound? Is that okay? We can lay naked and hold each other."

Callie was ambivalent about this new twist to their relationship. This was not something you did with a big brother or a father – *unless you are my mom.* However, she owed David enormously.

*What's it going to hurt to lie naked with him in bed if that's what he needs from me? I trust David. He would never do anything to hurt me.* "Okay," Callie agreed in a whispered voice.

"Thanks, baby girl. I need this right now," David uttered. He gave Callie one more, warm, grateful kiss. He got up from the bed then, and he left the room. David closed the door behind him. He told Callie that he would knock before he came back in to the room. This way there was no chance of him embarrassing Callie, if she was not fully hidden under the covers yet.

Callie's mind was still swaying from the drug. She undressed as quickly as she could, and she slid under the covers. Callie fully covered herself up to her neck. She turned onto her side, facing away from the door. The soft silky sheets caressed her now totally naked body. Callie did have to admit that even the feel of the satin sheets gave her a pleasurable sensation.

*What is it going to be like to lie naked with a man?* Callie all at once was looking forward to this experience. Her body was trembling with the anticipation of what it would be like to feel David's warm flesh against hers.

Callie heard David's quiet knock on the door. She told him it was okay to reenter the bedroom. She had to struggle to not let curiosity get the better of her. Callie wanted so badly to roll over and gawk at David's naked body. Callie had never seen a man totally naked before. Being high made her even more adventurous. Regardless, Callie managed to fight these strange new impulses. She stayed on her side, facing away from the door.

She heard David lay something on the bedside table. The blanket lifted, and the cool air rushed in. Then David's feverish skin softly slid up against hers. Callie also felt the slight bulge of his hardened manhood. It was pressing with slight pressure between her thighs.

"God, Callie, you feel amazing!" David declared.

Callie could feel his hot breath on her neck. Then David kissed her there. He also wrapped his arms around Callie's waist. He pulled them even tighter together. Callie was not at all prepared for the unfamiliar feelings and the incredible sensations that she was experiencing. *David feels amazing too. It feels fantastic the way he is holding me so tight!*

She could feel his manhood slightly moving and this ran pleasurable shivers throughout her entire body. *Is this because I'm high, or is this supposed to be this way?* Callie had no way of knowing. However, she was glad that David had suggested that they do this.

"Callie, would you want to roll toward me?" he asked after several more moments of warm cuddling. He had also planted many amorous kisses along her spine. Callie's whole body was tingling with excitement. *Should I turn toward David?* Part of Callie wanted to very much, but the other part of her was still a little frightened to do so.

"You don't have to do anything that you don't want to do," David assured her.

He slid his arms from around Callie's waist. David also began massaging her shoulders and kissing the side of her neck. David was working his magic to fully relax Callie. David's hands felt magnificent touching Callie's bare skin, and she could not help but feel the need to do as he had asked. Callie rolled toward David before she could change her mind. As she did, she could not help but glance under the blanket. When Callie saw David's perfect, erect member, she could not cease from staring at it.

"Would you like to touch it?" David asked in a voice hoarse with longing.

"Um…I don't know," Callie confessed and giggled a little in embarrassment.

David took matters into his own hands. He took a gentle grasp of Callie's hand and placed it on the object of her fascination. "You can pet it, it won't bite you," David said with a devilish smile and a rather wicked snicker. "Just take your hand and stroke it a little."

To help Callie farther along, David wrapped his hand around hers and gave her a little direction. Callie was getting more and more curious by the minute and less and less fearful. As David released her hand, Callie began on her own to lightly stroke her hand up and down David's erection. As she looked up for his approval, Callie watched David close his eyes, lie his head back, and slightly moan with pleasure. She was stunned by the reaction that her own mind and body were having to this. Callie was beginning to grow exceedingly aroused as well. The core of her was stirring in glorious response.

"David, is it supposed to feel this way? Or am I only feeling so excited, because I'm high?" Callie asked in a husky and sexy voice.

David opened his eyes and gave her a wide, adoring smile. "My sweet, innocent, Callie," he murmured and began to caress her erect nipples. "You are such a beautiful young girl. Sweet sixteen and never been kissed? " David mused.

"I've been kissed," Callie began to argue in a quiet little protest, though it was hard for her to focus. David's stroking of her breasts was making it difficult for Callie to even breathe. She had no idea that this could be so overwhelmingly pleasurable.

"You may have been kissed by boys maybe," David agreed. "But never by a man. Can I kiss you, Callie? Can I kiss you like a man kisses a woman? Will you let me do that? I want to kiss you all over. I want to taste your sweetness. I want you to experience pleasure like you've never imagined. Let's get high together, and then it will be even more intense for you."

"It's already intense, and I'm already high," Callie giggled in bliss. She did not want David to stop any part of what he was doing. Even the sound of his deep hypnotic voice was intoxicating to her right now.

"It won't hurt for you to take another hit. I want you to get high with me. Okay, Callie? Believe me, you will not be sorry that you did."

Callie hesitated from answering for several more moments. David removed his hands from her breasts and stopped touching her. *I want him to touch me some more!* Callie sensed that David did not intend to unless she got high with him.

"Okay, I'll take another hit with you," she agreed in an almost breathless voice.

"That's my sweet Callie," David praised with a huge satisfied grin. He took a second to give her an extended kiss on her pretty lips.

David sat up in bed. He prepared the crack for smoking; then he proceeded to smoke most of it. He gave Callie only one hit right before he extinguished the pipe. David laid it back on the table; then he settled back into bed under the covers with Callie. He took her into his arms. He proceeded to kiss Callie like she had never been kissed before. He urgently ran his tongue in and out of her mouth, and over her lips.

David soon moved his mouth and tongue to lavish Callie's breasts. For Callie, the whole room had begun to spin. The dreamy sounds of her moaning seemed far away. Callie had never experienced so much rapture in her entire life. She never wanted it to end. David trailed even lower on Callie's body. He settled between her thighs. Callie arched her back and had to struggle not to scream.

She was experiencing a multitude of awesome new emotions and sensations. Callie was completely overwhelmed, almost to the point of crying. She was overcome by ecstasy. She could hardly catch her breath she was so euphoric. Callie felt dizzy, inebriated and jubilant all at the same time.

The silent paradise Callie had fallen into was slightly disturbed. David's voice was saying, "Callie, I want to make love to you. Will you allow me to make love to you, Callie?"

Callie forced her eyes open. David's eyes were staring at her. They were full of desire. *Am I supposed to tell you to stop now? Why would I want you to stop?*

"Yes, David...please!! Please make love to me!" Callie found herself shrieking, in a rather frantic voice. "Now! I want you to."

"Oh my beautiful, darling, Callie. You won't be sorry," David pledged.

He began maddeningly trailing his tongue back up her body. David reached over to expertly tear open a condom. In a matter of seconds, he had secured it over his hot hard member. David sensually kissed Callie's lips. He slid his tongue into her moist mouth, and David positioned his lower body into perfect alignment with Callie's.

"You'll belong to me now, Callie. You'll be all mine forever."

"Take me, David. I want to be yours...forever," Callie affirmed with heated passion.

David entered her yearning body with caution. The scream came from somewhere within Callie's dreams, or at least she thought it had. Then the intense feeling of sexual pleasure took Callie over as their two bodies rocked together.

# Chapter 36

# *BJ*

His name was Benjamin James Rafferty, although only his family called him Benjamin. All of his friends called him BJ. Katie Rose had just turned sixteen and was starting her junior year of high school when she first met BJ. BJ was a new student, even though he too was a junior.

BJ's family's recent move had forced him to transfer from his high school to this new one. This was something BJ was having a hard time with. He was not good at making new friends. He did not play sports. He did not get into the band. He was not intelligent enough to get involved with the academic stuff in school.

BJ had merely been an average guy, getting average grades, and enjoying his life. Then his father had taken the offer for a promotion, and they had moved. Katie Rose found BJ wandering in the hall their first day of school.

She could tell that he was lost. The bewildered look on this boy's face was a dead giveaway. Katie Rose had never seen this guy before, and she had gone to school here since she was a freshman. She assumed he must be a new student.

Katie Rose approached the boy and asked, "Are you lost?"

"Slightly," he admitted with obvious embarrassment. "I'm looking for Ms. Monroe's English Lit. class. I have the room number here somewhere, but I've momentarily misplaced it." BJ was not the best-organized young man either.

"Well, you are in luck. That is where I am headed," Katie Rose confessed with an attractive, friendly smile. "So if you would like to follow me, then I can lead you right there."

*Yes, I'd like to follow you. I'd also like to get to know you. You're very cute.* "That would be great," he said with renewed enthusiasm, returning her smile. "My name is Benjamin, but my friends call me BJ. In case you haven't figured it out, today is my first day here." He held out his hand to Katie Rose.

"I *kind of* might have guessed that," Katie Rose revealed with an amused chuckle. "My name is Katie Rose. It's nice to meet you, BJ. Welcome to Holy Name Academy."

She took his outstretched hand in hers and gave it a friendly shake. As she released it, she turned to hurry down the hall. She did not want to be late to class, and they only had a few minutes.

"Lead the way," he replied and followed close at her heels to their classroom.

* * * *

It turned out that Katie Rose and BJ were in two more classes together as well. One of the classes they shared was their last class of the day. As if that was not enough of a coincidence, BJ's locker was in the same row as Katie Rose's as well.

BJ finished putting away some of his books for the evening and rushed to join Katie Rose's side. "Katie Rose, I wanted to thank you for all of the help you gave me today. Everyone else was avoiding me like I had the plague or something. I was beginning to dread being at this school, but you changed all that. I'm glad I met you," BJ told her with a grateful, toothy grin.

"It was no big deal. I was glad to show you around. I hope you'll like being here. It's a pretty good school. We have all kinds of great programs. Basketball, baseball, and we have a really good football team – made State the last three years. Then our academics are really good too. I am on the yearbook committee," Katie Rose shared.

"Well, it's definitely a *better* school since I met you. You are really pretty by the way."

"Thank you," she responded in a quiet voice.

It dawned on Katie Rose that this boy was not going to play any kind of sports; he did not look the part. *Then again, perhaps he might surprise me.* Katie Rose had been slightly embarrassed by BJ's nice comments. She was even more astounded to discover that she found herself somewhat attracted to BJ. She was not sure why.

BJ was far from being the most handsome guy in the school. He was only of average height, barely as tall as she was – about five foot seven. For a guy, he was on the thin side, with skinny legs and arms and not a very broad chest. BJ wore glasses and had a slight space between his teeth. His dishwater blond hair was cut a little too short. His bangs were cut straight across his forehead, which made him look a little nerdy.

*It's his eyes*, she found herself contemplating as they walked out of the school together. *He has nice eyes. Really different for a guy with blonde hair.* BJ's eyes were a deep dark chocolate brown. They made BJ appear warm and sensitive. Katie Rose found this appealing. It also did not hurt that she felt comfortable around him.

*Maybe we'll become good friends*, Katie Rose reflected.

The two of them walked out of the school building side by side. They continued to carry on a leisure conversation.

# Chapter 37

# *Adulthood*

Mason had just turned twenty-one, and he was graduating from college nearly a year ahead of schedule. He had earned a degree in Business Administration and Marketing. However, Mason was graduating far from the top of his class. He had struggled all throughout his college years to barely maintain a C average. Mason's main focus during all this time had continued to be his music. Nonetheless, he had made it through college and had managed to obtain the degree his father had wanted him to get.

Mason had gone to school year round. All through the Fall, Spring, and Summer semesters – so he had scarcely been home to visit his family in the past three years. Mason had only gone home for Thanksgiving and Christmas holidays.

Mason had formed a new band at college. He also called this band Savage Pride, since he had no idea whether his band at home was still together, plus they were miles apart from one another. The part-time music gigs Savage Pride managed to land had kept Mason going. They played somewhat regularly at many of the college clubs around town. He now had a business degree, but Mason's music was still the love of his life.

While he was away at college, Mason had changed a great deal. He had built his chest, arms, and legs up by spending the only spare time he had at the gym. Naturally, the fact that he had played on the college baseball team helped a lot also. Mason had allowed his hair to grow much longer. He now sported a full head of shiny, wavy, jet-black hair, now past the bottom of his shirt collar by a few inches. He also had decided to grow a mustache. Despite his Indian heritage, Mason's mustache was very full. All of this dark black hair seemed to positively accentuate his attributes. Mason's warm, golden brown eyes seemed ever more prominent, and his perfect, white teeth seemed to sparkle all the more.

Mason had matured into a handsome man. He effortlessly captured and held the attention of all the ladies. This being the case, naturally, Mason's social skills and romance life had also flourished during his college years. His initial loss of sexual innocence had been in his freshman year at college, with Belinda. Mason had fallen deeply in love with this woman. But Belinda had broken his heart. She had hardheartedly tossed Mason aside for her next sexual pupil. Mason had enjoyed only physical relationships thereafter.

This he had done with quite a few young ladies, over the course of the rest of his college years. Mason had never gotten emotionally attached again. He had learned a lot about how to immensely please a woman. As a result, Mason also left college with quite an extensive sexual education as well. Mason genuinely did not want to be tied down by only one woman. He had learned to like his sexual freedom a great deal.

\* \* \* \*

Katie Rose would be turning eighteen later in the month. She was anxious to graduate from high school. Unlike Mason, Katie Rose did not plan to start college until the fall, so she was looking forward to enjoying her summer beforehand.

Katie Rose also did not intend to go to school year round. She was graduating among the top ten in her class. Katie Rose had matured while Mason had been away at college, both physically and mentally. Mason was stunned by the changes he saw in his little sister each year when he came home for the holidays.

Katie Rose had grown another couple of inches in height, and now was the exact same height as their mother. She had pretty, sleek, long legs and a shapely behind. Her breasts had also significantly developed. Although Katie Rose's bust line was still not as large as Callie's – few young women's bust lines were – she had an attractive, curvy woman's body. Even Katie Rose's face had changed. Her cheeks seemed to be better defined, and her naturally ruby lips were much fuller. These sensuous lips begged to be kissed, and this fact the boys had not failed to notice.

The way that Katie Rose wore her hair now seemed to compliment her looks as well. Her beautiful, shimmering, ebony hair fell just past the middle of her back. She usually placed a few hot rollers in it to give it the body it needed to look incredible. Katie Rose's makeup was always applied lightly – rose-colored blush on her cheeks, pretty green shadow just around the corners of her eyes, several coats of mascara, and the slightest touch of gloss on her lips. All of this combined made Katie Rose look so enticing. Yet, she still had that innocence about her that every other young woman envied.

Katie Rose had enjoyed high school. She had made many good friends there, and she had made the most of the opportunities that were offered to her. She had taken enough college credit courses that she would be able to skip her first semester of college. Katie Rose had played volleyball, tennis and field hockey for her last two years. She had been appointed president of the student counsel her senior year. She had also been a runner-up for prom queen. Katie Rose knew she would truly miss her high school days.

As far as boys went, Katie Rose had dated only BJ. However, this had been more of a friendship than a romance, at least where she was concerned. Katie Rose was diligent about keeping this relationship at an arm's length. She had no desire to get serious about one guy at this point in her life. Katie Rose was determined not to allow BJ to tie her down. *He will* not *spoil my dreams.* Katie Rose had far bigger plans for herself. She wanted to help run her father's company. Her father might be grooming Mason to someday become president. But Katie Rose planned to earn at least some sort of management position within the company. *Maybe Mason and I can someday work hand-in-hand to run Greathouse Construction.*

The summer between her junior and senior year, Katie Rose had talked her father into giving her a summer clerical job at the company. She offered to take notes and type up the minutes from her father's negotiation meetings. She learned a great deal that summer. Katie Rose was excitedly planning to work there again this summer after graduation.

Callie would also be turning eighteen later in the month, although she looked much older. The intense strain of her last few, difficult years plainly showed in her face. She had developed a somewhat tired and hardened look.

Callie was far too slim for her tall, five-foot-eight inch frame. Her hollow cheeks, dull eyes, toothpick thin legs, concave stomach, and almost visible rib cage made her look absolutely anorexic. The only part of Callie's body that was large were her breasts. Because of the smallness of the rest of her body, Callie's full-bodied bust line drew even more attention from the male species. Even the sound of Callie's voice had changed. It had a slightly harsher tone to it now.

Callie had been through a great deal over the past few years, and little of what she had experienced had been pleasant. Her perpetual bad choices had put her where she was today. This was sitting in a secured area waiting for her father to pick her up from a drug and alcohol rehab center. Callie had been sent here a little over three months prior. This was after she had overdosed on a mixture of alcohol and crack cocaine. In doing this, Callie gave the authorities a chance to get their hands on her. They had placed her under arrest for being a runaway, and worse yet, for prostitution.

David had also been arrested now. He had been charged with drug trafficking and solicitation of a minor. He was now serving time in prison. Callie was relieved that he had been put away. She had believed that David loved her at first. However, when David had sold Callie into prostitution, this had all changed. Unfortunately, by this point, Callie had been hopelessly addicted to cocaine. She had scarcely had any option but to sell her body. Callie had needed to fund her habit. David had no longer been freely supplying the drug to her.

Now, Callie was about to go back home for the first time in over two years. Although, she was not at all certain what her home life was going to entail. She was looking forward to the comfort of her old room.

Jonathan had remained at home after Callie had run away. He had also remained there when her mother had gotten released from the mental institution. Jonathan and Mary Julia had been going to marriage counseling for over a year, but Callie got a strong impression that things were still very strained between the two of them. There was this nagging little question in the back of Callie's mind, *Is my dad still seeing Flora on the side?*

Callie's one saving grace was that she had earned her GED while at the rehab center. So if things at home became unbearable for her, she could always get a legitimate job. Then she could eventually move out on her own. The rehab center had given Callie coping tools to fall back upon, other than drugs and alcohol. Callie only hoped and prayed that she was strong enough to use these coping skills. She was glad to be leaving the rehab center, but she was still nervous about what her future would bring.

Callie had the support of the partner that had been assigned to her. She also would garner sustenance from the weekly meetings she had been court ordered to attend. Callie understood how lucky she was to have been put on two years probation instead of going to jail. A two-year sentence in a juvenile detention center was what had been originally handed down to her to serve. The kind judge had given her a choice of going to rehab or serving this sentence. Callie had begrudgingly decided to go to rehab.

*One day at a time*, Callie kept silently telling herself. She had been taught this line in group therapy. *Just one day at a time.*

\* \* \* \*

Jonathan was not sure what his feelings for Mary Julia were anymore. The only emotion he was certain existed in his life was tremendous guilt. Jonathan blamed himself for everything. He blamed himself for the mental breakdown that Mary Julia had suffered. He blamed himself for Callie's running away, due to his indiscretion with Flora. He blamed himself for Callie's drug and alcohol problems. He blamed himself for Callie having had to resort to prostitution to survive. He blamed himself for the breakdown in Mary Julia and Flora's long-standing friendship. And quite predictably, he blamed himself for the distrust that was causing the strain on his still failing marriage. That's all Jonathan could do was blame himself for not being man enough to be able to cope with his family's problems.

Needless to say, Jonathan was miserable at the present time. Regardless, he did his level best to try and put his own self-interests aside for the good of his wife and his daughter. Bringing his family back together and helping Callie get back on her feet was what was most important now. Jonathan was determined to undo some of the wrongs that he had perpetuated over the past few years.

* * * *

Mary Julia was not at all certain how she felt about Jonathan either. Since getting out of the hospital, a lot of her emotions were still numb thanks to the anti-depressant medications she remained on. One clear emotion she did feel, however, was anger. Mary Julia still felt angry whenever she thought of Flora and Jonathan kissing. Mary Julia distrusted Flora now, despite Jackie Lynn's continuous efforts to mend the momentous rift between her two best friends. Jackie Lynn still continued to be everyone's loyal friend. Jackie Lynn only wanted everyone to be happy and for them all to somehow be friends again.

Mary Julia's sole focus right now was on her family, especially on her daughter. Whether she loved Jonathan anymore or not, Mary Julia was determined to stay with this man. She believed they needed to formulate a plan to make their marriage work. Callie's life had not started to fall apart until her marriage to Jonathan had started to disintegrate. *If I can save my marriage, then I can also save my daughter.*

* * * *

Flora shared in Jonathan's pervasive remorse over the kiss that the two of them had shared. She hated how this kiss had negatively affected young Callie's life. Flora felt ghastly about all the terrible things the girl had been through in the last few years. She also felt beastly about having betrayed Mary Julia, one of her best friends.

Flora still could not comprehend nor explain what had happened. She and Jonathan had both been vulnerable at that point in their lives. Jonathan had been frustrated by his unruly teenage daughter's behavior. He had also been scared and felt guilty about Mary Julia's hospitalization and serious mental breakdown.

Flora had only been trying to help Jonathan with it all. She had only been his close friend, a confidant, someone to share his confusion and hurts with. Then Kenny had died so unexpectedly. Flora's whole world had crumbled. Jonathan had been there by her side. He had been such a total rock of strength for her. Flora had been spending far too much time with Jonathan.

Flora had begun to feel attracted to this man – attracted in ways that she should not have been. She should have parted ways with Jonathan. *So why didn't I? Why?* she would ask herself in agony over and over now.

Flora had never intended to act on her feelings. She had never intended to destroy her long-term friendship with Mary Julia. *How had it gone so wrong? How could Jonathan and I have been so stupid?* Flora felt wretched and totally alone now.

# Chapter 38

# *New Lives*

It was early Monday morning, but Katie Rose was up. In fact, she had already finished dressing. She had been unable to stay in bed. Katie Rose was exhilarated. She and Mason were supposed to be starting their summer jobs at Greathouse Construction today. She was standing outside on the deck. The sun was barely peaking over the trees. It was shining down on Katie Rose, and the picture was breathtaking.

Katie Rose's naturally glossy, ebony hair shone all the more. Her beautiful emerald eyes glistened as she looked up at the rising sun. She was silently greeting the quiet morning with a happy smile. Katie Rose had decided to wear a pale, moss green sweater. It was made out of light cashmere. She had also donned a black skirt that ended slightly above her knees. The skirt was flattering to Katie Rose's body and modestly showcased her attractive hips. A comfortable pair of low-heeled, black pumps finished her attire.

Katie Rose's sweater complimented her dark skin tone and her stunning green eyes. As usual, she had also applied some light green eye shadow and some mascara. This made her eyes even more striking. Katie Rose thought she looked professional. What she was totally oblivious to was the fact that men would find her nothing less than absolutely gorgeous.

\* \* \* \*

Her mother and her father soon joined her in the Kitchen. They all sat, drank coffee and ate breakfast together in silence.

Long Wolf and Katie Rose both took turns looking at and reading parts of the Wall Street Journal. Long Wolf looked at his watch a few times, glancing with expectation toward the entrance to the kitchen. He was waiting with impatience for Mason to make an appearance. A few moments later, Long Wolf's wish was at last fulfilled.

Mason sauntered through the archway to the kitchen. He was still dressed in his pajama bottoms and a white cotton T-shirt, and his hair was very tousled. It was obvious that he had just gotten out of bed. Mason wordlessly took a seat at the table with his family. He poured himself a cup of coffee and took a second to stretch and yawn. Katie Rose looked from Mason to her dad. Her father's apparent displeasure with her brother was plainly written all over his face.

Long Wolf's eyes were hard and disapproving and his mouth was set in a deep frown. He glanced at his watch again, and then he decided to address his son. "Mason, surely you haven't forgotten that today is your first day of work, have you? We need to be at the office by 8:00. It's 7:10 now, and it's quite obvious you haven't showered yet or anything. How do you expect to be ready to leave in fifteen minutes? This isn't a construction job, son. You need to be dressed appropriately for an office setting, in a suit and tie. I thought I made that clear."

Mason, unlike Katie Rose, was not at all excited about going to work at Greathouse Construction today. Quite the contrary, he had been dreading this day for some time. He would have been more than content to be working with the construction crew during the day.

Mason had formed yet another band and had already landed a band gig at a nearby restaurant and bar. His band had played rather late the previous night, 11:30 p.m. This was one of the reasons Mason had found it hard to arise so early this morning. He still did not feel totally awake. The other reason for his lethargy was lack of enthusiasm. Mason was not looking forward to what his day would hold.

"I showered last night when I came in, dad," Mason replied with sluggishness. "The only problem with playing in bars is you smell to high heavens like stale cigarette smoke when you leave. As to being dressed, I am going to go upstairs and get ready in a minute. I just came down to get a cup of coffee. I can't make it this early in the morning without at least one cup."

"What about breakfast?" Jackie Lynn questioned, like a typical mother. Her son might be twenty-one now, but she still had the impulse to coddle him.

Mason reached to a plate in the middle of the table. He scooped up three slices of bacon in one hand, and he grabbed his coffee cup in the other. "Thanks, mom," Mason said with a slight smile as he arose.

He popped one piece of bacon in his mouth and consumed it with swiftness. "This will carry me over. I'm not used to eating this early. I'll make up for it at lunchtime. We do get a lunch, right dad?"

"When we can find the time," Long Wolf answered. There was a notable edge to his voice. *Mason is already thinking about his lunch break when his workday has yet to begin.*

Long Wolf did not understand his son. He had chosen to overlook Mason's strange new look. His hair was far too long and unruly looking, and Long Wolf hated that his son had grown a mustache. *Facial hair on a man makes him look somewhat unkempt.*

Regardless of Mason's odd appearance, he had graduated from college with a business degree. *He should be ready to fully and enthusiastically embrace the business world, or more specifically the Greathouse Construction business world now.* Conversely, Mason seemed even more complacent than ever about learning to be a valued leader at Greathouse. This greatly disturbed and disappointed Long Wolf.

"I'll be ready to leave in less than fifteen minutes," Mason announced. He stuffed his mouth with the other two slices of bacon. He turned and meandered out of the kitchen. He still did not seem to be in any real hurry.

After Mason had disappeared from sight, Long Wolf grumbled to himself, "I guess this is what you get when your son hangs out in bars at all hours."

"Long Wolf, Mason is just settling back in," Jackie Lynn tried to defend. "I'm sure he'll be fine once he gets into some standard routine. You need to give him some time."

"Look at our daughter. She is settling into a new routine too. Yet, she was up and dressed before either of us. Katie Rose is excited about going into work with me. Aren't you, honey?" Long Wolf questioned.

"Yes, I am," Katie Rose was quick to admit. *But, dad, I love Greathouse Construction. Mason never has and probably never will.* Katie Rose did not say this to her father. She did not want to anger or dishearten him any more. Nor did Katie Rose wish to betray Mason behind his back.

"Katie Rose is barely out of high school, and yet she has initiative. Where is my son's initiative? All he seems to want to do is hang out in bars with that band. All of this band nonsense should be behind him now. It was fine when he was a boy, but Mason is a man now. He needs to start acting like one," Long Wolf freely complained. His voice was getting louder and louder.

"Long Wolf, please keep your voice down or Mason will hear you. Darling, you know that Mason's music has always been, and continues to be, very important to him. I think Mason wishes he could make a living doing something with his music, instead of joining you at Greathouse Construction. Mason is artistically talented, and he does have initiative. It is just tied to his music. This may disappoint you, but that is the way it is with him," Jackie Lynn pointed out.

She hated it when Long Wolf attacked Mason's obvious musical talents. She did not want her son to cut music completely from his life. Mason would not be happy if he did this. Jackie Lynn could not help but worry, though. *What kind of lifestyle would Mason carve out for himself if he chose music as his sole support?* Consequently, she did support Long Wolf getting Mason involved at Greathouse Construction, in some capacity. Jackie Lynn hoped Mason could find a way to balance both a career at Greathouse and music in his life. She was confident he could if he put his mind to it.

"So do you honestly think that I should let Mason run off with his band and try to make a living that way? This is total nonsense! He'll be living here with us forever or become some drunk living on the street. I want him to become a responsible man. And why did we send him to college? I'm a little confused," Long Wolf argued. The disdain in his voice was so thick that Jackie Lynn could practically cut it with a knife.

"I did not say that Mason shouldn't go into Greathouse with you and start using the business skills he learned at college.

I'm only saying that his music is equally important to him. You would do well not to dismiss this. You proclaimed that Mason is a man now, did you not? So isn't it true then that, if Mason is a man, he is capable of making adult decisions for himself? If you push him too hard and mock his interest in music, doesn't it logically follow that one of those adult decisions may be to totally turn his back on Greathouse instead of his music? I don't think either one of us want to see that happen, do we?"

Long Wolf could see that Jackie Lynn was in serious debate mode now. Many years of marriage to this woman – over twenty one – had taught Long Wolf well how incredibly stubborn she could be. Jackie Lynn was especially headstrong when she believed she was right about something, like now. Since she had been a successful attorney for many more years, Jackie Lynn was well versed in winning debates.

Long Wolf wisely decided that it was time to end this particular argument. Fortunately, he did not have to say anymore one way or another because Mason appeared in the doorway to the kitchen. This time he was much more appropriately dressed. His light blue, long sleeved dress shirt had been neatly tucked into his dark navy suit pants. His pants were secured by a like-new black leather belt.

Mason had slipped on the matching suit jacket but had not yet buttoned it. He had placed a pale yellow tie, with small gray and navy diamonds on it, loosely around his neck. He had on a brand new pair of black dress shoes and navy dress socks to match perfectly to the suit. These colors together complimented Mason's natural golden skin. His hair had also been wet down a little and combed to tame its usual windswept look. The only thing Mason had failed to do was shave.

In addition to his mustache, today, Mason also donned the slight five o'clock shadow of a beard. This was basically the style for young men. Long Wolf was not too thrilled about this, but there was no time for Mason to correct the situation by shaving. Besides, Long Wolf was not going to push his luck. Mason's appearance had been drastically improved.

Long Wolf stood back for a moment and admired his son. *This will someday be the next president of Greathouse Construction. We'll take it one step at a time, as Jackie Lynn suggested.* As Mason came closer to his father, Long Wolf could not help but notice his cologne. It was the same scent he wore himself, Coolwater. *The boy does have good taste. Mason merely needs some better personal grooming habits. Hopefully, this will come in time as well.*

"I'm ready to go whenever you guys are," Mason announced, with much more enthusiasm than he actually felt.

"Good. We need to be going," Long Wolf pointed out.

He leapt up from the table. Katie Rose also hopped to her feet. She was glad they were leaving. She had not liked the tension that had arisen between her mom and dad. It was rare to catch them in a quarrel, and she did not much like it.

Before Long Wolf walked out the door with his children, he bent down and gave Jackie Lynn a light peck on the lips. "I love you. Have a good day," he said. These were his usual parting words to his wife.

"I love you too," Jackie Lynn replied. She forced herself to give him a slight smile. She was still partially in fight mode with this man, but she needed to switch gears now. "I love *all* of you," she said glancing at Katie Rose and Mason with a big grin on her face. "You all have a great day!"

"We will," Katie Rose was fast to confirm.

She and Mason took turns giving their mother a small hug and a kiss on the cheek. They both told her that they loved her too. They were grown children now, but this show of affection between them and their mom did not make them feel uncomfortable.

Neither Katie Rose nor Mason had ever left their mother without hugs, kisses and those all-important words, 'I love you'. For that matter neither had their father. Today was not the first time that Long Wolf had ever disagreed with his wife. However, the two of them had long ago vowed to never leave with angry words between them, and they had always honored this pledge to one another. This perhaps was one of the reasons their marriage had remained so successful, and the love between them had only grown over the years.

Long Wolf, Katie Rose and Mason rushed from the house then. Katie Rose hoped this was the end of her dad's squabble with her mom over Mason, but she doubted very much that it would be.

\* \* \* \*

"Damn," Callie cursed.

She had been trying to call Katie Rose, but she had gotten the answering machine. It had taken Callie quite a bit of time to gather the courage to call, and now no one appeared to be home. It was still rather early in the day, 10:00 a.m. Callie wondered if Kate Rose had gotten a summer job.

*A job – this is something I need to pursue.* Callie needed to get on with her life. Her mom and dad wanted her to go to college, but Callie had no desire to go down that road at this time. *Maybe in a year or so. I want to take some time to settle back into 'normal' life first, if there truly is such a thing.*

When she had gotten home a few weeks ago, Callie and her parents had seemed to be walking on eggshells around each other. Their house had no longer felt like her home. Things had changed so drastically that Callie felt totally out of place.

When the taboo thought – *I could use a drink right now* – had uninvitingly filtered through her brain, Callie had wondered if she had left the hospital too early. She had gone to her bedroom, called her sponsor, and shared her apprehensions.

"I'm glad you called me, Callie. It's normal to have thoughts like this when you first get out of the controlled atmosphere of the hospital. Take it one day at a time, and you will be fine," her sponsor assured her. "Just remember, you can call me any time."

Even Callie's bedroom, which had been left virtually the same as when she had left, no longer seemed to fit her. The pinup posters that adorned the walls, of long ago favorite rock groups and teen idols, held no interest to Callie anymore. Callie took these down. She also cleaned off the top of her dresser and chest-of-drawers.

Callie put many items away on shelves in the closet. For one thing, she had tons of makeup sitting on her dresser, and Callie no longer wore so much makeup. Callie had also found several pictures of Mason scattered amongst the mess.

Callie recalled how she had tormented Mason. She also recollected how decent Mason had been to reject her advances. Callie had nothing but uttermost respect for him now. Mason had run off to college to get away from her, and Callie had been furious at the time. Nonetheless, she only wished him the best now. Callie hoped that Mason was doing well in college.

She made herself a mental note that, when she finally talked to Katie Rose, she would ask how Mason was doing. Although, Callie had no intention of chasing him like she once had. This foolish desire, like so many others in her life, had changed.

Things at home were gradually getting better, and Callie was settling in again. After the first two weeks, her parents had seen that Callie was not going to bolt from the house. They had also discovered that she was not going to sneak out to drink or do drugs. Mary Julia and Jonathan started to relax a little, and Callie did as well. Both her parents had gone back to work today. Callie was alone in the house for the first time. Mary Julia had taken a week's vacation Callie's first week home, and Jonathan had taken one her second week home.

Callie had taken advantage of the extra time with her parents. She had decided to follow sage advice from some of her hospital therapy. Callie had talked to both her mother and her father at great lengths. She had clearly let it be known that she did not blame them for anything that had happened to her.

Callie had talked openly with her mother about her addictions. She told Mary Julia that she forgave her for the affair she had had. Callie also told her mom that she could now better understand her sexual addiction. Callie commended her mother for having had the strength to overcome her addiction once more. She also praised Mary Julia for overcoming her mental breakdown.

Callie told Jonathan that, while she still could not understand his kissing Flora, she still forgave him for it. Jonathan and Mary Julia were stunned by how mature their daughter seemed now. Callie had grown up much too fast on the streets, but she had definitely grown up. Jonathan regretted that his little girl ceased to be a little girl anymore. Jonathan hated the hard edge Callie now possessed. He longed to have back all the time that he had missed with his daughter.

Mary Julia agonized over all Callie had been through over the past few years. She still felt responsible. Her illness had separated her from Callie and left her open to self-destruction. Mary Julia was thankful to God, however, that her daughter had survived. She wanted to try and help Callie heal her wounds.

The only other two people Callie still needed to resolve issues with were Katie Rose and Flora. Callie still was not ready to talk to Flora. Flora would be most difficult to confront and forgive.

Callie no longer held any grudges against Katie Rose. All Katie Rose had ever been guilty of was trying to be a good friend to her. If anything, Callie felt remorse over the way she had treated Katie Rose over the years. The last time Callie had talked to Katie Rose had been at the hospital, when she had nearly been raped by Ralph. Callie had found out that Katie Rose had snitched about her drug use. Callie had told Katie Rose that she no longer considered her a friend and never wanted to talk to her again. She had avidly avoided Katie Rose from then on.

Callie had wanted so badly to talk to Katie Rose today and try to make amends. She was more than a little disappointed that she had not been able to get through to her. *Oh well! There is always later today or tomorrow. Now that I've decided to do this, I will talk to Katie Rose. She may tell me she wants nothing to do with me now, but I can still apologize and let her know that I still consider her a friend.*

Callie got up from the kitchen table and walked over to the window. It was a beautiful spring day. There was not a single cloud in the brilliant, light blue sky. The sun shone so brightly that it almost hurt her eyes. Callie even noticed the sound of birds chirping and watched them flying to and fro. All at once, she felt very free.

*Wow! It feels good to be home!* It felt great – *and a little amazing* – to be genuinely happy about this.

## Chapter 39

# *Rebirth*

The *Help Wanted* sign in the window brought back many bad memories. *How many waitress jobs was I turned away from while I was living with David? If only I could have gotten a job back then, things might have turned out a lot different. Then again, would things have been any better? I still would have been out on the streets alone, and whether I wanted to admit it or not, I was already a crack addict. I wouldn't have kept the job long anyway. God, I'm glad I'm not held captive by that lifestyle anymore.* For the second time that day, Callie felt an immense feeling of freedom.

She entered the restaurant and gathered the courage to approach the counter. Callie asked for a job application. "For the waitress job posted in the window," she told the girl behind the counter. Callie pointed toward the sign she had seen, as if the girl would not have a clue what she was talking about. The girl said nothing, but in a robotic motion, she reached under the counter. She pulled out a few sheets of paper and handed them to Callie with barely a glance.

"Thanks," Callie said and gave the younger girl a slight smile.

"Uh huh," she inattentively replied. The girl went back to doing whatever she had been doing before Callie had walked in and interrupted her.

Callie turned with the papers in her hand. She started heading for the door. *I'll fill them out at home and bring them back in tomorrow.*

Callie was looking down at the application. One of the first questions on the first page was, 'Do you have a high school diploma or GED?'. Callie felt greatly relieved that she would be able to mark 'yes' this time.

*Maybe I'll at least have a chance at getting the job this time. After all, the sign also said 'No Experience Necessary'.*

She was still looking down at the papers and yet moving forward. Callie heard the bell on the door jingle, and she realized that someone was entering the restaurant. She glanced up and came to a halt. Callie could not believe she was standing face to face with *him*.

She had not seen Mason in nearly three years. Callie was shocked by how much he had changed. He had still been somewhat of a boy the last time she had seen him. Now, he was a handsome grown man. Mason's hair was longer; he had a full mustache; he looked as if he had grown another inch or so; and there was something else different about him that Callie could not quite put her finger on.

*Quit staring like some dumb schoolgirl! You're past all that! This was the only guy who was ever decent to you. Don't make him think you are still that stupid wild girl that drove him out of town with your dumb shenanigans.* "Hi, Mason," Callie spoke.

"Hello, Callie," he replied. "I had heard that you were back in town. How are you doing?"

Mason was astounded by how much older Callie looked also. She no longer looked the same age as Katie Rose. Katie Rose looked eighteen. Callie looked to be his age or maybe even older. *Her tough lifestyle must have aged her.* Katie Rose also still had some look of innocence about her, but Callie looked seasoned. Mason had heard about all the horrible things that Callie had been through, so he could understand why she had this look.

"I'm doing great!" Callie chirped. She gave him a wide arresting smile.

*She's still pretty*, Mason could not help but note. These days an attractive woman never escaped his notice, and normally, Mason would have been on the make. However, he still regarded Callie as 'off limits', even though she was certainly no longer an innocent girl.

315

"I'm glad to hear that you are doing well," he answered, still making casual conversation. "Katie Rose has wondered about you too."

Mason did not share that Katie Rose had spent many a day praying for Callie's safe return. When she had run away, Callie had been antagonistic toward his sister. Mason had no idea whether Callie still harbored the same ill will toward Katie Rose or not.

"I tried to call Katie Rose earlier today, but I didn't get any answer at your house. Has she taken a job someplace, or was she out somewhere else?"

"She's working at Greathouse as a clerical assistant to my dad for the summer. Then she'll start college in the fall. She should be home after six tonight if you want to try her again. I'm sure Katie Rose would love to hear from you," Mason shared.

"Oh, that's great! She has always wanted to work at your dad's company." *Actually she wants to* run *your dad's company, but Katie Rose can't because your dad expects that of* you. "So aren't you working there now too with your dad. You've finished college, right?"

"Yeah, actually I finished a little early, because I was going to school year round. I graduated last year, and I've been working at Greathouse ever since. Climbing the old corporate ladder like my dad wants," Mason revealed.

Callie could hear the underlying mockery in his statement. "I took the afternoon off. My band has a big gig tonight in the nightclub next door. I'm here to get stuff all set up early; then the rest of the band is going to meet me here in a little while for a sound check and practice session. If the nightclub likes us, we might get a regular gig playing there every other weekend. So, needless to say, tonight is important to us. Not that my dad understands that. I had to practically beg, borrow and steal to get a little time off this afternoon."

*He still has a band!* Callie was amazed to discover. She had not missed the way the tone of Mason's voice had changed when he had started talking about his band job versus Greathouse. His love was still his music and not Greathouse Construction. Callie was glad to hear this. *Mason is very talented.*

"Well, I wish you weren't playing in a bar, or I'd come and see you. I would love to hear your band play. I'm sure you're very good. You always were. It's good to hear that you are still doing what you love. Don't ever give it up, Mason."

"I don't intend to," he answered with steadfastness.

He was studying Callie a little oddly as their conversation lagged for a moment. *Is she for real? Callie sounds so mature. She isn't being flirty at all, or is this merely her latest tactic?*

"Well, I guess I better be going. It's a beautiful day, and I was in the middle of a nice long walk. Then I noticed the sign in the window. I stopped in here to get an application for the waitress job they have posted. My mom and dad aren't quite ready for me to leave their protective roof yet, but it's time I got on with my life. Getting a job will be my first step. But, in the meantime, I don't want to worry my parents. Lord knows, I've already done enough of that for a lifetime. So, I need to get back home. I hope your band audition tonight goes well, Mason. You're a great guy and deserve every happiness."

"Thank you," he replied and gave her a bewildered grin.

"Maybe I'll be seeing you again soon. That is, if we both get the jobs we are trying for," Callie concluded their conversation by saying.

*He still has the most handsome smile.* She had not been able to keep from observing. She also rather sadly took note of the innocent age-old longing that it produced in her. *How simple my life had been when all I had was a major crush on Mason. And he could have taken advantage of it big time, but he didn't.*

Regardless, Callie did not intend to act upon her attraction to Mason any longer. *There is no reason he would want a woman like me anyway. I'm used goods, and Mason can easily have any woman that he wants. He was always been such a great guy. It doesn't seem that he has changed at all. He deserves a special lady in his life.*

Callie continued out of the restaurant. She did not look back or say anything else to Mason.

\* \* \* \*

Callie drove over to Katie Rose's house that evening. She had come to the conclusion that she wanted to talk face-to-face, instead of over the phone. As she walked up to the front door, Callie felt a little unsettled being at this house again. She had so many great memories of spending time here with Katie Rose. It made her yearn for childhood again.

She knocked on the door and crossed her fingers that Katie Rose would be home. A few seconds later, her friend miraculously opened the door. Before Callie could get even one word out, Katie Rose grabbed her and pulled her into a tight embrace. When she pulled back several moments later, there were tears standing in her eyes.

"God, it's so good to see you again!" Callie was astounded to hear Katie Rose utter. She watched as her friend swiped a few escaping tears away. "I prayed so long and so hard that you would be okay. And here you are! How are you?"

"I'm...I'm fine," Callie stammered. She was blown away and extremely touched by Katie's Rose's warm greeting and kind words. She suddenly felt like crying as well.

"Well, come in!" Katie Rose invited with a wide smile. She stepped back from the doorway and made a sweeping welcome gesture with her arm. Callie suddenly felt like the Prodigal Son in the Bible.

She entered the house, and she and Katie Rose walked down the hallway and around the corner into the living room. It felt strange to be in this room together. Normally, they had always gone to Katie's Rose bedroom or to the playroom/den downstairs. Once again, Callie felt this odd remorse for the time she had lost with her friend.

She sat down on the couch and Katie Rose sat beside her. "I still can't believe you are actually here," she said with a gleeful laugh. "I'm really happy to see you, Callie." She couldn't believe how much her friend had changed. Callie was thinking the same thing about Katie Rose. They were both women now, and they had still been young ladies the last time they had seen one another.

"I didn't think you would be happy to see me," Callie confessed, casting her eyes down with shame.

"Why?" Katie Rose asked with confusion.

Callie made eye contact with Katie Rose and explained, "Because I treated you so badly before I left. I turned my back on you, and I told you I never wanted to see you again. I never was a very good friend to you, Katie Rose. It just amazes me that you are so happy to see me now," Callie said. Tears were now standing in her eyes.

Katie Rose pulled her into another embrace and consolingly rubbed her back. "Oh, Callie...how could I not be happy to see you again? You are so much more to me than just a friend. At the Reservation all those years ago, when we both got Indian names, Golden Fire and Emerald Sea, you became a sister to me. You will always be my sister, Golden Fire. We shared so many amazing things as children. It broke my heart when you ran away, and I worried about you the whole time you were gone. I was so relieved when I heard you were finally coming home. I'm sorry for all you had to go through. I love you, Callie."

"I love you too, Katie Rose...um...Emerald Sea. You are such a wonderful person. I'm so proud to be called your sister and to claim you as mine. I want so much for us to be friends again."

Katie Rose pulled back from Callie and looked her in the eyes once more. "If you mean you want to start talking again and spending time together, then great! I'm all for that! But, Callie, we've never stopped being friends," she assured her.

Callie's heart was so warmed by Katie Rose's actions and words. She truly felt unconditional love from this other astounding woman. She was genuinely proud to be claimed as her sister and was looking forward to striking up an active friendship with Katie Rose once more – a friendship that she would take much more care with from now on.

\* \* \* \*

Callie got the waitress job, much to her mom's chagrin. Mary Julia did not particularly care for Callie's choice of job – she believed her daughter could do better. Nevertheless, she intended to support Callie in any way in which she could now. Callie seemed convinced that getting this job was something important for her to do. For this reason only, Mary Julia attempted to put on a happy face about it.

Mason's band also got the job at the nightclub next door. Long Wolf was not at all happy about this. It would mean his son would be out late each night, and then Mason would be sluggish the next day at Greathouse. Long Wolf wanted Mason to learn the ropes of executive management at Greathouse, and he wanted him to learn them fast.

*Mason should be putting aside his musical* hobby. *His focus needs to be on his career at Greathouse.* Long Wolf freely shared these thoughts with his son.

Long Wolf's opinions greatly hurt Mason's feelings. However, Long Wolf had no idea how much he was hurting his son. Mason kept his pain to himself. He assured Long Wolf that he could have both Greathouse and his music in his life. He told his father that both were equally important to him. This was not true, however. Mason's music was vitally important to him, but Greathouse was not. Working at Greathouse was a frustrating obligation to Mason. Regardless, he did not intend to be a disappointment to his dad. So Mason would have both Greathouse and his music in his life.

\* \* \* \*

Mason had dinner a few nights a week at the restaurant. He and Callie began having some serious talks when she was on break. They commiserated about how their parents did not like their jobs. At least Callie could say that her mother and father were supporting her, even if they did not like her choice of job.

Mason could not say the same, at least not about his father. Callie heard the distress in Mason's voice when he talked about how his father *hated* his musical talents. "I think he wants me to give up music altogether," Mason shared with despondency. Callie praised him for keeping music in his life. She assured Mason that his musical talent was great.

Mason was astounded that he and Callie could sit and talk like this. He could not believe that she was not trying to come on to him, as she always had. The fact that he was becoming friends with a woman – *an attractive woman at that* – never ceased to amaze Mason.

Mason was also glad to see that Katie Rose and Callie had become friends once more. Callie and Katie Rose remained close, but Callie was spending more time with Mason now. BJ had come to fill the role of Katie Rose's best friend. Katie Rose invited Callie to go along with the two of them on occasion, but Callie always denied the invitation. She wanted Katie Rose and BJ to have time alone together, and BJ appreciated her doing this.

Callie asked Mason one day why he never brought any of his lady friends into the restaurant. He confessed with frankness, "Because I rarely see them over once. And this isn't to have dinner with them."

He then began confiding in Callie about all of his revolving door love interests. Mason did not know why he felt so comfortable talking to her about this. He guessed it was because Callie made it easy to talk to her about anything.

"Well, I guess if they will give it away for free, then you are entitled," Callie said with a little bit of a hard edge. Mason felt some pity for her.

"You make them sound like prostitutes. That's a little harsh, Callie. They are merely women who, like me, don't want to be tied down to one person," Mason tried to defend. Callie had made him feel a little bad for these ladies and for his own actions.

"Uh huh," Callie rather acerbically agreed. "If you can excuse it that way, then good for you. You're too great of a guy to keep using women like that Mason. And you know what? You deserve better too. You deserve a terrific woman who you can fully love and who can fully love you."

Callie's view of his treatment of women bothered Mason. He did not consider himself to be *using* women. "Let me tell you a little something about love and women, Callie. My first time with a woman, I fell head over heels in love with her. And come to find out she was using *me*. She had her little fun – teach the virgin – and then she moved on. I have never done a woman this way. Any woman who chooses to sleep with me knows up front that I am *not* looking for any kind of serious relationship, and they are fine with it. I would never hurt anyone like I was hurt."

Callie saw the disillusionment in Mason eyes. She also heard it in his voice. She knew that he was telling her the truth. Callie informed Mason that she could fully relate to what he was saying. Then she told him all about David. Callie relayed the sad story of how David had cruelly taken her innocence. She also admitted to how she had fallen deeply in love with him. She also revealed how humiliated she had been when David had so thoughtlessly used her as a prostitute.

"We are kind of in the same boat, Mason. I don't care if I ever get involved with a man again. And you only involve yourself with women to fulfill your needs. We've both been stung by love.

You know what they say, you should learn from your mistakes. Sounds like we both have."

Once again, Mason felt a pang of remorse for Callie. *She's only eighteen. She is awfully young to be so jaded about love. What a scumbag this David was. I'd love to get my hands on him. I'd make him sorry for what he did to Callie.*

From that day forward, Mason and Callie seemed to become even closer friends. There was not anything that they ceased to share with one another. She and Mason sometimes went to the movies together and out to dinner. When Callie had an evening off work, she even hung out with the band and watched their practices.

Both Mason and Callie were content with being good friends. They were relieved that all of the tension that had once existed between them was gone. They only wanted the best for one another now.

# Chapter 40

# *The Lecture*

Katie Rose and her mother were sitting at the kitchen table across from one another. Jackie Lynn gave her daughter an uneasy smile and reached to pat one of her hands. "Katie Rose, you are such a beautiful young lady. Both outside and in. I am very proud of you."

"Thanks, mom," Katie Rose replied with a slightly embarrassed giggle. Even though she knew her mom's comments were genuine, she inquired, "So what are you buttering me up for, mom? You said we needed to talk."

"I want to talk with you about BJ," Jackie Lynn hesitantly broached the subject. The instant change she saw in Katie Rose's facial expressions from happy and open, to disturbed and closed off told Jackie Lynn this was not going to be an easy conversation. Yet, Jackie Lynn needed to have this important talk with her daughter.

"Did BJ put you up to this, mom?" Katie Rose suspiciously asked.

"No, he did not," Jackie Lynn was quick to clarify. "I couldn't blame him if he had. That young man cares about you a great deal, and when a man is truly interested in a woman, he will go to every extreme to capture her heart. I could ask you why you keep dodging BJ's obvious affections, but I already know the answer to that. This is exactly what I want to talk to you about. Can I ask you a favor? Will you humor your mother and listen to what I have to say?"

"Mom, I will always gladly listen to what you have to say. But, I hate for you to waste your breath talking about BJ and I.

323

Because there is no '*BJ and I*'. At least not the way he thinks of it. BJ wants more out of the relationship than I do. I can't afford to be tied down right now. Not by BJ, not by any man. I know that is hard for you to understand."

"No, Katie Rose, that is where you are mistaken. It is not hard for me to understand at all," Jackie Lynn earnestly contradicted. "Because I look at you and I see myself many years ago. I didn't raise you to be like me. Your childhood was totally different than mine. I went out of my way to make sure your childhood was different. But, yet, you still turned out remarkably like I used to be regardless of how you were raised."

"What's wrong with the way I have turned out?" Katie Rose asked with confusion. "Didn't you say you were proud of me?"

"I did, and I am," Jackie Lynn assured her with a warm smile. "I can't imagine a parent who would not be proud of you. Nevertheless, what a parent wants most for their adult child is for them to be happy. And that is where I fear you may fall short of the mark."

"I don't understand why you would think that, mom," Katie Rose protested. "I am very happy. I have a family I love and who loves me. I have Callie's close friendship. I'm working my way up the ranks at Greathouse, and someday, I will be helping Mason run the company. And...I have romance in my life. I don't need any serious entanglements to be truly happy. That is probably hard for you to believe, since you and dad have been together since the dawn of time, but I sincerely don't need a man permanently by my side. In fact, having a man hovering over me would do the exact opposite of making me happy."

"Yes, that is exactly what I used to believe too. That is, before *the dawn of time*, when I met your father. You see, I fell head over heels in love with him, and he for me. Nonetheless, I was determined that if I professed this love, if I let this man permanently into my life, then he would somehow tear me down. I couldn't be a successful, independent woman and have a man in my life too. Sound familiar? Can you tell me that you don't feel the exact same way?"

"But, mom, you didn't meet dad until you were forty. You were already successful and had been independent for some time. I'm still young. I'm still climbing my way to the top. I need to prove that I can be independent. BJ could distract me from my goals if I let him," Katie Rose began to argue.

Before her mother could dispute her, she added, "I don't want to merely be BJ's wife and work at Greathouse. I want to be president...or...excuse me, vice president of the company. I can't be president, because dad has his mind set that Mason will assume this role. See what I mean about men holding woman back; even dad does it. Mason most likely will too. I have to work twice as hard as Mason does to prove myself to dad. I can't let anything, or *anyone*, get in the way of this."

"I have to give credit where credit is due. You are right in saying that you are young, and I was quite a bit older before I met your dad – not that age matters when it comes to true love. And you are also correct when talking about Greathouse, your father, his ideas for your brother's future, and his misconceptions about you," Jackie Lynn readily confessed.

Then she continued on her important crusade, "However, you are wrong when you assume that letting BJ into your life would distract you or hold you back from your goals. Quite the opposite, the love of a good man can help you to accomplish your dreams and goals, and make life easier. It will give you added strength, not cause you weakness. I can't sit back and let you make the mistake of pushing away the love of a lifetime. You have to at least give BJ a chance, Katie Rose. If he is not the one, then you will find that out soon enough and move on. It will take nothing away from you for giving him a shot. I know what I am talking about. I did everything I could to push your father away. Thank God, he was persistent and patient with me. I don't even want to think of what my life would be like now if I had remained stubborn, and independent minded, and pushed your father's love away."

Jackie Lynn paused for a second, as if to catch her breath. Then she doggedly persisted, "What I'm trying to tell you, Katie Rose, is that you *can* have it all, as I have, if you want. You can be a strong independent woman, have the career you want, but also have the love and companionship of a good man. Believe me, there was a time when no one would have ever believed that I would be saying these words to you. But they are true. I need for you to at least give them some thought. Can you do that for me?"

Katie Rose was silent for several moments. She was allowing her mother's words of wisdom to sink in. She trusted her mom. She knew that her mother would not be intruding in her life if she did not feel it was important. Katie Rose did have feelings for BJ, and he did seem to be a wonderful man. However, she had been afraid to explore these feelings for this man. Now, her mother had made her wonder if her decisions were wise.

*What if I am throwing away the love of a lifetime?* "I'll think about what you have said, mom. I honestly will," Katie Rose pledged.

"Good," Jackie Lynn said with relief. "Give it a lot of thought, Katie Rose. There is *nothing* that you can get in your life, not even if you could be president of Greathouse Construction, which can replace love. When the bible says, 'the greatest of these gifts is love,' it is never truer. Keep this in mind when making your decision. I can honestly tell you, I could not have been happier if I had every *thing* in this world. Not if I had not had your father…and of course you and your brother in my life. I'm a very happy, successful woman. You are a lot like me, Katie Rose, and I want you to have it all as well. Keep all of your options open."

"Okay," she agreed with some hesitation.

Katie Rose had not considered her relationship with BJ in this light at all. She had not thought of him as adding value to her life. Instead, she had convinced herself that he would be a huge distraction. Now, Katie Rose reflected on her mom and dad's relationship. She had always admired what her parents had. Truth told, Katie Rose secretly dreamed of finding someone special. She did want to share an everlasting love with a man.

*Is BJ this man?* Katie Rose was not certain. She had been afraid of cluttering her mind with thoughts of him. *Yet, have I been able to keep from thinking about BJ since he's been in my life?* Perhaps she was consuming more energy trying to push BJ away.

*Perhaps I should allow BJ to share more in my life. He does make me happy when I'm with him. Can I really have it all?* Her mom had opened her mind up to all kinds of questions. *Questions I'll have to find answers to.*

Katie Rose slid her chair back from the table. She stood and went around to the other side of the table. She gave her mom a hug and a kiss on the cheek.

"Thanks, mom," Katie Rose said with a smile of gratitude. "I love you."

"I love you too, baby girl," her mom replied with affection.

Jackie Lynn gave Katie Rose's body another squeeze before she released her. She watched as her daughter moseyed out of the room. Jackie Lynn could tell that Katie Rose was rigorously thinking over all she had told her. She was pleased to see this. BJ was in love with Katie Rose, and he struck Jackie Lynn as a decent young man. *A man that can fill Katie Rose's life with lots of love and happiness.* Jackie Lynn hoped that Katie Rose would freely embrace all the love that BJ could give her.

Her life was full because she had accepted Long Wolf's love so long ago. Jackie Lynn wanted more than anything for her daughter's life to be as well. However, Long Wolf was a big part of Katie Rose's problem. It was obvious that he had given Katie Rose the strong impression that all men tried to hold woman back.

*I must talk to Long Wolf about this. He needs to realize how important Greathouse Construction is to Katie Rose. He needs to acknowledge the talents and skills that she can bring to the business. Mason does not have, and never will have, the same passion for Greathouse as Katie Rose. One of his children is willing and able to eventually take over Greathouse Construction. However, that child may not be Mason. That child may well be Katie Rose. It is in Katie Rose's heart and soul to be a part of Greathouse Construction, not Mason's.*

\* \* \* \*

Katie Rose and BJ were sitting on the sofa in his basement. They were watching a movie they had rented. It was a comedy, and they both shared a hearty laugh several times during the movie. Katie Rose found herself clandestinely studying BJ tonight. After the conversation she had engaged in with her mother, she had given her relationship with BJ a great deal of thought.

*Am I being fair to him?* was one of Katie Rose's biggest questions. *BJ's a wonderful guy! He has a great sense of humor. I feel totally comfortable talking to him about anything. He's never been pushy with me, even though I can tell he wants to do more than kiss sometimes. So why am I holding back with him? Is my mom right? Could I be throwing away the love of a lifetime?*

The movie came to an end, and BJ noticed that Katie Rose was staring at him rather oddly. "What's going on in that pretty head? You're looking at me funny. Do I have pizza sauce on the side of my face of something?" They had shared a pizza while they were watching the movie. BJ took his hand and ran it over the side of his face.

"No," Katie Rose laughed. Then she kissed BJ with spontaneity, on the cheek he had been rubbing.

"Thanks. What was that for?" he asked with a happy smile.

*He's so easily pleased.* "I don't think I tell you often enough what a great guy you are. We need to have a talk."

"Um...I'm not sure I like the sound of this," BJ admitted. He gave Katie Rose a worried frown. "Why are you so serious with me tonight? What's up?"

"What is up is...well...I'm not sure I'm being fair to you. You're a terrific guy, BJ, and you deserve a woman who will treat you that way...."

"And that would be *you*. Why would you even think otherwise? Did I say something to hurt your feelings? To make you feel like you are treating me badly?"

"No," Katie Rose corrected him with haste. "You haven't done or said anything. You've been fantastic. I enjoy being with you so much. You've become one of my best friends. And the little bit of romance we share between us is fun, but is that enough for you?"

"Katie Rose, have I ever pushed you for anything else?" he questioned. "I love spending time with you too. I love the fact that you consider me to be one of your best friends. I feel the same way about you. I also love kissing and holding you. Do I hope that someday we might broaden our relationship? I'd be lying if I told you no. The fact that I care so much about you is why I can be patient. I'm willing to wait however long it might take for you to feel comfortable enough to take our relationship to the next level."

"Which is?"

BJ paused for a moment before he answered this question. His heart was racing with anxiety. He feared what the next words out of his mouth, which were inevitable, would do to Katie Rose. He did not want to scare her away. He would take whatever Katie

Rose was willing to give. He loved her deeply and only wanted Katie Rose in his life, whatever way he could have her.

"The next level would be us becoming…well…lovers; Whatever form this might take. If you want to wait until you are married to go there with a man, then the next level would be for us to become engaged. Then, depending on how long you would want the engagement to last, our next step would be to get married." BJ was speaking slowly. He was trying to be cautious and loving at the same time. "I can play this any way that you want. I care about you enough that I will do whatever you feel is right."

"BJ, people don't marry unless they are in love. Are you telling me that you are in love with me?"

Katie Rose was staring into his eyes with such intensity that BJ almost felt he needed to look away. *She'll see it in my eyes. She might as well. I can't lie to Katie Rose. I don't know what brought all this up tonight, but I guess it is time that I am completely honest with her. Oh God, please don't let Katie Rose run from me!*

BJ somewhat chickened out. Instead of heartily expressing his love for Katie Rose, he posed it as a question, "What if I was?"

*Didn't mom say BJ was in love with me? She was right! How could I have been so stupid, so blind? How do I feel toward him? I care about him…but love??*

After what seemed an eternity, Katie Rose responded with a question. "Why haven't you told me before? You are taking a huge risk at getting hurt, BJ."

"Well, you are willing to take that risk when you care…alright, I'll say it…when you love someone. Yes, Katie Rose, I am in love with you. And you know what? I don't care whether you feel the same way or not. I only want you in my life, and you have been. These past two years have been the best two years of my life, because you've been in it. I'll settle for whatever you are willing to give me. So don't feel like you have to say those words back to me."

Katie Rose felt a tugging at her heartstrings. She cared a great deal about BJ. However, she was not certain whether she was in love with him. After all, she had no other experiences with men. *How am I supposed to know what being in love with a man feels like?*

BJ took both Katie Rose's hands in his. He gazed into her eyes. "Katie Rose, I'm not sure where all this is coming from. But it doesn't matter. We are still the same two people that we were before we had this conversation. We are still best friends, and we can enjoy much more time together. I don't want you to make an issue of this. I'm begging you not to let this come between us."

"How could you loving me possibly come between us?" she asked with confusion. "I love you, BJ. I'm just not sure whether I'm 'in love' with you. I'm not quite sure what that means or how it should feel. But it would be unfair to you if I didn't try and find out."

"What do you mean by that?" BJ inquired with obvious nervousness. "Are you going to start dating other people?"

"No," Katie Rose promised him. "I don't want to date anyone else. I want to find out exactly what my feelings are for *you*. I've kept myself closed off from you, BJ, and that's been wrong. I've kept you at arm's length, but no more. From now on, I promise to look at you more like a boyfriend than only a friend. Then we'll see what develops."

Katie Rose could see the fear and concern in BJ's face, so she was fast to add, "I'll probably soon be telling you that I have fallen head over heels in love with you too."

*Oh, how I hope so*, BJ was wishing in desperation. His only fear was what would happen if Katie Rose discovered that she was *not* falling in love with him. *I'll cross that bridge if we come to it. In the meantime, I need to do everything in my power to help Katie Rose fall in love with me.*

"That sounds fantastic!" BJ said with a broad smile. "So does that mean I can kiss you now?"

"I wish you would," Katie Rose replied, and she meant what she said.

BJ pulled her into his arms, and Katie Rose began to return his persistent kisses.

*This feels right*, she was deciding. *It feels so natural to be in his arms. Maybe this **is** where I truly belong.* Katie Rose was not positive of anything, but she planned to do everything in her power to pursue her feelings for BJ. *I'm going to find out if BJ is **my** love of a lifetime.*

# Chapter 41

# *The Scare*

Long Wolf, Jackie Lynn and Mason had just finished having dinner together. Katie Rose had gone out to dinner with BJ. Mason had gone outside to wash his truck. So Jackie Lynn decided that this would be a good time to have a talk with Long Wolf about the children.

Long Wolf had retired to the living room. He was sitting in one of the recliners reading the newspaper. Jackie Lynn had a seat in the recliner beside him. She said in a soft but resolute voice, "Long Wolf, we need to talk."

He lowered his newspaper and gave her a hard stare. Seeing the serious expression on his wife's face, he laid the newspaper aside and asked, "About what?"

"About the children."

"The *children*? What about the children?" he asked with a puzzled look on his face. Both the children seemed to be doing fine, and Long Wolf was not aware of any problem either of them was having.

"It's more about your relationship with the children," she began to explain.

"My *relationship* with them?" Long Wolf was even more confused. "Care to explain that."

"I intend to," Jackie Lynn assured him. "I had a long conversation with Katie Rose yesterday about her relationship with BJ…"

"What's that got to do with me?" Long Wolf interrupted her. Jackie Lynn could tell he was somewhat on the defense now. She had not anticipated that this was going to be an easy conversation. Nonetheless, she felt it was one she vitally needed to have with this man.

"From what I ascertained during my conversation with Katie Rose, it has a lot to do with you. Katie Rose loves Greathouse Construction, and she would like to someday be President, but she feels that her father would not even consider such a thing. So she has concluded that all men hold women back. That's why she isn't actively pursuing her relationship with BJ."

"That's ridiculous!" Long Wolf argued. He got up out of his chair, in exasperation, and walked over to the fireplace. He turned and faced Jackie Lynn again. "I know that Katie Rose loves working at Greathouse Construction, but it can't have two Presidents when I pass away. Mason is going to be the President. Katie Rose can be his Vice-President if she wishes. It would be great to have both my children running my company."

"And therein lies another problem," Jackie Lynn contradicted. "Mason. He doesn't want anything to do with Greathouse Construction. Much less to be President someday."

"Where are you coming up with such nonsense, Jackie Lynn?!" Long Wolf demanded to know. He had raised his voice an octave. Jackie Lynn could tell that he was getting upset. She had broached the subject of Mason and Greathouse Construction on other occasions, and Long Wolf always turned a deaf ear. He did not want to accept the fact that his son did not share his dream of someday becoming President of his company.

"It's not nonsense, Long Wolf. You need to open up your eyes and see who your children truly are."

"I can't believe you just said that to me. You're acting like I'm totally disconnected from my children. That is so untrue!" he argued. He was digging in his heels now.

"No, you are far from disconnected from the kids. It's just that you refuse to accept them for who they are, and that is wrong."

"So I guess I'm ruining them by trying to shape their future. Is that what you are saying?" he questioned.

"I think it could ruin their lives if they follow dreams that aren't theirs – like Mason, or think that all men hold them back because they can't follow their dream – like Katie Rose."

"I can't believe you are saying these things to me, Jackie Lynn," Long Wolf said. He started to take a few steps forward. Then she saw him strangely grab his chest.

"Long Wolf, are you okay?" Jackie Lynn asked, rising to her feet.

"I..." he managed to mumble. Then he crumbled to the floor.

"Long Wolf!" Jackie Lynn shouted. She rushed toward him and dropped to her knees beside him. Just as she did, she glimpsed Mason in the hallway, out of the corner of her eye. "Mason!" she screamed and pointed to his father.

Mason had come into the house to get some wax out of the utility closet for his truck. Upon seeing his father lying in the floor, he instantaneously came to his father's aide. He ran over to him, dropped to the floor, and started giving his father lifesaving CPR. "Go call 911, mom!" he ordered his mother.

Jackie Lynn immediately ran to a phone and did so. She was so consumed with fear that she could hardly speak. *Thank God, Mason is keeping a level head, or we might lose Long Wolf.* The kind person on the other end of the phone kept assuring Jackie Lynn that help was on the way. Shaking and trying to control her tears, Jackie Lynn carefully answered the questions asked of her over the phone.

It seemed an eternity before Jackie Lynn had seen the ambulance pull into her driveway, but it had only been minutes. She pulled the door open in a flash. Jackie Lynn ushered the paramedics in with urgency. Mason rose from the floor and stepped out of their way. He was very relieved to see them too. He was out of breath from giving his father never-ending, life-giving puffs of air. His arms were also weary from the constant chest compressions he had administered. The paramedics praised Mason for his actions, however.

Everything that happened next was a total blur. The next thing Jackie Lynn knew she was sitting in the truck with Mason. They rushed along behind the ambulance that was taking Long Wolf to the emergency room. Once they arrived, the paramedics whisked Long Wolf directly back. The hospital gave Jackie Lynn a lot of annoying paperwork, which she filled out with shaking hands. She had been fortunate that she was organized. She had all the information they needed, including medical insurance cards. While Jackie Lynn took care of the paperwork, Mason called Katie Rose on her cell phone.

"Yes," she answered in a carefree, playful way. She had caller ID and knew it was Mason who was calling.

*How do I tell her this?* he was trying to decide. "Katie Rose, you need to come to Liberty Memorial Hospital," he slowly began to relate.

"The hospital? Why?!" she asked with alarm.

"I think dad has had a heart attack."

"A heart attack?!" she repeated with fear. "When? How? What happened?"

It took all of Mason's patient persistence to calm his sister down. BJ finally took the cell phone out of Katie Rose's hand. "Mason, it's BJ. Katie Rose will be fine. I'll drive her to the hospital right away."

"Thanks, BJ," Mason said to him. He was glad his sister was not alone. Mason trusted BJ to look out for her. He knew he cared a great deal for his sister.

Katie Rose collapsed into BJ's arms and cried for a few moments. BJ was happy to be there for her. He assured Katie Rose that her dad would be fine, even though he had no way of actually knowing this.

Jackie Lynn called Mary Julia from the waiting room and told her about Long Wolf. "I'll call Flora and tell her," Mary Julia graciously offered. She realized that Flora would want to know, and Jackie Lynn was certainly in no shape to make another call. "We'll be there soon," she also promised. "Just hang in there, Jackie Lynn. I'm sure Long Wolf will be fine."

Jackie Lynn, Mary Julia and Flora were seated in the waiting room of the ICU now. Jackie Lynn appreciated the companionship and the support that both Mary Julia and Flora were providing. She was also thankful that Mary Julia and Flora were working on mending the rift in their relationship. They likely would never have the intimate friendship they had once had. Regardless, Jackie Lynn was glad to see that the two of them were talking civilly now.

Callie had come to the hospital with her mother, to lend support to both Katie Rose and Mason. More so Mason, since Katie Rose had BJ there to lend her comfort. Callie liked BJ and was glad to see that Katie Rose was at last opening up a little more to him. She hoped that something more serious might develop between the two of them.

Long Wolf had suffered a serious heart attack. They had rushed him into surgery to perform a triple bypass. The nurses gave Jackie Lynn and everyone else updates on the surgery from time to time. It was hours later before Long Wolf's surgeon at last made an appearance. He announced that Long Wolf was still in serious condition, but he had come through the surgery fine and was resting in ICU.

It was then that Mary Julia embraced Jackie Lynn. She hugged her tightly and whispered in her ear, "See, everything is going to be fine. Long Wolf is not a quitter. He won't give up."

Flora also arose and gave Jackie Lynn a supportive embrace. With tears in her eyes, she said in a barely audible voice, "I love you both so much. I know in my heart that Long Wolf is going to be okay."

She and Mary Julia also gave Katie Rose and Mason a hug. They assured the children that all would be okay. Mary Julia decided she should leave and go home. It was after midnight. She wanted to get some rest, so she could come back up to the hospital later that day. This way she could better continue to lend her support to Jackie Lynn and the children.

Mary Julia grabbed Callie's hand to prod her to leave as well. But Callie told her mother that she wished to stay. BJ was lending support to Katie Rose. She intended to do the same for Mason. Flora told Mary Julia that she would walk out with her. Mary Julia and Flora assured Jackie Lynn that they would see her later that day. They had Jackie Lynn promise that she would call them if she needed them before then. Both ladies headed for the elevator then, to go home and to get some much needed rest.

\* \* \* \*

The rest of the early morning hours passed at a snail's pace. Each hour seemed like an eternity. Jackie Lynn had only slept when she had inadvertently dozed off, which had been every now and then. She was still very troubled about Long Wolf, and she was eager to be able to visit with her husband. However, what Long Wolf needed most right now was solitude and rest. So Jackie Lynn continued to lie on the small couch in the ICU waiting room. At least the hospital had provided her with a clean pillow and blanket for the night.

Mason, Katie Rose, BJ and Callie also spent the night in the ICU waiting room, worrying with Jackie Lynn. Mason awoke to the sun shining in his face through a window directly across from him. He thought he was the first to stir, but as he looked around the room, he did not see his mother. After checking to be certain that she was in with his father, he took it upon himself to head down to the hospital cafeteria to get coffee and breakfast for everyone.

* * * *

It was shortly after 9:00 a.m. when Mary Julia returned to the hospital. "So how are you holding up?" Mary Julia asked Jackie Lynn. She patted one of Jackie Lynn's hands. Jackie Lynn and the children were sitting in a row of chairs in the back of the waiting room. She had just finished eating breakfast.

"I am doing okay; really, I am," Jackie Lynn replied in a weary voice.

She shared with Mary Julia that the doctor had told her that Long Wolf had a restful night. "He said Long Wolf was doing well considering the extensive surgery he has undergone." The doctor had assured Jackie Lynn that, with physical therapy and time, Long Wolf had the possibility of making a full and healthy recovery.

Mason and Katie Rose both revealed that they had also visited with their father earlier that morning. They had both been relieved to see that he seemed to be doing well – especially considering all of the trauma his body had been through. It was then that Jackie Lynn suggested to the children that they should go home for awhile.

"After all, I have the companionship and support of a good friend to keep me company now. Why don't the two of you go on home for awhile? That way you can get a couple hours sleep, freshen up, and eat a decent meal. You can come back and relieve me a little later."

Mason and Katie Rose were a little ambivalent about leaving their mother. But Mary Julia assured the children that she would stay there at the hospital by Jackie Lynn's side until they returned. Mason told Callie that he would be glad to give her a ride home, and of course, BJ would be taking Katie Rose home.

As the children were leaving, they were happy to pass Flora getting off the elevator. Their mother would have even more support while they were away. They gave Flora a brief update on their father, and then they went on their way.

Terrible guilt about Long Wolf's heart attack besieged Jackie Lynn now. As Flora was sitting down next to Mary Julia, Jackie Lynn broke down in tears and began confiding in them both, "This is all still so unreal to me. I'm so eternally grateful that Long Wolf made it through the surgery, but I feel terrible that he had a heart attack. I shouldn't have been pushing him so hard about the children. I believed it was important that he grasped, once and for all, the effect his 'Greathouse grand scheme' for Mason and Katie Rose was having on the two of them. Both Mason and Katie Rose are getting bitter about the decisions their father has made regarding them both, even though they plainly adore Long Wolf. I only wanted all of them to be happy. I hadn't meant to create so much stress. I helped bring on this heart attack."

"We all make mistakes" Mary Julia commiserated. "Lord knows I have with Callie. I tried so hard to protect her that I drove her to the very life I was trying to keep her away from. I think that all parents naturally have illusions about their children. We believe that we can protect our children from our childhood hurts and that our children will turn out a certain way. Long Wolf is no different. But you are right, Jackie Lynn. It was important that you enlightened Long Wolf to the fact that he is hurting Mason and Katie Rose with his illusions. He needs to see this for himself and let those children begin to live their own lives. I wish I had seen the light a lot sooner and that Callie hadn't had to go through all that she did because of my foolishness. But I don't for any reason think you caused this heart attack; this was something that had been coming on for some time. Long Wolf always has worked too hard and too many long hours. He needs to relax more and look at what a wonderful family he has. Maybe this will make him see he needs to let someone else help with the company and that might not be his children. You were only standing up for them, trying to convince Long Wolf that he was pushing them too hard and driving them away. He is trying to make them into something they are not."

"What you are saying is definitely true," Jackie Lynn concurred with a strained smile. "Look at how Katie Rose has turned out. I did not raise her to be so fiercely independent, and she is already pushing men away. It's scary. It's like looking at a carbon copy of me, only I always thought my childhood made me the way I was. Yet Katie Rose's childhood was so different than mine. So, as you say, we definitely do live with false illusions when it comes to our children. Long Wolf is a good, intelligent man. He surely will come to realize this as well. He loves his children so much; he wanted Mason to be part of his world, to have the opportunity to enjoy the benefits of a company that was already successful. It is so hard for him to see that it is Katie Rose that would stand beside him and run that company, but he only sees that working if a man steps in, not a woman. I need to be more patient with him. Hopefully, he will come to accept that our children are who they are, and we can't change that. We are lucky that they are good kids."

"Be patient with him, but don't back down," Mary Julia further advised. "You have to fight for your children's futures, and letting them be whoever they choose to be is the only way they will ever be happy."

"It's so good to see that you have recognized this at last," Jackie Lynn shared with a wider, more contented grin. "You've been through a great deal yourself. I'm glad that you are so healthy now."

"Me too," Mary Julia agreed with a happy chuckle. "I've learned…the hard way… that the past is the past and that is where it needs to be left. I'm living for today and for the future that I will have with Jonathan and my daughter. I'm able to be here to support Callie and not try to shelter her from everything. It's a shame that it took me so long, but wallowing in guilt will do me no good. So I'm moving on and looking forward to whatever tomorrow may bring, especially where it concerns my daughter. Callie knows I'm here to support her now and not to hold her back."

"Well, that is great." *I hope that I can get Long Wolf to somehow see the light, and that he will someday support Mason and Katie Rose in the same way.*

Flora was thinking to herself, *I feel almost useless. These two women have their children in common. I don't think they need me at all.*

Flora gathered the courage to speak and said, "It seems the two of you are doing fine. If you don't need me anymore, I should be on my way." She gave a soft laugh, trying to carefully conceal that her feelings were being hurt.

Jackie Lynn and Mary Julia glanced at one another in confusion for a moment. Then it suddenly dawned on them that they had been going on as if Flora was not even there. They both reached over at the same time and gave Flora a much needed hug.

Almost in unison, they began assuring their other friend, "We'll always need you, Flora."

This surprised Flora, but it astounded Jackie Lynn to hear Mary Julia also speaking these kind words. This terrible incident had brought Mary Julia and Flora closer again. Jackie Lynn was very glad to see this.

They sat back and began to converse about things other that Long Wolf's heart attack, or their relationships with their children. The three women eventually fell into a pensive silence, completely content. Each was in her own way thanking God for their families and the deep friendship they shared.

# Chapter 42

# *Callie and Mason*

Mason, Katie Rose, BJ and Callie all rode the elevator down to the lobby together. Exhausted, they were all quiet. However, mainly, they were all grateful that Long Wolf was going to be okay.

Mason had not shown it, but he had been scared half out of his wits when he had seen his father unconscious on the floor. His first thought had been to start CPR. There had been a time, during the CPR, where Mason had not been sure whether or not his father was dead or alive. The realization that his father might have just died had been excruciating.

His dad had still not looked his best earlier when he had gotten to visit with him. Mason was still thankful that he had gotten to talk with him a little before they had left. Mason assured his dad that he did not need to worry about anything. He vowed to take care of everything at Greathouse, and Mason fully intended to keep this promise. He would not let his father down, no matter what. Mason realized now more than ever how much he loved him.

Mason, Callie, Katie Rose and BJ walked out of the hospital. Callie and Mason said their goodbyes to Katie Rose and BJ. Callie hugged Katie Rose and reassured her one final time that Long Wolf would be fine. Then she hugged BJ and whispered in his ear, "Thanks for being there for Katie Rose. Take good care of her."

"I will," he pledged with a slight smile.

Mason gave his sister an extended hug and a kiss on the cheek before they parted. He shook BJ's hand and playfully swatted his arm. Mason also thanked BJ for being there for Katie Rose.

After their goodbyes, Katie Rose and BJ headed to BJ's car. Mason and Callie headed to Mason's truck, which was on the opposite side of the parking lot. Once they were settled inside the truck, Mason turned to Callie and said, "I want to thank you for all of your support. You didn't have to spend the night up here with us. That was sweet. You've changed a lot, Callie. I'm sorry that you had to go through so much, but you've turned out to be a really great lady."

"Thanks," she gushed with a silly giggle. Mason's nice comments were making Callie feel self-conscious. "It was no big deal. I wanted to be here for you guys. I'm glad your dad is going to be all right. He's a wonderful guy. You guys are so lucky to have him. I was jealous of all the attention and affection that he showed Katie Rose. I wished so many times that my dad could have been like that."

"He probably would have been had it not been for your mom," Mason pointed out.

When he thought more about what he had said, he apologized, "I'm sorry, Callie. I'm not trying to put your mom down or talk badly about her. She couldn't help being the way she was. Not that she was a bad mom to you...oh, I'm really tired...so this is all coming out wrong...."

"It's okay," Callie assured Mason. She reached over to tenderly pat his hand. "I know exactly what you mean. You're not offending me with your comments. My mother went through a terrible ordeal when she was a child, and it left her with some mental problems. Under those circumstances, she did the best job she could of being a mother. I don't have any hard feelings toward her at all anymore. It's weird. It's like we've become friends now. Does that make any sense?"

"Well, unfortunately, you've got some things in common now. Ironically, your mom drove you to the very place that she was trying to protect you from. Life is so weird. I was so mad at my dad right before he had his heart attack, because he is always pushing me so hard when it comes to working at Greathouse and never supports my music. But when I thought he had died, none of that mattered. I only remember pleading with God not to take my dad. And he gave him back to us, so I'm going to do everything I can to make my dad proud of me. I can still have my music. It will have to take second fiddle to running Greathouse right now."

Callie's heart went out to Mason upon hearing his last statement. If he was willing to sacrifice his music for his dad, it showed that Mason loved his father a great deal. Callie hated to see him put his music on hold, but she understood why he would do such a thing.

"Mason, you are such a wonderful guy!" she candidly asserted.

Callie allowed her emotions to get the best of her. She slid across the seat, and she engulfed Mason in a tight embrace. When Mason placed his arms around her as well and pulled them even closer, Callie was so moved that she almost felt like crying. They held one another for several moments. Callie was thinking that Long Wolf should already be so proud of Mason. *He is so giving and unselfish. And so talented! Why can't Long Wolf love him the way that he is?*

Mason released his strong grip a little, and Callie pulled back to gaze into his warm, dark brown eyes. She had always been drawn to Mason physically. Yet, now, they only shared an endearing friendship. Nevertheless, presently, Callie was unable to fully identify what she was feeling for Mason. The depth of her emotion right now for this man was almost staggering. *I must be overly tired.*

Mason was noticing a strange magnetism towards Callie as well. *God, she smells good. She's turned into this amazing woman. She is so pretty, even though she hasn't fixed her hair and her makeup is a little messed up from sleeping in it. I don't want to let her go, not yet.*

The thought barely registered before Mason found himself drawing back in close to Callie once more. This time, however, he did not pull her into a hug. This time, Mason brought his lips to Callie's. She was astounded, but at the same time, Mason kissing her felt so totally natural to her. She relaxed and began to heartily respond.

Mason was completely blown away by the passion that Callie aroused in him. The last time they had kissed she had been but a girl, and he had still been somewhat of a boy. Now they were grown – a man and a woman – and her kisses were knocking him for a loop.

When their fierce lip lock ended, Mason declared in a breathless voice, "Callie, I don't want to take you home."

"You should," he was disappointed to hear her say.

*Maybe it's for the best. Things could easily get out of hand anyway.* Mason started trying to rein back in his extreme desires. Callie saw the disappointment in his eyes, and she knew that he would stop if she insisted that he do so. However, in her heart she did not want Mason to stop. She wanted to hold him, to caress him. It was simple: Callie wanted to make love to Mason.

Before she lost her courage, she chattered, "My dad has to work all day, and my mom will be at the hospital for quite awhile with your mom. We would have the house all to ourselves." In saying this, Callie candidly revealed her desires for Mason as well. "Why don't you take me home?" she half pleaded in a husky voice. She pulled her legs up underneath her and was practically sitting on Mason's lap as she persistently began kissing him once more.

He did not say another word. Mason merely started the truck and raced off toward Callie's house.

\* \* \* \*

Callie and Mason dashed into Callie's house. They were embracing and obsessively kissing as they stumbled sideways down the hallway to her bedroom. In an insane rush, they practically ripped the clothes off of one another's bodies. They fell into bed, hands, mouths and tongues moving everywhere on one another's bodies.

Overwhelming desire flooded Mason's body and his mind. His need to be joined with Callie was so all-consuming that he almost felt as if he was going to lose his mind. The knowledge he had gained, from his experience of having been with other ladies over the past few years, came in handy now. Otherwise, Mason would have moved much too quickly.

Time and time again, Mason allowed the passion between him and Callie to take him close to the edge. Then he was careful to channel these desires before he reached the point of no return. By the time Mason succumbed at last to the furious demand of his body, Callie was literally begging him to become one with her.

Callie arched up towards Mason's body. She wrapped her legs around him so that she could be as close as possible to

Mason's warm, moist erection. The desire inside Callie's body was totally overtaking her senses. She had to feel Mason inside of her, filling her needs, her desires, her wanting for this man.

Mason at long last brought their bodies together as one. With only a few hard thrusts, they both completely soared to a new height, to a new feeling of awareness. The heat of passion had consumed them. The world outside no longer existed. They both surrendered to the glorious sensations they could bring one another.

As Mason still lay on top of Callie, both of them working to bring their breathing back to normal, his mind began to wander. He had not been prepared for the scope of intensity that had roared through his body. He had never felt this kind of heat, this kind of passion; not even with Belinda had it ever been this tremendous.

Mason was slow to roll his body off of Callie's. He weakly collapsed on the bed beside her. As their eyes met and held, Mason was not at all prepared for Callie's next odd response. She burst into tears, crying and sobbing so fiercely that her entire body was shaking.

Mason mustered his strength and pulled Callie into a warm, comforting embrace; the feel of her warm damp skin against his was again dangerously arousing him. But, using fierce control of his manhood, he tenderly began stroking Callie's long hair, as he softly whispered in her ear, "Shh…Callie, it's okay. I didn't mean to hurt you. I…Callie, I'm so sorry. It all got out of hand…please don't cry, baby. It will be alright."

*Where did the* baby *endearment come from?* This was not the way Mason normally addressed women. Nor did Mason understand where the deep feelings were coming from that were overtaking him at this moment. All Mason knew for certain was that he desperately wanted to take Callie's pain away and make her stop crying. He felt guilty and helpless right now.

After a few more, long, tense moments, Callie was able to gain control of her haywire emotions. She gradually stopped crying. Mason remained silent and continued to hold Callie and caress her head and back with gentle strokes.

"Are you okay now?" he finally dared to ask. Mason pulled back a slight bit so he could gaze into Callie's watery eyes.

"Yes," she answered, still sounding a little unsure.

"Why were you crying? Were you regretting what happened between the two of us?" Mason dared to ask.

He could not take back what had transpired between them. An even stranger feeling was that he did not want to. Nevertheless, Mason intended to do everything in his power to make things right between the two of them again. *If this is something Callie has decided should not have happened.* All at once, Mason was more than a little rattled. He did not want to lose having Callie in his life. Yet, Mason was used to his relationships with ladies ending after their sexual encounter. *What have I done?* he worried in silence.

"Regret what happened? Are you kidding me?" he was rather stunned to hear Callie reply. "No. I don't regret it. The whole experience blew me away. It's never been like that for me before. Not even with David; not with any man. You made me high without drugs. The feelings were so intense I...I can't even begin to describe it. No, you have not hurt me. I've never felt so much pleasure, so much passion. Thank you."

Callie brought her lips to Mason's and gave him a warm, endearing kiss. Then she gave him a gleeful smile, but her big beautiful sapphire eyes were still glistening with more unshed tears. Mason was profoundly moved. He usually wanted to leave right after having relations with a woman, but right now, here with Callie, he only wanted to continue to hold her, stroke her and softly kiss her. He did not want their time together to end – *not ever.*

*Geez...have I fallen...am I in love with Callie?* This nagging question in the back of Mason's mind startled him. He gently pushed Callie away from him a little and laid on his side, staring invasively into her adoring eyes. *Could she be in love with me? Or is what I'm seeing in her eyes only satisfaction from a great sexual experience?*

He reached out and caressed one of Callie's cheeks with tenderness. She moved her face so that she was kissing his fingers. More tears escaped and rolled down her cheeks. Mason reached to softly brush the tears from Callie's beautiful pink cheeks; she still felt flushed.

"Callie, I have to know something," he told her. Mason took a deep breath, and he bravely asked, "What do you think you are feeling right now?" Callie now had a frightened look in her eyes, but Mason had to continue. "I need for you to tell me. What do you feel in your heart? And you must be honest."

"Um…you may not want to hear it," Callie began with hesitation. She was fighting not to begin sobbing again. She was completely overwrought with emotion right now.

"Tell me, Callie. You can say anything to me," Mason assured her. He affectionately kissed her forehead and both her wet salty cheeks.

"I…I may be falling in love with you, Mason. That's probably not what you want to hear. You don't want to be tied down by a woman. What just happened was probably an accident to you. I'm used to that with men. Things got out of hand like you said…oh…I'm sorry. That cheapened things. I didn't mean to suggest that you treated me like a prostitute. Never… you are so loving and giving…you deserve a wonderful woman in your life. I'm used goods. I don't expect you to feel the same way about me. I… I'm sorry, Mason… I'm talking too much… Please forget everything I said. All I want from you is to still be your friend. We can pretend like today never happened. That's what we will do…"

He stopped her with a deep, engulfing kiss that literally took Callie's breath away for a few moments.

"No. We won't pretend like today never happened. And I won't forget what I heard you say. Except for maybe the part about you being used goods and not being good enough for me. Do you know why I won't forget any of this? Ever."

Callie shook her head. She could not talk. Her speech was being choked off by the sob that was trying to escape from her throat. She waited with nervousness for Mason to continue.

"I won't forget any of that, because I don't want to. You say I deserve a wonderful woman in my life. You are right, Callie. And I've found her. She is lying right here beside me. It's you, Callie. I love you too, baby."

The honest confession of his feeling for her touched Callie's heart. It had her uncontrollably sobbing all over again. Mason pulled her back into his strong arms, rocking and cradling her like a child. He patiently waited for her tearful escapade to end once more.

"God, Mason, where do we go from here?" Callie questioned, when she had regained control of her feelings again.

"I don't know all the answers right now. We'll have to take things as they come. But I do know that I probably should be getting out of your bed and putting some clothes on before your mother comes home from the hospital. She will at long last have her chance to lynch me. Lord knows, she has wanted to do that for years."

"None of that was your fault. I treated you so bad when I was younger. I just...I felt so rejected by my dad back then, that I couldn't take your rejection as well. I can't believe we are together like this now."

"It's still a little unreal to me too," Mason divulged with a chuckle. "But you know, it feels so right. Maybe I've been in love with you for years. I was definitely attracted to you back then. I never acted on it because I didn't want to take advantage of you."

Callie kissed Mason again then. "And you wouldn't believe how much I respect you for that now. It makes me love you all the more. God, it feels great to say that, Mason."

"It does feel great; I love you too. We'll figure it all out, Callie," he promised her. Mason laughed out loud with overpowering joy.

He kissed Callie again. Then he reluctantly climbed out of the warm bed and started picking up his clothes off the floor. Callie followed suit and got dressed also. She and Mason walked arm and arm to the front door.

"I'll call you when I get home," Mason told her with a contented smile. He gave her one final, long, smitten kiss.

"Drive safe," Callie instructed. She was slow to release him. Callie stood in the doorway and watched as Mason walked to his truck.

Before he climbed inside the truck, Mason turned to face her and said, "In case you should forget....I love you, Callie Roberts."

She gave him an enormous smile as she dashed out the door and ran to him. Callie threw herself into Mason's arms for one more, yearning kiss. "I love you too, Mason Greathouse!" she gushed.

Callie could not believe that all of this was actually happening. It was like a dream come true. *How many times did I dream of this when I was younger?* It was finally happening, like a fairytale coming true. Callie was so delighted that she could hardly stop grinning and jumping around.

# Chapter 43

# *The Reckoning*

Long Wolf had a great deal of time to think about what Jackie Lynn had said to him about their children. He spent a month and a half recovering at home after he got out of the hospital. Samuel took over the day-to-day running of the company for him. Mason was at Samuel's side, learning the ropes of being in management.

Mason continued to assure his dad that all would be okay. He promised that he would do everything he could to learn as much as he could, in the shortest amount of time. Mason temporarily stepped into his father's shoes until Long Wolf could return.

However, each day as his children came home from work, Mason would mechanically relate the details of the day with only slight interest. Katie Rose, on the other hand, would chatter away with enthusiasm. She wanted to tell her father about each and every detail of the workday. Katie Rose went on and on about every contract that they had landed or had the opportunity to land.

It was hard for Long Wolf to accept, but he had to admit that Jackie Lynn must be right. He was forcing his son into a life he did not want, but one that his daughter would embrace with open arms. Long Wolf had never even entertained the idea that Katie Rose, and not Mason, would be the one who wanted to be passed the reins of management, and ownership, of Greathouse Construction.

It was clear that Mason only wanted to be a musician, or at least spend his life doing something in the music industry. This unsettled Long Wolf a bit. The music industry was a difficult arena to be involved in. Regardless, he recognized that it would be wrong for him to squelch his son's dreams. *What kind of a father would that make me?* he questioned himself in secret. *Not the kind of father that I want to be.*

* * * *

The week before Long Wolf was planning to go back to work, on Friday evening, he requested a family meeting. After dinner, Long Wolf, Jackie Lynn, Mason and Katie Rose all retired to the den together. Mason and Katie Rose had a seat, side by side, on the sofa. Long Wolf and Jackie Lynn sat down in the two recliners in the room. These chairs were on a swivel base, so Jackie Lynn and Long Wolf positioned them so that they were facing the children and slightly facing one another.

This was not the first family meeting they had ever had. Over the years, Jackie Lynn and Long Wolf had participated in many family powwows of this nature. Often, either Jackie Lynn or Long Wolf requested these meetings, but the children, from time to time, had also requested a family sit down of this manner to discuss certain matters that were important to them.

When they were all seated and comfortable, Long Wolf began by sharing, "I asked that we all get together to discuss Greathouse Construction."

No one in the room seemed surprised by Long Wolf's announcement. They were all expecting him to return to work on the following Monday, so they expected that he might like to talk to them about how this would affect them.

Long Wolf began again. "The first thing I want to do is apologize to your lovely and insightful mother and put her mind at ease. Jackie Lynn, you were right about what you said about Mason and Katie Rose and Greathouse Construction. I've had blinders on, and the last thing in the world I want to do is hurt either of our children. I love you, and I appreciate you speaking up."

Jackie Lynn was awestruck by Long Wolf's words, and she could not help but wonder if she truly understood what he was saying. Long Wolf could see the uncertainty and doubt in not only Jackie Lynn's eyes, but also his children's, so he continued, "Katie Rose, I want to apologize to you next. You are daddy's beautiful baby girl, and you shall always be this to me. But, you are also a lovely, wise and determined, young woman, much like your mother. I'm very proud of you and you bring me great joy, but I don't think I've shown this to you."

"Yes you have, daddy," Katie Rose interrupted. She was bewildered by why her father was saying these things. She was suddenly very worried about him. *Is he thinking that since he's had this heart attack that he might die soon, and so he needs to apologize to all of us for any of his shortcomings?*

"Not in all the ways that I should have," he contradicted. "I've overlooked one important fact, Katie Rose. I've ignored your love of Greathouse Construction. You share the same passion that I do for this business, and you long for me to recognize this. Well, now I have. You also want me to acknowledge that you could run this company as well as, if not better than, your brother. I've made you feel inferior because you are a woman, and this was not right. I tell you now that I do believe that you could run Greathouse Construction as well as Mason, if not better, and I will support you in your endeavors. Don't let your father's foolishness cause you to be bitter toward all men and think that they want to hold you back. I've been wrong, Katie Rose, and I intend to correct this situation starting today."

Katie Rose had a look of utter amazement on her face. She gaped at her dad in awe, but said not a word. *Am I dreaming?!*

Long Wolf was quick to turn his attention to his son, lest Mason think he had been forgotten. "Mason, as with your mother and sister, I also owe you an apology. My dream has always been to pass the reins of the company on to my son, as my father did to me. The problem is that this was *my* dream, but *not* yours. Your true passion lies in your music, but instead of supporting your passion and your dreams, I have totally disregarded them and tried to stamp them out at every turn. I have been wrong, and I'm glad that you have fought for what is important to you. You would never be happy as President of Greathouse Construction, and your happiness is what is most important to me. As I told Katie Rose, from this day forward, I also intended to begin to support you in your passion and dreams. I will no longer force you to do something that you hate either. I'm very proud of you as well, even though I have not properly shown this."

There was an awkward silence in the room for several beleaguered moments. Mason broke the unwelcome stillness by exclaiming a simple, "Wow!" *Is this for real?!*

His dad further emphasized that it was *for real* by inquiring, "So, Mason, what time is your band playing tonight?"

"We start at nine," he rather absentmindedly answered. Mason was so unused to his dad asking anything about his music that he hardly knew how to respond.

"Mind if your old man comes and watches you? I've never even heard this band play," Long Wolf admitted with some shame.

"Um…well…wow!!" Mason uttered again. "This is a lot to take in all at once, dad," he confessed.

"I know. I understand. If you don't want me to come, then that's okay…."

"No!" Mason interrupted. "I'd love to have you come. I've always wanted you to want to come and hear me play. It's hard to accept that you are truly interested all of the sudden."

"I'm very interested," Long Wolf assured him. "I'd also like for you to be thinking about what role…if any…you would like to play in Greathouse Construction. You've always been interested in construction work in the past. If that's the only part you want of the company, then I'd be happy to have you back in that capacity. If not, then that's okay too. You're a grown man, and I need to start trusting you to make your own decisions about your life. You've put your life on hold far long enough to support my dreams. I appreciate all you've done, son. Especially while I've been recovering from my heart attack. You saved my life. Now, I'm trying to return the favor by giving you yours."

Mason rose from the couch, approached his dad and unabashedly pulled him into an embrace. "Thank you, dad. You don't know how much this means to me. You're a great dad. I love you."

"I love you too, son," he professed, giving Mason a tight squeeze.

Katie Rose followed her brother's lead. She rose from the couch and walked up right behind Mason. "Hey, can I get in on this?" she asked.

Mason gave her a smile and started to step back to let her into their father's arms. "No," she protested. "Why don't we do a group hug? Mom?"

"Sounds like a wonderful idea to me!" Jackie Lynn agreed with a wide happy smile. She hopped to her feet and frolicked with delight over to her husband and children. They all linked arms and converged in a secure group hug.

A new life was about to begin for all of them, and each of them was excited and pleased. The veil of illusions, which had struck them all blind for so long, had at long last been lifted. Truths had been revealed, and the future was a wide-open adventure for both Mason and Katie Rose. They could not wait to begin their new lives.

## The End

**Continue the journey…**

Now that you have had the opportunity to completely lose yourself in our second novel, *Illusions*, we invite you to continue following the lives of the characters that have warmed your hearts, and that you know so well.

Be on the lookout for the final novel in this trilogy, **Indecisions**. It should be available for purchase before the end of 2005 or early in 2006. Check www.sissymarlyn.com often for updates on the progress of this new novel and enjoy reading our free monthly short stories in the interim.

Now, we invite you to sit back and enjoy reading a short preview of *Indecisions*:

## Chapter 1

# *Death*

The day was warm; there was not a cloud in the picturesque blue sky; the sun was shining brilliantly. Regardless, all was cold, dark and gloomy in Jackie Lynn Greathouse and her children's world. Their father, Abraham 'Long Wolf' (he had been half Indian) Greathouse had just passed away earlier that day. Now, the remaining family members were all sitting together in the funeral parlor, about to begin making arrangements for Long Wolf's viewing and funeral. They were all devastated by his death. They had all loved him a great deal.

Long Wolf had died from a fatal heart attack. It had not been the first attack that he had ever suffered. He had encountered the first one five years ago. Even though it had done a fair amount of damage to his heart, a triple bypass had saved his life. Since then, Long Wolf had changed his diet, had begun eating healthier and had cut down significantly on his stress. He had begun working less and less at Greathouse Construction, the company he had been President of since his own father's passing many years before. Long Wolf's children, Mason and Katie Rose, had begun to take a much more active role in working at the company. This fatal heart attack had come as quite a shock to all of them.

Long Wolf's oldest child, Mason, was now head supervisor for all of Greathouse's construction crews. He was a staggeringly handsome, twenty-six year old man. Mason was tall and well built – years of working construction and being an avid athlete had paid off to build muscles in all the right places. Mason looked a great deal like his father, with jet-black hair and handsome, dark chocolate eyes. He had been quite the playboy with women while he was away at college. He had a degree in Business Administration, which his father had pushed him to get. At one point, Long Wolf had been grooming his son to take over the reins of President of Greathouse Construction.

However, when Long Wolf had suffered his first heart attack, he had come to terms with the fact that running Greathouse Construction was not Mason's dream, but his own. Mason's true passion rested in his musical talent. He was a great songwriter; he enjoyed organizing bands and playing nightly to cheering crowds. Long Wolf had merely been grateful that Mason had continued to have some small role in the construction business. His son had always loved working construction jobs, so moving up the ladder to supervise the crews had been a natural, and pleasant, progression for Mason. Long Wolf had begun supporting his son in his musical endeavors as well.

Mason had been on top of the world right before his father's death. He had recently moved into his own apartment. He was in love with a beautiful woman. He had never felt closer to his dad. And his musical career was starting to show some definite promise. A talent scout had expressed interest in him making a studio recording of one of his songs.

His younger sister, Katie Rose, had also been very happy with her life. She was twenty-three years old and had been out of college a year. She also had a degree in Business Administration and was going for her Masters. Katie Rose had convinced herself that she was also in love – with BJ, her boyfriend of several years. BJ and Katie Rose had always seemed to make an odd couple. She was tall, beautiful and smart. As Mason greatly favored his father, Katie Rose looked a great deal like her mother. She had long black hair and the most alluring emerald green eyes. She also had a very attractive body with a nice bust line.

In contrast, BJ was only average in everything – in height, in looks and in intelligence. BJ stood barely as tall as Katie Rose. He was shorter than her if she was wearing heels. He had sandy brown hair and grayish blue eyes. Since his eyesight was bad, he also wore glasses. BJ was happily content working as a mechanic at a nearby muffler shop.

Regardless of their physical differences, things had recently turned intimate between Katie Rose and BJ. Katie Rose was attracted to BJ for his caring nature and close friendship, rather than his appearance or intellect.

Katie Rose had always dreamed of someday taking over the reigns of management at Greathouse Construction from her father. Long Wolf had resisted this most of her life and had mistakenly tried to push her brother into this role. Yet, this also had changed when Long Wolf had suffered his first heart attack. Even since then, her father had been fully supporting Katie Rose in her career choice, and she had begun to quickly climb the ladder at Greathouse Construction.

Presently, both Katie Rose and Mason's career dreams came to a crashing halt. The entire family was all encumbered by grief. They were all centered on doing whatever it took to fully support one another at this heart wrenching time.

\* \* \* \*

After they made all of the arrangements at the funeral home, Mason took his mom and Katie Rose home. He stayed with them for a short while before he left to return to his apartment. After he left, Katie Rose called BJ. They only talked on the phone for a few moments, because he told Katie Rose that he was coming over. Katie Rose was fine with BJ coming over. She wanted to see him. She knew BJ would comfort her, and Katie Rose needed all the comfort she could get right now.

BJ did not live far from Katie Rose, so he was there within ten minutes. When Katie Rose opened the door to him, BJ pulled her into a warm and loving embrace. Katie

Rose began to freely cry. She thought she had already cried all of the tears that she possibly could and was amazed to find that she could find more.

BJ securely cradled Katie Rose in his arms and whispered comforting words in her ear. He was trying to convince her that everything would be okay. His heart was breaking for Katie Rose. BJ loved Katie Rose deeply, so her pain was his pain. He merely wished to remove it whatever way he could.

"I'm here, baby. I'm so sorry about your dad. But I'll be here for you. I'll do anything you need me to do."

Katie Rose eventually pulled back from BJ. She gave him a strained smile, and she kissed his lips with affection. Katie Rose's heart felt full of love for BJ at this very moment. BJ had always been there whenever Katie Rose had needed him.

"I should invite you in," she said. She stepped backwards a few steps. Katie Rose pulled BJ forward through the doorway. BJ reached to shut the door. He followed Katie Rose down the hall and into the living room. They had a seat side by side on the couch.

"How are your mom and Mason?" BJ asked with concern. He liked Katie Rose's whole family a great deal; this had included her dad.

"I think Mason is still numb. He hasn't cried yet. He's just been there to support my mom and me. My mom is crushed. They had an everlasting love for one another. I want the kind of love they had to be a part of our life."

"I'd sure do my best to give it to you," BJ said with a caring smile. He gave Katie Rose another kiss, this one a bit more passionate. Katie Rose earnestly returned his kiss.

They had become lovers only a few months ago, but it had all come so naturally between them, as had their whole relationship. Katie Rose believed that they must surely belong together. Some day she hoped to marry BJ. Katie Rose dreamed of living happily ever after with BJ as her mom and dad had lived together.

"Katie Rose, why don't you come back to my apartment with me and spend the night," BJ proposed in a husky voice. "I don't want you to be alone tonight. Let me comfort you."

She had yet to spend the night with BJ, because she was still living at home.  She had not wanted her parents to know what she and BJ were doing.  Katie Rose was very tempted tonight.

However, she did not want to leave her mom there alone to dwell on the wretchedness of this whole situation.  Her mom and dad had rarely been parted.  She could not imagine what it might be like for her mom to be alone.

"I can't," Katie Rose told BJ with noted disappointment. "I want to be here for my mom tonight.  Do you understand that?"

"Of course I do," BJ told her, putting his own selfish desires aside.  "Do you want me to stay here too?  I can sleep on the couch.  Then if you need me, I'll be here for you."

"You are so sweet," Katie Rose cooed.  She gave him several more little kisses on his lips.  "I love you, BJ."

BJ never tired of hearing Katie Rose say these words to him.  "I love you too, Katie Rose.  With all my heart.  Just tell me what you need, and I'll do it."

"I need some time alone with my mom tonight.  But I will call you if I need you."

"Deal," BJ agreed.

He hugged Katie Rose.  He also kissed the side of her neck.  "I'll be here in a flash if you call."

Katie Rose felt warm and loved in BJ's arms.  She took a second to thank God for allowing her to have him in her life.  Katie Rose still could not quite comprehend why God had so cruelly taken her father away from her or her family.  She remained cuddling with BJ for quite awhile, gathering strength from his great love for her.

* * * *

When Mason got home, his girlfriend, Callie Roberts, was waiting for him in the living room.  She had been crying.  Callie sprinted toward Mason.  She enfolded him in her arms.  Callie and Mason were living together.  They had been together as a couple for five years.  Both had been living at home with their parents when their deep friendship had unexpectedly turned romantic – the day Mason's father had suffered his first heart attack.

Growing up, no one would have even convinced Mason that Callie would have become the love of his life.  She had been a ravishing young girl, with long, shimmering, naturally curly, blond locks; the most beautiful sapphire blue eyes; and a very attractive and well-rounded figure. However, Callie had been a very wild teen.

She came on to Mason at every turn, but he refused all of her well-planned advances. She had been his sister's best friend and his mother's best friend's daughter. Callie was Katie Rose's age – three years younger than him. Mason had watched these girls grow up together. Since their birthdays were only a day apart, he even watched them celebrate most of their birthdays together. At first, Callie's flirtations turned Mason off. He considered Callie to be like another little sister.

Mason had even decided to go away to college to get away from Callie's constant tormenting. While he had been at college, Callie's family had fallen apart, and she had run away from home. She turned to drugs, alcohol and prostitution to survive. When Mason returned from college, Callie also come home, and he discovered that she was a very different person. Her harsh life, going through rehab and learning to forgive her parents had changed Callie a great deal. She was no longer the unruly girl he had known.

Instead, a wise, mature, lovely woman returned home. She and Mason became good friends, using one another as constant sounding boards. The intense romance that followed had taken them both by surprise. At first, they attempted to hide the fact that they had become lovers. They were not sure how their families would react, particularly Callie's mom. She had always threatened to harm Mason if he ever laid a hand on her daughter. Of course, this had been when Callie had been only twelve through fifteen – the years when Callie had been chasing and trying to seduce Mason.

Katie Rose was the first one to discover that they had become much more than friends. She came home early one day and almost ran into a completely nude Callie. Callie had been coming from her brother's bedroom. Callie had been embarrassed, and Katie Rose had been a little hurt that Callie had not confided in her. Callie's relationship with her brother had plainly evolved into something more than merely friendship. Katie Rose convinced them to come clean with everyone else about the fact that they were in love.

Mason told the rest of his family first. He asked his mom and dad if he could convert the garage into his bedroom. He explained that he and Callie needed privacy until he could get a place of his own. This arrangement had been a little uncomfortable for Jackie Lynn and Long Wolf, but they agreed to Mason's request. Their son was a man now and Callie was a grown woman. They had not wanted them to have to sneak around to share their love. They would have preferred that the two of them were married since they were being intimate. However, Jackie Lynn and Long Wolf had lived together for awhile before they had married.

As expected, Callie's mother, Mary Julia, had been a little more upset about their 'affair'. She had not wanted Callie to be used by Mason 'just for sex'. Mary Julia believed that Callie's proposed love for Mason was true, but she was not as convinced that Mason felt the same way. Mary Julia had been molested and sexually abused as a child. She had been hospitalized for this twice, once before Callie had been born and once right before her daughter had run away. Mary Julia still had a basic mistrust of men. This is what finally ended her marriage to Jonathan, Callie's father. They had been in the process of getting a divorce when all this news came about. Jonathan, unlike Mary Julia, was happy for the young couple.

Fortunately, Mary Julia did not take a stand against Callie's love for Mason. She had received enough therapy that she realized that acting in such a manor would not work to her advantage. Mary Julia wisely realized that this would only drive her daughter farther into Mason's arms. Hence, she also somewhat gave their relationship her blessing in the end.

Mason and Callie practically lived together in the garage for the next few years. In the meantime, they also saved money, with the intention of buying furniture and moving into an apartment together. They had accomplished this goal about six months ago. Mason and Callie were still very much in love. Mason had it in the back of his mind that he intended to propose to Callie very soon. He wanted her to become his wife. Mason could envision having a family with this woman.

Now, Callie was holding Mason in her arms and trying her best to comfort him. "Mason, honey, I am *so* sorry," Callie emphasized and began to cry again. Callie's heart was breaking for the entire family. She had known all of them her whole life. Callie felt as if she had just lost a family member as well.

"Are you okay?" Callie asked Mason. She pulled back from him and stared into his hard, somber eyes. *He hasn't been crying. He almost looks angry.*

"I don't really know how I feel right now," he confessed. "I don't think it has all sunk in yet. It's just extremely hard for me to believe that my father is actually gone...dead. I just feel....I feel.....actually, I don't feel anything. I'm numb. I just expect to wake up and find out that this has all been a terrible nightmare."

"I truly wish it were," Callie commiserated. She stifling another sob and wiped a few remaining tears from her cheeks. "Are you hungry? Do you want me to fix you some dinner?"

"I'm not hungry," Mason answered Callie after several moments of pensive silence. "But thanks for offering to fix me something. Have you eaten?"

"No. I wasn't really hungry either. I've been waiting for you."

"I'm glad you're here," Mason professed. He gave Callie a warm, grateful kiss.

"I wouldn't want to be anywhere else," she told him and gazed at him with overwhelming love in her eyes. "What can I do for you?"

"Just come to bed with me, and let's hold one another. I need to feel you next to me. To know you are there. Your love will help me make it through this," Mason told her in a soft voice, an extreme sadness suddenly overtaking him. He did not even realize he had started crying until Callie started to tenderly kiss his tears away.

"Come on, honey. Let's go to bed. I'll be there for you. I'll hold you all through the night. It will all be okay. You'll see," she said. Callie took Mason's hand and quickly led him off to the bedroom.